PRIORSFORD

PRIORSFORD

BY

O. DOUGLAS

THOMAS NELSON & SONS, LTD
LONDON, EDINBURGH, PARIS, MELBOURNE
TORONTO, AND NEW YORK

First published in this edition, September 1936

TO

MAUD

A GOOD COMRADE

PRIORSFORD

CHAPTER I

" There's comfort for the comfortless
      And honey for the bee,
      And there's nane for me but you, my love,
      And there's nane for you but me."
                                    WITCH WOOD.

IT was high summer in the Cotswold country, and the
old house of Mintern Abbas dozed in the peace of the
August afternoon.

At its back, beyond the home-woods, was a remote
land of sheep-walks and forgotten hamlets ; at its feet
the young Thames, in lazy reaches, wound through
water-meadows. The house itself was of Cotswold
stone, grey and bleak in rain, but in summer honey-
coloured as if it had absorbed the sun. It was as much
a part of the landscape as a boulder on the hill-side.
Built in many periods and many styles, it had been so
subtly blended by time that it seemed a perfect thing,
without beginning, as long descended as the downs that
sheltered it.

The heat which had laid a spell on the place had
evidently no effect on a group of children camped on
a corner of the lawn sloping to the river. Two boys
tumbled about with a cocker-spaniel puppy, while a fat

little girl was absorbed in threading berries. On a wooden seat in the shade of the copper-beech their nurse sat sewing—a large woman with a broad comely face. Presently she spoke, and her voice sounded oddly in that English pleasaunce.

"Mind, Peter, that wee dog 'll bite ye. Dinna torment the puir thing."

Peter lay on his back holding the puppy suspended in the air.

"He can't hurt, Ninny: his teeth are too young; besides, the Black Douglas likes being tormented."

"I doot it," said Ninny dryly. "Hoo wud *you* like if a muckle giant held you in the air like that?"

Peter twisted round to see his nurse's face as he said in an interested voice:

"Am I like a giant to Black Douglas? Ho, ho! Here comes Giant Cormoran. Fee-fo-fum, I smell the blood of a—black puppy with floppy ears."

Peter stopped with a gasp, for the small Quentin had suddenly thrown himself on his brother's prostrate form, and for a few minutes there was an inextricable tangle of boys and puppy, the Black Douglas at last emerging triumphantly on top.

Suddenly Alison, the girl, who had shown no slightest interest in the mêlée, left her berry-threading and started to run up the lawn. In a second Peter was after her, and, as he was seven and slim and Alison was five and solid, he was soon well ahead of her.

"It's Mummy," Quentin remarked, but did nothing about the matter, being well content to remain with Ninny, who was his providence.

" Ay, it's yer mother," she said, watching the scene with kindly eyes. " Peter micht hae let Alison beat him, but he maun aye be first, that laddie."

The girl whom the children ran to meet seemed absurdly young to be their mother, a wood-elf of a creature, rather small and brown, very light and graceful. Her eyes were like moss-agates at the bottom of a burn, and there were yellow lights in her brown curls. She had hardly changed at all since that day, more than nine years ago, when, as Jean Jardine, she had married Lord Bidborough, and she stood now, her hands raised to shade her eyes, smiling at the light-foot lad running so easily, and the fat little girl so earnest in her endeavour.

Peter flung himself at his mother's feet, laughing, while she held out her arms to her moist, crimson-faced little daughter who panted : " Oh, Mummy, it was me saw you first."

" But I *reached* you first," said Peter.

" And so you should," his mother told him ; " you're two years older and your legs are two years longer. Alison should always have a good start—that would make it fair."

" All right," Peter agreed. " Come on, Alison, and I'll race you back."

" It's much too hot for racing," Lady Bidborough said, mopping her daughter's forehead.

Alison held up her face like a sunflower to the sun, saying gratefully, " I do like your hankeys, Mummy. They smell like the leaves in the greenhouse that you pinch."

" We're having tea in the Crow-Wood," Peter announced. " It was my turn to choose and I chose that because it's a place the Black Douglas can enjoy himself. Yesterday Alison chose the Dutch garden, and he sat on all the best flowers, and Mr. Webb was mad."

" And he's eaten the claws off the tiger," Alison said, making round eyes.

" The tiger ? "

" She means the leopard, Mummy," Peter explained. " You know, in Daddy's own room—the one he shot in India or somewhere. They made him sick."

His mother laughed. " Puppies are like that : they want to taste everything," and added: " Here he comes," as a black object was seen walloping towards them. " Poor little fellow, he's all ears and flat feet."

" He's *beautiful*," Peter said, rushing to embrace his new possession, while Lady Bidborough, with Alison holding her hand, walked down the sloping lawn to where her youngest offspring played beside his nurse.

" And what's my baby thinking of things," she said, sitting down with him on her knee.

" Mummy," said Quentin, with a welcoming grin, but in a minute he had slid from her lap and made off after Peter and the puppy.

His mother looked after him rather wistfully.

" Ninny, he's quite a boy. I've no baby, now."

" Weel," said Ninny, with great good sense, looking critically at her seam as she spoke, " ye surely wadna want him to bide a bairn. He's a steerin' callant, an' as gleg as a hawk ; naething passes him. Speerity too, stands up to Peter. See that noo ? "

Lady Bidborough laughed and sighed almost in one breath.

"It's quite true, Ninny. Of course it's mere silliness to regret the nursery days, but it's such a happy time and it's over so soon—How long have you been with us, Ninny? Seven years, isn't it?"

"Ay. I cam' when Peter was a month old. Me that kent naething about bairns, takin' charge o' the heir! I dinna ken hoo I daured!" Ninny laid down her work and looked at her mistress. "Were ye no feared, Mem? . . . Of course your ain nurse stayed on till I kinna got into the way o' things—I was terrible handless at the stert."

"Oh, no, Ninny, you weren't. The moment you took Peter into your arms you were just right—as I knew you would be when I saw you at Laverlaw and stole you from Mrs. Elliot."

"Eh ay." Ninny nodded reminiscently. "I hed been there as laundry-maid for twae years when you cam' doon to the laundry ae day wi' Mistress Elliot. Ye crackit to me, I mind; askit aboot this an' that— sic a lassie you lookit! I couldna believe it when they tell't me that ye were Lady Bidborough. . . . Then, a while after, the mistress sent for me to her ain room. I couldna think what she wantit wi' me; I thocht mebbe I was to get ma notice. An then she tell't me that her sister-in-law, Lady Bidborough, had got a little son, an' she wantit me to gang awa' to England an' be his nurse. Me! I near drappit on the floor, I got sic a fricht."

"No wonder!" Lady Bidborough shook her head at her own temerity. "It was rather calm when you come to think of it, to demand a valued laundress from one's sister-in-law, and expect her to leave all her friends, and the place where she had been brought up, and come away to England to take unfamiliar and very responsible work ! But, you see, Ninny, my need was great. All the nurses I interviewed were so highly trained, so certain that they knew everything there was to know about bringing up a baby, so condescending to me, I knew exactly what sort of nursery they would make, and it wasn't the kind I wanted. I had so often thought of you as I had seen you that day at Laverlaw, in your spotless print, ironing the clean clothes, your face so kind and contented, speaking such soft, beautiful Tweedside Scots, and I just longed to have you here to look after my baby. So I wrote to my sister-in-law and asked her to sound you and see if by any chance you would consider it, but Mrs. Elliot thought it better to wait until Peter had arrived, and then she asked you plump and plain. And you took your courage in both hands and came—and you've been everything I dreamed of and more. From the first you made the nursery the happiest, serenest place ; I always felt welcome, never an intruder : you've given the children quiet nerves and good health, and you've been the greatest comfort always."

" Weel—" Ninny seemed rather at a loss. She took up her work, smoothing it out as she said : " I'm sure I'm gled ye're pleased. . . . Of course I ken fine I've nae manners. I ca' ye ' Mem,' for I canna get roond ' your ladyship,' an' I speak terrible broad. . . ."

" But that's one reason why I wanted you—that the children might be familiar with the Scots tongue."

Ninny shook her head. " They're terrible English, puir lambs. Ye see, there's his lordship, an' you, an' Elsie in the nursery, an' a' the servants inside an' oot, a' speakin' English, but I dae ma best, an' they ken what a' the auld words mean. Peter aye asks aboot it if he hears me use a new word : he's a great yin to speir——"

She was interrupted by a shriek from Quentin, and sprang forward to receive and comfort her youngest nursling :

" Was Peter bad to ye, ma bonnie lamb ? Wait an' I'll sort him."

Peter strolled up unabashed. " He was pulling the puppy's ears, so I pulled his hair to see how he liked it. He's not hurt, Ninny ; he's only shouting for fun."

Alison, who had begun again to thread berries, now looked up, saying : " Mummy, come to tea with us in the Crow-Wood. You haven't been to tea with us for *weeks*."

" Darling, both Daddy and I had tea with you on Sunday."

" Well, but you hurried, and went away to give all the visitors tea in the drawing-room."

" Why do visitors come to stay ? " Peter asked. " It isn't as if they were poor and needed food, like the poor tramps. Why don't we ask tramps to stay ? " He did not wait for an answer but went and stood on his head for a minute. When he came back he had got on to a different train of thought. " Where's Daddy ? " he asked. " I had my ride with Jim this morning."

"Daddy went to London yesterday to see poor Uncle Tim, who is so ill."

"Is he ill *still* ?" Alison asked ; "and I put him in my prayers three nights."

Alison's prayers were a great feature of the nursery life at Mintern Abbas. She insisted on saying them aloud and liked an audience. Every night she mentioned by name all her special friends ; she also prayed for any one who was ill, but was apt to become exasperated if an immediate cure was not the result.

"Why does Uncle Tim want Daddy if he's ill ?" Peter wanted to know.

"Wouldn't you want Daddy if you were ill ?" his mother asked.

"Oh, yes, but Daddy's my relation. He's not Uncle Tim's relation. Uncle Tim's not our real uncle, not like Uncle Jock, or Uncle Davy, or Mhor."

"*Isn't* he ?" said Alison.

"No." Peter had been going into the subject of relationship with Ninny. "To be a real uncle he'd need to be a brother of Mummy or Daddy, and Daddy hasn't any brother and only Aunt Pamela for a sister."

"But, Peter," Jean said, "it's just because Daddy has no brother of his own that Uncle Tim means so much to him. They've been friends all their lives. They played together, worked together, travelled together, and fought together. Out in France, in the great fighting, when Daddy was lying with his leg broken, Uncle Tim, though he was badly wounded himself, managed to drag him into safety. So you see, none of us can ever do enough for Uncle Tim—." She turned to Ninny—"I think it's the effects of that old wound that trouble him now. He seemed to get over the pneumonia all right, then there came one relapse after another, and now his nerves seem to have gone all to pieces, and that's the worst of all."

Ninny looked serious. "'Deed it is," she said. "Bad eneuch for a woman but a heap waur for a man. I wadna thocht Major Talbot wud hae gone like that, he was aye so blythe and cheery-like."

"Uncle Tim's my godfather," Peter reminded the company. "He sends me a present every birthday—a good one."

"And you don't even say him in your prayers," his sister reproached him.

"Oh," said Peter lightly, "I might put him next to Mummy and Daddy before I come to—Quentin, let *go* the puppy's tail."

Lady Bidborough rose to go, amid protests, Alison remarking bitterly, "Mummy *never* stays long enough."

"I'm so sorry, darling, but Daddy may be back any minute now and I want to be on the doorstep to welcome him. . . . Enjoy your picnic, and perhaps I'll bring Daddy out to the Crow-Wood after tea. Don't overfeed the puppy; it's mistaken kindness. Goodbye, my ducks."

Jean walked quickly until she reached the rose-garden. From there she could see the bend of the drive and the approach of the car.

As she stood in the warm, delicious afternoon among the roses, listening to the contented hum of the bees, knowing that every minute was bringing her beloved nearer, she sighed with sheer happiness.

From one rose-laden tree to another she went, bending over the blossoms, blush pink, pale yellow, glowing crimson, revelling in their sweetness, and humming to herself words that had run in her head all day :

> " There's comfort for the comfortless
> And honey for the bee. . . ."

Comfortless ! She smiled as she thought of her brimming cup, then sobered, remembering those whose cups were empty of aught but bitterness. How strangely, almost waywardly, things were portioned out in this world. Certainly it was not always the most deserving to whom the good things came. Perhaps—but this was not the moment to puzzle over the decrees of fate : the car was coming up the beech avenue.

She was at the door as it drew up, and in a second Lord Bidborough was up the steps.

" Jean, my blessed girl, what a refreshing sight you are ! Yes, I am a bit hot and dusty. I'll change, if you don't mind, before tea. I shan't be many minutes."

Lord Bidborough was forty-two, ten years older than his wife, but as he was neither fat nor bald, he still had the appearance of youth, and certainly he had the spirit.

" Well, this is good," he said a little later, as they sat together in Jean's own room. She had appropriated it the day she had come as a bride to Mintern Abbas, saying that it reminded her of the living-room at The Rigs. It was a small room, panelled, looking out over lawn and river and away across woods and meadows to the hills, and Jean had given it the touch she was able to give to any room she occupied.

Looking round it, her husband gave a satisfied sigh, saying :

" This room is so like you, Jean. I'd know it for yours anywhere. It's always meticulously neat—like yourself: a trifle austere perhaps." He nodded towards a bureau on which stood the miniature of an old lady, with white hair and a mouth that folded sternly. " Great-Aunt Alison dominates it, doesn't she ? "

Jean looked at the miniature and smiled.

" Poor Great-Aunt Alison ! I don't think she'd think the room very tidy ; too many flowers ; but I can't resist them against the old oak. . . . Am I very old-maidishly tidy, Biddy ? "

" It's part of you : it goes with all the rest. You wouldn't be yourself if you allowed yourself to lounge, or if you smoked, or were loose in speech or manners. I like the hint of austerity." He leant forward, smiling. " . . . I wonder if you remember a talk we had the day we were married, when you told me you thought it would be *stawsome* (you translated it as ' rather sickening ') if we had nothing to do but *love* all the time."

Jean blushed and shook her head. " Did I say that ? Surely not."

" Oh, yes. You said it. I was amused at the time, thinking it rather an unusual remark for a bride to make, but I've often thought of it since, when I saw couples who began with raptures, shipwreck, or descend to a dreary jog-trot, having obviously lost all interest in each other. I realize the wisdom of having reserves. . . . Well, what have you been about since I left you ? "

" Tim is worse " thought Jean to herself : " Biddy

dreads beginning to tell me about him. We'll talk about other things till he's rested," and she began an account of how she had spent the hours while he was away.

"I lunched yesterday with the Maynards: a large *hot* luncheon. After it the ominous words : ' *Now* you must see the garden.' It's dreadful of me, but I am so sick of garden, and oh, I know, it's like saying I'm sick of Spring or the Bible, but I can't help it. This summer has been so hot, and people's gardens are so large, and so similar. You wouldn't think you could get tired of herbaceous borders, but you can. And so many of them are making rock-gardens, and you're expected to poise on boulders and be intelligent. . . . The Maynards spare one nothing. We trailed, quite a party of us, along hot ashy paths, while Mrs. Maynard pointed out how large this blossom was, and what a wonderful colour the other. . . . I managed to ooze away before we reached the vegetables, and rushed home hoping to have tea with the children, but some people arrived—Americans— Doria Manson brought them. They asked to see over the house, and were nice, and interested, but it took so long that I only saw the babes at bed-time. . . . After dinner I sat here and wrote letters—worked off quite a heap—and thought of you in airless, August London."

Her husband lit a cigarette and remarked : "It's a very good imitation of the Sahara."

"And poor Tim lying in that grim Home ! " Jean went on. "I do think if he would only make the effort and come here it would do him good. He could come in an ambulance with his own nurse, and he'd have perfect quiet. This house is so big the noise of the children would never reach him. And at least he would smell roses instead of disinfectants. Don't you think you could persuade him, Biddy ? "

Lord Bidborough smoked for a minute in silence.

" No," he said at last, " he won't come here. I did suggest it, but I don't think he even listened. He was too full of his own plan. Yes. Something—nobody seems to know what—has roused him from the state of apathy he's been lying in all these weeks. He's taken the most tremendous desire to be on a ship. He would be well, he thinks, if he could wake up and hear the water swishing past. And of course the doctors are only too glad to encourage him in his idea."

Jean lifted a delighted face to her husband.

" Why, Biddy, that's *splendid* news ! It means that now he will recover, for the sun and the sea will do wonders for him. Of course he'll take a nurse with him, and a doctor too, if he's wise. Oh, Biddy, how glad you must be ! And I was thinking from something in your voice that he must be worse."

Lord Bidborough carefully placed the end of his cigarette in an ashtray as he said : " You haven't heard it all. Tim's idea is not only to get away from London —you can't wonder he loathes the place—but to get away also from doctors and nurses and everything that would remind him of his illness."

" But he can't go *alone*," Jean said, her hands clenching in her lap.

" No," said her husband, " he can't go alone ; he wants me to go with him." He got up and looked out of the window, and came back and sat down beside Jean.

" . . . You know how desperately unselfish Tim always was, never thought half enough about himself, but now it didn't seem to occur to him that I'd even hesitate. As a matter of fact I believe he's forgotten the years between, forgotten your existence and the children's; to him there's only the two of us again— and he needs me."

Jean leant forward and straightened a rose in a bowl on the gate-table. Presently she said:

" Tim is quite right to forget everything but that, Biddy: I'd hate that he should remember me as an obstacle and a hindrance. Of course you must go with him. Will it—will it be for long ? "

" All winter, I'm afraid. The doctors are keen on a long voyage, and he musn't be back in England until spring. His own idea is to go to Canada, then on to New Zealand. . . . Of course if he improved rapidly I might be able to leave him, but——"

There was silence in the room. Lord Bidborough smoked by the open window, staring at a scene he did not see, while Jean gradually realized what this would mean. She grudged even a day away from Biddy, and this would mean a whole winter out of their lives. A winter. Summer was delicious, but it was a restless time : they were much away, and when at home streams of people came and went. Winter was their own. How she loved the falling of the leaves, the first frosty mornings, the chilly grey-blue mists at twilight, the whistling wind ! Mintern Abbas was such a perfect place in winter, she thought, so cunningly lighted ; warm, with central heating for comfort and huge log fires for show ; smell-

ing deliciously of apples and chrysanthemums and burning wood.

The burden of a great house lay but lightly on Jean's
shoulders. True, Miss Hart, the housekeeper, kept her
place less because of her efficiency than because her
mistress's heart was tender. She sat in her room and
wrestled with accounts, but the house was really run by
Mrs. Watts, the cook. Not only did Mrs. Watts keep
everything going smoothly indoors, her beneficent in-
fluence extended to the village, where she was every
one's friend and comfort. Very large, very placid,
nothing upset her, nothing was a trouble. She spoke
little but listened with intelligence. With two such
women as Mrs. Watts and Ninny, Jean always felt that
she was armed against all slings and arrows of domestic
misfortune. They had made such plans for the winter,
she and Ninny and Mrs. Watts, plans to give every one
a good time. . . . Already Jean was looking forward to
the Christmas Tree and storing away gifts for it. . . .
And the gully below the lily-pond that she and Biddy
had meant to work at in the autumn and transform.
And the—Oh, but there were a hundred things that
would not be worth doing if Biddy were away. . . .

And as Jean realized all it meant she drooped so
pathetically that her husband cried :

" Don't look like that, Jean, girl. After all, it mayn't
be for long. I *may* be home for Christmas."

Jean sat up straight, and, though her face looked
pinched, she smiled bravely.

" Of course you may," she said. " Why, this is only
August. When d'you sail ? "

" Oh, there's nothing fixed. I had to see you first, of course. Probably September. I suppose I ought to be jolly glad to get the chance to do something for Tim, and I am glad, but——"

" There are no buts, Biddy. I'm glad too. It was just when I remembered all we'd planned for next winter. . . . But we'll do them yet—if we're spared. (Great-Aunt Alison always made us add that. Why, I don't know, because if we weren't spared no one would expect us to do anything !) Anyway, nothing would have been much fun with Tim lying lonely and ill. That he should get strong again is what matters most. And now, let's go to the Crow-Wood where the babes are picnicking, and let's try to forget that there are such things as partings in the world."

She took his hand and they went out together.

CHAPTER II

" Women never have half an hour that they can call their own."
FLORENCE NIGHTINGALE.

" BIDDY," Jean said to her husband as they sat at breakfast next morning, " Biddy, let's get all the plans for
your going away made at once, and then we can banish
the thought of it, so that the time we have together won't
be spoiled."

" All right, darling. There'll be a deuce of a lot to
arrange. . . . Sausage ? Bacon ? Mushroom omelette ?
Cold ham ? "

" Sausage, please. Yes, a tiny bit of bacon. One
thing I know, you won't taste anything so good as
sausages made by Mrs. Watts till you get home again."

Lord Bidborough came back from the sideboard and
sat down to enjoy his breakfast, remarking as he unfolded his napkin, " That's a true word. But to me
everything at Mintern Abbas is perfect, so whatever
the wide world has to offer me will be second best."

" Very nicely said, but it's the wrong spirit to go
travelling in. Besides, you know you love wandering.
Confess that the very idea of taking a steamer ticket
thrills you ! It always amazes me that you're content
to be a stay-at-home. Have I tethered you, Biddy ?
I haven't meant to. When we were married I made
all sorts of vows to myself about being unselfish and
letting you go off on expeditions with Tim. It would

ill become me to make a fuss and play the martyr now, when I've had nine undisturbed years of you."

"You're not playing the martyr, blessed child. It's I who feel a martyr. I want to be tethered, as you call it. Taking it all round I suppose I've had about as varied a life as any man could have, but I can say with perfect truth those nine years have been worth all that went before—By Jove, these sausages are good! I must have another."

"Sausages and sentiment!" Jean mocked. ". . . I've just realized that there'll be no stalking for you this year, poor lad. The children, too, will miss their time in Ross-shire. Pamela is so good to them and they adore the moors and burns at Kinbervie. Biddy, d'you think I should take the children to the seaside after you sail? It would be a melancholy kind of holiday, but it would brace them up after the hot summer."

Biddy carried his plate to the sideboard, and when he was seated again he very deliberately buttered a bit of toast before he said:

"Jean, I've been thinking, wouldn't it be a good plan for you and the children to spend next winter at Priorsford?"

"At Priorsford?" Jean laid down her cup. "But —but what about Mintern Abbas? Who would look after everything, the house and the gardens and—Oh, and the Institute, and the District Nurse, and the——"

"I know: that's just my point. They've got far too much into the habit of leaving things to you. It's high time somebody else took a hand. I know quite well if I leave you here all the people round will bully

you into doing things—meaning to be kind, I admit.
And this place would be a burden to you. I can see you
creeping about at night after Simson has retired majestically to rest, trying the fastenings, and looking under
sofas for possible burglars. You're scared at night,
though you're too proud to admit it, and I'd hate to
think of you alone in this big place, listening to the owls
hooting. I confess I'd go away much happier if I knew
that you and the children were comfortably settled in
some place near Priorsford, with Pamela and Lewis
within call if anything happened to worry you, and
people round that you've known since childhood. There's
sure to be some place to let. I'll write to Pamela.
Wouldn't you like the children to have a winter in
Priorsford? Think of Ninny's delight!"

"Ye—es," Jean said, "it would be lovely in many
ways—if I didn't feel a shirker."

Her husband laughed. "O Great-Aunt Alison!
That conscience of yours!"

"If we went to Priorsford," Jean continued, "why
shouldn't we go to The Rigs? You know we got electric light put in, and it's in perfect order. It would
hold the children and myself and Ninny. Of course
there would be the boys in the holidays, and——"

"And Miss Barton and her typewriter."

"Yes. But we might get a furnished house quite
near The Rigs and take a couple of maids and Elsie.
I don't know . . . but it might be managed."

"I'd like to think of you in The Rigs; and Mrs.
McCosh is a tower of strength."

Jean nodded. "I'd like it to be The Rigs myself.

It was nice of you, Biddy, to think of such a plan—
but don't let's talk about it any more just now. We'll
enjoy this summer day as if no black cloud were coming
over our particular bit of sky. Are you fairly free?
Could we do something with the children? . . . Here's
a letter from Pamela. Isn't it odd that, when we are
parched for want of rain, they are drowned out? She
says they might just as well be in Lincolnshire for all
they see of the hills! Mist to the doorstep. It *is* bad
luck. And they've got such a large party, rather heavy
in hand, I gather. Pamela says—where is it? Oh, yes.
' *At present there is nothing to report but rain; it's like
living in the middle of a wet sponge; everything squashy
and dripping. Even the most ardent sportsmen are daunted,
and show a tendency to sit about in the house. . . . The
women aren't so bad. The wise ones stay in their rooms
till luncheon, but the girls have a nasty trick of coming down
to breakfast and hanging on my hands most of the day. In
despair I suggested theatricals, a performance for the Nursing Association, and they have embarked on* Quality Street,
*chosen because there are several female parts—the female
being always more ready for impersonation and acting than
the male—(which sounds like a sentence from an eighteenth-
century novel)—and because Daphne Morris had played
" Phoebe " before. Fortunately I came across trunks of old
dresses in the attics, and they are happily rummaging among
them. Would it were September and you dear people here!
I wouldn't care then whether it rained or snowed or blew—— !* '
Pamela will be disappointed, Biddy."

" Yes, and I'm sorry to miss Kinbervie, but, after all,
that's a small part of the missing."

Jean turned to her letters. " I see they've sent the plans for the addition to the Cottage Hospital. They could be getting on with the work, couldn't they, even if—— What is it, Simson ? "

" Mrs. and Miss Marston in the library, your ladyship. They will not detain you more than a few minutes."

Simson removed his portly presence, walking delicately as one long accustomed to slippery oak floors.

" Institutes," said Jean resignedly. " When I lunched at Lovell on Tuesday we talked for two hours on the subject. Mrs. Marston must have thought of something fresh to say."

" But why should Mrs. Marston rise betimes and disturb people's breakfasts to talk about Institutes? Don't go till you've finished."

" Oh, I finished long ago. I was just idling. Coming ? "

" Lord, no, I'm taking Peter out riding at ten. Get rid of your visitors and come and see us start."

Mrs. Marston was a woman of fifty who would have been strikingly handsome if her head had not been a trifle too large for her body. Her daughter Sara, a perfectly nice girl, was handicapped by a bad manner. She was very good-looking, though Lord Bidborough, who shrank from her supercilious stare, said she made him think of Buffalo Bill and the Wild West, and christened her for his own satisfaction, *Rain-in-the-face*.

Mrs. Marston gripped Jean's hand with enthusiasm, and spoke rapidly in a high clear voice.

" How are you ? Forgive this shamefully early call. No. No breakfast, thank you. Sara and I are on our way to London. An absurd place to go to in this heat, but Jemmy has chosen to arrive there this afternoon, and we couldn't have him un-met after three years' absence, could we? . . . My dear, how lovely this room is. Those flowers! And such a business-like writing-table! You have one side and your husband the other? Isn't it perfect, Sara?"

Sara, after a brief greeting, had begun to march about the room, staring at water-colour drawings of the three children ranged along the ledge of a bookcase, and pulling out a book here and there. She made no response to the remark addressed to her by her mother, who continued:

"What I came to say was that after you had left the other day it occurred to me that it would be rather a scheme if our Institute joined yours for the October meeting, seeing you are having a special speaker. I know our people do love to come here, and it would be a nice beginning of the Session for them. I shall be away for October myself, so it would fit in very well. . . . And then, didn't you go in for the acting competition last year? I wonder if you would come over and give us some hints? Or let us come and see you? It would be such a help. You are all so talented at Mintern Abbas, and Chipping-on-the-Wold has a lot to learn. Now please say yes, and Sara and I'll rush off and leave you in peace. No, positively I mustn't sit down."

"Please do," said Jean, "until I explain. Since I saw you on Tuesday we've got news that changes all our plans. My husband has to go abroad for the winter with an invalid friend: I may go to Scotland with the children, and I'm afraid the Institute 'll have to look after itself.

Luckily, there are several members quite capable of
taking charge."

Mrs. Marston sat down suddenly. " Oh," she said,
and again, " *Oh.*" Then, " This *is* bad news. I wish
I'd never promised to be President. I was leaning on
you, my dear.—Sara, isn't it dreadful ? Lady Bidborough's going to be away all next winter in Scotland ! "

Sara turned her piercing gaze on Jean and said :

" Scotland in winter sounds pretty foul. But it
can't be worse than Chipping-on-the-Wold. Get up,
Mother."

Her mother rose obediently. " I'm dreadfully dis-
couraged," she murmured. " Of course it isn't your
fault, and sick friends are so selfish, but you shouldn't
be so helpful, really you shouldn't. Yes, Sara, I'm
coming—Oh, could you write me out the names of
some one-act plays ? Nothing about dream-pedlars or
Jacobites : something really funny without being low
—you know the sort of thing I mean : suitable to a
village audience."

When the door had closed behind her visitors, Jean ran
out to the garden to have a minute with the children
before she interviewed the housekeeper. It was not her
first sight of them, for she always took the nursery on her
way down to breakfast. It made, she said, a good beginning for the day, the sight of the three small figures with
the morning sun on their gilt heads, supping porridge
vigorously, in a nursery from which, Peter boasted, you
could see the young crows in their nests when the wind
was singing " Rock-a-bye, baby," to them.

She was in time to see Peter start off proudly with his

father, mounted on a mild pony that could not be persuaded to curvet.

"Take care, my dears," Jean cried. ". . . You'll
find me in the library, Biddy. . . . Alison, you will soon
be going out with Daddy, too."

The child shook her head. "Ponies have such slippy
backs," she said.

As Jean turned to go into the house she was told that
the rector's wife wished to see her and was waiting in
the hall. She sighed when she heard it, for Mrs. Turner,
with the air of desiring above everything not to be a
nuisance, was apt to put off much time.

"No, thank you," the lady said to an invitation to
come to the library. "I won't think of coming farther.
I know how busy you are in the morning, but there was
something I thought I ought to discuss with you, something that has worried me a good deal; in fact I have lost
sleep over it ; and I said to Herbert this morning while
we were at breakfast : ' I'll go and consult with Lady
Bidborough,' and he said, ' I would most certainly.' "

The Turners were a childless couple with a comfortable
private income, who spent their own time worrying about
trifles, and Jean's heart sank when she heard that she was
to be consulted, for she knew it would be a lengthy
business.

"Do sit down," she said, "and tell me what's worrying you."

"No," said Mrs. Turner firmly, "I won't sit down.
If I once sat down I might be tempted to sit too long."

Her large earnest eyes were fixed on Jean's face as
she said : "I always think it is a crime to waste people's

time, for I know how *precious* the hours are to me.
Herbert said only yesterday that he did not know
how I got through so much, but I told him it was simply
because I map out every hour and never waste a minute.
Yes. Breakfast at 8.30, then prayers : see cook :
correspondence : flowers : visiting, and so on. Then
when evening comes I can fold my hands—don't you
think there is something very sweet and pathetic in the
expression to *fold* one's hands ?—and feel that rest is
sweet at close of day to workers. . . . Herbert has just
gone off on his bicycle to Woodford to see dear old
Amelia. You know she was cook with us for long, and
so interested in everything—the dear dogs and the church
services. I could even leave her to do the flowers. But
she began to get a little *peevish*, poor dear : old servants
are so apt to develop tempers, I can't think why, for
housework is so soothing. At times she was quite rude
to me. Yes, everything I said seemed to irritate her ;
wasn't it sad ? I would have borne with her, but
Herbert said ' No.' It was demoralizing, he said, for
Amelia herself, and bad for my nerves." Mrs. Turner
smiled wistfully. " I used to get so upset when I received
a snappish answer to a kind question, and she was just
eligible for an old-age pension, so we got her a dear little
cottage at Woodford, which happened to fall vacant—
so providential. . . ."

She stopped.

" Yes," Jean prompted. " You wanted to discuss
something. . . ."

Mrs. Turner glanced round the hall and, lowering
her voice, said, " It's Mrs. Hastings."

" Mrs. Hastings," Jean reflected. " Isn't that the nice woman who has come to the cottage by the ferry ? I think she'll be a great help to the Mothers' Union."

" But can we allow her to help, dear Lady Bidborough ? She is not a widow as we supposed : I've found to my great regret that she is *living apart from her husband*. Of course, I have mentioned it to no one but Herbert : you know what *he* feels about the sanctity of marriage ? "

Jean felt that at least she could guess, and a spasm of inward laughter seized her as she thought of that gentleman's decent, cod-like countenance.

It was with great difficulty that she persuaded the rector's wife that it was the kindest as well as the wisest thing to say nothing.

" You see," she said, " we don't know the circumstances nor what the poor woman has had to bear."

" But is it *right* to pass it over ? Is it not our *duty* to make it known ? "

" I don't know," said Jean, " but it doesn't seem to me that it's ever any one's duty to make things harder for another. I think if you were specially kind to Mrs. Hastings——"

Mrs. Turner brightened : she liked to be kind.

" Yes," she said, " and Herbert might make a special point of preaching on the sanctity of the home, and the duty a wife owes to her husband. She might, who knows, see things in a better light. . . . I am so glad I came to you, Lady Bidborough. Now I must fly back to my neglected household."

Jean walked with her visitor to the door, thinking

what a decent soul she was after all, and regretting that she had so often tound her tiresome and her Herbert dull.

" I wonder," she said, " if Mr. Turner likes grouse. He does ? Then I'll send down a brace. They came from Scotland yesterday, the first of the season. . . . There's a chance that we won't be at Mintern Abbas this winter. . . . I think you've met our great friend Major Talbot ? Yes. He has been very ill for months, and the doctors think that the only chance for him is a long voyage and a winter in sunshine. There is no one to go with him except my husband. . . . I may take the children to my old house in Scotland. It *is* a turn-up, isn't it ? "

The rector's wife was aghast. " What dreadful news ! What shall we *do* ? Mintern Abbas means so much to us all."

" You will manage beautifully," Jean assured her. " I'll try not to put more on you than I can help. We'll arrange for speakers for the Mothers' Union and the Institute before I go, and make plans for the Christmas festivities. . . . I want you to be my almoner."

Mrs. Turner's troubled face lightened a little.

" Of course," she said, " I'll do my best, but how we shall miss you and the children and all the cheerful bustle of this house ! It keeps us all interested and alive. I don't really see how I can face having no one to come to for advice."

Jean, looking about sixteen in a white frock belted with green, laughed aloud : " You make me feel so old," she protested. " When I go back to Priorsford

no one will think of asking me for advice : they'll give
it me—and I'll feel young again ! "

" It's quite true, dear Lady Bidborough, quite true.
You are really only a girl and we all lean on you.   I
was saying so to Herbert only the other night. . . .
What Herbert will think of this news I simply *don't*
know.   I'm afraid it will quite spoil his lunch," and
shaking her head, Mrs. Turner departed.

That morning, one thing after another cropped up
demanding attention, and it was nearly luncheon-time
before Jean was free.

" Anyway," she thought, " I'll have Biddy to myself
for lunch," and, remembering that she had said she
would do the flowers herself, she seized a basket and
scissors and ran out to gather them.   But about a
quarter past one Simson came stepping delicately
among the roses to announce that Her Grace the
Duchess of Malchester and Lady Agnes Chatham were
in the drawing-room.   " In the *drawing-room*, m'lady,"
said Simson impressively.   He only put the fine flower
of the county into that sacred apartment : the library
or the boudoir were good enough for ordinary callers.

Jean handed Simson the roses she had cut and went
off to wash her hands, feeling rather out of patience
with the world at large.

The Duchess of Malchester was a round, little woman
with a soft voice and a merry laugh.   She was con-
sistently pleasant to every one, but as her circle was
enormous and she had no memory for faces, she seldom
knew to whom she was talking.

She kissed Jean affectionately as she said :

" It is really too bad of us to descend upon you like this, but the fact is Agnes and I have simply run away. Yes. You see this is our month for entertaining relations, and the house is packed with them—both sides ; and they're all taking the opportunity to tell us home-truths—So ungrateful, isn't it ? Last night, after dinner, my sister-in-law—Jane Dudley, you know—who doesn't play bridge, made me sit beside her while she tore poor Agnes to pieces. At breakfast this morning —my dear, they *all* come down for breakfast !—an aged aunt on my father's side criticized me severely. We didn't know who would attack us at luncheon so we made off to find refuge with you."

" We came to you, Jean," Lady Agnes said in her soft deep voice, " to have our feathers smoothed down : you're better at smoothing than any one I know—— Hallo, Biddy ! "

Lord Bidborough remarked, after greeting his guests, that he thought they had a houseful of visitors.

" It's because of them we're here," the girl told him cheerfully. " We've just been explaining to Jean that the house is full of relations who all think they've a right to be rude. We thought we might just stand them at dinner if we'd had a rest from them at luncheon, and I said : ' Let's fly to Jean.' You've got rid of your lot ? "

Jean laughed suddenly. " I like," she said, " the note of true hospitality in that remark ! We *have* got rid of them : in other words, we have parted regretfully from our delightful and delighted guests." She nodded at Lady Agnes as she added : " They were, you know."

" But they weren't relations," Lady Agnes insisted.

" No, but relations don't terrify us as they do you. We can count all ours that matter on the fingers of one hand."

Jean held out her hand and ticked each finger off. " Pamela and Lewis, Davy, Jock, Mhor. Five."

Lady Agnes looked across the table at her mother, crying :

" Oh, Mums, aren't they lucky ? We've got aunts and grand-aunts, and uncles and grand-uncles, all full of proper family feeling, all determined to spend some time every year under the family roof-tree. They look and dress like ordinary mortals, but they might have come out of the Ark so far as their ideas go. Nothing must be changed at Malchester. Though their own houses are quite modern and comfortable they resent any change there. We had positively to fight for electric light and central heating—hadn't we, Mums ? And old great-uncle John patrols the house in a dressing-gown every night, scared to death in case we go up in flames. I got the fright of my life when I met him at midnight in the Picture Gallery : I thought it was the family ghost."

Lord Bidborough looked across at the Duchess. " Does this romantic miss frequent the haunted gallery at midnight ? "

That comfortable lady merely shrugged her shoulders, smiling. She was enjoying her lunch and her company.

" Tell me, Jean," she said, " when do you go to Scotland ? Is it the very beginning of September ? "

Jean looked at her husband.

" Alas ! " she said, " our plans are altered. Biddy is going abroad, and I am taking the children to Scotland for the winter."

Lady Agnes laid down her knife and fork. " *What !* " she said. " That's my last outpost gone ! Jean, are you and Biddy going to separate ? . . . And I *banked* on you two."

" Really, my dear ! " her mother warned her, " you go too far. Jean—what has happened, my dear ? "

" Biddy, you tell this time," Jean cried. " I seem to have been recounting it all morning."

" What a nuisance," said the Duchess, when things had been explained. " I quite see that you can't very well do anything else, but still . . . And I was relying on you, Jean, to take Agnes out next winter and let me be lazy at home."

" And *I* thought you'd help with the play we're doing in October," Lady Agnes said ; " there's a perfect part for you. Oh ! and my ball in December ! It's too bad, Jean."

" I shall miss you all sadly," Jean said.

" I wonder ! " Lady Agnes munched a salted almond and studied her hostess. " Biddy, I think you're rash to let Jean go back to Priorsford. She loves it too well. . . . And there's something so very nymphish about her, I'd never be surprised to find her becoming the shade under the beech-tree or whatever it was the girl became in the story."

" Most unlikely," said the Duchess comfortably. " Though I'm selfishly sorry we're to lose you for a winter, I think Jean will be greatly the better of getting away from us all for a little. I hope you will get a rest from responsibilities, my dear."

Her daughter scoffed. " Not she! The Priorsford people—horrible creatures I'm sure they are—will have ' the face ett off her.' Are you going back to The Rigs? Really, Jean? Well, I'm coming to stay with you whether you ask me or not. Yes, I'm determined to see Priorsford with my own eyes, and Mrs. McCosh, and Bella Bathgate."

Jean nodded. " Of course. We'd love to have you. But don't come expecting too much, and be disappointed. I'd *hate* any one who didn't appreciate Priorsford."

When the luncheon guests had departed others arrived for tea, and it was not till dinner was over that the husband and wife could finish their morning talk.

" Wasn't I right, Jean, not to leave you here? As Agnes puts it, elegantly, the neighbours would have ' the face ett off you!' You're too popular, my girl."

Jean was leaning back in a chair by the wide open window enjoying the evening air that came in sweet with a thousand scents.

" Not so much popular," she said lazily, " as soft. It's easier for me to do things than refuse, and people have found that out—I've written to Miss Janet Hutton, Biddy, to ask if there's a furnished house to let for the winter near The Rigs. I didn't want to trouble Pamela when she is away. Besides, Pamela really doesn't know much about Priorsford. She and Lewis keep themselves very much to themselves in their green glen at Laverlaw. . . . Did you ring up the steamer people? "

Lord Bidborough came over and sat on the window seat.

"They can give us the accommodation we want on a ship sailing on the 25th September—the *Duchess of Inverness* or something. I've written to Tim sending him all details—he'll be in a fever until things are settled."

"Oh, Biddy, it makes it so dreadfully definite, a fixed date. As Ninny says ' a set time soon comes.' "

Biddy nodded gloomily. "I'm wondering why I ever considered going. To leave you with so many responsibilities—the children, two places to run, and all your own money to worry about! If anything happens, if you're too worried, cable, and I'll come as quick as I can be brought."

Jean patted his hand reassuringly. "Don't let's be silly," she said. "Just think of soldiers and Indian civilians and other people who spend their lives parting from their best beloved! I've been reminding myself all day how little I have to complain about. Indeed, I won't cable for you. You're quite capable of trying to fly home from Australia and arriving with a *dunt*."

CHAPTER III

> " You know how one sits on a fresh day in May
> or October and wishes one could have a fire in the
> parlour, but cannot because it is not the season of
> the year? Miss Mitford is as if you lighted the
> fire and it blazed up bravely, and you sank down
> in the sofa and toasted yourself snugly and said,
> ' Ah, that is just what I was longing for.' That
> is what it is like when she comes into a room."
>
> MISS BARRETT'S ELOPEMENT.

MISS JANET HUTTON's parlour—she liked the word—
was as pleasant a room as you could wish to see. It
looked out to a small bright garden, the burn at the
foot dividing it from wide fields, which mounted on one
side to the hills, and sloped on the other to the river.
It was a most un-fussy room, with its plain old furniture and bare spaces of floor. There were many books
in it, the newest as well as the oldest, flowers, and—
except in the few hot days of a Scots summer—always
in the grate a fire that sparkled.

One afternoon, late in September, Miss Hutton was
in her parlour with her friend Mirren Strang. They
were looking out at the flaunting autumn flowers that
still made the garden gay, and Janet Hutton said :

" They're holding their own, but a night's frost will
finish them. We get more frost in Priorsford than you
get in Muirburn."

Mrs. Strang nodded. " Hopewaterfoot is sheltered.
I believe I'll have my chrysanthemums for another

month." Her eyes wandered to the quiet fields and the blue hills beyond. " Your room, Janet," she said, " is like yourself, it has a pleasant outlook. I always think you look at life with such serene eyes."

" Do I ? Well, you see, it can't hurt me now."

Mirren stared. " My dear, that's a rash statement for any mortal to make."

" I know, but don't you think the real hurting is seeing those we love hurt ? Since my mother died I've nobody of my own, no people so close that I must suffer if they suffer : I mean, no one to agonize over. Surely I can bear what is sent to myself without making a fuss."

Mirren shrugged her shoulders. " I call that disgustingly stoical. When my time comes I promise you I'll make fuss enough for half a dozen. . . . You and I are alike, Janet, in being almost alone in the world. It has its advantages of course, but sometimes . . ."

Miss Hutton looked down at the sock she was knitting. " Robbie would have been over thirty," she said. " Married, probably."

" There might have been children. It would have been funny—and nice—to see Robbie's children." Mirren's voice sank, then brisked up as she added : " But more than likely I wouldn't have got on with the wife. . . . Janet, how many tea-parties d'you suppose are given in Priorsford in one afternoon ? As I came along to you to-day I met numbers of women that I know vaguely, all obviously going out to tea : clean gloves, tidy hat, *you* know."

" I know. I was invited to two myself : Mrs. Jowett's and the Miss Duncans'."

"What I've made you miss! I know Mrs. Jowett's parties. The good soul is too full of the milk of human kindness to be a very entertaining companion. . . . The Miss Duncans I don't know. Don't they live near the old golf-course?"

"Yes, on the top of the hill. The view is marvellous, and they have their dining-room upstairs, which is such a nice thing to have. I shall never forget last Christmas-time when I went to tea there. It had been snowing all day and had cleared to glittering frost. When we went into the dining-room I just stood and gasped. There were silver candle-sticks on the polished round table and bright red berries: the blinds were up and the moon was rising over the white hills. The fire-light and candle-light, the red of the berries, the sparkle of the silver, the gold of the moon . . . ! They've promised to ask me again the first snowfall we have."

Janet sat back in her wide wooden chair with arms and smiled at her recollections, and her friend watching her thought what a wholesome, heartsome creature she looked, with her greying hair, her firm rosy cheeks, and wide humorous mouth.

"Dear Janet, with the brindled locks! I love the way your hair is quite black in some places and white in others: it's so attractive, with the rose of your cheeks and the blue of your eyes. I don't remember what you were like in your youth, but I don't think you could ever have been as good looking as you are now."

Miss Hutton took Mirren's compliments with great calm.

" You couldn't remember me in my youth for I'm almost ten years older than you are. Yes, I'm sixty : and a very nice age I find it."

" *Do* you ? I'm fifty and I think it's horrible. Half a century sounds so terrific, and birthdays occur with such alarming frequency. Kirsty Home's small girl, Fanny, since she was two and could toddle, has always appeared at Hopewaterfoot on my birthday morning in March with the first daffodils (generally kept on the nursery mantelpiece for days to bring them out), and really, you know, it seems as if the child were constantly there ! I'm fairly appalled at the shortness of life. You are young, and before you know where you are your youth is gone. That's why I don't think we should ever be angry at youthful follies and impertinences : even while the young things are scoffing at age it is upon them. . . . I suppose I should be rather ashamed to confess it, but, fifty and all as I am, I've still got a great zest for life. I enjoy everything—getting up in the morning and having my cold bath : going down to eat a good breakfast : my letters : work (though I malign it) : motoring about our adorable Tweeddale : my friends : my books : my holidays : the seasons as they come : bird song : the sunsets. . . . It's a great life I tell you, Janet, given decent health, and even with poor health there are compensations. I wish I could get Rebecca Brand to enjoy things : she will never *own* to being happy. Isn't it odd ? "

Miss Hutton carefully picked up a dropped stitch, then said :

" As to odd—living with an enthusiastic eager creature

like you might make a person as naturally contrary as
Rebecca become all the more apathetic. How is
Rebecca ? ''

" Oh," said Mirren, " as well as ever woman was. I
think she's glad to be back with me, at least she's glad
to be near the Manse and her brother. She gets on well
with her sister-in-law, and the baby is a great delight.
She must have been miserable in that place in Edinburgh,
for Rebecca was never intended by Providence to be a
companion to an old lady. To begin with she never sees
anything to do, and when she sits down to sew or read
she doesn't at all like to be disturbed. I can imagine
the impotent wrath of the old lady waiting for cushions
and hot-water bottles that never came ! ''

" But is she any real use to you ? ''

" Well, I wouldn't call her useful, exactly, but I like
having her. She isn't stupid, and there is something
so utterly honest and decent about her that I can't
help respecting her. And she makes the place seem more
like home. I'm always glad to go back to her. And
you know, Janet, it isn't every one who is supportable
as a companion. If I got one of the really helpful and
agreeable kind I'd probably weary of her and curse
her.''

Janet smiled : she knew her friend. Presently she
said : " I'm glad you've got Rebecca. I never liked
your living alone. I am alone, but, being a ruminative,
cow-like creature, I don't mind, and, besides, in Priorsford I'm in the middle of a busy brisk little community.
Hopewaterfoot is removed from the haunts of men. . . .
By the way, have you heard the latest news ? Lady

Bidborough is coming with her children to Priorsford for the winter."

"Lady Bidborough? Little Jean Jardine! Whatever for? Hasn't she houses and lands in England? This is great news. Where are they going to live?"

Janet laid down her stocking. "I am the fountainhead of knowledge, so to speak. Jean wrote to me about a month ago asking if I knew of a house to let furnished anywhere near The Rigs, and told me that her husband had to go for a voyage with his greatest friend, who was recovering from a severe illness. . . . There is a house just behind The Rigs, rather a nice place, called 'The Neuk,' owned by people who only use it in summer, and she has taken that. Jean herself wants to stay at The Rigs with her children; The Neuk will be used as an overflow. I think she said her secretary would live there, and the boys when they come. . . . Three maids are coming from Mintern Abbas."

"Dear me, this is great excitement. . . . How long is it since Jean left? Nine years, is it? Won't Priorsford *buzz*!"

Janet looked up quickly. "Why should it?" she asked. "Everybody assumes that a country town is a hotbed of gossip; it's most unfair. In Priorsford we certainly take a friendly interest in our neighbours, but we are *not* gossips,—with one or two exceptions."

"Yes, I know the exceptions! But I believe you're right. 'Let live' is more or less the motto of Priorsford. . . . Well, *I'm* vastly excited about Jean coming back into our lives. She was a duck of a child, but I didn't

see much of her after she grew up : I was away so much.
Were you in Priorsford when the romance was going
on ? ''

" No. Mother and I were abroad that winter. I
wish I had been here to see a fairy tale come true. For
the whole thing really was a sort of fairy tale. But it
seems to have stood the test of time. Nine years, and
this is the first time they have been separated, and it's
evidently a great wrench. It was Lord Bidborough
who thought of the Priorsford plan. Jean herself wanted
to hold the fort at Mintern Abbas : she always had a
conscience, the child.''

" She could hardly escape it," said Mirren. " You
remember old Miss Alison Jardine, the great-aunt who
brought them all up ? An old terror ! ''

" She was, rather. But you'll admit her training was
very successful. She managed to give Jean a certain
distinction, to make her just a little different from other
girls. Jean's manners were so good. She was neither
affected nor offhand, but frank and natural, rather like
a nice boy. And remember she was left at the age of
eighteen to look after not only her own two brothers,
but little Gervase Taunton, her stepmother's child by
a second marriage.''

" *Mein Gott!* It sounds like ' Ministering Children.'
How did she escape being a horrid little prig ? ''

" I know. But Jean was gay as well as sedate, and
it was a very happy home. . . . Yes, I wish I could have
been here when Miss Pamela Reston took Bella Bathgate's rooms, and Lord Bidborough arrived to visit his
sister. You were away too, I think ? ''

Mirren nodded. " Most people were glad to settle down after the war, but Peace sent me wandering. . . . It made things so final somehow. The bells on Armistice Day ! I don't think I ever realized that Robbie was really gone until old Watty Somerville began to pull the Muirburn Kirk bell because Peace had come. I had hardly cried through it all, but that day I wept myself sick." She stared out at the autumn flowers for a minute, then turned to her friend with a laugh. " Life's a comic business. D'you know, I'm rather sorry Jean's coming back. She's grown into a legend. Jean, Lady Bidborough, who was an ordinary girl in Priorsford till the ' baron's heir ' appeared and carried her away to reign amid unimagined splendour. And here she is walking out of her fairy tale and back to the little house in the little town, bereft (for the time) of her husband and accompanied by three (probably very ordinary) children. She may even have grown stout . . . perhaps a little pompous. . . ."

" Oh, no, Mirren," Miss Hutton protested. " Jean pompous is unthinkable. . . . Oh, dear, this sounds like a caller."

" Mrs. Duff-Whalley," the maid announced.

A small woman came into the room, with an important air, and stopped in the middle, surveying the two occupants.

" *Actually* I've found you in, Miss Hutton ! How d'you do ? And Mrs. Strang. *How* d'you do ? Quite a pleasant day, isn't it ? " She chose a chair and sat down, while her companions meekly resumed their seats. Wherever Mrs. Duff-Whalley was she elected

herself mistress of ceremonies, relegating her hostess
and every one else to the background.

She began : " Did you motor down from Muirburn,
Mrs. Strang ? Oh, you *have* a car ? Then you aren't
quite cut off from society."

" Not quite," Mirren said gravely.

" And of course you have the Homes fairly near you
and Lady Carruthers, dear woman. D'you see much
of the Laverlaw people ? "

" When they are at home they are hospitable. But
they are away a good deal in winter, and of course you
know they go to their place in Ross-shire from July to
October."

Mrs. Duff-Whalley reared her head in a way she had,
as she replied, " *Of course,* I know that. When I met
Lady Tweedie yesterday at lunch at the Olivers' she
told me she had been visiting them. Kinbervie is the
name of the place. Quite a large place it seems, but
very wild. . . . Mrs. Elliot is delightful of course, but
it's a pity she seems to care so little for society. She's
almost as bad as her husband. I often say to Lewis
Elliot when I meet him, ' Now, *when* are you coming
to dine with me ? ' and he blushes like a girl ! Odd
that people in their position should positively shrink
from their own kind ! "

Mirren looked sceptical as she said, " But d'you think
they do? They're a very popular couple up with us,
and certainly don't shirk their responsibilities : they
help with everything, and Laverlaw is quite a hive of
industry."

" And how are the Homes ? " Mrs. Duff-Whalley

inquired. "I've been meaning to call on them all
summer, but there are so many demands on one's time.
Is that marriage really a success? Colonel Home
always struck me as such a crabbed individual, lame
too, and much older than his wife. But of course she
was glad of a home."

Mrs. Strang laughed. "I don't think pretty Kirsty
was in any crying need of a home."

"Of course, I forgot, she has money."

"She has, but I'm not thinking of that. . . . Kirsty
got the man she wanted, she adores her children, and,
indeed, it would be difficult to find a happier home
than Phantasy."

"I'm sure I'm glad to hear it," Mrs. Duff-Whalley
said without warmth. "It's *too* distressing to hear of
so many unhappy marriages. I can't help sometimes
being thankful that Muriel has so far been obdurate.
. . . I heard some astonishing news this morning, that
little Jean Jardine, Lady Bidborough, you know, is
coming to winter in Priorsford. Do you know anything
about it, Miss Hutton?"

Janet, who had been calmly knitting while she listened
to the conversation, turned her deliberate gaze on her
visitor, and said:

"Yes, Lady Bidborough is coming to The Rigs.
Lord Bidborough has had to go with an invalid friend,
who has been ordered a sea voyage."

Mrs. Duff-Whalley's small keen eyes searched her
companion's face, as if suspecting something hidden in
her simple statement.

"Very sad," she said at last. "It's quite obvious to

me that there's been a rupture. I never did think that marriage would prove a success. Too much disparity in *every* way. Lord Bidborough so aristocratic, and Jean such a plain little thing. Lady Tweedie said to me only the other day, ' In these levelling days, when Jack's as good as his master, we old county people must make a *stand*.' It's really deplorable how lax we are becoming. Young men marry beneath them, bring chorus girls to their parents and expect a welcome for them—Ridiculous ! . . . And Jean is actually coming back to The Rigs ! Why, it's a *hovel* compared to what she's accustomed to. Dear, dear, I feel quite distressed about it."

" Oh, but you needn't. You will be glad to know that it is not as you fear. Major Talbot, who is Lord Bidborough's greatest friend—I believe he actually saved his life in the War—has been lying dangerously ill for months and must be out of England for the winter. He has no relations and is sick of hired help, and his old friend felt it his duty to go with him. I'm very sure Jean supported her husband in that. Lord Bidborough wanted Jean to be near his sister and away from the responsibilities of a big house and estate, so home she comes to Priorsford. She wanted to be in The Rigs with the children—sentiment, that,—and they've taken The Neuk—that nice house in the big garden, just behind The Rigs—to overflow into. It is really all very simple."

Mrs. Duff-Whalley sat silent for a minute—it was obviously a disappointing explanation—then she reared her head, remarking, " It's very astonishing. . . . Well, I *hope* everything is all right and that it really is a sick friend that Lord Bidborough has gone off with, but as a woman of the world—Well, well. She has taken The Neuk, you say. My daughter, Mrs. Egerton Thomson, wanted a house for a month or two in the summer and I took the chance to look through several. The Neuk isn't bad, quite decently furnished, and a billiard room : six bedrooms, I think, and fairly large public rooms. But if Lady Bidborough was coming back would it not have been much liker the thing if she had taken a *place* : there are several nice places in the neighbourhood she could have had. It's not as if money were any object. I wonder how she spends all she has. You know she got a large fortune from that old man—what was he called ? Peter Reid. He must have been insane. Was there no one to contest the will ? ''

Mrs. Duff-Whalley rose to her feet and Miss Hutton asked mildly : '' Why should any one have contested it ? The old man had a perfect right to leave his money as he pleased. . . . Must you go ? ''

'' Indeed I must. . . . Good-bye, Mrs. Strang. Muriel and I mean to call on Mrs. Home one day soon— perhaps Tuesday next. We might see you at the same time if you are free that day.''

'' Would you like to lunch with me ? '' Mirren asked.

'' Well, that would be nice, and give us a long after- noon for calling. That's settled then. Tuesday. One- thirty, I suppose ? . . . Good-bye, Miss Hutton, you must come and lunch with me some day. I'll ring up.''

Mrs. Duff-Whalley stepped into her car and was whirled away to her residence, The Towers, which stood on the outskirts of Priorsford. A very large, staring

villa, with many bow-windows and pepper-pot turrets,
it had been built for twenty years ; but wind and
weather seemed to have no effect on its red and white-
ness, and it looked almost as glaringly new as the day
it was finished.

Mrs. Duff-Whalley found her daughter Muriel in the
morning-room, rather listlessly trying over a new song.

" You're in, Muriel. . . . Evidently there's a tea-
party at Glenoliver : odd we weren't invited : they
owe us a tea-party. Did no one call this afternoon ?
. . . I've been to tea with the new people who've bought
Archfield. They are still in a great turn-up. I don't
think Mrs. Forbes can be much of a manager ; there
seemed a lack of a head : servants dodging about in
each other's way——"

" They wouldn't be keen on a visitor for tea."

" No, the invitation was rather halting, but it was
tea-time, so I stayed. I doubt if they'll be much use
in the county. One daughter, married, a son in Kenya
or somewhere, and a young son at home. . . . They
seem a quiet couple. He likes books and talked away
about some coloured prints. . . . Then I went to Miss
Hutton's to get the truth about Jean Jardine. She
says Lord Bidborough has had to go for a voyage with
a sick friend—a *very* queer story !—and Jean *is* coming
to The Rigs ! "

" But surely," said Muriel, " that's absurd. The Rigs
is a mere cottage ; there isn't a decent-sized room in it :
where will she put nurses and children ? "

" They've taken the house just behind—The Neuk.
You remember I looked at it for Minna ? . . . I must

say it seems to me a very odd arrangement. It's all very well for Janet Hutton to talk about Lord Bidborough having to take a sick friend abroad, but I think he must have been glad of the chance. Men in that station are always rovers, and I never did think Jean would be able to hold him, quiet, dull little thing that she was. Now you, Muriel, have some *go* in you. If you had had the chance . . ."

Muriel moved impatiently. " Well, I hadn't. And now I'm thirty-four."

" You don't look it," said her mother quickly. " You don't look a day more than five-and-twenty."

" The fact remains. . . . In a year or two I'll be one of the spinsters of Priorsford."

" Oh, no, Muriel, don't say that. Don't get such a thing into your head. People marry later now ; you've lots of time. Why, look at Nancy Burnett ; she must be forty if she's a day, and no one thinks of putting her on the shelf. She's always the centre of everything."

" Nancy Burnett has brains, and can fill her life full of so many things that I don't suppose she even gives marriage a thought. With me it's different. I've only brains for a house, and they're not needed, for you see to everything. It's no pleasure to me to sit on committees : I loathe them. I'm not religious, so I get no comfort from putting flowers in the church and attending early services. I never was taught to read good books and it's too late to acquire the taste, so I only read novels, and I'm sick of them. I'm quite good at games, but there are so many young girls coming up, and—oh, what's the good of talking. . . . And now here comes Jean Jardine, with her title and her children, to remind me how many years I've been hanging round this dead-alive place.''

"Muriel,''—Mrs. Duff-Whalley's face was firm with purpose,—" Muriel, we'll go away for the winter. You've wanted to, often, but I wouldn't stir ; but I'll go now. I don't deny it'll be a wrench, for I like winter in Priorsford, but I'll go. We might take a cruise to the West Indies. I see numbers of titled people are doing that. It would be a complete change for you. I can see I've been selfish. I'm so taken up running the house and looking after the servants, and sitting on committees, and keeping things going in Priorsford—they're such an apathetic lot I don't believe they'd ever do anything if some one didn't stir them up—that I never realized that you might be bored. We'll write for information about cruises, and then we can say to Lady Bidborough, ' How too bad of you to come just as we are leaving. . . .' Well, I'll get my things off. Why, it's about half-past six ! "

As she was going Muriel said :

" It's very good of you, Mother, to be willing to go away, but I think we won't cruise this winter. You'd hate it, and I don't believe I'd like it much. . . . By the way, Madge Williamson telephoned when you were out asking me to dine with them to-night. They are having that Mr. Hamilton who has come to Drykeld, and they want a fourth for bridge."

Mrs. Duff-Whalley gave a snort. " The farmer of Drykeld ? Dear me, I remember the time when a farmer wouldn't have been asked to dinner."

" This man's come home from India," Muriel said
indifferently, " and wants to sheep-farm. I suppose he
must be all right, and after all, in this spinster-haunted
place, a man's always a man—especially if he can play
bridge."

CHAPTER IV

"... But do not think you can at all,
 By knocking on the window, call
 That child to hear you ...
 For long ago, the truth to say,
 He has grown up and gone away ... "
      A CHILD'S GARDEN OF VERSE.

Mrs. McCosh, the guardian of The Rigs, was a woman of sixty, the widow of one Andrew McCosh, a Clyde riveter. She had come from her native city of Glasgow after her husband's death to be housekeeper to the Jardines, first to old Miss Alison Jardine, and then to Jean and her brothers. When Jean married she had continued to look after the little house for which the Jardines had so great an affection.

This afternoon Mrs. McCosh was taking a final look round, to be sure that everything was as right as she could make it for the return of the owner.

Accompanying her was a neighbour, Miss Bella Bathgate, who owned a cottage called Hillview and let her rooms to people desiring rest and change in Priorsford. Tall and high-coloured, with a broad Priorsford accent, and a high opinion of her own walk and conversation, she was something of a terror to frailer folk, for she never disguised her opinion of their comparative unworthiness.

"This 'll make a big difference to you, Mrs. McCosh,"

she was saying as the couple returned from the kitchen, after making a tour of the house. " It'll not be easy after nine years' peace, as ye might say, to start again with a mistress an' three bairns. I wouldna be you ! "

But the serene face of Mrs. McCosh showed no apprehension as she replied in an accent as redolent of Glasgow as her friend's was of Tweedside :

" Weel, Bella, ye maun mind that it's Miss Jean, an' Miss Jean's weans, an' that mak's a difference. I've been mistress here ye may say, an' I've gotten into ways o' ma ain, but Miss Jean 'll understand that. I'll no' be ill-aff wi' the weans, I like them fine, an' Ninny's an auld friend. The extra maids are to bide at The Neuk an' juist to come in here to help, ye ken. The secretary's to be there to keep an eye on them."

Miss Bathgate pulled down her long upper lip.

" What secretary ? " she asked suspiciously.

" Her wee leddyship's secretary, Miss——, I canna mind her name. Wi' a' that siller Miss Jean needs somebody to dae accounts an' add up things for her like. . . ."

" I never right understood hoo she got that money," said Bella.

" Mercy, d'ye no' mind o' the auld man comin' here to his tea ? Mr. Peter Reid ? I'm sure I tell't ye aboot it at the time. He had been a Priorsford laddie, brocht up in The Rigs, but he had been in London aboot fifty years or mair. . . . When he felt that he was comin' near his end he took a notion to come back hame, an', thinks he : ' I'll gang back to The Rigs an' end ma days where I began.' He hadna a relation in the warld, an', bein' a cankered kind o' man he'd never made friends. He'd made siller, though. . . . It seems he said to somebody that he'd leave his fortune to the first person who did anything for him for naething. Did ye ever ! Up he comes to Priorsford, gey frail, puir body, and comes up to tak' a look at The Rigs. Miss Jean sees the auld frail man an' asks him in—that was her wy : and the laddies cam' hame and they a' hed their tea thegether, and Miss Jean gied him some auld sang-book he'd taen a notion o', an' syne he gaed awa' an' there was nae mair aboot it."

" But I thocht ye said he meant to live in The Rigs himsel' ? "

" Ay, but ye see he died no lang efter. Mebbe he hedna time to see aboot it, or mebbe he thocht it wasna worth while, but onywey, he made his will and left everything tae Miss Jean."

" It was a queer thing to dae," said Miss Bathgate, " wi' so many infirmaries, no' to speak o' the Foreign Field."

" That's so," said Mrs. McCosh. " Eh, will I ever forget that awfu' nicht when the news came ! It was the nicht Peter cam' hame efter bein' lost for three whole days—Puir Peter, I miss him mair every day that passes."

" Mercy, wumman, ye would think it was yer man ye were mournin', no' a dowg."

" Weel, Bella, Andra wasna a bad man to me, an' I was real vex't he died so young, but a' the same he wis niver the comfort to me that Peter wis. Mony a time

I think I hear him at the back door. . . . But I wis speakin' aboot Miss Jean's fortune." She rose to sweep away a cinder that had fallen from the glowing ribs, and stood with the brush in her hand as she went on with her story.

"We were juist gettin' ower Peter's hame-comin'— I mind Miss Pamela was at her tea—when the six post cam' in wi' a letter for Miss Jean. I forgot to pit it on a tray. Ma bein' a pew-opener afore I gaed into service I wasna weel up in leddy's ways, an' I whiles forgot the wee things they pit sic value on, like sayin' ' Mem ' an' ' Sir,' an' pittin' things on trays."

Mrs. McCosh gave a tolerant laugh. " . . . In I gaed wi' the letter. Miss Pamela, Mrs. Elliot I *should* say, wis sittin' on the sofa wi' her work on her lap, an' a' her silks spread oot aboot her : Miss Jean wis mendin' : Mr. Jock wis daein' his lessons, an' Mhor (as we ca'ed him then) wis lyin' on the rug, an' in a meenute, by the tearin' open o' an envelope, ye micht say, the whole world was changed to them. Ay, that wis an awfu' nicht. Puir Miss Jean grat, she didna' ken whit to mak' o' the news."

"It brought great changes," said Miss Bathgate, "whether for good or ill who can say. It brought Miss Jean a lord for a husband——"

But here she was interrupted.

"That's where ye're wrang, Bella,"—Mrs. McCosh's voice was meek and final. " Lord Bidborough speired her afore there was a sough o' the siller. I ken that for a fac'. She wadna look at him the first time but——"

"It brought great changes," Miss Bathgate repeated firmly. "I'm no' sayin' Lord Bidborough mairret Miss Jean for her siller (I kent fine he was efter her from the first, but she was quite right no' to tak' him till the money had evened things up a bit), but what I'm sayin' is this: they were a' oot o' The Rigs in three months—Miss Jean mairret, an' the laddies aff to English schools. They were kinna nice laddies then, though wild, of course."

"They're nice laddies noo," Mrs. McCosh said. "Weel, ye can hardly ca' them laddies, for Mr. Jock's twa and twenty an' Mhor—Mr. Gervase—maun be sixteen. When they were at Laverlaw aboot a year syne—I think you were at Portobello—they cam' here, an' went ringein' through the hoose like bloodhounds. They were that gled to see their bits o' auld things again. I've aye keepit them juist as they left them."

"Mhor wasna a bad callant," Bella said in her grudging way. "He used to come and ask me for tea-biscuits for Peter. 'Not Abernethy, please, Miss Bathgate, Peter doesn't like them.' (The imitation was given in a high English voice, very unlike Bella's native wood-notes wild)—"But what I'm wonderin', Mrs. McCosh, will ye get to the Women's Guild on the Wednesdays? Wi' the Sale comin' off in November we need all our workers. I'm at ma twelfth semmit, an' I've made six pairs of socks, an' six pairs of boys' stockings."

"That's good," said Mrs. McCosh, quite unruffled by the note of conscious superiority in her neighbour's tone. "*I* hevna made as much as a garter, but of course I'll bake for the Provision Stall—black bun an' shortbread,

the same's I dae every year. Na, Miss Jean 'll no' object.
I gie the materials masel', there's juist ma time.''

" Mrs. Duff-Whalley's to open it,'' Bella said gloomily.
" Suggested hersel', I wadna wonder. Impident ? As
a packman's powny. An *she*'ll no buy mair than she
can help : juist provisions, likely ; an' there's sma'
profit on them. . . . If Mr. Thornton hed waited we
might hev hed Lady Bidborough. That's the worst
of a young unmarried minister—he's at the mercy of
unprincipled women.''

Mrs. McCosh had begun to make preparations for
the meal that the mistress was to partake of. Emerging from the scullery with a bright frying pan, she
said :

" Wud ye ca' Mrs. Duff-Whalley unprincipled ?
She's kinna impident an' angersome, but I wadna say
she meant ony ill. She'll hae her ain troubles dootless,
puir sowl.''

" Ay, she's unprincipled,'' said Bella firmly, " for she
doesna do things from a right motive. . . . What are
they gettin' for their dinner the nicht ? ''

" A drap o' soup, a cutlet, an' an omelette. There's
juist Miss Jean and the secretary. The bairns 'll get
their supper an' awa to their beds, an' Ninny an' me 'll
hae oor supper an' a crack, rale cosy. I'm lookin' furrit
to them a'.''

" And are the maids at The Neuk ? ''

" Ay.'' Mrs. McCosh was getting down a snowy bak-
ing board, and diving into what she called her " meal
ark '' for flour.

" Ay, they cam' in here the day, three o' them : said

her leddyship hed gien them orders to report theirsel's
to me. Rale wise-like young women, and pleasant-
spoken : no' flee-awa (though one o' them hed earrings
an' powder on her nose !) : English, of course. They've
a' been at Mintern Abbas for years, an' ye see it's hame
to them. They're six mile frae the nearest toun, so they
think this is fair Piccadilly. I tell't them we hed twa
picture-houses an' a public bath, an' twa parks wi' seats
an' a band-stand, an' a golf-puttin' green, an' they were
fair excited. I'm thinking they'll see life in Priorsford."

Bella shook her head. " Priorsford's no what it was.
I mind when it was a quiet nice bit where we a' kent
one another and were friendly thegether, and now I
dinna ken half o' the folk I see walkin' aboot. An' the
auld folk are mostly a' away. I just lookit round the
kirk last Sabbath at the elders takin' up the collection,
an' they were a' young men : no' a venerable head among
the lot. And eh, the difference in the congregation !
There used to be seat after seat filled wi' big families,
an' the faither at the end. *Everybody* gaed to the kirk :
it never entered ony body's heid to stay away. But
everything's changed noo. They play tennis and golf
on the Lord's Day. I wonder they're no' feared ! . . .
I'm never oot o' the kirk morning or evening, an' I spend
the rest o' the day readin' a guid book. I've never
countenanced entertaining on the Sabbath : I wasna
brocht up to it."

" Oh," said Mrs. McCosh, " I see no harm in giein' a
friend a cup o' tea on a Sunday. I'm real glad to see
onybody, an' I aye tak' care to hev a cake in the crock.
They whiles come in on their way to the evenin' service

—Mrs. Beaton, the keeper's wife up at Peel, an' ithers —an' we hae a cup o' tea an' a crack an' nae harm done."

" Gossip on the Sabbath Day canna be pleasin' to the Almighty."

" Hoots," said Mrs. McCosh, " the Almighty's mair to dae than listen. . . . Sit doon, Bella, I meant no ill."

But Bella rose majestically to her feet, saying :

" Ye're like a' the rest o' them, Mrs. McCosh—light-minded. It's the fault of the age. I said that to Mr. Thornton when he visited me last Thursday. It was his pastoral visitation, intimated from the pulpit, an' I hed a cup of coffee ready for him. He's a right-think-ing young man, Mr. Thornton. I gave him some advice. I said——"

" Open the oven door, Bella. What time's that ? Oh, mercy ! "

" I'll away back to ma peaceful hame, Mrs. McCosh. This is a terrible stir for ye."

" Stir ! No. It 'll mak' me young again : I've been slippin' into auld ways. . . . I think I'd be as weel to pit a match to the fire in Miss Jean's room. It's no' cauld, but a fire's aye a welcome, an' she'll be dowie enough, puir thing, comin' here an' her man awa' ower the sea ! "

" She'll likely be in to see me the morn," Miss Bathgate said importantly, " she was never one to forget old friends. I'll just treat her as I aye treated her. Rank's no' a thing I bother aboot."

" I'll hae to try an' mind to ca' her ' ma leddy,'

though I ken ma tongue 'll aye be slippin' back to
' Miss Jean.' "

Bella pursed her mouth. " Very daft-like that would
sound to the mother o' three bairns."

" So it would. . . . Gude-nicht then, Bella. I'll
likely be seein' ye sometime the morn."

It was a good thing that Mrs. McCosh was not easily
upset, for the arrival at The Rigs of a small army of
people, and a pile of boxes, not to speak of the cocker-
spaniel puppy, Black Douglas, might have caused the
bravest spirit to quail. The little house looked so in-
adequate to house such an invasion. But it looked a
very welcoming place, with lights twinkling from every
window, and Mrs. McCosh on the doorstep.

Jean came up the flagged path leading Alison, who
was murmuring with deep content, " It's like Wendy's
house. . . . Peter, it's Wendy's house." But Peter was
already on the doorstep, thrusting into Mrs. McCosh's
hands what had been such a charge to him all day.
It's my gold-fish," he explained. " I nearly spilt him
on the platform and they let me keep his bowl in the
wash-basin on the train. He's called ' Baxter.' Don't
let Black Douglas get him."

" An' wha's Black Douglas ? " asked Mrs. McCosh,
accepting the gold-fish in its bowl with the placidity
with which she accepted most things in this world.

She was not long left in doubt. A black object came
careering up the steps, charged into her, and vanished
through the door.

" Keep us ! " said Mrs. McCosh.

" So here we are," said Jean, as they all stood looking

round the little square hall with the Chinese rug and the grandfather clock with the clear face; the oak chest, and the old brass. "Nothing's changed, Mrs. McCosh. . . . You know Ninny, of course. This is Elsie. Miss Barton will stay at the Neuk; the luggage has gone on there, but she kindly came in to see if she could help, and we'll have some dinner together before she goes. . . . Betty, this is Mrs. McCosh, who looked after us all when we were children and is going to look after us again."

The tall young girl nodded, but Mrs. McCosh, in her friendly Glasgow way, held out her hand, remarking: "Pleased to meet ye."

"Now then, babes, supper and bed."

"Not till we've seen the house, Mummy," Peter pleaded, and bounded into the drawing-room, followed by Alison and Quentin. Then upstairs and down again.

"It's a lovely house," Alison said; "there's no nursery."

"I've got Uncle Jock's room," Peter boasted, "and there's a ship on the mantelpiece. I knew it was there: he told me himself—Ho! Good! Fish for supper. Alison, fish for supper."

"This is a treat," Jean said. "I thought I told you bread and milk, Mrs. McCosh?"

"Oh, so ye did, but I thocht that was a wairsh kinna meal for comin' aff a journey. It'll dae them no' ill. If ye want mair milk there's plenty. . . . Mrs. Elliot brocht a' thae flowers the day an' pit them as ye see them: an' I was to tell ye she'll be here the morn's mornin'."

Later, Jean and her secretary sat over their coffee.

" You will be glad to go to bed," Jean suggested, as Miss Barton tried unsuccessfully to conceal a yawn. " Two of the maids are here, Mrs. McCosh tells me, to take you to your own quarters. It's only a minute's walk. One gets odd impressions of a new place, arriving at night, but things look better in the morning." The girl agreed politely, and asked if she were to come to The Rigs in the morning, or work at The Neuk.

" Well—when things are in their usual place I'll come to you every morning, just as I do at home, but to-morrow—to-morrow, I fear, will be a very unsettled day. Just work away by yourself, will you ? There'll be rather an accumulation of letters to go through, I expect. Bring them over to me at tea-time."

They rose and stood by the fire. Jean said : " You have everything you need ? You are sure ? I hope they have a good fire in your room, and everything comfortable. I'll see it to-morrow. . . . Good-night, Betty, sleep well. I expect you feel rather far from home."

" Oh, no, thank you, Lady Bidborough. I can't feel far away from what I haven't got ! Good-night."

The door closed behind the girl, and Jean stood looking about the empty room. How familiar it was, and yet how strange !

Pamela had filled the place with chrysanthemums, the single ones that Jean loved : they were beautiful, against the yellow walls. . . . Every one was kind, and it was absurd to feel so desolate. She gathered together some belongings and proceeded upstairs to bed.

A murmur of voices from the kitchen meant that Mrs. McCosh and Ninny were enjoying their talk.

All was peace upstairs. Peter lay asleep in Jock's old room, with Black Douglas in his basket beside him.

Alison shared a room with Elsie, who was making everything tidy before going to bed. Quentin was with Ninny.

Jean went into her own room. Her things were unpacked and put away; her dressing-gown and slippers toasted before a bright fire. It was cosy and welcoming, but how small the room seemed, and shabby. . . . She had been so proud of this room: the Indian rug had seemed such an extravagance: she had made the curtains and bedcover herself. . . . It was cruel to look critically at it, for once it had seemed so fine, but—it was Jean Jardine's room, not Lady Bidborough's.

" You can't go back," Jean told herself, rather bleakly. " You *can't go back*."

She sat down by the fire and tried to think over what had been happening. The past six weeks seemed to her like a confused dream. There had been so much to arrange, such endless plans to make, so many people to see, and over everything had brooded the thought of parting. " Anyway," Jean told herself, " that's over. Now that Biddy's really away, every day is bringing him back. At least—— " She sighed as she thought of the waste of waters that already lay between her and her love.

She rose and took a step to the writing-table, and stopped.

" No," she said to herself. " I shan't begin a letter

to-night. It'd be sure to tell how home-sick I was. In the morning I'll be better.''

Before Jean got into bed she opened her window wide and let the cold clean air, smelling of autumn, rush in.

The sound of Tweed over its pebbles mingled with her dreams.

CHAPTER V

" He dwelt in a house by the high road and gave entertainment to all that passed by . . . "

ILIAD.

THE next day went, as Mrs. McCosh said, like a cried fair.

Breakfast was hardly over when Mrs. Elliot arrived from Laverlaw. She was greeted with enthusiasm by Jean and the children.

Jean sprang up from the rug where she was playing with Quentin, crying : " Pamela, how good of you to come so early. And look at your flowers ! It was so cheering to find them here last night."

Pamela Elliot was taking off the long cape she wore.

" Yes," she said. " I thought flowers would be the best welcome. I'd have come myself, but I was afraid I'd merely be in the way. . . . Well, this is fine ! I don't believe Quentin knows me : he's hiding his face. . . . Jean, I think Alison is like me."

Jean regarded her small daughter, such a square little figure beside the tall elegance of her aunt.

" I hope you're right," she said. " I'd like her to have your height and grace, but I confess I see little sign of it at present."

" I was rotund at that age, too."

Jean shook her head. " I can't believe it. I can't

picture you anything but long and slim. But you do
look well, and so young: younger than you looked
ten years ago when you came first to Priorsford, and
stayed at Hillview with Bella Bathgate, and lived
almost entirely on a diet of duck eggs and stewed steak
and carrots! Why did you do it, Pamela? I never
really understood what brought you to Priorsford."

Pamela laughed, as she settled herself in a corner of
the sofa.

" This was my special place, you remember? I used
to sit here with my embroidery and spread my silks all
about. . . . Is it ten years, Jean? Unbelievable! "

" Ten years," said Jean. " In some ways it seems
much longer. . . . Pam, dear, why *did* you come to
Priorsford? "

" For one thing, darling, I liked the name. It
beckoned to me, like *St. Anthony in Roseland.* . . .
As a matter of fact, when I first knew Lewis he used
to talk to me about the little town among the hills,
and when it suddenly came over me that I was growing
old (now, at fifty, I feel quite young!) and that I had
done nothing worth while with my life, I longed for
simplicity, for time to think; and, remembering Lewis's
little town, I set out for it. . . . I had written for
rooms, but how could I judge without seeing them?
When I met Miss Bathgate and her chilly welcome
and crept to a bed that seemed to be stuffed with cannon-
balls, I all but turned tail and fled back to London.
. . . In which case, Peter, my lad, you wouldn't have
been in the world."

" Not me neither? " Alison asked.

" Not you neither, nor Quentin : you're all part of the Red King's dream."

" That's from ' Alice,' " said Peter. " Aunt Pam, are there any puppies at Laverlaw ? "

" Three," his aunt told him, after a minute's thought.

" Oh, Mummy, I'll take Black Douglas to see them ? "

" Who ? " said Pamela.

" Peter's puppy," Jean explained. " His whole name is ' Black-Douglas-tender-and-true.' "

" I must see him. Fetch him, Peter, do." And as Peter ran willingly on his errand, Pamela turned to her sister-in-law, saying : " Do you know, Jean, I sometimes positively shiver when I think of the little accidental happenings that mean so much. When I think how easy it is to miss one's happiness. . . . It's quite true, if I hadn't come to Priorsford in all probability I'd never have met Lewis again, Biddy would never have found you—It hardly bears thinking of."

" But," said Jean, " if you believe that everything is ordained from the beginning——"

There was a sound of scuffling and Black Douglas burst into the room, knocked over Quentin, leapt on Pamela and licked her face, then threw himself in the air in an attempt to reach the ham which had not yet been removed from the sideboard.

" Heavens ! " cried Pamela, " he's not a dog, he's a tornado ! "

" I've got a gold-fish, too," said Peter, " called ' Baxter.' "

Pamela, vainly trying to protect herself from the puppy's affectionate onslaughts, became convulsed with helpless laughter. " Take him away, Peter," she gasped, " and fetch the gold-fish : he'll be a more restful companion. . . . Ninny, how do you put up with this all day long ? But you seem to thrive on it."

The children and the puppy were removed, so that a peaceful talk was possible. At last Pamela said : " I'm taking up all your morning. What should you be doing now ? "

" Nothing," said Jean, " nothing that matters. Some time I'm going to see The Neuk and Betty Barton."

" Betty—oh, the secretary. I remember her. Let's go now, shall we ? "

The two eldest children were waiting, ready, and, as they all went down the flagged path bordered by lavender bushes, Jean said :

" Hadn't we better shake hands with Miss Bathgate ? I haven't seen her for an age. . . ."

Miss Bathgate herself opened the door, dressed at that early hour in her best brown coat-frock and cairngorm brooch, and, after greeting the party, took them into " the good room," where a fire was burning.

" Would ye like a piece ? " she asked the children, and, on the principle of never refusing a good offer, they promptly said they would.

" Oh, don't trouble, *please*," Jean pleaded, but Miss Bathgate, remarking " They're in the lobby press," stalked out of the room and returned with a plateful of sugar-biscuits.

" Bairns like fancy biscuits," she said. " . . . And how are ye yersel', Lady Bidborough ? I hevna seen ye for an age, but ye're no *that* much changed."

She turned to study the children. "That laddie," she said, indicating Peter, "is like his faither. When Mhor was his age he was an awfu' bonnie laddie. . . . I dinna ken who, the lassie's like."

Pamela thought it the moment to thrust herself into the conversation.

"I had such a happy time in this room," she said.

"Ye hed that," Bella agreed. "But I daresay ye hardly recognize it noo. I've improved it a lot." She looked proudly round. "This suite was made for me: the sideboard's a beauty. I got the carpet at a sale. It's an Axminster, an' I keep a crumbcloth on it when I let ma rooms." She added, "I've got to be careful who I let into my rooms since I refurnished them."

"Quite," said Pamela, while Jean stooped to pick up the crumbs left by the children on the carpet. "You've no one at present?"

"Ma last lot went last week—two maiden ladies from Arbroath. I never tak' men: they've nesty ways—tobacco smoke in ma curtains an' hot suppers." Jean got up to go, explaining that they were on their way to see The Neuk.

"Ay," said Miss Bathgate, "it's a braw hoose. A daft-like thing to keep a secretary and servants in't. Ye'd be better there wi' the bairns than in The Rigs."

"Perhaps," Jean agreed meekly, "but I wanted to be in the old place. Sentiment, I suppose." She smiled as she held out her hand. "It *is* nice to see old friends again. Say 'Thank you,' children, for the biscuits."

" Never," said Pamela, as they found themselves out on the road, " never did I know any one who could so put one in one's place and keep one there as Bella Bathgate ! "

" She certainly doesn't encourage conceit," Jean said. " I gather that she found me changed and aged, the children almost painfully plain : you far from reaching the level of what she thinks a boarder should be. . . . It's rather refreshing, don't you think ? Mrs. McCosh is another who is entirely unimpressed by any one's importance. No deference to be expected from that couple—This is The Neuk. What a nice garden ! Look, Peter, a swing ! "

The Neuk was a solid, well-built villa, complete with all modern conveniences and comfortably furnished.

The sisters-in-law found Miss Barton installed in a small sunny room opening into the garden. She had arranged the typing machine, her books, and stacks of papers very neatly on a plain oak table, and, trim in a tweed frock, was working busily when discovered.

" We've met before," Mrs. Elliot said, as she shook hands, " How do you find yourself ? It all looks very business-like, and this is a pleasant writing-room, quiet, and out of the way."

" Yes, quite." Standing very erect, Betty Barton was almost the same height as Mrs. Elliot.

" Well, I think you'll like Priorsford. We'll hope to see you all at Laverlaw one day soon." She turned away to look at the pictures on the wall, while Jean turned over some letters.

" Bring these in this afternoon, will you, Barty ? "

" Yes, Lady Bidborough."

" Coming, Pamela ? We're going to look over the
house, Barty. Good-bye, just now."

Mrs. Elliot was pondering as they looked through the
rooms.

" When the boys come they'll put up here, of course.
Will Miss Barton preside over things ? "

" Yes," said Jean, " I suppose so. I hadn't really
thought of it."

" She's very young, you know, and quite remarkably
good-looking. Is it quite wise, d'you think ? "

" You mean, it isn't quite fair to Barty ? She's a
nice girl, you know, Pamela."

" I'm sure she is. I don't care much myself for that
type of chill young woman. Very assured. Very
competent. Where did you get her ? "

" Some one told me about her who had known her
people. Her father was killed, and her mother died,
leaving Barty and a younger brother. There was
enough to educate them and leave a little over. Barty
was at Somerville and did very well. She's far too
good for what I require, but I can't spare her : she's
such a stand-by to me, and I've learned to trust her
judgment : over and over again she's proved right
and I've been wrong."

Pamela shook her head. " No wonder Miss Barton
has an omnipotent air. Very bad for the young woman
to be always in the right. But it's a blessing you have
such a person when Biddy is away." She looked at her
wrist-watch. " Half-past twelve ! I must be getting
back. . . . I've people coming for luncheon."

" Oh—I hoped you'd stay with us. When will you and Lewis come ? To-morrow ? Saturday ? "

" Saturday would be nice ; and you must come in a body to Laverlaw and spend a long day as often as you can. . . . Jean, I want to know, how d'you mean to live at The Rigs ? "

" Live ? " Jean looked questioningly at her companion.

" Yes. Are you going to be content with the children, with Lewis and me, and perhaps one or two of your old friends, or are you going to enter into the life of Priorsford (which I understand is a perfect welter of tea-parties and bridge), and be at every one's beck and call ?—as you are, my dear, at Mintern Abbas : they take advantage of you : I know it."

Jean grinned broadly. " You make me sound something between a worm and a busybody ! No, I don't mean to fling myself into the giddy whirl of Priorsford— I've neither the time nor the desire for it—but I shall enjoy seeing my old friends, dear Mrs. Hope, and Miss Janet Hutton, and others, and while I'm living here I'll help in any way I can. . . . Biddy thought it would be quite a good plan for Peter and Alison to go to school. I'm sure Miss Main would give Peter a taste of school before he goes to Evelyn's. I must go and see her at once. I wish Elspeth was still there."

" The daffodil girl ! She's married, isn't she ? "

" Yes, to a naval man ; and they've got a beautiful blue-eyed boy, exactly like Elspeth, I'm told."

" How nice. Well it seems to me you'll be a very busy woman all winter, Jean, girl, with two houses to run, and the children, not to speak of the worry of administrating Peter Reid's estate."

" That's the real snag," said Jean. " I never feel myself anything but a steward, and I've got to worry much more than if it had been my own."

" But what about the boys ? I thought you divided it up."

" I tried to. I wanted us all to share and share alike. But the lawyer didn't approve, and when he said Peter Reid wouldn't have approved, I had to give in. Of course they each got so much ; quite a lot really. Davy and Jock have got theirs—Gervase gets his when he's twenty-one—Davy needs his, for he doesn't make much at the Bar, and he goes out a lot and entertains."

" And likes everything of the best," Pamela added. " Jock's in an office, isn't he ? "

" Yes," Jean laughed. " He's supposed to be learning something of finance, but I'm afraid his heart's not in it. Give him birds and beasts and the open air. Natural history is his craze. Oh, Pam, there's Miss Hutton. I must speak to her."

Jean flew on, and when Pamela made up on her, she was saying to her old friend : " I hardly dared hope you'd be staying at home this winter. You generally go away, don't you ? "

" Generally, but last winter disheartened me. It was really worse weather in the Riviera than it was in Priorsford. It seems silly to leave one's own fireside and friends, brave the Channel, and bore oneself with strangers, all for the sake of sunshine which often isn't forthcoming. So this year I thought I'd risk a winter at home." Miss Hutton turned as Pamela came up, remarking : " Lady Bidborough looks well."

" Oh, *don't*, Miss Janet," Jean protested. " I've been Jean to you all my life and I won't be anything else. Tell me, how is every one ? "

" More or less well, I think. The Miss Watsons are not so clever on their legs, but their tongues are as nimble as ever : they are still the town-criers ! "

" And Mrs. Duff-Whalley," said Jean : " what of her ? "

" That awful woman ! " said Pamela. " One would almost need to barricade oneself against her ! Snubbing has no effect. She's worn down every one else, and I know she'll wear me down in time."

" Oh, I know," said Miss Hutton, " but I'm not sure that Mrs. Duff-Whalley isn't good for us. She hunts us round and gives us something to talk about. Life in Priorsford would be much duller without her."

" I can't agree," Pamela declared. " If she were clever or amusing or even wicked, but she's only the worst sort of climber. I'm sorry for the daughter : she has a hunted look. . . . Where has Jean gone now ? "

Jean had noticed the Miss Watsons, two small, very voluble elderly ladies, hanging round, obviously in two minds whether to stop or walk on. When Jean called to them they started with well-simulated surprise.

" Fancy ! Lady Bidborough ! You here ! Who would have thought it," they exclaimed in unison.

Jean knew that the two ladies were probably primed with every detail of her coming to Priorsford, the why

and wherefore of it, The Neuk, the secretary, the maids
—but she smiled at them and said :

" My husband has had to take a sick friend for a
voyage, and I've come with the children to spend the
winter in Priorsford. You must come and see us."

The Miss Watsons beamed and murmured : " Oh,
I'm sure. How kind : very pleased indeed : how
nice," while Jean ran back, rather conscience-stricken,
to her sister-in-law.

" Pam, dear, I am so sorry to keep you waiting, but
I *had* to shake hands with the Miss Watsons."

" Jean," Pamela said solemnly, as they went round
to get the car, " before you know where you are you'll
be in a vortex."

" I know ; Biddy said so too. Somehow, I seem to
collect people ; I suppose because I like them and am
interested in them. I'm terribly sorry, Pam, but I'm
afraid I could never be exclusive."

Pamela laughed as she kissed her sister-in-law.

" You like," she said, " to live in a house by the high
road and be a friend to man—and what's more, you'll
always manage it ! "

CHAPTER VI

"... with his satchel
and shining morning face, creeping
like snail unwillingly to school."

AS YOU LIKE IT.

Two days after their arrival in Priorsford Peter and
Alison made their first acquaintance with school.

They came down to breakfast looking rather over-
awed, and started on their porridge in silence, but
Peter, who was never quiet long, began as if continuing
a recent conversation :

" Of course it isn't a real school or Alison couldn't go
to it ; I'm going to a real school when I'm nine ! this
is mostly girls."

Alison looked anxiously at her mother as she asked :

" What'll they do when they find I don't know anything ? "

" Why, darling, they don't expect you to know anything : you're going there to learn."

" She can't even say her alphabet," said Peter, and
added boastfully, " I can say it backwards."

" He can say it backwards," echoed Alison dismally.

" It won't do him much good," her mother assured
her. " They've got new ways of teaching, and I don't
know that they pay much attention to the alphabet
now. I know children aren't taught as we were taught :

a b ab, s o so. You'll be able to tell me about the new ways."

" Mummy," Peter said, dealing with an egg, " what's the teacher like ? "

" There are two teachers. Miss Main has been keeping school since ever I knew her, and her hair is quite white, and she's very wise. She's taught more boys and girls than she can remember, but I don't expect any of them have forgotten Miss Main. Although she's so clever she's very patient and won't expect too much from little girls who are only five. As a matter of fact, you'll probably be taught by Miss Callard, who helps Miss Main. She is so young that I'm sure she hasn't forgotten her first day at school, and her face is round and pink and sweet. Somehow, she made me think of nice things to eat, or is it that her name recalls ' butterscotch ' ? Anyway, I know you'll like her. . . . There are twelve girls and three boys at school just now, beginning at five and ending at ten. I saw them all running about in the garden yesterday. They get out at eleven for ten minutes, and morning school finishes at a quarter to one. Elsie will fetch you home and you won't go back in the afternoon. . . . Run up now, and wash your hands and get your coats on. I'll take you myself this morning, and you'll be able to show Elsie the way to-morrow."

It was a fine morning, with a touch of frost in the air : mist lay in the valleys, but the hill-tops were sharply clear against the pale blue of the sky. The trees in their burning autumn beauty were reflected in Tweed's quiet waters.

"Look," said Jean, laying a hand on Peter's shoulder, "aren't these peaks beautiful, piercing up behind the roundbacked hills ? They're called the Shielgreen Kips, and some day we'll go there, perhaps when Jock comes, and Mhor : they love the Kips."

"That's the Tweed," Peter said. "It's rather a small river, isn't it ? "

"It's a *lovely* river," Jean cried jealously. "Peter, you're almost as bad as the American who called it 'a creek.' I'd rather have the man who declared, with no regard for the truth, that it was as wide as the Hooghly at Calcutta."

"Oh, I *like* it," Peter hastened to protest. "Jock told me it was the best river in the world, and he's going to take me to fish in it some day. . . . Barty says that in America the rivers are so big you can't see to the other side of them. Silly sort of rivers they must be ! "

"Well," said Jean tolerantly, "America's such a huge place—gigantic mountains, rolling prairies, houses and hotels sky-scraping—so I suppose they've got to have rivers to match. . . . But I've seen Tweed big enough. When a thaw comes suddenly, and the snow melts on the hills and the rain pours, then Tweed comes roaring down in spate, carrying away sheep and gates and trees, and when it gets to Priorsford it sometimes floods out all over the place. I've seen swans swimming on Tweed Green and people rescued from top windows ! "

"Oh, I hope it does it soon," said Peter.

"I hope *not*. It's very poor fun for the people who get all their belongings ruined with water and mud."

" It can't get to The Rigs," Alison said comfortably,
" so it doesn't much matter."

Jean, amazed at the heartlessness displayed by her
offspring, felt she ought to improve the occasion with
a homily on thought for others, but they had reached
the gate of the school, and Alison's hand had tightened
on hers.

They went up to the door of the pretty creeper-
covered house, and rang the bell.

" To-morrow," Jean told the children, " you'll go in
at the back with the others, but this morning I want to
introduce you to Miss Main."

They were shown into a drawing-room containing
some fine old furniture and many portraits of dead
and gone Mains. They had no reason, these dead men,
to feel ashamed of their descendant. The same spirit
that had kept them going through the Indian Mutiny
and the Crimean War was alive in Miss Agnes Main.
She taught and trained these children with all the care
and energy she was capable off. It was her job and she
did it. People said it was absurd that a brilliant scholar
such as she was should so waste her time, but Miss
Agnes did not consider her time wasted.

She was very small, with delicate colouring and snow-
white hair : very gentle in her voice and ways—but a
terror to evil-doers !

She greeted Peter and Alison affectionately, telling
them that she had taught their mother and their uncles.

" Don't give us away, please, Miss Agnes," Jean
begged.

Miss Agnes shook her head, smiling. " I'm like the

sundial," she said : " I only record the sunny hours.
It's funny, when a pupil, even one of the worst, leaves,
you forget all the stupidity and inattention and mis-
chievous ways and only remember that he was a queer
wee boy and oddly likeable. You'd be surprised, too,
how many of them come back, grown men from the far
parts of the earth, and stand sheepishly and say, ' You
won't remember me, I was——' But now, what about
these young people ? "

" Alison hasn't learnt anything yet," said Alison's
mother, " she's only five. Peter has done lessons regularly for a year with the rector at home. I think he's
got a good deal of miscellaneous information, but you'll
find that out for yourself. It's a great delight to me,
Miss Agnes, to think that you will start them. . . .
But I must not take up your time. . . . No, I'll let
myself out. Good-bye, Miss Agnes. Good-bye, darlings. We'll hear what school's like at one o'clock."

It was only a little after nine o'clock, so Jean went
for a walk. She went up through a narrow lane bordered
with high beech hedges, climbed a dyke, and came out
on the hill-side.

Beneath her lay the town with Tweed running through
it like a shining highway. A blue haze from smoking
chimneys hung over it : cheerful morning sounds came
up to her. . . . All round were fields cleared of the
harvest, and woods and hills and valleys. . . . " There's
no place like it," Jean told herself, with a kind of surprise.

At ten o'clock she sauntered into The Neuk to find
Miss Barton busy at her desk. She jumped up and

wanted to know if the children had gone happily to
school.

" Alison," she said, " was rather worried last night,
and even Peter had tremors. But of course it's only
the first plunge. To-morrow they'll feel as if they'd
been going to school all their lives."

" Yes," said Jean, " and it'll be so good for them doing
things with other children. Peter's apt to get bump-
tious, and Alison is touchy, but I'm hoping school will
do a lot for them. Miss Main is so interesting ; you
must meet her. . . . Well, how are things going here ? "

" Quite well, I think, Lady Bidborough. Marriot
goes down early to The Rigs and stays all day, and the
other two keep this house, and help Marriot when she
needs them. It's a holiday for them, really. They're
quite excited exploring the place, and town is a treat
to them after the heart of the country. There are constant entertainments of one kind and another in the
evenings."

" Priorsford was always a whirl," said Jean. " I'm
glad you think things are going to go smoothly. . . .
Is there much for me to see, Barty ? "

Miss Barton laid several documents before her, saying,
" Would you decide about these, please ? "

Jean read through the topmost letter. " It's a sad
case," she said.

" They're all sad cases," said Miss Barton.

" How many can we help ? "

" Three out of the six."

Jean sighed as she took up the next letter.

" It's so trifling," she said, " so temporary, what we

can do, but I suppose it helps. The ex-officers with children, out of work, and savings gone, aren't so hopeless ! There's always the hope that things will take a turn and trade improve, and it's only a case of keeping their heads above water till then. It's the women who break my heart, the women who love the comforts and prettiness of life and who, in old age, are left stranded in a world grown bleak and unfriendly. To be young and poor isn't so bad, but to be old and poor and ill. . . . Barty, I'm haunted by the thought of winter coming on, and poor souls, many crippled with rheumatism, not daring to light a fire (when a good fire is one of the few comforts left in life) and hating to let any one know how poor they are. . . . *Couldn't* we help all these cases, Barty ? ''

Miss Barton shook her head inexorably. " We've already exceeded—I don't think you need worry too much about these cases. They sound very pathetic, I know, but if you saw the people you'd probably find them very complaining, ungrateful, and far from attractive."

" Oh, I dare say." Jean sat with her chin in her hand pondering over the sad details on the paper before her.

Presently Miss Barton said : " I've one or two cases here that it might be as well to see personally. . . . Edinburgh isn't very far from Priorsford ? ''

" A little over twenty miles. We might all go in on Saturday—that would be a good enough day for the purpose, wouldn't it ? I'd like Peter and Alison to see the Shrine, and Saturday's their only day. I envy your seeing Edinburgh for the first time. No, forget I said that. Go to it as to any other large city, expecting nothing but tall tenements and ugly streets and railway stations."

Miss Barton smiled, and presently said, " There's this woman in Glasgow. I think I'd better go and see her : there's something about her letter that I'm not sure of."

" You demand truth in the inward parts, Barty. These are terribly searching eyes of yours, and you never soften."

" I've no use for sentiment," said Miss Barton, " and there's a sickening amount of it in the world. The number of slushy people——" She nodded towards a daily paper on the table. " There's a murder trial going on just now : all the sympathy is for the murderer : not a thought for the soul he sent into the darkness."

" Oh, I'm with you there. If a man in his right senses deliberately murders a fellow-creature he ought to die, if only to discourage others from attempting to do likewise ! All the same "—Jean's eyes grew dark with feeling—" it's awful to think of the murderer, perhaps coming handicapped into the world, bred in misery, knowing nothing but evil in life, going violently out of it. The only comfort is that his soul goes back to God Who made it, and Who knows why."

There was a moment's silence, then Miss Barton said : " Well, is that arranged for Saturday ? Could we be in Edinburgh about eleven ? I shall have to see this Mr. Paterson in his office, and offices close early on Saturdays."

" Of course. We can start directly after breakfast.

I do hope it will be a day like this. Take a walk this afternoon, Barty : it's lovely on the hills."

" Yes, thank you, Lady Bidborough."

" I had promised myself I'd show you the walk over Cademuir to-day, but I've been summoned to see my oldest friend—Mrs. Hope. She lives in that white-washed house standing in the woods by Tweedside. Look, you can see the chimneys from this window. She is very old now, and frail, and can't see many people, but her daughter telephoned last night that I might go this afternoon for a little. But we'll have our walk another day."

CHAPTER VII

"Thy thoughts and feelings shall not die
  Nor leave thee, when grey hairs are nigh,
      a melancholy slave.
  But an old age serene and bright,
  And lovely as a Lapland night
  Shall lead thee to thy grave."

WILLIAM WORDSWORTH.

HOPETOUN HOUSE was about a mile from The Rigs, a white-washed Georgian house standing on a knoll by the river. Jean walked slowly up the avenue, glad to see again the lovely bend of Tweed, the sloping lawns, and Hopetoun Woods behind. There was no change here, she told herself, and shrank from the thought of the change she would see in her old friend.

But she need not have feared. There was nothing unsightly about Mrs. Hope's years. She was as scrupulously neat as ever she had been, with her white hair dressed high and covered with a square of lace tied under her chin. Her soft black dress showed grey silk stockings and buckled slippers, and a little coat of brocaded velvet kept her warm.

She sat where she had always liked best to sit, in the drawing-room, a room full of books and flowers, and lit by four long windows. Two of the windows looked out on the lawns and the stone figures chipped by generations of catapult-owning boys : the other two

looked across the river to the Hopetoun Woods. With
her was her daughter Augusta, all that was left to her,
since her three sons had found graves in the far corners
of the Empire.

Augusta was sixty, seeming, with her long, kind,
patient face, almost older than her ageless mother.

" My dear Jean ! " said Mrs. Hope, holding out her
arms, and Jean was glad to hear that the voice was the
same : the clear definite speech had not failed.

" Jean, let me look at you, child. . . . Do you know
that it's eight years since we met ? Yes. You came
the first year after you were married, but after Lewis
and Pamela fell heir to Kinbervie you forsook us."

Jean drew forward a stool and seated herself, as she
said :

" Ah, but not willingly, my dear ; not willingly.
Twice I've been at Laverlaw and came to Hopetoun,
but with no luck ; you were seedy and not seeing people.
. . . But you're getting stronger with the years, it
seems. There's not a day's difference in you, and
you're prettier than ever ! "

" Do you hear her, Augusta ! "

" You agree, don't you, Miss Augusta ? And what I
want to know is, how is it done ? I'm sure beauty-
doctors would give anything to know the secret of your
complexion. And it isn't only your looks. The letters
you write would shame the young women of to-day.
Letters are no use now : people are so busy that they
can only accomplish a scrawled sheet of exclamations.
Your hand-writing is a joy to read, and I know that
Biddy finds your letters a joy to listen to. I hope you

don't mind, but I always read them aloud to him. It's a red-letter day when there's an epistle from you. And I keep you well posted up in everything that happens to us, so, though parted, we are very well acquaint. Oh, but how poor letters are to the spoken word." She looked round her. " Back in this quiet room with you and Miss Augusta, I can hardly believe that I'm not Jean Jardine, and that Davy and Jock and Mhor are not waiting for me at home."

" Tell me about the boys. How is my Jock ? "

" He is still your Jock ; I never saw any one change so little in appearance ; indeed, in everything. He has still the surprised blue eyes and the unruly hair. His chief interest is natural history. He hates dancing, and all social things ; very unlike Davy, without whom no gathering is complete. . . . Mhor is very happy at Eton, where he's doing fairly well."

" Mhor was an attractive child."

" Yes," said Jean, " and he's as attractive as ever, with beautiful manners, and out of the ordinary good looks. He and Jock are the idols of my boy Peter."

" Your boy Peter. Ah, my dear, I'm glad I've lived to see your children. When will you bring them ? "

Jean looked for guidance to Augusta, who nodded, so she said : " I'll bring them any afternoon you like, but a few minutes of them will suffice : they're restless children."

" Tell me about them."

" D'you know I'm afraid there's nothing to tell. They're healthy and world-like, and to Biddy and me seem everything that is most adorable, but to the outside world quite ordinary and uninteresting. No, they're not good-looking ; rather plain, really."

Augusta smiled. " What a detached mother ! "

" No, I don't think so, but it would be absurd of me to imagine my children brilliant and beautiful—I wouldn't like them half as well if they were ! "

Mrs. Hope patted her hand, remarking, " Anyway, I needn't ask if you are happy, Jean. Your face answers for you."

Jean nodded gravely. " When Biddy is at home, there's simply nothing I could wish for—I'm *frighteningly* happy. But just now it's a case of just getting through the days. Of course, it's much easier here at Priorsford than at home. Biddy saw that. At Mintern Abbas there would have been a blank every way I turned, here it is different. I have all you dear people to help me through, and the interest of the old life. I mean to keep myself busy every minute, and, happily, that will be easy, for there's lots to take up my time."

" My dear, you must be a very busy woman always. I can see from your letters how much you have to get through. . . . I'm specially interested in all you tell me about Peter Reid's money."

" Yes, Biddy helps me with the big yearly sums to hospitals and such like : it's the personal part, the portion I keep in my own hands to distribute, that is the real worry. Barty—that's my secretary, Miss Barton—and I wrestle with cases until we're both dazed ! Reading the letters that come take one into quite a different world, such a hard, sad, suffering world, that one's little teaspoonful of help is lost in an ocean of misery. But I'm sitting here talking about myself when it's *you* I want to hear talk." Jean, on a low seat, looked up into her friend's face as she had often done as a child, and Mrs. Hope, smiling down at her, said :

" And what have I to talk about ? We just sit here, Augusta and I, day in and day out ; read *The Scotsman* and *The Times*, sometimes play patience, sew a little, read a little, talk a little, and think a lot. I never see strangers or irrelevant people. Pamela I enjoy, and Janet Hutton. Mirren Strang is an understanding creature and sometimes amusing. . . . How does Priorsford strike you coming back ? "

" More lovely than ever. I'm loyal to my birthplace (though I must confess to a great affection for the land of my adoption), but there are sad changes : blanks that'll never be filled."

" The Macdonalds," said Augusta. " We knew you would miss them badly."

" Will you tell me about them ? I didn't want to hear from any one else. I only know that they went, practically, together."

" Yes," said Augusta, and went on in her quiet way, " You know Mr. Macdonald came every week to see Mother, always on Thursday afternoon if it could be managed. Mrs. Macdonald often came too, and we looked forward to those Thursdays. The last time he came was in June, a day so warm and still that we had tea out on the lawn. Yes, Mother too."

" It was a perfect day," Mrs. Hope said. " The rhododendrons were at their best, and the laburnums

and lilacs still blooming : the beech trees and larches in
their new green against the dark of the pines, and Tweed
silver in the sunshine——"

" I can see it," said Jean, " and Mr. Macdonald with
the smile he wore when he saw anything very lovely,
as if he were saying to himself, ' *What* a world ! ' . . .
And did Mrs. Macdonald not say that tea in the garden
was all very well, but for her part she preferred it in the
house ? "

" Yes, I believe she did," said Augusta. " She always
hated picnics."

" But that afternoon," Mrs. Hope said, " we sat
enchanted. . . . Mr. Macdonald fell to talking of old
times, and told old stories, and we laughed, and we
cried, and we couldn't be separated. . . . He stayed
long in the Manse garden that evening, they told me,
looking at the hills and walking among his flowers, and
went to bed to all appearances in perfect health. He
died in his sleep, went out as the summer dawn came
in. . . ."

There was silence for a minute, then Augusta said :

" On the funeral day Mrs. Macdonald took pneumonia,
and in a week she followed her husband."

Jean winked away her tears as she said :

" How beautiful that it happened like that. I'm so
glad Mrs. Macdonald hadn't to drag on without him.
But how they must be missed ! "

" They were very fond of you, Jean : that visit they
paid to you last summer was a great delight to them.
They came and gave us every detail, didn't they,
Mother ? "

" It was a delight to us," said Jean. " They always promised to come, but, as you know, they were great home-keepers. Then I heard that they were actually to be in London at their son's wedding, so Biddy went and fetched them to Mintern Abbas, and we had such a happy time together. You can imagine the delight of showing the house and the children to Mrs. Macdonald ! and Mr. Macdonald went off with Biddy and scoured the whole country-side. We never had more delightful visitors. . . . I'm glad it's winter and I shan't have to see another minister in the Manse garden with the lupins. But I'm told the new man is quite nice."

" Very nice," said Augusta. " Clever too : he preaches well. Mother quite liked him when he came to call."

" A pleasant youth," Mrs. Hope said : " but I'm too old for new people, Jean. At ninety one should be excused. . . . Nine years ago, when you went away, I was waiting like Christiana for the summons : but the messenger tarries. Not that it has seemed long,"—she said her hand on her daughter's as she spoke—" Augusta and I never weary. . . . Are you going already ? Well, when am I to see the family ? "

" I'll bring them any time. If Miss Augusta will ring up and say when you feel like it."

Jean leant down to kiss her friend good-bye and Mrs. Hope looked rather wistfully into the young face as she said : " Life's at its fullest with you, my dear. Rejoice in it. . . ."

It was beginning to get dark as Jean went up the flagged path to The Rigs. Peter came hustling out to meet her, accompanied by Black Douglas. The lights were lit : tea was ready : Quentin was shouting with sheer joy of living.

With her mind still running on the quiet house she had left, Jean said to herself : " It must be strange to have nothing to do but die."

CHAPTER VIII

" She saw a lady sit on a throne,
  The fairest that ever the sun shone on !
A lion licked her hand of milk,
And she held him on a leish of silk ;
And a leifu' maiden stood at her knee,
With a silver wand and melting e'e . . . "

KILMENY.

NOTHING happened to prevent the carrying out of the plan for Saturday, and they set off in the car immediately after breakfast.

It was a misty morning and Jean deplored the fact that Miss Barton was not seeing the Pentlands to advantage.

" Perhaps coming home," she consoled her, " we may yet get a clearer view, and you will see Swanston that Robert Louis Stevenson loved so much. . . . This is Leadburn Moor, supposed to be one of the coldest places in the world."

" I can well believe it," said Miss Barton, looking with some distaste at the bleak landscape.

Peter, much interested, spelt out the name of the first town they passed through. "' P e n i c u i k.' What a funny name ! "

" Pronounced Pennycook—but some of the places round here have the most lovely names : Hawthornden, Rosslynlee, Pomathorn. And there's a place—I

4

don't know where or what it is, probably a mining village—called ' Little France.' Isn't that delicious ? "

" Is this Edinburgh ? " Peter asked, as rows of bungalows in neat gardens rose out to meet them.

" The suburbs," his mother told him. " The real Edinburgh is the Castle and Holyrood : the Lawnmarket and the Canongate. . . . Where is it you want to go to, Barty ? "

Miss Barton consulted a paper : " Castle Street. Is that far away ? "

" Just off Princes Street. It's where Sir Walter Scott lived. You remember, Alison, we read about him fetching Pet Marjorie in the snow-storm, and carrying her in his plaid to his house in Castle Street ? "

Alison nodded. " And she taught him ' Onery twoery tickery seven.' "

" Yes, and got very angry when Sir Walter laughed. Here we are, Barty—we've a little shopping to do and then I thought we'd go up to the Castle. Try and get up there before lunch ; anyway, we'll meet at the North British Hotel at one o'clock. Is that all right ? . . ."

The children were full of interest in all they saw at the Castle : the kilted soldiers, the bugles, the equestrian statues excited them, and they asked so many questions that their mother was sorely put to it to find answers.

As they stared at the Crown Jewels, " Who wore them ? " Peter asked. " What was the names of all the kings ? "

" Don't you remember any ? " asked Jean, who couldn't at the moment recall one.

"Robert the Bruce," said Peter promptly.

"And the last was Mary Queen of Scots, whose son ruled over both England and Scotland—James VI. of Scotland and First of England," she added glibly.

"There's a poem about her," Peter said. "Ninny knows it, about ' the scene was changed.' They chopped off her head. Why did they do that ? "

"She was beautiful," said Jean, "and it was an unsafe time to be a queen and beautiful."

"I'm glad I'm not a queen," said little fat Alison.

As they crossed the courtyard to the Shrine, Jean tried to make them understand what they were going to see.

"Peter," she began, "you know about the Great War ? "

"Which one ? " said Peter importantly. "I know about the Wars of the Roses."

"Oh, that was hundreds of years ago : English people fighting each other : what is called a civil war."

"Is it ever civil to fight, Mummy ? " Peter asked.

"Well, no, not really," said Jean hurriedly. "But I'm talking about the war that Daddy and Uncle Tim fought in, when almost the whole world was fighting. . . ."

Alison twisted round to watch another child, while Peter said in an unconcerned voice : "Why were they fighting, Mummy ? "

His mother hesitated before she said : "It's a long story, Peter, and indeed I don't know if anybody knows the real reason. Anyway, Britain couldn't in honour keep out, and for four years nations struggled together, and hundreds of thousands were killed, and some countries had very little food, and no fires in the bitter weather, and children starved for want of milk ; and great Zeppelins came over to England and dropped bombs on houses and factories, and people were killed—not fighting men, but often women and little children."

They were standing on the steps outside the Shrine watching the people pass through the door in a steady, orderly stream.

" When peace came back," Jean went on, " every village, every town and city built a Memorial to the men they had lost. This is Scotland's Memorial to the Scots who died. The name of every man who gave his life is here : no one has been forgotten. . . ."

As they came out they met Betty Barton going in and Jean greeted her. " Take as long as you like. We can easily wait a bit for lunch. We're going to walk slowly down to the hotel now.

Motoring back to Priorsford the children chattered of what they had seen : the shops, the Castle, the hotel where they had lunched.

" What did you like best ? " Miss Barton asked them.

" The lemon-squash at lunch with straws in it," Alison said promptly.

" I liked the Castle," said Peter. " Mummy, *everybody* wasn't killed in the War. Daddy wasn't. Did Uncle Davy not fight ? Or Jock ? "

" They were too young," Jean told him : " only boys at school."

P'r aps there'll be another war," Peter said hopefully.

" I hope not, my son."

" But fighting's good fun, Mummy. Everybody fights in books."

" Fighting could never be fun," his mother said ; " though, perhaps, it wasn't so bad long ago, where everything, even war, was conducted in a leisurely way. But to-day war is so terrible that it doesn't bear thinking of. Nobody will ever know what the soldiers in the Great War suffered. The men in the trenches were not only in constant danger of being killed or terribly wounded, but they had to live in filth, and see and hear and smell horrible things all the time."

" I'd have come home," said Peter.

" They had to stick it for four years—" Jean turned to Betty Barton, saying : " Barty, didn't you think it was marvellous how in the Memorial they've forgotten nothing ? Even the friendly beasts that helped us— I liked that best of all. . . . I've seen it three times now, and every time it seems more wonderful."

Miss Barton nodded. " It's magnificent—but heart-breaking. Peter "—she laid her hand on the child's bare knee—" Peter, get it into your head and never let it out again that war is the *silliest* thing that the mind of man ever thought of. The futility of it ! " She turned to Jean—" And these poets who glorify blood-shed, and sing of drinking death like wine, should be gagged. Patriotism is answerable for a lot."

" Perhaps," Jean said, after a pause. " But all the same I'd hate if we didn't put our country first. I believe every decent, right-thinking man is willing to give himself if the need arises. What we've got to see is that the need doesn't arise. . . . But don't let's argue about it. How did Edinburgh strike you ? "

Miss Barton gave a little laugh. " Well—I wasn't disappointed. . . . It's a poem of a place. I haven't had the chance to travel much and see cities, but I should think that that street, so fine with its shops and clubs and hotels, facing those green slopes crowned with the towering Castle Rock, would be difficult to beat. A prince of streets indeed ! But it was the High Street and the Lawnmarket that took hold of me. I felt compassed about——"

" With ghosts ? " said Jean. " I know. Even at twelve o'clock on a Saturday morning, which almost seems to me the most commonplace, not to say stodgy time of all, there is something about those streets, something about those high tenements and dark entries, something that seems to be waiting and watching. . . . What they've seen, the oldest of them ! Montrose in his carnation silk stockings, John Knox in his Geneva gown, Prince Charlie keeping brief state at Holyrood, Mary Queen——"

" Yes, Mary above all," said Miss Barton. " I've felt positively obsessed by that woman to-day."

" I'm glad to hear it, painfully practical person that you are ! Queen Mary's magic grips the most unlikely people. You remember the farmer in Barrie's story who ' couldna sleep at nichts for thinkin' o' her ' ? Barty, I see that Edinburgh has got you in her thrall."

" Oh, I admit it. But I find that I'm disgracefully ignorant of Edinburgh's past. I must read it up."

" Let's read aloud at night," Jean said, " all the best

books about Edinburgh. We've got them by the dozen —at least, I know of three. . . . Oh, by the way, was your interview with—Mr. Paterson was it?—satisfactory?"

In a moment Miss Barton ceased to be woman and became the efficient secretary.

"It was short," she said. "Mr. Paterson was going off to play golf, so he didn't prolong things, but he gave me all the information I wanted. Then I took a taxi and saw the two cases we were considering; luckily they were both in the same direction, over 'the Bridges' to 'the Meadows'—at least it sounded like that. I went first to Mrs. McEwan, you remember the one who wrote and said she was in great straits."

"She had some connection with Priorsford, hadn't she?"

"She said so, but I found it didn't amount to much. I couldn't see any sign of the 'straits' she referred to in her letter. She keeps house for a son and two daughters all in good jobs. Keeps it very badly, it seems to me : it was un-aired and dusty, and the breakfast things had never been removed. She was inclined to resent my presence, and said she had expected to deal with you. She implied that you and she would have been more likely to understand each other."

"Then you don't think she really needs help?"

Betty Barton shrugged her shoulders. "She needs money," she said, "and always will, no matter what she gets. She has a small income of her own, apart from what her family gives her, but she is lazy and fond of good-living, and probably deep in debt. She reminded me of a great soft spider, sitting in her dusty web. It was sheer cheek that made her write to you. She's probably in some hole for money and doesn't want her family to know, and it occurred to her that something might be got out of you. Obviously she expected a cheque by post, not a visit."

Jean sighed. " And the other people ? " she asked. " The people Dr. Kelly wrote about ? "

" The Gordons," said Betty. " That's a perfectly *pukka* case."

The girl's face became eager and animated as she proceeded to tell her tale. " They live in Forth Street, somewhere near ' the Bridges,' one of those depressing streets that have decayed, and is now given over largely to people who keep lodgers. Not very clean lace curtains, aspidistras in pots—you know the sort of thing. I was put out at a door with six bells with a name above each, and when I rang the one marked ' Gordon,' the door opened as if by magic, and I walked into a stone passage. I climbed three flights of stone stairs and on the top found my quarry. Standing by an open door was a boy, who explained that when their bell rings they have to pull something which opens the street door, so that they always get warning when a visitor approaches."

Peter, who had been listening with interest, said :

" You could open the window when the bell rings, and look over, and if it was some one you didn't like you could pour boiling oil on them."

" Yes," Alison agreed contentedly.

" What fiends I have for children ! " said Jean. " Go on, Barty."

Miss Barton continued :

" As the boy told me this he grinned broadly, and explained that he'd been cleaning brass when the bell rang and had rushed to wash his hands. ' My mother's an invalid,' he said quite simply, ' and my sister's in an office all day, so I help a bit.' He wasn't in the least ashamed of it, and said he'd invented a jolly good brass polish which he thought he might make a fortune out of some day. . . . And I must say the brass shone."

" How old is the boy ? " Jean asked.

" About nineteen. He's getting through college by the aid of bursaries and tutoring fees. They've evidently a great struggle, but are quite gay about it. I liked the boy, and the mother couldn't say enough about the goodness of her children. Everything was so above-board. They had obviously nothing to hide. Very unlike the furtive Mrs. McEwan ! . . . I was rather at a loss to explain my visit. They are gentle-folk and might easily have resented it, but I told them as tact-fully as I could—I did wish you had been there to do it yourself—that you were steward of a sum of money which you wanted to put to the best advantage, and that your desire was to help people over tight places, especially young people beginning life. I said that through some private source you had heard of them—and so on, and so on. The mother wept a little. . . . Of course I asked no questions, I had no right to, but she told me everything with a sort of simple dignity. I confess I was impressed."

Jean looked at her secretary and said solemnly,

" D'you know, Barty, that is almost the first time
you've ever spoken with any enthusiasm about people
who have needed help. I was beginning to feel that it
was all no use. We so often do things for the best and
they turn out for the worst. Over and over again we've
done more harm than good. But even if we fail fifty
times and succeed once, it's worth while. . . . That
must be a good boy and it's splendid training for him.
But I'm so sorry for a young man who has to be unlike
his companions. It's so hard for them to go shabby, for
most of them adore smart clothes and socks and ties.
When Davy went first to Oxford he had to be very
careful : we were poor then."

" It's good for a young man to have to be careful,"
Miss Barton said primly ; " it keeps them out of mischief. I always despised the undergraduates who loafed
about, opulent and idle."

" But the opulent aren't always idle," Jean protested :
" some of them are very serious workers. . . . Children,
Aunt Pam's coming to-day. Isn't that fine ? "

" Uncle Lewis, too ? " Peter asked.

" Well, perhaps. . . . I wonder what Quentin's been
doing all day, nice fat thing that he is ! "

" Kicking Ninny, I should think," said the elder
brother. " He's only just found out that he can kick,
and he goes about kicking everybody."

" What a fellow ! Well—here we are back in Priorsford, and the sun is actually shining ! . . . Better play
in the garden, darlings, till Ninny brings Quentin in from
his walk. Barty, we'll see you at tea ? "

" Thank you, Lady Bidborough. I'll go to The Neuk

now and write some letters that have to go off to-night."

Jean had changed from tweeds into a house-frock and had settled herself comfortably in a corner of the big sofa by the living-room fire with a pile of weeklies by her side, thinking there would be time for some reading before tea. But she had hardly opened *The Weekend Review* when she heard the front door open, and the sound of voices. Pamela had come early. Delightedly, Jean sprang up to welcome her sister-in-law, but the door opened and the servant announced : " Mrs. Duff-Whalley, Miss Duff-Whalley."

How awful ! At tea-time, and the Laverlaw people arriving any moment. . . . Still—

Lady Bidborough smiled as she greeted her visitors, and Mrs. Duff-Whalley said firmly :

" Well, *Jean*, it's an age since we met. Muriel and I meant to be the first to welcome you, but you know what a whirl our life always is. It's absurd of course, in a place like Priorsford, but we never seem to have a moment to ourselves : do we, Muriel ? To-day we were lunching with dear Lady Tweedie : she's to be with us till after Christmas, I'm glad to say : it's too *triste* when our friends depart. . . . Of course you will have lost touch entirely with the people here."

" Not really," Jean said. " True, I hadn't seen any of them for years, but when I met Miss Janet Hutton and the Miss Watsons we might have parted yesterday."

" Oh, Priorsford people," said Mrs. Duff-Whalley. " Very worthy creatures, of course, but— When Minna

—you know, Mrs. Egerton Thomson ?—is here she's too funny. Really very naughty. She'll come in and say : " All the oddments were in the Highgate this morning. The Miss Watsons with their chatter, Janet Hutton with her big boots, Mrs. Jowett out of a band-box '—Minna can do them all to the life. It's as good as a play when she starts."

" It must be very amusing," Jean said gravely.

" Minna is apt to carry it too far," Muriel said : " and there's nothing she resents so much herself as being taken off. . . . Jean, you haven't changed one little bit."

" Haven't I ? Oh, ten years must make a difference, inside and out."

Muriel laughed. " ' Inside and out.' You always said odd things, Jean. I can't believe that it's all that time since you left. Now that you're back, don't you feel as if you'd dreamt the years between ? "

" I hear," Mrs. Duff-Whalley broke in, " that Lord Bidborough has gone on a voyage ? "

Her tone was heavy with the questions she desired to ask and Jean began a little wearily the explanation she had already given so often.

" Ye—es," said Mrs. Duff-Whalley, when she had finished ; " well, they'll have a great time together, the two men, while you vegetate through a Priorsford winter, poor Jean. Of course you have your sister-in-law. I seldom see Mrs. Elliot : she's become almost as great a recluse as her husband : it was always like pulling teeth to get him to come to dinner."

The door opened, a voice said, " May we come in ? " and Lewis Elliot entered the room, followed by his wife.

Jean was afraid Lewis was going to turn and fly on beholding the Duff-Whalleys. He certainly recoiled, but in a moment he steadied himself, and, after greeting Jean, turned to the visitors.

Mrs. Duff-Whalley was pleased to be arch.

" Here you are," she said, " to answer my charge in person."

" Yes ? " Lewis said politely, looking down at the little woman with the sharp nose and darting eyes. He was a man of fifty-four, shy, with a scholar's stoop, and a gentle smile. Alone, he was utterly incapable of dealing with Mrs. Duff-Whalley, but behind him stood his wife who had more than once done battle with that formidable lady.

" I was just saying to Jean, Mrs. Elliot, that you were becoming as much of a recluse as your husband."

" Is that all ! I thought we were going to be accused of something exciting. How d'you do, Miss Duff-Whalley !—Yes, I'm afraid we are very fond of shutting ourselves up at Laverlaw. You see, we are so much away, that the time we have there is very precious."

Betty Barton came into the room, and stopped, hesitating, when she saw the visitors. Mrs. Elliot turned to smile at her, and introduce her to her husband, while Jean murmured : " Miss Barton—Mrs. and Miss Duff-Whalley," and at the same time Marriot announced that tea was in the dining-room.

" You'll have tea with us, won't you ? " Jean said.

" Oh, thank you," said Mrs. Duff-Whalley, who had come with no other intention. She was engaged in eyeing Miss Barton and trying to place her. If she were a guest, a friend of Jean's, she might be worth cultivating—she was certainly very decorative : but noticing that the girl kept herself rather in the background, she decided that she was probably some sort of companion, and decided to waste no efforts in her direction.

Mrs. Duff-Whalley ate a large tea with much content, being the only really pleased person at the table. Pamela was aggrieved at being cheated out of a pleasant hour : her husband disgusted that he had been dragged from his books only to find himself in the clutches of his *bête noire* : Betty Barton had seen and resented Mrs. Duff-Whalley's appraisal of herself : Muriel was self-conscious, miserably aware that again her mother had thrust herself in when she was not wanted. Jean was wishing heartily, if inhospitably, that this old acquaintance had remained that afternoon in her flamboyant residence, and not shattered her tea-party at The Rigs.

The talk went on. . . . " Do tell me," Mrs. Duff-Whalley said to Lewis, " how you put in your days. I'm sure I envy you your leisure. Life to me is such an utter rush. My daughter, Mrs. Egerton Thomson, writes to me of her London rush, lunching here, dining there, theatre parties, and so on ; but I write back and say, ' Don't talk to me about London : Priorsford is a *vortex*.' "

" I quite believe it," said Pamela. " After Priorsford one is grateful for the comparative peace of the metropolis."

" Of course," Mrs. Duff-Whalley continued, " I interest

myself in everything that is for the good of the town ; I feel that to be my duty. And then we have such a *wide* range of acquaintances, really they comprise three counties, and always extending."

" That," said Jean, " must make life very interesting."

" Yesterday we were lunching near Jedburgh : next week we have engagements in St. Boswells and Kelso. It's lovely down Tweed. I must say I prefer it to this part."

" Oh, I *don't* agree," said Pamela. " Could anything be more exquisite than the road from, say, Holylee, up to Tweedsmuir ? Stobo, Dawyck, Drumelzier ? And those lovely green glens—Stanhope, Hopecarton, Gameshope ! and Tweed singing beside you most of the way."

" I like place-names," Miss Barton said suddenly.

" Oh, so do I," said Jean. " ' Almost singing themselves they run.' I was telling Miss Barton, Lewis, about the lovely names of the stations you pass going to Edinburgh. But where, I wonder, is ' Little France.' Doesn't it make you think of gentlemen in flowered satin waistcoats and red-heeled shoes, and ladies with lace about their delicate hands ! "

Mrs. Duff-Whalley paused in the act of conveying a bit of cake to her mouth and remarked : " You were always very fanciful, Jean." Presently she turned to Pamela Elliot, saying : " It's very sad for the poor child to have her husband go off like this. I almost wonder she came back to Priorsford : very brave of her, I'm sure."

Pamela stared at her. " Brave," she repeated. " Why brave ? Surely, when my brother had to go with his friend it was the most natural thing in the world that he should wish his wife and family to be near relations. We wanted them all to come to Laverlaw, it would have been the greatest treat for us—but you wouldn't, you obstinate Jean."

" Oh, *I* understand," said Mrs. Duff-Whalley soothingly, " but people are apt to be so ill-natured. I needn't tell *you* that, Mrs. Elliot."

" Well, I wouldn't have known it otherwise. I've never noticed any particular ill-nature about the people in Priorsford ; but why they should give a moment's thought to my sister-in-law's affairs I can't see. . . ."

Jean turned to Muriel asking : " You still do Guides, don't you ? I remember you used to be very keen. I wish we had you to help us at Mintern Abbas : we have just started them there. I'm so sorry, Mrs. Duff-Whalley, that the children aren't in this afternoon, they're having tea at The Neuk. . . . Some other time, I hope. . . ."

When tea was over the visitors departed.

Pamela sank into a chair. " Jean, *couldn't* you have got rid of them ? "

" Only by being rude, and that's never worth while. The poor soul doesn't mean any harm : it's just her heavy-footed way. . . . Here come the children ! Anyway, we've got a *little* time to ourselves. . . . But I wish this hadn't happened, with you of all people."

Pamela laughed. " Fie, the honeypot ! " she mocked.

CHAPTER IX

" . . . THREE weeks to-day, Biddy, since you left us, and it seems a long, long time. We have got into a peaceful routine. Every morning Peter and Alison march off importantly to school, and Quentin in his pram, attended by Elsie, proceeds to take an airing. I've just seen them off now : and in a little I'll go and work with Barty.

" The weather is fine—still, autumn weather, as if Nature were holding its breath for its winter blasts. The leaves are falling so quietly, fluttering down in the still air, and as the black branches begin to show, the leaves that are left glow more golden. The Hopetoun Woods are a sight to see. Mrs. Hope sits by her window and looks and looks. It must be queer to see the leaves fall when one is very old.

" I posted a large letter to you yesterday which may not reach you for weeks if you are wandering about.

" It was a great relief to get your letters posted as you landed. I was *afraid* about Tim. But he had known himself what was best for him. It's perfectly amazing to hear how he has benefited already. I am so glad for your sake, for now he will really be able to enjoy things, and you won't be anxious about him. Your letter was frightfully interesting. I'm just realizing one of the blessings (so to speak!) of this trial! If we had never been parted I should never have known what splendid letters you could write. You have the seeing eye, and can describe what you see. And you have so much to write about: hosts of new people and vast continents. I feel my tittle-tattle from Priorsford is very small beer indeed!

"I can understand how you must grudge being out there, as you say, simply loafing, when you used to hunt and climb, but *don't* say you are getting old. Forty-four is the prime of life, and you know you are as good as ever you were on the hills: the gillies at Kinbervie said you had them beat. . . . For the matter of that I'm getting pretty old myself. Mrs. Hope upbraids me for being so staid—but I was always that, if you remember? Davy, at nineteen, feeling that something was amiss with me, used to beg me to wear earrings and powder my nose and use slang; but it seemed to me rather a heroic remedy! Pamela is one of the lucky people who grow handsomer with the years. She and Lewis make the most perfect couple, that fact strikes me afresh every time I see them.

"We all spent yesterday at Laverlaw: went up to luncheon and stayed to tea: all of us, the children, Barty, even Quentin and Ninny.

"When I think of what Laverlaw used to be like when Lewis stayed there alone; except for his own room it was about as cheerful as a tomb, and now—. Pamela has kept it as 'country' as ever, simple, even austere, but the *comfort* of it! I wonder if Lewis, bless him, ever notices it. He can't see past Pamela. The way his eyes follow her as she moves about the room (here is Beauty!); when she speaks how he listens (here is Wisdom!). Knowing nothing about clothes, he will suddenly touch something she is wearing and say, 'That's nice stuff: that's new,' and Pamela smiles, and disguises the fact that she has worn it many times.

"But I was talking about the comfort of Laverlaw. . . . I was never so struck with it as yesterday, for it was a grey day, misty and cold: the glen was grey rather than green, and the Laverlaw water was a very wan water indeed. . . . The only colour was the rust-red of the brackens and the beech-hedges, and they smouldered sullenly like a dying fire. We felt chilled as we got out of the car and looked round us, but that was only for a second, for, before the bell was rung, Pamela herself opened the door (getting in front of old Oliver, who was sorely affronted), and Pamela looking like the spirit of autumn, all in brown and orange.

"I've often told you, haven't I, Biddy?—rather insisted on it, perhaps—that I liked a little house best. . . . Well, I'm not so sure that I do! When I found myself in Laverlaw (after three weeks of The Rigs) I almost wept with home-sickness for Mintern Abbas. It was the smell, compounded of wood-smoke and apples, and furniture rubbed with beeswax and turpentine—you know how smells bring things back more than anything? and the spaciousness and the dignity. I enjoyed showing Barty the Raeburns and the other

treasures. Pamela—you won't be surprised to hear—
does not greatly care for my secretary. While admit-
ting her good looks and her competence, she says she
is not a person she would want in the house with her.
She says that though Barty never obtrudes her opinions
she (Pamela) has always the feeling that there is a regular
volcano of dissent heaving in her bosom when we
discuss politics and the questions of the day. . . . I
know there is, for Barty and I often have talks about
things, and I can't help being amused when I watch
her eyeing Pamela as she inveighs against something
Barty holds most dear. Some day there will be an
eruption !

"But things went very smoothly yesterday. Lewis
is such a peaceable soul, he disarms even born fighters
like Barty. I suppose that is really his weakness. If
he had been more of a fighter he would never have been
contented to settle down at Laverlaw and let the world
go by him ; to be absorbed (as Mrs. Hope says bitterly)
in *sheep*. I thought that Pamela would have wakened
him up, and perhaps persuaded him to go into politics,
but probably she saw that it would be a mistake. He
would never have been a good politician, for he has the
great disability of seeing both sides of a question, and
he is thoroughly happy as a sheep farmer. He and
Peter are great friends. He gets on well with children,
for he never rags or ridicules, but takes them very
seriously.

"Ninny greatly enjoyed being back at Laverlaw and
seeing her friends. Except for kitchen-maids, who in
the nature of things must be evanescent, Pamela has

the same servants as she had seven years ago, when
Ninny left her to come to us. (That must be something
of a record : I'll ask Barty what she thinks of it !)

"Quentin had tea with us, and sat with his hair
burnished beside Peter, proudly munching bread and
butter. Having become aware of the existence of rail-
ways, he visits the station every morning with Elsie
and watches the trains come in. He is going to be a
porter, and carries luggage about all day. History
repeats itself. You remember Mhor had a perfect
passion for trains ?

"I'm glad you think we made a good choice of books.
One needs something really long, and the fat omnibus
books are ideal. It's always fun, if you're fond of an
author, to read through all his books, till you become
soaked in the atmosphere he creates, but if you've
read all those detective stories you're likely to be a
criminal by this time ! I'm glad you've got some
' Lives ' with you as an antidote.

"Barty and I have begun a course of reading. The
children are in bed early, our dinner is over shortly
after eight o'clock, so we have long evenings. Barty
wants to know more of Edinburgh and its history
(I'm ashamed to say I'm disgracefully ignorant on
the subject) so we've got Chambers's *Traditions of
Edinburgh*, James Bone's Edinburgh book, a book
called *Haunted Edinburgh*, and Morton's *In Search
of Scotland*. We read aloud in turns and enjoy our
evenings.

" . . . . I'm expecting to hear news of you to-morrow.
The cables are a great comfort, they keep us in touch.

. . . A letter from Mrs. Watts this morning gives all sorts of interesting details about the health and doings of every one in Mintern Abbas, not to speak of the pickles and chutney she is making. Quite evidently we are not missed ! "

CHAPTER X

" But suppose, madam . . . suppose, after all, that I found this great world not very different from the world I know ? Its setting, clothing, scenery would be more magnificent, but in it, my sense assures me, I should find as many foibles and absurdities, as much weakness and vulgarity of mind, as in my own. . . . I am assured, madam, that your story, and the stories of your friends, would suggest to my irreverent mind a thousand parallels in the lower life I know so well. I have never been a party to those who can see romance only beneath a coronet, and the beauties of nature only when they are framed by strawberry leaves. Greatness and littleness of soul are, they must always be, independent of circumstance. . . . "

From *The Hornbeam Hedge*, by WINIFRED F. PECK.

OCTOBER finished in sheets of rain and a hurricane of wind, and Tweed ran between bank and brae.

The children came in with their faces rosy from battling with the elements, and prodigious appetites. Finding that The Rigs seemed to shrink as the weather grew bad and the garden became impossible, Jean arranged a play-room in The Neuk, to which they repaired every day after their one o'clock dinner, when the ways were too heavy and the wind too cold for anything but the shortest of walks.

Jean herself was undaunted by the weather. She liked to get up to the hill-side and, with the leaves dancing widdershins around her, wrestle with the wind ; she wanted to shout and sing when a mighty blast swept across the valley, and the trees bowed, trembling, before it.

Coming across the fields one afternoon she did not go doucely round by the gate but climbed the dyke, and landed with a flying leap almost on the top of the Miss Watsons, who, swathed in waterproofs, and protected by umbrellas and goloshes, were obviously bound for a tea-party.

They stared at Jean in her beret and mackintosh, and Miss Teenie said : " My, Lady Bidborough, have you been for a walk this awful day ? "

" Why not ? " said Jean. " It's grand up on Cademuir. If you lie back on the wind it carries you along, at least, it nearly does."

Miss Watson shivered. " I wonder you're not frightened, all alone up there. Suppose you met a tramp ! "

" Tramps keep to the highway : I only met innocent things like sheep. . . . When are you coming to have tea with me and make the acquaintance of my family? Do you remember how Jock and Mhor loved seeing your treasures ? My Peter would love them too. Have you still the ostrich eggs, and the lumps of coral, and the Chinese scratcher ? "

The Miss Watsons looked both pleased and affronted. They shook their heads and Miss Teenie said : " Fancy you remembering about that old rubbish ! It's somewhere in the attic : we only see it at spring-cleaning times. Our father being a captain. . . . Funny how fond children are of those sort of things, even when they've got beautiful toys of their own. How are they liking school ? "

" Oh, immensely. It's such fun for them being

with other children. Peter and Ian Burnett are inseparable, and Alison has found a little girl of her own age
called Margot. Margot has the loveliest flaxen plaits,
which are the envy of poor Alison. . . ."

" I'm sure," said Miss Watson, " it's an honour for
Miss Main to have them."

Jean laughed. " Far from that. If there's any
honour about it's mine. Everybody knows Miss Main
is far too good for her job. It's absurd that she should
waste her time with little scallawags like Peter and
Alison, but it's a jolly good thing for them that she
doesn't seem to think so. Well, I mustn't keep you
standing in the rain. What about next Wednesday ?
Would that suit ? That's splendid. Round about
four o'clock."

" Oh, *thank* you," said Miss Watson. " We're going
to tea to-day at Mrs. Jowett's, in connection with a
Nursing entertainment we're getting up in aid of the
town nurses, you know. Funds are low ; Teenie, here,
is treasurer, and we get quite worried about it. It
makes an awful difference when trade's slack, the people
can't give in the same way. We've been doing what
we can—just privately, you know, making woollies and
shawls and selling them among our friends."

" I'd like some woollies," said Jean. " And seeing I'm
a resident this winter, shouldn't I send a subscription ? "

" Delighted," said Miss Teenie, briskly. " Never can
get too many of them ! "

" And be sure and let me know when the entertainment is coming off. Good-bye. Don't forget next
Wednesday ! "

Passing Miss Hutton's, Jean looked over the white garden gate at the wide lawn that was tidy even in an October gale, and the firelight through the parlour window tempted her to ring the bell.

Janet Hutton was sitting sewing in her own particular chair with the wooden arms and the chintz-covered seat.

"No, don't get up, please," Jean said. "You look so comfortable sitting there, 'sewing a fine seam.' . . . May I stay to tea with you? I've just met the Miss Watsons sallying forth to a tea-party, and the sight filled me with a desire to do likewise."

"They do 'sally,' the Miss Watsons. I like the pleased expectation on their faces when a tea-party is in prospect. . . . Of course I'll love to have you to tea, but alas! if one swallow doesn't make a summer, it takes more than one middle-aged woman to make a party! I don't even know if there'll be any cake, unless Skinner has baked on chance: it's so discouraging to keep sending things in that are never touched."

"I can trust Skinner," said Jean. "May I take this thing off my head?"

"You look about fifteen in that hat. Sit in that low chair and get warm and tell me the news. I haven't been over the doorstep for two days, and no one has come in. It's amazing the number of things one can find to do in one's own house! I've been most happily busy in the attics these two days."

"Why," said Jean, "that seems the fashionable employment of the moment. I met Bella Bathgate to-day, and she said she had been 'howkin' in the garret.' . . .

The Miss Watsons were on their way to Mrs. Jowett's :
a party to arrange about some entertainment for the
Nursing. I don't think Mrs. Jowett should worry herself with such things : she isn't able."

Janet Hutton paused, with her needle in mid-air, as
she said : " You think she looks ill ? "

" Well—she had always a fragile, transparent look,
like a delicate bit of old china, that was natural to her,
but now she seems to me to be receding. I mean, her
voice is even softer than it used to be, her manner gentler,
her colour more delicate : one has the feeling when she
is talking to one that she might just fade away, and one
wouldn't be talking to any one."

Janet Hutton resumed her sewing. " I'm sorry you
think that," she said. " Seeing people constantly, one
doesn't notice changes."

" And another thing," said Jean, watching a maid
wheel in a table and spread a cloth on it, " Mr. Jowett
sounds quite angry when he speaks to her. That's how
anxiety takes most men. . . . Mrs. Jowett's the sort
of person who would suffer in silence rather than worry
the people round her. But perhaps it's only that she's
getting older. Age makes some people coarse, others it
fines down. . . . "

Jean surveyed the tea-table, then grinned triumphantly at her hostess. " I knew I could trust Skinner.
How's that for a party tea ! "

" Well, sit in and enjoy it while everything's hot. . . .
Skinner certainly has risen to the occasion. She never
gives me sandwiches and hot cakes."

" You don't encourage her to—nibbling a bit of bread

and butter. Don't you remember Mrs. Macdonald's
disgust if you didn't ' make a meal of your tea ' ? "

Miss Hutton smiled, then sighed, as she said : " *Indeed* I do. . . . Have you met Mr. Thornton ? "

" No. I haven't even heard him preach. It's silly,
but I can't bear to think or him in Mr. Macdonald's
place. You like him ? "

Miss Hutton nodded. " I do. He's a good fellow,
I think, and sincere. Rather cock-sure, of course,
being young. . . . I know what you feel about the
Macdonalds : they're missed by every one. Their going
seemed to cut a bit out of all our lives, and every way
you turn there's an emptiness. Mr. Thornton tells me
that in his congregational visiting most of the conversation consists of deploring the loss of the former minister.
It is rather disheartening for the young man ! It's a
good thing he hasn't a wife, for no matter how good and
clever and helpful she was, she would suffer in comparison with our dear Mrs. Macdonald. I wish you'd come
to luncheon one day and meet Mr. Thornton : will you ? "

" I'd love to. I hear he has the sense to appreciate
Priorsford ? "

" Yes. Indeed, he was the real reason for my
' howkin' ' in the garret this morning. He is anxious
to read all he can get hold of about Tweeddale. I
lent him the three volumes of the County History
which he devoured (he's a rake at reading), and I
wanted him to read the *Memoirs of Robert Chambers*
but when I went confidently to get it from the shelf
it wasn't there. I was afraid it had been lent to some
nefarious person who had not returned it—some people

lose all their honesty when it's a question of a book—
and as I value it I made a thorough search, and eventually found it in the attic among a lot of old books.
How it got there I don't know. . . ."

" Oh, may I have it when Mr. Thornton's finished
with it, if I promise to return it carefully ?—I *am* enjoying my tea. These little sultana cakes are the most
delicious things . . . can you really forbear ?—You see,
we have long evenings alone, Miss Barton and I, so we've
got into the way of reading aloud : one reads and one
works, and it's more sociable than each poring over a
separate volume. At present we're reading books about
Edinburgh, and we're specially enjoying Chambers's
book, which I'm ashamed to say I'd never read—*Traditions of Edinburgh*. There are such delightful tales of
the old ladies of quality who lived in the ' lands ' in the
Canongate. And he is most learned, is Mr. Robert Chambers, about women's dress at the end of the eighteenth
century. I love his description of the ' gypsy straw hat
tied down close over the ears with a coloured ribbon '
and the ' white frock with a flaunting sash and white or
black *mode* tippet.' And the *calbash* and *bongrace*, and
lappets, pinners, rumple-knots ! Next, I thought, we'd
read about Tweedside and the Borders."

Janet Hutton looked over her spectacles at the girl
as she said : " These long evenings, are they not very
dull for you, Jean ? For myself, I love them, and never
weary for a minute, but you are different : you are
young."

Jean gave a replete sigh and wiped her sticky fingers
with her handkerchief. " I feel," she said, " as if I

should say with the children, ' Thank God for my good tea.' . . . No, I can't say I find the evenings long, being naturally tranquil—or is bovine the better word ? If I wanted to I could go out a certain amount—people have been most kind about inviting me to dinner—but it isn't much fun going out alone, and it means leaving Miss Barton in solitude. No, books are the real solution."

Janet Hutton took up her seam. Jean, lying back in her chair, watched her lazily.

Presently the older woman said : " It seems to be working well this arrangement. When you wrote to me about it I was just a little doubtful."

" I was more than a *little* doubtful," said Jean ; " but so far things have gone smoothly. The children are very happy—you can't think how glad I am that Peter and Alison are beginning their school-life with Miss Main !—and of course it makes all the difference to have Pamela and Lewis at our backs, so to speak. . . . Biddy was right. I'd have been crushed by the responsibility of Mintern Abbas, and the claims that every day brings there."

" Yes, it can be no light task to fill your position. . . . But you enjoy it ? "

" Oh, I do. You see I have Biddy : I can always turn to him if things go wrong, and he's there to laugh with me when people are funny—as they so often are ! "

" Yes." Janet smiled agreement over her work. " And I don't suppose they vary much. The people round Mintern Abbas will be very like the people in Priorsford ? "

Jean sat forward, her elbows on her knees, her face cupped between her hands. "I wonder," she said, "if you happened to read a story in the *Cornhill* some time ago, called 'The Hornbean Hedge'? No? Well, it was delightfully amusing—and so true! The story of an encounter between a novelist (obviously Jane Austen) and a fashionable London lady. A wheel comes off the coach of the lady (Mrs. Damer by name, a sculptor of note), and she seeks shelter in what she thinks is the inn, but which is really the home of 'the demure, inconspicuous spinster.' Refreshments are offered and accepted, courtesies are exchanged, also confidences, and in the end Mrs. Damer makes the amazing proposal that Jane Austen will write her memoirs. 'I have had a wonderful life,' she says; 'I have lived with the greatest minds of my age. I have seen love and hate, virtue and vice in conflict in the very highest circles. It shall be for you—yes, for you, madam, to give the story of my life to the world.' . . . Of course 'Jane' won't do it, objecting that though criticism may be imparted, inspiration can never be. . . . But what is so delicious is that the writer of the tale gives the parallels that pass through the novelist's mind as the lady tells her of her experiences. I can only remember one—'I had my share of good looks,' says Mrs. Damer, 'but it was for me to make my niche in my world by my talents rather than by my appearance.' ('Our Patty,' reflected the listener, 'told me that as her mother was so handsome, and her elder sister so popular, she made up her mind that her's would be the lightest hand at pastry.')"

Miss Hutton laughed appreciatively, and said:
" Child, what a memory you have ! "

" Always had. I used to make myself a nuisance
quoting poetry to the boys, till they rebelled. But
this story appealed to me specially, because I, in my
small way, have felt much the same : I was lifted
(most people would say) out of a narrow world of small
things into a wider, fuller life. But I found very little
difference : people are the same everywhere, and the
same things, more or less, happen to all."

" It somehow sounds," said Miss Hutton, " rather like
Ecclesiastes ! But I daresay you are right. The setting may be different, the clothing and the scenery, but
the same foibles and absurdities, the same greatnesses
and littlenesses are to be found in every circle. There's
something rather comforting about that thought : one
feels one isn't missing anything. If you can find that
story, I'd like very much to see it. . . . Oh, you're not
going . . . ? "

" I fear I must : my neglected family call to me.
. . . It's been lovely this afternoon. . . . And I hear
I'm to have the great pleasure of taking you up to
Hopewaterfoot for luncheon next Wednesday. I had
a letter from Mirren Strang this morning. I do wish
you'd tell me, now that you haven't a car of your own,
any time you want to go anywhere. It would be a
real kindness to Phipps (the chauffeur), for I'm not a
great deal out, and the poor man lives a life of cultured
ease, and is bored to distraction. Haven't you any
long calls you ought to make ? Try and think."

" Thank you, my dear." Miss Hutton laid aside her

work and rose to say good-bye to her guest. " I'll
remember your kind offer. Come again soon: I've
enjoyed you immensely. . . . And, Jean, when you've
time, run up and see Mrs. Jowett. She's a lot alone,
and it's dull for her."

" Yes. I'm worried about her looking so frail. . . .
She *was* so kind to us when we were little. . . . That's
one of the sad things about coming back to Priorsford,
finding old friends failing—and the blanks."

CHAPTER XI

" More needs she the divine than the physician."

MACBETH.

THE very next afternoon, rather late, so that Mrs. Jowett's afternoon rest should be over, Jean walked up the drive of The Knowe. It was, she decided, quite the prettiest place in Priorsford. Divided by a meadow and a belt of trees from the other houses, The Knowe, its long low front covered with creepers and roses, looked across its lawn to the hills. Inside and out it was without speck or flaw. Which was not to be wondered at, as Mr. Jowett had had nothing much to do for twenty years but walk about and think how things might be improved. He considered himself a stern task-master, but indeed the gardener and the chauffeur lived lives of the greatest comfort and ease. True, Mr. Jowett was subject to eruptions of wrath as sudden as they were violent, but they passed as quickly as an April shower, and were as little heeded. The gardener was " Johnston—decent man," and the chauffeur " Crawford—poor fellow," but when enraged, their master, like Shakespeare's shepherds, used " grosser names."

Mr. Jowett was a small man, with a red face, and something vaguely nautical about his gait. He was almost completely idle, but his great desire was to be considered a man of affairs. He sat on various boards, acted as secretary to several societies, and was a god-send to cranks of all descriptions.

That afternoon he came trotting down the drive, his hands full of papers, so preoccupied that he almost passed Jean without seeing her.

" Ah," he said, " how are you ? My wife 'll be glad to see you. . . . You must excuse me. As you see I'm in a great hurry. These telegrams must be sent off at once. Most important. I'll be back shortly." He lifted his hat, gave a funny little old-fashioned bow, and still murmuring, " Back shortly," disappeared out of the gate.

Jean went on and rang the bell, and the sight of the maid who opened the door made her smile. She was so entirely Mrs. Jowett's maid. No one else could produce anything so respectful, so gentle-voiced, so fresh, in her demure grey, with apron and mob-cap, cuffs, and collar of spotted muslin.

Mrs. Jowett, some one said, collected maids as other people collect china or first editions ; she had all a collector's joy in securing a perfect specimen. But she not only found perfect maids, she managed to keep them—a more difficult matter.

Jean was taken through a blue and white hall, warm and flower-scented, to a drawing-room, all soft pinks and blues and mauves, with delicate water-colour draw-ings on the white walls.

It was a constant wonder to less perfect housekeepers how Mrs. Jowett's curtains always looked as if they had been freshly put up, her chintzes newly laundered.

Mrs. Jowett was sitting on a couch before a fire. She was dressed in mauve, her favourite shade, with a little velvet coat trimmed with grey fur. Her beautiful silver-white hair was carefully dressed, and she made a pleasant picture among the cushions in the pretty room, but Jean saw that her face was small and drawn.

"I'm so glad it's you, Jean," she said, in her sweet, smooth, rather precise voice. "When the door opened I was afraid it might be callers."

"I'm not a caller," said Jean, "but I hardly feel fit to enter this room. I dread the effect of my rough tweed on your chintzes and cushions. . . . May I sit on this stool?"

"Don't be absurd, child. . . . I like you in that brown tweed with the orange. Come and sit near me and tell me what you've been doing, and how the children are, and everything. I'm so lazy these days I'm seldom out." She held out her hands to the blaze. "The cold seems to wither me, somehow."

"Priorsford winters try the hardest. What about a winter abroad?"

Mrs. Jowett shook her head. "Timothy would hate it. But we have a warm, comfortable house, and if it's dreary outside it's cheerful indoors, and I ought to be very grateful." She leant back on her cushions. "Talk to me, Jean. What news have you from your husband?"

Jean lifted a bright face. "The best," she said. "Biddy is very well himself, and he's positively amazed at the progress Tim Talbot is making."

"Why, is he a Timothy too?"

" No, not really. He was christened Algernon, so of course he had to have another name : he's always been Tim to his friends. . . . Biddy says he can walk quite a long way, and enjoy his meals : he even takes an interest in the people they meet. And not much more than two months ago we had almost given up hope of him. It's marvellous what a complete change and a sea-trip can do ! "

" The trouble must have been removed."

" Yes. It was pneumonia, and then his old wound gave trouble, and the doctors were afraid that he would slip out of life simply through not caring enough to live. At this moment they're on their way to New Zealand. It'll be nice when they've stopped moving farther off : it's such a desperate long way to New Zealand. Sometimes at night I get dreadfully scared thinking Biddy may be ill, accidents can happen so easily. But of course that's silly. He sends me a cable every week, and that's a great comfort. Moving about all the time letters must be uncertain, and the cables keep me up to date. I suppose when you were in India you and your husband would be separated quite a lot ? "

" No," Mrs. Jowett said, " we were very little apart. Having no children I could be with Timothy most of the time. I only once left him to go to the hills. He always wanted me to go, but I think he was quite glad when I stayed."

" I'm very sure he was ! He doesn't like you out of his sight."

Mrs. Jowett gave a quick sigh. After a minute she

said : " Timothy has been put on two more committees. I'm so thankful, for he enjoys meetings. If he can feel himself busy then he's happy. . . . Perhaps it was a mistake to retire so soon, but we had had more than twenty years in India, and we did long for a place of our own in our own country. We used to picture to ourselves, sitting all damp with heat on the veranda of an evening, just what our garden would be like : lawns green like velvet, not burned brown : flowers that smelt sweet, mignonette and sweet peas, pansies, stocks, pinks : roses, of course : high hollyhocks against a grey wall, lupins and delphiniums—the very names seemed to bring coolness. . . . And the house. We thought we'd like it long and low, harled in cream, with the window frames painted black : inside white and blue. I don't know why, but we always liked the idea of white and blue—white paint and blue rugs and curtains. The drawing-room was to be all my favourite colours— pink and blue and mauve."

" And so it is," said Jean : " just as you pictured."

" Just as we pictured," Mrs. Jowett repeated. " We couldn't have been happier than we've been in Priors- ford : kind friends round us, and such *good* servants. But I might have done more for people, Jean ; I feel that now."

" Why, you did—and you do—far too much for everybody," Jean assured her. " We haven't forgotten how good you were to us as children, and it can't have been easy to let three wild boys rampage through your pretty house. And everybody turns to you for help when it's a question of getting up money. You give your drawing-room for meetings—only yesterday I met the Miss Watsons on their way to drink a dish of tea with you over the Nursing. . . ."

" Yesterday ? Yes. I was very tired before they went away."

" That's what I say," Jean protested. " You've got run down and you're not well enough to trouble entertaining people. . . . What about a week in bed ? "

" Oh no, it would worry Tim dreadfully. He hates to be alone, poor dear."

Jean thought some angry thoughts about the absent Tim, but all she said was : " Dear Mrs. Jowett, you spoil everybody, your husband not excepted."

" You see, I'm a mid-Victorian," Mrs. Jowett smiled, and laid her hand on Jean's. " It was the fashion to spoil husbands in my young days. It's different now, but I'm too old to change, even if I wanted to. . . . Ah ! here is Tim."

Mr. Jowett bustled in, announcing that he had got the telegrams away.

" Couldn't Crawford have gone with them ? " his wife asked.

" Oh, Crawford—poor fellow, he was very busy in his garden so I didn't trouble him. I didn't mind the walk, enjoyed it indeed, but it's the time it takes. I assure you, Jean—Lady Bidborough, I mean—that I hardly know what it is to have a spare minute. It's often tea-time before I get my morning letters read."

Jean expressed surprise, but remembered that her old friend had always had a fancy for running about brandishing unopened letters and protesting about lack of time. What struck her as new was the way he furtively and anxiously watched his wife, even as he babbled of his own affairs.

Presently he announced: " My wife has been a bit off colour lately: run down, easily tired, that sort of thing. I tell her imagination has a great deal to do with it. Eh, Janetta ? "

Mrs. Jowett smiled and agreed that it might be so.

" Doctors are such unsatisfactory fellows," Mr. Jowett went on, trotting up and down the room as he spoke. " Nothing to be got out of them. Fact of the matter is, they know nothing, even the big-wigs. We went to see a man who has a great name, and, would you believe it, all he said to Janetta was to go home and sit in the garden and enjoy the flowers ! Even when I tackled him I got no satisfaction. I was prepared for anything, an operation, a winter abroad, *anything* —but that was all we got. Preposterous ! "

" But, Tim, dear," his wife protested gently, " surely it was a very pleasant prescription ? "

Mr. Jowett snorted. " Pleasant enough, if it had done you any good ! " He went on angrily: " You know quite well you've less strength than you had a month ago, and you don't care to take even a short drive now. . . ."

Mrs. Jowett turned her head on her cushion, as if weary of the discussion, and her husband, after a rapid turn through the room, pulled up opposite Jean and said :

" I've simply no use for these intangible ailments. With appendicitis and such things you know where you are, but to see a person lose strength and weight for no apparent reason—I must say it is most annoying, most *annoying.*"

He rubbed his hand over his rather stubbly hair in such a perplexed way that Jean could not but feel sorry for him. Murmuring that she must go, she made a movement towards her hostess. Whereupon Mr. Jowett said in a loud voice: "Janetta, rouse yourself. Lady Bidborough is going."

"No, *don't* rouse yourself," Jean besought her. "Yes, I must be home for the children's tea."

"I must make a party for them," said Mrs. Jowett.

"That would be lovely—later on, perhaps. . . . Oh, d'you remember the party when poor Jock covered himself with disgrace by spilling his tea all over everything?"

"I remember. Dear Jock, I'd like to see him again."

"So you shall: he's coming for Christmas. . . . It is so nice to be near you again."

Mr. Jowett conducted Jean to the front door, and stood staring out at the darkening garden.

Jean said, after a minute, "It's a bad time of year for any one who isn't quite well; the days shortening, and nothing much to expect but rain. . . ."

"She had a long summer of sunshine and it did her no good," Mr. Jowett said.

Jean was silent.

CHAPTER XII

" In winter's tedious nights sit by the fire . . . "
KING RICHARD II.

MUIRBURN, a village about ten miles farther up Tweed
than Priorsford, was where Mirren Strang had her
abode. Her house, Hopewaterfoot, was really what
the house-agents call " a commodious cottage," standing
in a big walled garden. She was alone, except for her
companion, Rebecca Brand, the sister of the minister
of the Parish. Poles asunder, the two women agreed
on almost no point, but lived and wrangled together
quite happily.

Mirren Strang was by way of being a novelist, but
she always made light of her claim to the title.

" I make money out of it," she said, " and that's a
blessing, for otherwise I'd have to do without much
that I enjoy, but I'll never be anything but a sort of
amateur. Enjoy writing ? No, of course I don't.
Does any one ? Yes, I believe some do ; the writers
who can sluice it out. But the odd thing is, although
I've such a slack tongue, I've a very slow-moving
pen, and a brain that's simply not worth talking
about. It's very rarely that a thought passes through
my mind. No, it's a fact. As for plots, I simply can't
think of one ! How I respect the people who can work

138

out intricate stories of crime. But there are worse
jobs than writing. On cold winter mornings it's a good
excuse to hug the fire. To sit in an armchair with a
writing-pad on one's knee, toasting one's toes, listening
to the rain on the pane, while one thinks out, lazily,
conversations and situations—that's very pleasant. But
when things become serious and the MSS. has to be
produced on a given date, to have to sit ten or twelve
hours on end, feverishly scribbling, with your mind as
dry as a nut, while the summer sun shines outside, and
you long to be working in the garden, or picnicking with
friends ! Always I begin with the best intentions about
getting things forward and not having a rush at the
end—but I always fail. But it doesn't matter, the books
do get written. Whether they're *worth* writing is another
matter, but anyway they're as good as I'm capable
of. . . ."

Mirren was writing one morning in November, in the
living-room. She liked to work in the living-room, hating
the feeling of being shut away. For her sort of writing,
she declared, quiet did not matter, and she rather welcomed interruption and stray callers. They all went into
her conversations, she said, and gave them verisimilitude.

This morning as she sat by the fire scribbling, Rebecca
Brand came in, conning a list she carried in her hand.

" *My love,*" wrote Mirren, " *you have made my life
blossom like a rose.*"

" We need washing soda," said Rebecca, " and
powdered bath-brick, and some bars of common white
soap for scrubbing—I simply don't know how Martha
gets through so much soap : you'd think she ate it ! "

"Yes," said Mirren absently, writing ' *She smiled up at him and all the glory of the sunset*. . . .'' What did you say, Rebecca? I'm writing.''

"Oh," said Rebecca, in an ill-used voice, " I'm afraid I'm interrupting.''

Mirren laughed. "Not really, I'm only writing it down to see what it looks like, and it's no better than I expected! . . . Are these the week's groceries? I suppose we can get most of them at the village shop? ''

"Ye—es," said Rebecca doubtfully, " I daresay we can. But there are some things we must get at Priorsford—Bath Olivers—the small thin ones, cheese, icing sugar—quite a lot. . . . Will you be going down to-day? ''

"M'm . . . I'm going to Hopetoun to tea. I'll leave the list at Cranston's—unless you care to go yourself? ''

"Have you forgotten," said Rebecca, " that it's Robin's birthday? I am going to the Manse to eat a bit of his birthday cake.''

"Of course. Imagine Robin with a birthday! It seems no time since he came into the world—I've a plush dog for him in my present drawer.''

"Robin's very far on," said his aunt proudly. "He can stand alone, and Stella says he points to my photograph and says ' Bec.' *I* don't believe it—but there's no doubt he is intelligent.''

"Oh yes," Mirren gravely agreed, " he's got a most alert look. No wonder you're all proud of him. . . . They're a very happy couple, your brother and Stella, Rebecca.''

"Oh, I think so. Of course it's a struggle on a

minister's income, and Stella hasn't got a penny of her own. But she's a good manager, I'll say that. Much better than I was. Her economies aren't so apparent as mine were! And she has the knack of dressing well on little, which I never had. I still think Rob would have done better to marry money, but he thinks he's been the luckiest of men—and perhaps he's right. . . . Chrissie's broken the glass box on your dressing-table. Quite defiant about it too. Not a word of regret, just tossed her head, and said, ' Accidents will happen, and I didn't do it on purpose.' What that girl breaks is prodigious, she must break her wage every year. And if she were quick and smart, one could understand it, but she's a slow worker. I told her *she* had no call to be impudent."

" Oh," said Mirren, " and what did Chrissie say to that ? "

" Muttered something. I took the opportunity when Gladys was clearing the breakfast-table to speak to her about coming in so late the other night. I must say I'm disappointed in Gladys. I thought she was a nice girl."

Mrs. Strang sighed, and said ruefully, " You seem to have roused a hornet's nest this morning, my dear. I wish I weren't going to be in to lunch. I hate an angry atmosphere."

" You're much too inclined to pass over things," her companion told her severely. " The servants would just do as they liked if I weren't here."

Mirren laughed as she pushed away her writing-pad.

" I believe they would," she said. " . . . I don't

feel like doing any more work. I've got to get some books looked out to leave at Miss Hutton's. Oh, and I want to cut some of those tawny chrysanthemums for Lady Bidborough. She admired them the day she came to lunch."

"Lady Bidborough 'll get lots of flowers from Laverlaw."

"I daresay she will," Mirren agreed, "but I think she would like some from Hopewaterfoot as well; anyway, it'll be a pleasure to me to give them."

"You couldn't call her *pretty*," Rebecca began in an argumentative voice.

"No?"

"But it's an interesting face to watch. It stands looking into. Her forehead is so smooth and calm; and her eyes are lovely. . . . I felt myself staring at her across the table as if she were a heroine out of a book."

"It's been rather a fairy-tale-ish life, Lady Bidborough's, when you come to think of it."

"She's got too much," said Rebecca: "a peer for a husband and a fortune as well."

"And would have been contented with so much less," Mirren said.

"Things," said Rebecca, "are unequally divided."

"It's a common complaint. . . . Leave the list on the hall-table, will you? and I shan't be so likely to forget it. I shall just have time to change before lunch."

Rebecca Brand was not a great deal of use at Hopewaterfoot. She was an indifferent housekeeper and given to quarrelling with the servants : she had a heavy hand with flowers : she was often in the way, and generally out of it when wanted ; but Mirren was glad of her, for, as she said, she was some one to come home to, some one who was deeply interested in her doings, and the news she brought in.

On this day of which I write Mirren Strang did not get back from Priorsford till late, and went straight upstairs to change, but after dinner, sitting comfortably before the fire, Rebecca with her knitting—she kept her brother in socks and her small nephew in woollies —they recounted to each other the events of the after-noon.

A question from Mirren started Rebecca, who told with gusto all that had happened at the birthday party, finishing with :

" . . . And Mrs. Home was there with Archibald and Fanny. Don't you think Fanny's an absurdly early-Victorian name to give the child ? It's after the old aunt who used to live with them at Little Phantasy."

Mirren nodded. " Dear little Aunt Fanny," she said. " Always wrapped up in soft white shawls, afraid of everything—draughts, burglars, mice, but especially of death. She used to sigh, and say, ' A step in the dark,' if the subject came up. It worried Kirsty Home : she said she couldn't bear the thought of the little sheltered soul going out into the cold. . . . But we needn't have feared. Nothing became Aunt Fanny so well in this life as the leaving of it. She was only a few days in bed, not suffering, except with weakness; dignified and sweet to the end. ' Don't keep me,' she said at the last, and stepped out like an explorer. . . . I'm certain Kirsty misses Aunt Fanny to this day, though she has her husband and children and all she wants in this world. . . . Young Archibald ages with Robin, doesn't he ? "

" Yes," said Rebecca, bending over a tangle in her wool. " They rolled on a rug together and clawed each other's hair. Did I tell you Stella had baked and iced a beautiful birthday cake ? Yes. Rob kept telling us it had been made at home—as proud as Punch. She has the dining-room table bare—she must have got it all done up, for it was ink-stained and disreputable in my day—and I must say it looked very well, with the lace mats on it that you brought her from Italy. . . . Mrs. Home said she liked my new tweed, but it's second nature to that woman to say the pleasant thing. Colonel Home came with the car to take them home. He's lost that lean, hungry look he used to have, and is getting quite fat. . . . I used to think he looked like a knight in a picture, now he's only an ordinary contented married man."

" There are worse things," said Mirren Strang lazily. She was stretched out in a most comfortable chair, her feet in the fender, her head pillowed in cushions. On a table close to her hand lay two new books, a novel, and somebody's reminiscences ; beside them a box of hard-centred chocolates : the shade of the electric lamp was just as she liked it : this was the happiest hour in Mirren's day.

"And what kind of afternoon 'had you?" Rebecca asked.

"Very pleasant. I went first to Janet Hutton's with the books, and found her sitting with a large atlas spread out before her on a table. She looked at me over the owlish spectacles she had put on, and said, 'No, she wasn't thinking of taking a journey, she was merely refreshing herself with the size of the world, after having entertained some very circumscribed people to lunch!'"

"Dear me," said Rebecca, "she must be getting queer; and she looks so sensible."

Mirren laughed, and continued: "Then I ran in to The Rigs with the chrysanthemums, and met the children returning from their walk. Friendly little creatures, they seemed. I went in with them, as they assured me 'Mummy' would be in the 'shiproom.' You've never been to The Rigs? It's quite small, with one large living-room. That always seems to me the ideal thing —a small house with one spacious room. This room is an unusual shape, long and rather low-ceilinged, with one end coming to a point, like the bow of a ship. There's a window with a window-seat in the bow, and as the house stands high on a slope and faces west you look straight across the river to the hills, and almost feel that you're sailing into the sunset." Mirren paused and looked into the dancing flames, smiling to herself. Then she turned to her companion and said:

"They're lucky little people, those children of Jean's, to have this time at Priorsford. For one thing, they're getting their mother to themselves. At home Lady

Bidborough must be a very busy woman, her days
filled to overflowing with all manners of duties and obliga-
tions. Here she can devote most of her time to her
children. . . . I wish you could have seen that room
to-day. It was full of shadows, and through the end
windows you saw the last of the sunset and the glint
of the river. Tea was laid on a gate-table before the
fire, a children's tea, with high chairs and feeders!
Jean was kneeling on the rug, toasting slices of bread,
which a very pretty girl in a red dress, with absolutely
raven-black hair, buttered and put in a covered dish.
. . . And in a second I was received into the warmth
of the circle. Lady Bidborough turned round a fire-
scorched face, and gave a joyful shout at the sight of
me and the chrysanthemums—yes, she *sounded* glad
and I believe she was—and said: 'You've come to tea.
What good luck!' And a comfortable broad-faced
nurse brought in the children with their golden heads
shining; they clambered into their chairs, full of news
about their walk, and the pretty dark girl helped to tie
on their feeders, and their mother—you would have
called her pretty to-day, I'm sure—listened and laughed.
To leave that little house, brimful of young life and
merriment, and go through the dark Hopetoun Woods
to that quiet room where Mrs. Hope sits with Augusta,
was almost too much of a contrast. Yet Solomon
said that the end was better than the beginning. I
wonder!"

Rebecca was not greatly interested in Solomon, nor
in Mrs. Hope, so she went back to the subject of The
Rigs and asked: "Who was the dark girl?"

" The dark girl ?—oh, she's Lady Bidborough's secretary, a Miss Barton. They call her ' Barty,' and she seems quite one of the family. Few people would care to have such a decorative secretary, but Jean quite obviously delights in her beauty. I hardly spoke to the girl—I wasn't in the house more than ten minutes —but I got an impression of rather hard efficiency. . . . Jean came with me to the door and told me she'd had a long letter from her husband that morning and a cable as well. That was why not only her eyes but her very curls seemed to sparkle ! That's a thoroughly happy woman."

" She has every reason to be," said Rebecca, knitting briskly.

Mirren picked a chocolate from the box, bit it, and sank deeper into her cushions. Presently she said :

" I've known Jean all her life, but chiefly through other people's eyes—prejudiced, kind eyes like Mrs. Hope's and Janet Hutton's, and, like you, I've sometimes wondered whether fate had not been too lavish to her. But now that I'm getting really to know her, I realize that old Peter Reid knew what he was about when he left her his fortune, and that Lord Bidborough was a lucky man to persuade her to marry him. She is good, but not too good to be likeable : she has her prejudices and weak spots like every one else, and is as unreasoning as the rest of us in her likes and dislikes. But there's something finer than the ordinary about her ; a gentleness that goes right through, a deep clear sincerity, and with it, a great sense of the ridiculous, and a liking for the queer waifs of life. . . ."

Rebecca pursed her lips and shook her head as she remarked :

" I'm afraid Lady Bidborough will do more harm than good with her money : she sounds sentimental and tender-hearted."

" But," Mirren objected, " sentimental and tender-hearted are two entirely different things. The senti-mental are content with feeling ; the tender-hearted help. Jean has a passion for helping. Even as a child, they say, when she had nothing, she was a real " Madam Liberality,' and now that she has the means . . . ! "

" Well," said Rebecca—she had finished the woolly she was knitting and now stretched it, contemplatively, on her knee—" Well, some people get a great deal from life, but most get very little, and at the end we'll not worry how much or how little we've had—nothing will matter then."

" That's true," said Mirren. " And I suppose in a way it's a comfort. . . . "

She looked round the pleasant room, with its books and prints, its rugs, and carefully kept old furniture, and her eyes came to rest on the mantelshelf, where, between two Ming parrots, stood a framed sampler. It was worked on very fine Chinese-yellow canvas : amazing trees, pre-posterous fowls, done in exquisite stitches, and a poem which began : " What availeth beauty of the skin."

At the end :

Easter Backler Wrought this in the year 1706.

Mirren read the last words aloud. " *Easter Backler*

Wrought this." "I wonder what else she did! Loved, married, brought up children? Or sat in sedate spinster-hood writing out receipts for possets and face washes? Was she pretty or plain? Virtuous or wanton? A saint or a shrew? 'Tis more significant she's dead. Dead more than two hundred years, little Easter Backler who wrought this. . . . And in a few short years we, too, will be gone and forgotten, and only the inanimate things will remain, the Ming parrots, Easter Backler's sampler . . ."

"I quite forgot," said Rebecca, "to ask you to order toilet soap. The lavender kind you like is all done: there's only that highly-scented stuff that came from Paris; a horrid smell it has."

Mirren looked over at her companion. "Really, Rebecca," she said, "need you break into my delicate fancies with your sordid domestic details? . . . It occurs to me that I might bring Easter Backler and her sampler into the chapter I'm writing. The heroine is *swithering* (good word that!) whether or not to accept an offer, and sits trying to fore-fancy her fate if she refuses. . . . Her name is Cynthia. She's a fool," Mirren added gloomily.

"Most people in books are," said Rebecca. "Either they're too good to be true or too bad to be true. I seldom meet any one in a book that I can be bothered with."

Mirren Strang looked up at the Ming parrots as she remarked: "It would be a sad job for writers if there were many Rebeccas in the world!"

Rebecca replied with a sniff.

CHAPTER XIII

"I wrote my love a letter . . ."

OLD SONG.

JEAN was writing to her husband. She sat curled in a corner of the sofa, with a writing-pad and a fountain-pen.

"Nov. 30th," she wrote. "It's a tremendous satisfaction to come to the last day of a month. I can't hustle the weeks away fast enough, especially a week that brings no letter. The cables, though a comfort, are not very *satisfying*! But after you land in New Zealand letters will come regularly.

"I wonder how you are enjoying the voyage? I rather envy you. You'll see so many new things and meet so many new people that you yourself will be renewed. Perhaps we were getting rather groovy, you and I, too utterly satisfied with our lot, thinking that our house and our neighbours made the world. I daresay we needed to be thoroughly shaken up. But life is so *short*, Biddy! Six months is a lot to lose. I get quite frantic sometimes at the thought of missing so much of our time together. . . . I've just been seeing the babes to bed. They've got into the habit of coming into my room after their baths, to say their prayers and play about a bit. Quentin is such a duck, so round and

tubby and smiling! He has taken to calling Alison
'Sister' in a pompous early-Victorian way. To-night
he was sitting on a low chair by my fire, a comical figure
in his stripped blue and white sleeping suit, gravely sipping a glass of water. Alison was pirouetting about
asking, 'Shall I say my prayers to Mummy or to Ninny?'
Quentin looked at her over the brim of his glass and said
rebukingly, 'Say your prayers to God, Sister.'

"Peter has got an atlas and is marking out your
journey: it has given him quite an interest in geography.

"Two months are gone, Biddy! I always come back
to that, though, really, I don't know why I should make
a fuss, for the days pass quite quickly and pleasantly.
Barty and I have busy mornings together, for there are
many poor and needy in these bad times. I'm afraid
this is going to be a dreadfully scarce winter: it's bad
enough in Priorsford, and what it must be like in some
districts I daren't think. When the children come in,
all glowing from the cold air, and make the food vanish,
it's awful to think of the mothers who can't rejoice in
the sight, for they haven't the wherewithal to satisfy
their children. And they are so patient under it; that's
what's so heart-breaking. I simply hate Mrs. Duff-
Whalley when she talks as if the dole were a fortune, and
rails against the extravagance of the working-classes.

"She came here yesterday, that same lady, accompanied by her daughter, and announced that Priorsford
was terribly behind the times on the question of Community Drama. She had been meeting somewhere
somebody sufficiently important to impress her, who
had been greatly interested in the subject and had wanted

to know why Priorsford had not a team. Mrs. Duff-Whalley had promised to see about it at once. (As a matter of fact, I believe some of her projects have died on her hands, so she's rather out of a job !)

" She seated herself on a high chair and began in challenging tones, ' Of course, you are interested in Community Drama ? '

" I replied with truth that I was, and began to tell her about our Institute successes, but she brushed me and my experiences aside. ' My friend, Lady Brockle-bank,' she said, ' tells me that it's a most uplifting thing, and she wants as many teams as possible to compete in the Border Festival. Now, why should Priorsford remain outside ? Always so slack : no en-terprise : no real Border spirit : never enthusiastic about anything : half-hearted.'

" I tried to stop the flood by asking her what she suggested.

" She replied : ' To start a team of course. I know nothing about acting myself, but I'm sure Muriel here could act if she tried. Any one could. It's not like singing. You just walk on and say your part—that's all.'

" ' And who,' I asked, ' would produce for you ? '

" ' Produce ! ' she repeated. ' Oh, stage-manage, you mean. I'm sure I don't know. It would need to be a man, I suppose. Here there are no resident un-attached young men, and the young married men are too lazy. The times I've tried to get them to take a proper interest in politics ! ' (You must imagine the good lady seated on the very edge of a chair, gesticulating with both hands, her eyes darting from Muriel to me.)

"'It's nothing short of scandalous their slackness. Then they complain about the Labour Government and taxation, but whose fault is it, I'd like to know! Leaving the meetings entirely to the working-classes, and Mr. Baldwin giving votes to sluts of girls. No wonder the country's going to rack and ruin. I've done my best, but I can't stop it. . . . What do you say, Muriel . . . *who* could produce?'

"'I don't know if he'd do it,' Muriel said, 'but you might ask him: Mr. Hamilton who has come to Drykeld.'

"'The *farmer*!' said her mother, her tone implying that tillers of the soil were without—with dogs. Muriel flushed (has she an interest in the man, I wonder!) and said that Mr. Hamilton had done a lot of acting in India, and had asked her if there was no dramatic society in Priorsford.

"'Well,' said Mrs. Duff-Whalley, 'we might ask the man to dine some night—of course letting him know that it's for a purpose, so that he won't presume—and have some likely people there and see if he can make up a caste.'

"With that she whipped out a notebook and pencil.

"'I'll put you down, Jean?' (She keeps calling me 'Jean' very firmly, especially when there are other people there!) 'I'm sure you'll be glad of something to do. And Muriel, of course. I wonder if Rosalind Tweedie would join? I'll phone to-night. . . . The men are the puzzle. Can't you think of any one?'

" I could only think of the young minister, Mr.
Thornton, and Mrs. Duff-Whalley received him with
no enthusiasm, merely remarking, ' We'll fall back on
him if we have to, but surely there are others we might
try first. I don't suppose it would be any use trying
Mr. Elliot. . . . I tell you what, Muriel—the new people
at Archfield ! There's a son lurking about, I know.
We'll call there now. . . . I want to get as many county
people interested as possible : no use making it a town
thing. . . . Come along, Muriel.'

" And off she went, as eager as a ferret in a rabbit-
hole. I don't expect her victims will even put up a
fight ! "

Three days later the letter was finished.

" Before I post this," Jean wrote, " I must tell you
about Mrs. Duff-Whalley's Community Drama dinner !

" I took Barty with me : she's really the only person
who knows anything about acting ; besides, I wanted
her support.

" We had a very good dinner and quite an amusing
evening.

" Our hostess was most ingratiating to certain members of the party, civil to Mr. Thornton (who was there
faute de mieux), but rather haughty to Barty and Mr.
Hamilton.

" The latter seems a very nice fellow. He was a
planter in Behar, but finding that he was losing money
he thought he'd come home and take a sheep farm.
About forty, I think. He went to the war from India.
I liked his enthusiasm about Tweedside.

" Rosalind Tweedie has grown up the jolliest thing,

with very yellow hair, very red cheeks, very blue eyes, and very high cheek-bones! She talks without stopping, simply because she's so interested in everything, and is as natural as a border burn. Mr. Thornton I had met before at Miss Hutton's. He came in Mr. Macdonald's place. He is very young, not more than six-and-twenty: tall, good-looking, with very neatly-fitting hair, and beautiful teeth. The third man, by name Malcolm Forbes, was a very nice boy, and painfully shy. You could see he feared his hostess greatly. Fortunately he sat between Rosalind and me, so we could protect him.

" When we left the dining-room, Mrs. Duff-Whalley said, almost threateningly: ' Seeing we are met to-night for a purpose, we shall expect you in the drawing-room *very* shortly,' so the poor men arrived almost on our heels!

" The first snag was the choice of a one-act play. . . . As you may suppose, Mrs. Duff-Whalley has no love for ' kitchen drama.' Low, she calls it, fit only for village players who haven't the accent for anything else. Maeterlinck was what she harped on. Lady Brockle-bank had mentioned Maeterlinck, and he sounded superior.

" Mr. Hamilton was doubtful. ' I don't know much about him,' he confessed, ' but I suspect he takes some acting. Now—well—can any one here act ? '

" Rosalind laughed aloud and joyfully confessed that she couldn't; Young Forbes shook his head convulsively ; Mr. Thornton said he'd never tried, so he didn't know ; Muriel said that was her case too, while I announced proudly, that though I wasn't much good myself, my friend, Miss Barton, was something of a star.

"Mr. Hamilton said it was obvious we must begin with something simple, and named a few plays, which were turned down at once by Mrs. Duff-Whalley, who was still set on Maeterlinck. After a couple of hours we parted to meet again next Wednesday—this time *after* dinner—and quite right too. Mrs. Duff-Whalley can't be expected to feed us *all* the time !

"Darling, I don't know why I'm writing all this to you, except that I can so well imagine you listening benevolently as you smoke your pipe that it seems to bring you nearer. . . .

"Well, I think I've told you every single thing that has happened this last week. A lot of the people I mention you won't know : some are new-comers to the district ; others were away when you came to Priorsford. I don't think, for instance, you ever met Mirren Strang ? I think you'd like her. She's a little dark woman, both keen-eyed and kind-hearted, who lives in a charming cottage near Muirburn with Miss Rebecca Brand, who is by way of being a companion, but is more like a thorn in the flesh, for she constantly says and does the wrong thing. They are the oddest couple, the one so light and quick and glancing ; the other stolid, plain, stupidly outspoken ; but they've lived together now quite happily for about six years, since Miss Brand's brother (the minister of Muirburn) married and she lost her home at the Manse. Once she got it into her head that she was being kept as a charity, and went off to be with an old lady in Edinburgh. The old lady hated it (which was to be expected), but the odd thing was that Mirren Strang was lost without her morose companion, and when Miss Brand quarrelled finally with the old lady, received her back with open arms !

" Mirren Strang writes : pleasant books with a Scots flavour. I have them all in my own room at home. You have heard me quote from them many a time, but I'm only now getting to know her as a woman, for she wasn't much at home when I was growing up in Priorsford. She lost her young husband in the Boer War, and her only child on the Somme. And she can laugh, that is the amazing thing. . . . Here come the children ! It's Alison's turn to post your letter in the pillar at the end of the road. Peter goes with me to see that it's correctly done !

" Good-bye, beloved,

" JEAN."

CHAPTER XIV

> "The best actors either for tragedy, comedy, history, pastoral, pastoral-comical . . . Seneca cannot be too heavy, nor Plautus too light . . . "
>
> HAMLET.

MRS. DUFF-WHALLEY had no intention of being deprived of the distinction of introducing the study of dramatic art into Priorsford.

"That man Hamilton," she said to her daughter as they breakfasted together one morning, "takes too much upon himself : that class is always upsetting."

Muriel demurred. "Mr. Hamilton isn't 'that class' any more than the rest of us. Less, in fact, for his father was a W.S. in Edinburgh, and he himself was educated at Loretto : I can't imagine anything more respectable."

"But he's a farmer."

"Well, what's wrong with being a farmer, Mother ? "

"Oh, nothing, of course," said Mrs. Duff-Whalley, "but I've always made it a rule not to know any one below a certain standard. One must draw the line somewhere, and I draw it at people who keep a general servant."

Muriel took a bit of toast, buttered it, and asked for the marmalade. With the spoon in her hand, she said: "Mr. Hamilton has a good housekeeper—it's all a bachelor needs. . . . And, Mother, I've heard you say yourself that when you and my Father were first married you did all your own work."

Mrs. Duff-Whalley flushed. "Yes," she said defiantly, "I had to help your father to rise. And rise he did. There was nothing grovelling in my disposition. I was always aspiring, always after the best. And you may thank me, Muriel, for the position you're in to-day. You're like your father—he had always a taste for consorting with his inferiors: Minna and Gordon are more like me. I believe if you'd been left to yourself you'd have been hand in glove with people like the Miss Watsons, but my efforts have given us the entry to the best houses in the neighbourhood."

Muriel gave an impatient sigh. "Oh, I agree," she said. "You're a wonderful woman—but is it worth it? To be a climber takes constant effort."

"In Priorsford," said her mother, "if you don't draw attention to yourself, you're completely overlooked. I know I'm a climber and I admit it's a struggle, but, bless me! if I gave up and vegetated, life wouldn't be worth living. If I didn't constantly worry people to come to lunch and dinner, and get up bridge-parties, and do whatever is asked of me in the way of helping things, like the Nursing, and politics, and so on, I'd be dropped. But it's the breath of life to me to do things and have people to the house. Of course, there are some people who won't be friends with us—the Laverlaw people, and the Homes at Phantasy, and that impudent woman who writes, Mrs. Strang—but we needn't bother about them, they don't really count for much in the district, though Pamela Elliot, if she had liked, might have taken a foremost place ; what an opportunity she's missed ! "

" I don't suppose she cares," Muriel said. " Mrs. Elliot has everything she wants, and more."

" Well," said her mother, " it's no business of mine, but what I say is that she can afford to be a law unto herself, and we can't—I wish I saw you, Muriel, with more appreciation of all I've done for you. . . . Now, about this man Hamilton, I'm simply going to tell him what I want done. What's all this talk about ' producing ' ! You rehearse, I understand, and compete ; that's all there is about it."

" I'm afraid there's a lot more than that, Mother. Not only must the acting be as good as you can make it, and the exits and the entrances and so forth carefully thought out, but every detail of dress and scenery and deportment will be noted and marks lost if they're wrong. I don't know much about it myself, but the other day, when we were lunching down at Hangingdean, I sat next a woman who was mad on Rural Institutes, and she told me a lot about this Community Drama stunt. Even tiny, out-of-the-way villages have their teams and study hard all winter, and motor, sometimes, forty miles in the snow, to whatever festival they are competing at. She said even the middle-aged women in the Institutes love it. I suppose we have all, more or less, got acting in our blood."

" I daresay," said Mrs. Duff-Whalley, " but I've never been aware of it in mine. . . . The point is, ours must be no town affair. What shall we call it? *The County Players?*"

Muriel shook her head and said, "I'm sure that wouldn't do. There may be half a dozen other teams in the county who would resent it—rightly. We must leave it to the company to decide the name."

"I don't see it. Much better come to a decision beforehand, and simply intimate what it is to be. . . . I don't care for that secretary person, Miss Barton. I wouldn't be surprised if she made herself disagreeable. The way she looked at me when I called Lady Bidborough Jean! A girl I've known all my life! And an insignificant little thing at that."

Muriel looked thoughtful as she said: "All the same, I wonder if you should call her Jean. And I don't agree that she is insignificant. She is not assertive, but she always had—and now it's more marked—a sort of serenity that sets her apart. I was trying to decide the other night what it was, and I think it's her brow—it's lovely, smooth and white and untroubled—and the clear, steady eyes underneath. I don't know, but—somehow—I think it would be more fitting if we called her Lady Bidborough, as the other Priorsford people do. Yes, even Miss Hutton, who was a really great friend: we were never anything but acquaintances."

Again Mrs. Duff-Whalley's cheek-bones flushed.

"Really, Muriel," she said, "I've never heard such nonsense. It's the only chance we'll ever be likely to get to call a peeress by her Christian name."

Muriel laughed suddenly. "Well, that's true. If you put it like that—why not? I'm sure Jean herself

6

doesn't mind, though her secretary may mind for her, and Mrs. Elliot looks as if she could slap you every time you do it."

" Toots ! " said Mrs. Duff-Whalley. " Well, that's lunch to-day with the Olivers. We might just run in to Fairmile and see if it's all right about the 10th. I *wish* the Scotts would ask you to Cowdenglen to the Hunt Ball. I hinted pretty plainly to Lady Scott, and she does owe me something for all I've done for her ' Girls on the Land ' scheme ; but some people have no gratitude. However, perhaps the Olivers will ask you to go with their party."

" Well, please don't hint, Mother. It makes me so ashamed. After all, why should they drag round a woman of my age, when there are hosts of pretty girls just out and longing for fun. . . . I've had my day, and I'd like to stop going to balls. I feel out of it."

" Nonsense, you're better looking than ever you were." And Mrs. Duff-Whalley meant what she said, for she sincerely admired everything that was her own, including her daughter.

Muriel raised her eyebrows and her shoulders, and shook her head.

" No," she said. " And it's time I found some interest, for I lead an aimless life. I should have struck out for myself ten—fifteen years ago, but I thought, and you thought, that I'd marry."

" And you could have married," said her mother quickly, " several times."

" Well—twice, to be exact. But not suitably. We can think of both suitors without regret. I had no luck.

It was for Jean the prince came riding. . . . It's a pity I can't settle down to be a perfectly contented and happy Priorsford spinster, but I can't. I'm like one of the characters in those horrid novels people are so fond of writing—frustrated.''

Mrs. Duff-Whalley was getting really angry : she had borne a good deal from Muriel in the past few months.

" Muriel," she said, " don't talk like that : it's positively unhealthy, and—and not very decent. If Providence means you to have a husband, you'll have one. And I'm sure you've nothing to be discontented about ; a good home—indeed, a luxurious home, and everything you want in the way of clothes and amusements. You're the envy of many. Poor Minna, fighting away with her dyspeptic husband and two spoiled brats of children, often says to me, ' Muriel has the best of it.' . . . Egerton Thomson was no great catch, though she makes the best of him. Minna's like me, she keeps her end up. . . . But for any favour, Muriel, do get out of this mopy state you've got into : it's fatal for a girl to lose hold. What's thirty-four ! Nothing, nowadays. . . . . There's the telephone ! No, I'll go."

Mrs. Duff-Whalley loved to answer the telephone. She had a special voice for it, suspicious a little when she said " Hallo," then warming into pleased acceptance or becoming mournfully regretful when she had to decline. . . . Invitations were the delight of this good lady's life, and it really hurt her to have to refuse even the dullest. Especially she liked the telephone to begin at breakfast time : it gave her a rushed feeling that was very pleasant.

"Yes," Muriel heard her say. "Yes. Will you hold on a second while I look at my book." Pause for so doing, though she did not move from the spot. "Yes, thank you, we shall be *charmed*. Too good of you. Wonderful weather for the time of year, is it not? Yes—Thursday at 1.30. Good-bye."

Mrs. Duff-Whalley came bustling back into the dining-room, and in response to Muriel's raised eyebrows said:

"Lady Scott. Just when we were speaking of her. Lunch on Thursday. That's this week pretty well filled up. I must ring up Moran's and tell them to have my new tweed out by Wednesday. It's so difficult knowing what to wear to lunch-parties. I believe myself in dressing—it shows more respect for your hostess, *I* think—but you feel rather a fool if you go smart and find every one else dressed in woollies. Then you think you've had a lesson and you turn up in tweeds only to find every one else dressed up to the nines! I'm sure I wish there was some rule."

"You can't go wrong with tweeds," said Muriel, and took up *The Scotsman*, while her mother seized on the *Daily Mail*.

Wednesday evening came, and the company gathered. The hour was eight-thirty. ("I'll give them coffee and sandwiches," said Mrs. Duff-Whalley, "but I'll not waste another dinner on them.")

That lady took the chair with an air of standing no nonsense.

"My friend Lady Brocklebank," she began, "has sent me a list of one-act plays suitable for beginners. I'll read them out."

This she proceeded to do, and there was a silence until Mr. Hamilton said :

"Any one of them would be quite suitable. The only thing is they're all desperately hackneyed. I think we might be able to find something a little out of the common run."

"What about *Riders to the Sea*?" Rosalind Tweedie asked. "It's Irish, of course——"

"No, no," said Mrs. Duff-Whalley. "We want nothing Irish or mystical, or about Jacobites or dream-pedlars. High-bred comedy is the thing."

The company looked at each other.

"You mean," said Jean, "something adapted, say, from Sheridan or Jane Austen?"

"Ye—es. *I* thought of Galsworthy or Noel Coward. Barrie, too, is always popular."

"I'm told," said Miss Barton, "that adjudicators have a special down on Barrie. They take off marks for the choice of a play."

"What impertinence!" said her hostess angrily, "when you think how the papers write him up!"

"It's nothing against Barrie," Miss Barton continued calmly. "Simply, he suffers from over-popularity. *Old Lady* has shown her medals until every one is sick of them, and the same thing applies to his other short plays."

"It's a pity," said Mrs. Duff-Whalley coldly, "because we can always depend on him being refined. . . . What about *The Knock at the Door*?"

"There's a corpse on the floor when the curtain goes down," Mr. Hamilton said. "I may be wrong, but I think a corpse is out of place in a one-act play."

Mrs. Duff-Whalley looked at the speaker severely. "Death," she said, "is never a subject for jesting."

Rosalind Tweedie began eagerly: "I read such a funny one about a Registry Office; the servants coming in, and the mistresses, and two poor men sent by their wives. The questions they ask! And no one could feel hurt, for the mistresses are as silly, if not sillier, than the maids. I'd adore to do a maid."

Muriel smiled at the girl as she said: "Registry Offices are too sore a subject for jesting for most of us."

Mr. Hamilton suggested that they might adapt a scene from one of Sir Walter's novels. "It would be very fitting for a Border company," he pointed out.

"But so out of date," said Mrs. Duff-Whalley.

Mr. Thornton, the minister, turned to Jean, who sat next him, and said, with a wary eye on his hostess, "That being so, I needn't suggest Shakespeare."

Jean shook her head, smiling. "I'm afraid not. It's a pity; there's nothing so repaying. Where I live, in England, the village women adore acting Shakespeare. After a hard day's work they come up to the house to rehearse, perhaps a scene from *Midsummer Night's Dream* or *As You Like It*, full of enthusiasm. And they do it so well too!"

"Where is it?" Mr. Thornton asked—"In the Cotswolds! Then they're almost Shakespeare's own people: no wonder they enter into the spirit of it. . . . When I was at Oxford I had many a happy day tramping in the Cotswold country."

" What was your college ? " Jean asked, and on being told " Brasenose," she beamed on the young man delightedly.

" My husband's college," she told him. " . . . Were you a member of the O.U.D.S. ? "

" A most inconspicuous one. I never attained to a part. ' A loud voice off ' was about my bit." He grinned boyishly, and added, " I didn't like to refuse when Mrs. Duff-Whalley made such a point of it, but I'll be no earthly use in this show. Happily, there's not likely to be a part for me, whatever play they decide on : it would be a terrible ' speak ' in Priorsford if the minister appeared on the boards. Think of Miss Bella Bathgate's face ! "

" I daren't," said Jean, with a chuckle. " But I agree. It would be too brazen for you to take a part. . . . And yet a preacher needs to have a sense of the dramatic, or his sermons are apt to be quite ineffective. I don't mean, of course, that he should *try* to be effective, but born preachers are unconsciously dramatic, don't you think ? "

" I suppose they are," said Mr. Thornton. " But there are precious few born preachers—most of us just toil along."

" I haven't heard you preach—yet. Since we came to Priorsford I've been taking the children to the church nearest us. The fact is, I dread going to your church. The Macdonalds were my greatest friends, and—oh, I know it's silly—but I can't bear to see another in Mr. Macdonald's pulpit. . . . What did you say, Mrs. Duff-Whalley ? No, I'm afraid I never heard of it. . . . There are some quite good light little plays that go down well——"

" Vulgar, I suppose," said Mrs. Duff-Whalley severely.

" No, merely funny. Of course if you want to be profound——"

At that moment the coffee was brought in and the subject, for the moment, was dropped.

As Mr. Thornton helped Jean to sandwiches he said :

" I understand very well what you must feel about a stranger in Mr. Macdonald's pulpit. Indeed I sometimes feel that the whole parish resents me being there ! I wish I had known Mr. Macdonald : he might have left me the fringe of his mantle."

Something rather forlorn in the young man's tone touched Jean's kind heart. " I wish you had known him," she said, " for he was the most lovable of men. And I've just been thinking how glad he would have been to see you in his beloved church. He had a great idea of the dignity of the Ministry, and from all I hear you carry on his tradition. . . . Come and see us, won't you ? Not as a pastor but as a friend. And I'm going to get over my silliness and go back to my own church, for I hear you are too good a preacher to miss. ' Here's fame ! ' say you."

When Mrs. Duff - Whalley felt that enough time had been spent over the viands she had provided, she rapped smartly on a table with a paper-knife, remarking :

" So far we have done nothing but talk this evening. A decision must be come to before we separate. Mr. Hamilton, what do you suggest ? "

That gentleman smiled rather ruefully. " Well, I have suggested three plays," he reminded his hostess.

" All most unsuitable," said Mrs. Duff-Whalley coldly. She rummaged among the litter of books on the table and lifted one. " This now." . . . She adjusted her eye-glasses and read, " *Noblesse Oblige.* A good title to start with. . . . The scene seems to be laid in Russia. . . . Characters : *Lady Elsie Davenant, General Strickland ;* three women wanted and three men. We could manage that, couldn't we ? Well, Mr. Hamilton, I suggest that you take this home and study it, and let me know by telephone your opinion of it. To me it seems just what we want. Russia is always so thrilling, and the number of characters just right. Well—shall we meet here next Wednesday at the same time ? "

Mr. Hamilton looked doubtful, but his hostess was on her feet, and meekly the company rose and departed.

CHAPTER XV

"That will ask some tears in the true performance of it . . ."
A MIDSUMMER NIGHT'S DREAM.

FOR some time the health of Baxter, the gold-fish, had been a source of anxiety to its owner. Though constantly given clean water, and fed assiduously, Baxter had drooped, swimming ever more slowly round his bowl, till one sad morning he was found lying at the bottom, dead.

It was a Saturday morning, so the children had time to give full vent to their grief, and a sad breakfast it was with Peter's tears salting his porridge, and Alison sniffing mournfully over her egg.

What was left of Baxter had been wrapped in a clean handkerchief and encased in a small wooden box with a sliding lid ; presently it would be decently buried beside Peter, the fox terrier, near the lavender bushes.

" You must ask Barty if she'll make you a tombstone," Jean said.

" I went with Ninny to Priorsford cemetery," said Alison, in a small chastened voice. " There were heaps of tombstones, and they nearly all said ' sacred ' ; it's a nice word."

" But hardly the word for poor little Baxter," her mother told her. " What about—

> ' Here lies Baxter,
>   A gentle gold-fish.'

That has the merit of being true."

Peter looked doubtful. " Doggie Peter has a nice tombstone," he said. " It says, ' The faithful friend and companion ' . . . Isn't that true ? "

" Well—only partly." Jean smiled as she said it. " Peter was so much the friend of everybody that he had very little time to bestow on his own household. He would start for a walk with us, but he met so many people and dogs that he knew that we lost him almost at once. ' Faithful ' hardly describes Peter."

" Mrs. McCosh says he was ' a general favourite,' " Alison reminded her mother.

" Oh, so he was, though he wasn't very well behaved. He chased sheep and attacked postmen and frightened errand boys, but he had a large circle of devoted friends who made light of his faults and extolled his virtues. When he died he actually had a column in the Priorsford *Reporter !* . . . Dry your eyes, my son. You mustn't mourn too much for Baxter. A marauding character like Doggie Peter has a great life, but it can't be much fun being a gold-fish. Think how dull to swim round and round a bowl all day ! "

Quentin paused in his breakfast. " I'll dig his grave with my new spade," he volunteered helpfully, but Peter glared vindictively at his young brother as he said :

" No, you won't dig Baxter's grave : I'll dig it myself."

At this rebuff Quentin gave a piercing yell, and Jean shook her head at her ungracious elder son.

"Well," said Peter, defending himself, "why should that little beast dig Baxter's grave when he's not sorry that Baxter's dead? Alison may dig it if she likes, for she gave me her best hanky to wrap him in."

Jean dried the facile tears that were pouring down Quentin's face, and said soothingly: "Quentin only meant to be kind. . . . I'm sure poor little Baxter wouldn't like to be the cause of rudeness and quarrelling, Peter. . . . Now, let's change the subject. D'you know that it's only four weeks to Christmas? High time we were beginning to make preparations."

A gleam of light came into Peter's face, while Alison said, "*Does* Christmas come to Priorsford? Barty said it wasn't the same in Scotland."

Her mother smiled at her reassuringly. "Did you think you were to be cheated of your presents, poor Alison! Oh, yes, Christmas comes to Priorsford. It won't be the same to us with Daddy away, and we'll miss the Christmas Tree to the village, and all the excitements we have at Mintern Abbas, but we'll have our own fun. Mhor will be here, and Jock, and Uncle Davy, and perhaps we'll have a Tree, and invite Ian Burnett and Margot, and as many more as you like. And there will be presents just the same of course!"

"Presents," said Quentin, smiling, with tears on his lashes.

Peter said, "He doesn't really remember about Christmas and Santa Claus."

" I does," said Quentin, busily engaged with an egg
and bread and butter.

" Of course he does," said Jean, catching the egg as
it seemed about to descend to the floor. " Don't wave
your spoon, darling. . . . You remember hanging up
your stocking, don't you ? "

" Yeth."

" What did you get in it ? " Peter asked suspiciously.

" Eggs," said Quentin.

" It's Easter he's remembering," Peter said.
" Mummy, he was only two last Christmas. Nobody
can remember till they're three. . . . I don't expect
he'll know Daddy when he comes home."

" Nonsense," said Jean. " Well—what are we going
to do this fine Saturday ? After we put poor little
Baxter safely to sleep, we might have a walk."

" I've to do sums for an hour," Peter said gloomily.
" Miss Main told me to. I had them all wrong yesterday."

" Sonnie ! I'm afraid you don't pay attention."

" Yes, I do, Mummy. It's just that I can't do sums."

" Oh, but that's feeble. They can't be so very
difficult, for think of all the millions of boys, some of
them quite stupid, who have conquered them. Tell
Miss Main that you don't understand and she will
explain how to do them."

" Explanations make it worse," Peter insisted.

" I'll tell you what," said his mother, " we'll have a
class for sums after tea to-night, with Barty as teacher.
Arithmetic has no terrors for her, and perhaps she
could make us understand. . . . Oh, here's Ninny and

Black Douglas. Catch him, Alison, he's making for
the ham. . . . Ninny, Peter's beginning to feel the
responsibilities of age. Arithmetic has got him in its
toils."

" Puir bairn ! " said Ninny. " I never could dae
sums masel'."

" Nor I," said Jean. " Happy Douglas who knows
no such troubles."

" Ay, I whiles think a dog's life's no bad. Hunger
an' ease I've heard it ca'ed. Nae worry in life an'
nae responsibility in death. . . . When ye think o't,
we never want for worries efter we're aboot five year
auld ! An' there's sae muckle expected noo frae
bairns ! When I hear ither nurses crackin' aboot it
I feel fair vext for the bit things. Ye never heard
the like o't. Every meenute o' the day they're at it.
Into Edinburgh for a dancing class or something, lang
hours at lessons, an' the rest o' the time bein' rushed
aboot to enjoy theirsel's—pairties, pantomimes, an'
such like. If they'd let the bairns alane ! They'll
be worn oot afore they're twenty. I canna but be
thankfu' that Mintern Abbas is such a quiet bit an'
oor bairns get leave to hing as they grow."

" Yes," said Jean, " I notice some of them have rather
a hunted look. But, on the other hand, perhaps it's
only fair to give them every advantage. Some one
I met the other day told me she was having her three
girls taught golf and tennis by professionals, bridge,
too, and, of course, dancing : everything, indeed, that
she can think of, so that they may start fair. Will
Alison upbraid me, I wonder, in after years ! Ninny,

what a good thing two are boys ; life is so much simpler
for the male sex."

" It was aye that," said Ninny.

Peter saw to it that Baxter was mourned in his burial.
The entire household was paraded at the grave.

Mrs. McCosh was dragged, floury-handed, from the
making of an apple-dumpling for lunch, Marriot and
Elsie from putting clean sheets on the beds : Quentin,
in Ninny's arms, viewed the proceedings with a slightly
cynical eye.

A box of carnations had arrived that morning from
Mintern Abbas, and Alison had begged some to make
it, as she said, a proper funeral.

It was a bright day, quite warm in the sheltered
corner where Peter had dug the grave, and the company stood and watched the two chief mourners as
they patted down the earth and arranged the gay
carnations. Alison thrust a grubby hand into Peter's,
and the two stood comforting each other. . . .

And when it was all over and the various members
of the household had returned to their duties, " Now,"
said Jean. " we'll have our walk. Where shall we go,
darlings ? "

" We've never seen the dungeons in the Castle,"
Peter said.

" Haven't you ? Then we'll go to Peel. But first
I want to take some carnations to Mrs. Jowett."

" Oh, Mummy, we shan't have time for both. Why
must you go to Mrs. Jowett's ? "

" Because Mrs. Jowett is ill," Jean said, tying up the
carnations as she spoke, " and the days are long to

her, and any little thing, like a short visit from some
one, or a gift of flowers, helps to fill the hours. We'll
see if she wants to see us—she may not feel able—
and if she does, I'd like you and Alison to do your very
best to interest her. Tell her anything you think
would amuse her. . . ."

" *Mummy!* " Peter's voice was shrill with horror,
" there's nothing amusing to tell."

Jean looked at her son and daughter for a minute
without speaking, then she said :

" Run and wash your hands and get on your coats,
and try to imagine what it must be like to be shut up
always in the house. Here you are springing about
full of health ; surely you can spare a few minutes to
some one who has to lie all day on a sofa. Perhaps it's
too much to expect you to amuse Mrs. Jowett, but at
least you can answer nicely if she speaks to you. Don't
keep thinking about yourselves and wanting to get
away to Peel ; think of somebody else for a change."

They came upon Mr. Jowett in the garden of The
Knowe, and he led them, talking loudly all the time,
straight into the drawing-room where his wife was
lying on a couch by the fire.

" I've brought you visitors, Janetta," he announced.
" Dear me, those are very fine carnations. Surely
not Priorsford ? "

" Mintern Abbas," said Jean, laying the flowers on
a table near the sofa, and kissing Mrs. Jowett's hand
in greeting. " It's such a good Saturday we're going
to walk up to Peel to see the dungeons, and we've
looked in just for a minute to bring you the flowers. . . ."

Mrs. Jowett smiled at the children, who stood awkwardly beside her. Peter was conscious of a terrible sense of responsibility. His mother was talking to Mr. Jowett, he must try to say something to this invalid lady. But what? He fumbled in the empty pockets of his mind for some small change of conversation. . . .

But Mrs. Jowett was speaking. " When Mhor was about your age," she said, " he used to come to see me on Saturday mornings and get an eleven-o'clock lunch. Wouldn't you and Alison like some ? "

Peter unclenched his hands, his tongue which had seemed like a dry stick in his mouth loosened. " Please," he said, and gave a sigh of profound relief.

Hopefully he and Alison watched a befrilled, grey-clad maid lay a lace-trimmed cloth on a small table, and produce, as if by sleight of hand, cakes and fruit and lemonade.

Jean, helplessly watching her offspring eating as if for a wager, turned to Mrs. Jowett, saying, " How history repeats itself ! I used to be so ashamed of Jock and Mhor, afraid that you would think I didn't feed them properly at home, and here are my own, worse, if possible. Dear Mrs. Jowett, why do you encourage greed ? "

Mrs. Jowett was watching rather wistfully the evident enjoyment of the children. " Ah, my dear," she said, " don't grudge me a pleasure. It does me good—I who dread my meals—to see how they make things disappear. It must be heartsome work to cook where there are children ! "

The refreshment seemed to brighten Peter's whole outlook on life. Of his own accord he went and stood by Mrs. Jowett and thanked her earnestly for her hospitality, and then he found himself telling about Baxter, and from Baxter he went back to his pets at Mintern Abbas, and so absorbed was he in what he had to tell that his mother had to remind him that they weren't leaving much time to inspect the dungeons.

" Come and see me again," Mrs. Jowett said. " Some wet Saturday you and Alison might like to explore the attics."

" That's a good idea," agreed Mr. Jowett, pleased to see his wife interested. " There's any amount of queer things up there that we brought from India and couldn't find room for. A regular rubbish-heap."

Jean laughed as she said : " I can't imagine anything approaching a rubbish-heap in this tidy house. But the children would love to see the Indian things some day. You'll let Elsie come with them to see they don't damage anything. . . . Come now, children, we must hurry."

CHAPTER XVI

" O gentle, tender lady mine,
   The winter wind blows cold and shrill."

                                    W. M. THACKERAY.

THE casual summer visitor probably thinks of Priorsford as dead in winter, but to its true lovers it is never dull. At Christmas time especially, when the shops are hung with holly and gay with gifts, when almost every family is preparing to welcome home absent members, when every house is redolent of savoury bakemeats, it positively radiates good cheer.

At The Rigs life had to be rearranged for Christmas.

" Let the boys come to me," said Pamela Elliot. " Indeed why not transfer the whole household to Laverlaw ? There's room and to spare, and Lewis and I would simply love it. No, Jean, don't protest. We'll consider that settled. It all arranges itself beautifully. Davy and Jock and Mhor will all sleep in the west wing ; you and Ninny and the babes in the south wing, beside us—I suppose Miss Barton will be on holiday ? "

" Well " said Jean. " I wanted her to take a fortnight, thought she might like to go to friends, but she doesn't seem very keen. Her brother is going home with a college friend, so she can't have him, and she has no one else, poor girl. Of course she *could* go to London

and do a round of plays, but I expect her friends 'll
be out of town, and it's a dreary thing to be alone at
Christmas time."

" We can easily **put her up**," Pamela said. " The
turret room's the very place for her."

" Oh, but," Jean protested, " we simply couldn't
plant ourselves on you like that. We might go on
Christmas Day, if you'd have us, but . . . I think we
could easily manage between this and The Neuk.
Davy will only be for a few days, you know, and Jock
for a week. We'll have Mhor for three weeks—longer,
perhaps, if he doesn't go to Piggy in Devonshire."

" I'm quite determined." Pamela got up and stood
on the hearth-rug, looking down at her small sister-in-
law on the fender-stool. " Don't be obstinate, little
Jean."

Jean looked up, quite unimpressed, with a laugh
in her moss-agate eyes. " What ! Nothing but low
and little ? Pamela, if you think to intimidate me
by your height . . . Sit down, there's a dear."

" Well." Pamela sat down. " You are coming to
us for the length of Davy's visit, and longer if you'll
stay. My dear, I can quite understand you want the
boys to yourself for a little, but don't keep Lewis and
me outside altogether. Can't you think of us as lonely
souls that need cherishing ? That seems the only road
to your heart ! . . . Here we are, done out of our usual
Christmas visit to Mintern Abbas ; are we to have no
compensation ? I know Biddy would like to think of us
as all together."

Jean nodded. " I know he would. And there's

nothing we'd enjoy more than being with you and Lewis.
We've always had our Christmases together. . . .
Thank you, darling. I gratefully accept."

"Good child. Forgive the seeming condescension,
but you're a baby to me, Jean girl. You can't think
how Lewis and I are looking forward to having you at
Laverlaw. This will be my first Christmas at Laverlaw.
. . . . We'll all go to the school-treat on the twenty-
fourth. . . . Our own Tree will be on Christmas Day,
of course. After luncheon ? or perhaps after tea ?
We can arrange that later. What joy to have you to
myself for the best part of a week—I never can see you
here without some of the Priorsford rabble breaking
in."

Jean expostulated. "*Rabble!* Oh, Pamela ! "

" I take it back. Let's call it ' the happy little world
of Priorsford.' By the way, is Mrs. Duff-Whalley still
making a nuisance of herself about Community Drama ? "

Jean grinned. "She has at last chosen a play—
Noblesse Oblige. She thought it looked ' high class.'
They're all coming here to rehearse on Tuesday.
Mhor 'll be here, but I wonder if I dare admit him.
You know the fits of helpless laughter that overtake
Jock and him ? . . . Barty and Mr. Hamilton are
the only two who know anything about acting at the
moment : Muriel may be quite good, but Rosalind
Tweedie does nothing but giggle."

" What part have you ? "

"None," said Jean. " I'm to be prompter when
such a thing is required, but I can see them clinging
to their books for some time to come."

Jean seemed amused, but her sister-in-law looked far from pleased.

"It's ridiculous," she said, "that you should trouble with them. Be firm, Jean, and tell Mrs. Duff-Whalley to run her own stunts."

"It's all very well to talk of being firm," said Jean ruefully, "there's something about our friend that saps my moral courage! But anyway, Pamela, it's great fun to rehearse a piece. You'd think it would be black boredom saying and listening to the same words—often dull, stupid words—time, and time again, and yet there's a fascination about it I can't explain. Hear it once, it bores you to tears. Hear it ten times and you can hear it fifty!"

"Well, I'll take your word for it, Jean. I don't think I have the proper community spirit. But anything that amuses you, my dear, I'm grateful for. Lewis and I often worry about your long evenings alone."

"Oh, but I'm *not* alone. When the children go to bed, Barty and I have dinner very comfortably together, and then we read aloud, and tell about all sorts of things. It's my own choice. I know you'd be willing to have me to dinner every night, and I daresay, if I wanted to, I could play bridge with people two or three nights a week. People have been very good about asking me, but now I think they've given me up as hopeless. Did I tell you one night we went to Edinburgh for a lecture? Yes. That woman, Alice Marvel, who writes those clever, queer stories, was the lecturer, and I persuaded myself and Barty that it would be interesting

to hear her. . . . It wasn't much of a success. There was
a fog, an East *haar*, the lecturer had a bad cold, and the
hall was decidedly chilly. I'm sure the lecture was very
clever, but my feet were too cold to let me listen. I only
remember that we were urged not to live intellectually
but temperamentally—like Robert Burns ! The fog
eddied through the hall, the lecturer sniffed and sneezed,
and none of us felt in the *least* like Robert Burns ! I
don't think we'll go to any more lectures. . . . I ought
to be very grateful to you, Pam, for getting the reputa-
tion of being rather a recluse ; it helps me to play the
same game."

" What ! Why, Jean, you know you simply love
being friendly with all your neighbours, and taking an
interest in their affairs, and——"

" Oh, so I do, so I do. I like to be friendly and
helpful—don't groan, I know it sounds awful—but only
through the day ! My evenings must be my own. And
the people I like best—Miss Hutton and the Hopes and
Mirren Strang—don't want to be bothered in the evening any more than I do. We sit and read and meditate
and let the others junket as they will ! "

" Quite so," said Pamela, " only I hold on to more
than the evenings. I never would tolerate people
descending on us any old time. Ours is by no means
the ever-open door ! Lewis would hate to find the
place always littered with people. I don't mind entertaining, but I like it kept within bounds. We find it a
good plan to do most of ours at Kinbervie."

" And you do it handsomely there. I can vouch for
that," said Jean. " Biddy and I sometimes excuse to

each other our very frequent evenings alone by saying they must come to an end as the children grow up, when Peter wants to fill the house with his friends : when Alison comes out. How odd it is to think of little Alison in court-train and feathers ! ''

" Let us hope she won't be as rotund as she is now ! '' said Alison's aunt.

That evening Jean laughed over the conversation with Betty Barton.

" We were talking," she said, " about Alison coming out, and her aunt thought her *rotundness* would be against her success. ' If to be fat is to be rated.' Poor Falstaff ! ''

" Not only fat," said Betty, " but so religious ! I fear the gay world would have little use for such a débutante. But she has time to change.''

Miss Barton was sewing busily at something she was making for Christmas. After a pause she said : '' Lucky girl she is, with all the world can give, a perfect background, an assured position, the entrée everywhere. I just hope she'll appreciate her good fortune.''

" I hope she'll be happy," said Jean. '' Barty, are you sure you can see there ? Turn on the other light. . . . Girls are such a problem. So many of them spoil their lives out of sheer waywardness. The fortunate ones meet early a man they can care for and, all things being well, they marry and settle down and are absorbed in their homes and their babies. But there are so many with whom life doesn't run smoothly. They're too difficult to please, perhaps too capricious, unstable ;

anyway nothing goes right with them, and they spend
their time driving their parents crazy. Some want
publicity. They think, poor innocents, that because
they can act a little they'd make a success on the
stage; but most of them don't know what they want.
I hear both sides, for sometimes it's the mother and
sometimes it's the daughter who pours her plaint into
my shrinking ear. I'm sorry for them both, but sorriest
for the mother—though I expect if we go back to first
causes it's largely the mother's fault. .... I'd like to
bring up Alison to be a useful person in the world. I
don't want her to feel that she has to compete with
other girls, to stand in the market-place and be ap-
praised, but to have so many interests that she won't
bother too much about the thought of marriage. If
love comes, so much the better : if not—well, if she
has a sane outlook on life she'll feel that she must fill
her life with other things."

Jean stitched for a few minutes at a bag she was
making for Pamela, then she continued :

" It all amounts to this, bring up a girl to think of
others and she won't have time to worry about herself
and her feelings. But it's "—Jean sighed—" it's a
counsel of perfection."

Miss Barton laid down her work and said, in the
quick business-like way that contrasted so oddly with
her appearance : " If you can get a girl to think of
others before herself you will be cleverer than most.
Selfishness is the commonest failing of this age in every
class—girls have no monopoly of it ; but I think you're
right about most girls being spoiled by their mothers.

Weren't you amused at that woman who called yesterday? I forget her name: attractive looking, with a pretty young daughter."

" Mrs. Arthur Fraser ? " said Jean.

" Yes. Well, you heard how she went on about her girl ? ' Poor Veronica has so little, but I must say she *does* make the most of her small pleasures. The child has really a *sweet* disposition.' Then it transpired from the conversation that ' the child ' went to every single ball in the neighbourhood: golfed at North Berwick: skated in Edinburgh: attended every Point-to-Point: went to London every few months, and Biarritz every spring: next autumn will probably go to India for a cold weather. I ask you ! "

" Oh, I know." Jean laughed, and then she said: " Did you really think Veronica pretty ? I thought her the most shaved-looking, hard-eyed little object I'd ever seen. I could have pinched her with pleasure."

A gleam of fun lit in Betty Barton's dark eyes and she said demurely : " How nice to hear you've got such unregenerate impulses, Lady Bidborough ; I thought they were all left to me. I'm sometimes chockful of bitterness and envy. I admit it. Oh, it must be so *restful* to have parents, to feel you've some one behind you, that you're not facing the world solitary. . . . I don't believe my brother Pat feels it. He's got such a pleasant, careless sort of nature that he just takes things as they come and doesn't worry. The gods generally send some people sugar-plums. He always has invitations to spend his holidays with people, and is quite happy so long as he isn't entirely penniless.

It's my job to see that that doesn't happen, and with the generous salary you give me it's easy."

Jean said nothing. Her secretary had been with her over a year and in that time had hardly mentioned her own affairs. Now, it seemed, the barriers were coming down. The girl went on: " Eight is too young to begin and face the world. My father was killed in 1916 : my mother was an invalid until she followed him. We had no near relatives except an aunt in India, so after my mother died we had nowhere to go for the holidays. It was all right for Pat, he was so tiny and fubsie that some one's heart was always melted, and he was really much happier than he had been in seaside lodgings with a sick mother. But for me . . . My mother needed me and leant on me, and I was proud to have the care of her. When she went I lost everything. No one wanted a repellent little girl with a sulky temper. . . . I didn't mind term-time. I liked the work and I was good at games ; it was when the girls talked of home and planned for holidays. . . . College was better. There were others like myself, solitary, who had come to prepare seriously for their life-work. I made one or two friends, not many: I haven't a generous enough nature to make many friends. I'm too parsimonious in giving love to get much love."

(" She seems proud of it," said Jean to herself.)

Miss Barton went on: " It was a tremendous stroke of luck to get this job, not only because the salary's good but——"

Here Jean interrupted her with a question.

" Are you happy with us, Betty ? I'm never quite sure."

The girl flushed. " That's my unfortunate manner, I'm afraid. I don't suppose you can realize what it meant for me to find myself received into your home-life at Mintern Abbas. . . . My goodness, when I hear girls talking as if all that mattered was that they might get away from home—home !

" And yet," she added, smiling at Jean in a shame-faced way, " if things had been differently ordered and I had found myself snugly set in a home, I daresay I'd have been the first to shout about freedom ! "

" I think you would," said Jean.

CHAPTER XVII

"... As ithers see us ..."
ROBERT BURNS.

It was always something of a surprise to her acquaintances that Miss Bella Bathgate kept her rooms well let, that the same people came back time and again, for not only was she a poor cook, she took no trouble that she could help, and had a particular aversion to putting on a fire in the " good room," dreading the effect on her new and treasured suite of oak upholstered in crimson moquette.

The Miss Watsons were talking of it one afternoon as they sat working together. " Fancy ! " said Miss Watson, " going to Bella Bathgate's when you might go to Miss Baker or Mrs. Alston, who cook beautifully and never grudge fires, and are always pleasant and obliging. Miss Bathgate just glowers if you ask anything. Mrs. Bryce who had her rooms—and you couldn't want a nicer boarder—said she got positively nervous at the way Miss Bathgate glared suspiciously round the room as she brought in the food, as if she suspected Mrs. Bryce of pocketing some of the ornaments. It's not that she means any harm ; it's the sort of face she's got. It's the same at the Guild. When she gets up to ask a simple question you'd think she was declaring war. I'm sure it takes all the good manners and Christian charity

that the rest of us possess not to be rude to her. In her
way she's as bad as Mrs. Duff-Whalley."

"And with no reason," said Miss Teenie. "After all,
Mrs. Duff-Whalley's rich and important and you more
or less expect to put up with a lot from such as she, but
in Bella's place it's just impudence. You and I have far
more reason to set ourselves up."

"It's too late," said her sister, struggling to thread a
needle. "We've been door-mats far too long. People
expect pleasantness from us—we've taught them to.
They say, 'Ask the Miss Watsons, they won't mind,
they're so obliging,' and they pile one thing after another
on us. If we objected it would be like sheep showing
fight. Teenie, could you thread this needle? It beats
me."

"Mercy! I'm as blind as you are," cried poor Miss
Teenie, and chuckled as she added, holding the eye of
the needle to the fading light, "Age does make a fool of
folks! Here are we blind and lame that used to be so
gleg and active."

"It's a good thing you can laugh about it."

"Well, there's not much use in greetin'. And we're
a great deal better off than some, with a nice wee house
and an assured income and kind friends. But what
annoys me is that we're older for our years than we
should be. After all, we're hardly on borrowed times
yet—you're only just seventy and I'm sixty-eight—
and our legs have failed us. Whereas at ninety Mrs
Hope is still quite agile, I'm told, though she never
leaves the Hopetoun policies."

"From what I can hear," said Miss Watson—she

spoke with difficulty, her mouth being full of pins—
" Mrs. Hope just sits most of the time. I asked Lady
Bidborough about her and she told me that in winter
she's never outside the house. But she's as erect as
ever, and very pretty, Lady Bidborough said."

" Well, we were never beauties," said Miss Teenie,
" so we haven't that regret. It must be an awful vex
to watch good looks going. . . . Mrs. Hope used to be a
picture when she drove about in her victoria—that's
one thing I always coveted, a victoria—with her Queen
Mary bonnet and her pretty cloak. We were never asked
to Hopetoun."

" It wasn't to be expected," her sister said, " though
the Honble. Pamela Reston entertained us to tea, and
she's had us to Laverlaw."

" Well, that hardly counted. It was in connection
with the crippled children, you remember, to see what
we could all do to help. . . . It's Lady Bidborough
that asks us just for kindness, and seems to find it a
pleasure. It's a big difference having her at The Rigs.
I was kinda losing interest in things, but with Miss Jean
here, waving in as she passes, lending us a book at a
time, sending the children in with flowers and fruit
from their English home, I feel quite brisked up. . . .
Talking about Bella Bathgate, I met her yesterday,
and d'you know where she was going ? To the Manse
to tell Mr. Thornton that she doesn't like read prayers.
The impudence ! I'm sure it's hard enough for a young
man like Mr. Thornton to make two new sermons every
week without getting up and praying extempore. I said
to her, ' Far better a read prayer, well thought out and

expressed, than a confused rigmarole such as we often get.' But she's as obstinate as a mule. Off she went to worry the poor man."

" Mr. Thornton 'll know how to take her," said Miss Watson soothingly—the pins were now safely pinning down the hem. " Bella's very susceptible where a man is concerned, and he's a nice-looking, well-set-up young fellow." She gave a little kindly laugh at the weaknesses of her fellowmen, and said, " There, that's all I'll do to-day, it's getting too dark to sew. I think, Teenie, I'll do some babies' semmits next, just for a change. There won't be the bother of threading needles, and I like making things for babies : they're wee and soft like the babies themselves. I really wonder if we're wise taking such a lift with the Guild Sale. When you think of all the people in the congregation who do nothing —never even put in an appearance at the Sale ! "

" We'd miss the work," said Miss Teenie, " and the Sale's always an excitement. Besides, think how much the money is needed. I could hardly sleep the other night after we heard yon address about Missions : so much work stopped for lack of funds. I'm sure if semmits and socks and things can help I'm glad to go on making them, and I was thinking we might have a Missionary box . . . Oh, I know we're not good at asking people who come in, and it's apt to get put away in a drawer, but when money's so much needed we must just *make* ourselves remember. We might keep all our threepenny bits for it. Priorsford's an awful place for threepenny bits. . . . As you say, a lot of people are very shabby about the Sale, but we can do without them.

I thought it was specially nice this year, with the whole family from The Rigs, and Mrs. Elliot of Laverlaw with them, all so willing to buy."

" It's easy to buy with a full purse."

" Oh, that's so. . . . And Mrs. Duff-Whalley certainly put on her best clothes for us, and she bought a good deal—what she called ' common garments ' for the Needlework Guild ! But she's not what I call a good buyer. I'd like to hear what Bella Bathgate thought of her, but of course I wouldn't demean myself to discuss a lady with her."

Although Miss Bathgate believed in Spartan treatment for her boarders there was always a great measure of comfort in her own premises. She had had the grate taken out of her kitchen and replaced by a neat little fireplace ; there was a carpet on the floor, a crimson cloth on the table, a canary in a cage, and a comfortable sofa on which, on an afternoon, Bella sat crocheting long strips which eventually became a bed-cover.

Sometimes, when lunch was over and peace had fallen for a brief space on The Rigs, Mrs. McCosh would step over the way and pass the time of day with her friend.

" Ye're there, Bella ? " she would say, putting her head round the kitchen door, and then, with a well-pleased smile, she would sit down on the wicker chair between the window and the fire and proceed to enjoy a talk. . . .

" I hevna seen ye, Bella, for mair than a week, no' since the Sale. I hope ye were pleased ? I thocht

7

it was a real nice Sale masel', an' ye made a heap o' siller."

" Oh, ay," said Bella. " Considerin' the state o' trade in Priorsford it wasna bad—but it might hev been a lot better." She gazed sternly at her crochet as she said, " Ye couldna expect the workin' folk to do more, but there's plenty folk in Priorsford whose incomes are not touched by the general depression, an' they're the worst givers of any."

" Mebbe ye're right," said Mrs. McCosh.

" Oh, I'm right," said Bella, as if it were unthinkable that she could be anything else, " an' there's far too many o' that kind in oor kirk."

" An' what did ye think o' Mistress Duff-Whalley ? " Mrs. McCosh asked.

Bella grunted. " If Mr. Thornton had consulted me she would never have been there. She has nothing to recommend her as an opener. Ye couldna call her a good speaker, she's far ower long, an' ravelled. An' what's an opener for but to buy the articles we want rid of ? D'ye ken all Mrs. Duff-Whalley bocht ? I just watcht—a flannelette chemise and night-shirt frae the Miss Watsons, a brace o' pheasants that came frae Laverlaw, an' some tablet tied up in pokes. Miserable ! But I expected nothing else." She sniffed, and crocheted rapidly.

" Oh, weel," said Mrs. McCosh, " in that case ye'll no' be disappointed. For ma ain pairt I'm aye vext for the leddies that opens Sales. They must be fair sick o' the sight o' dressing-jackets and pincushions and lavender bags. Usefu' things ye can gie away, provee-

shions ye can eat, but a' the ither things just fill up
drawers.   Sic a stuff the mistress brocht hame ! "

" Ay. I saw the Miss Watsons loadin' her up wi' a'
the semmits and socks and shawls they've been knitting
for months.   It's a great chance to get the haud of somebody who has baith the money and the heart to give.
But Lady Bidborough 'll find a use for them.   She visits
a lot down the Water-side, an' there's plenty bairns
there who'll be glad o' them."

Miss Bathgate let her crochet lie in her lap as she
looked over the top of her spectacles at her old friend
and said very slowly and impressively : " I've a very
clear judgment, Mrs. McCosh.   Mr. Thornton just said
to me the ither day : ' Miss Bathgate,' he said, ' you
weigh your neighbours in the balance.'   I said, ' I do,
and generally find them wanting.'   There's not one
in Priorsford, from the ministers downwards, that I
couldn't point out serious faults in, but I will say this,
though Lady Bidborough's far from being perfect, on the
whole I believe she tries to do her best."

Mrs. McCosh smiled a singularly sweet smile as she
said : " Ay, Bella, d'ye think sae ?   An' whit hev ye
been hearin' aboot Miss Jean to mak' ye say that the
noo ? "

" Well—I was visitin' Jessie Baird yesterday ;   we
were at the school together and hev aye kept up a friend-
ship, and we fell into a crack about auld days and folk
that are away."   Miss Bathgate pulled down her long
upper lip as she went on : " Jessie's no' like me.   She's
a sort o' sentimental cratur' : likes to recall our school-
days, and mind me o' this or that ; and I tell't her we

werna' a bit happy in thae days; it's just that she's lookin' back through rose-coloured spectacles. The folk that she thinks were so bonny and kind were just verra ordinary."

" Oh, Bella," Mrs. McCosh interrupted, " ye were aye the yin to tak' the gilt off the gingerbread."

" Weel, and what guid does the gilt dae the gingerbread ? It's better off. . . . Jessie thinks when folks are dead we should just mind the nice things they did and think o' them as perfect. That's nonsense. I'm no goin' to forget folks' faults because they're dead— no likely. Onyway, we were crackin' away and she was mindin' me o' the days when she used to sew for auld Miss Alison Jardine, and mak' Miss Jean's dresses and the like, and I said something about Miss Jean havin' done weel for hersel'. I meant no harm, I said no ill of her, but ye'd have thought by Jessie's face that I'd spoken blasphemy. ' Dinna misca' Miss Jean,' she said —me ! I wisna misca'in' onybody—' she's the best friend I hev in this world.' It seems that when Mrs. Baird was dying and Jessie couldna get oot to sew there was practically nothing comin' in. Miss Jean heard aboot it through Mr. Macdonald, and arranged that the auld body should hev every comfort, a nurse comin' in, and fruit and champagne sent frae the place in England. An' she pays Jessie's rent and taxes an' gies her plenty sewin', so that she's braw and comfortable. I aye wondered hoo she was so bien. . . . And Jessie said to me, ' *I'm no' the only yin.* ' "

Mrs. McCosh nodded assent, and Bella went on : " Of course I pointed out to her that Miss Jean was glad to

find a road for her siller, that it was nae credit tae her
to be generous, but, as I said, Jessie's a sentimental
cratur' and she would hev it that Lady Bidborough is
little short o' an angel. Sic blethers!"

"Angels!" said Mrs. McCosh. "I never likit the
soond o' them. Harps an' a' that. Puir wee Miss
Alison has an awfu' wark wi' angels. She's a rale
releegious wee thing an' as guid-herted as she can be,
though naebody could ca' her bonnie, but she'll likely
turn bonnie later on ; but whit I was sayin' is, that since
I've seen whit Miss Jean's like as Lady Bidborough, I've
mair respect for her than ever. To read about the gentry
you'd think they were a' alike, daft jades, then ye see
Miss Jean leavin' a place like Mintern Abbas (Ninny
tells me it's a fair palace) an' comin' tae a wee plain
hoose like The Rigs, as contented as ye like, that pleased
tae see her auld friends again, that ta'en up wi' her weans,
learnin' them, playin' wi' them, an' aye watchin' the post
for letters frae her man, just that kind o' *innocent* : that
I can but think if there's mony like her there's no muckle
wrang wi' the aristocracy. Jessie Baird's mebbe right
aboot Miss Jean being an angel."

"Hut," said Bella, beginning to crochet angrily,
ruffled by such extravagance, "it's easy to be an angel
in this world if ye've every mortal thing ye want."

CHAPTER XVIII

" . . . There was a man . . . I shall tell it softly:
Yond crickets shall not hear it."
THE WINTER'S TALE.

MHOR, otherwise Gervase Taunton, arrived at Priorsford
a week before Christmas. It was a case of coming home
to Mhor, for he had spent his childhood at The Rigs,
coming to it from India a baby of two. He was no
relation to Jean and her brothers. Their mother had
died when Jock was born, and their father, who was in
the Indian Civil Service, had married a second time, while
home on leave, a beautiful penniless girl. He died
shortly after they landed in India. The young widow
stayed on and presently married a soldier, Gervase Taunton. With him she was supremely happy for three years,
when he was killed playing polo. Broken-hearted, the girl
slipped out of life, leaving instructions to send her baby
to Priorsford to Jean, and Jean, herself little more than
a child, accepted the trust, welcomed the baby warmly,
and he at once became the pet and plaything of the household. Now he was about sixteen, a tall Etonian, adored
by Peter, who followed him about with dog-like de-
votion.

Mhor was delighted to be back at The Rigs, and
explored every nook and cranny of it the moment he
arrived.

" You're to sleep at The Neuk," Peter told him.
" It's a house behind this."

" Ho, you needn't tell me where it is. I used to
trespass in it with Jock and Peter when it stood empty.
Great sport. . . . When's Jock coming ? Oh, good !
. . . I say, I've brought you . . . Oh, but my things have
gone to The Neuk. Come on and we'll unpack before
any one else gets at my baggage. I've got things that
mustn't be messed about."

Very willingly Peter trotted beside his friend, delighted that this splendid fellow expressed appreciation
of the arrangements made for his comfort.

" This isn't a bad room." Mhor looked out of the
window. " Got a burglar run too. If Jock was in the
next room I could pay him a visit. Lean out. D'you
see ? I'd get my leg over there, and the rest's easy.
Come on now, let's unpack."

Mhor's system of unpacking was to turn everything
on the floor in a heap. The treasures that he had been
anxious about were put safely into a drawer, and all the
rest of his belongings were left lying for the housemaid
to put away.

" Have you a wireless here ? " he asked. " No ?
that's good. I'll make you one. We'll go down to
Bothwell's after lunch and get the things. Come on out
and see where we can fix an aerial."

It was pleasant to have Mhor at meals, Jean felt, and
Mrs. McCosh said it did her good to see the way things
disappeared. " I'll mak' the toffee-tart for him," she
promised herself, " he aye likit that awfu' weel." And
Jean laughed and told Miss Barton that they must

expect nothing now but schoolboy fare, for Mrs. McCosh was determined Mhor should be considered first.

During lunch, on that first day, he touched on the question of a wireless. " I'll make you one," he said handsomely.

Jean looked uncertain, remarking that personally she didn't care much for the wireless, but Peter's eager " Oh, *yes*, Mummy," made her accept the offer.

" Then," said Mhor, " can you let me have some money ? I'll have to get a lot of things and I haven't a copper. I gave my last shilling to a porter at Symington this morning. Luckily Phipps was on the spot at Priorsford and saved me a porter. Bothwell's, the iron-mongers, is the place to go."

" Oh, then, that's all right," said Jean, " we've an account with Bothwell. And here's some change, but, whatever you do, don't feed the children up with sweets and make them ill."

" Thanks," said Mhor, pocketing the money, " thanks *awfully*, Jean. . . . I must go in and see Miss Smart at the sweet shop. She'll be glad to see me again, I should think. And Mr. Bothwell, if he remembers me, and, I say, what about old Miss Bathgate ? "

" Don't let her hear you calling her old," Jean warned him.

" No, of course not : but she must be pretty aged. What ? Does she still draw down her upper lip ? She used to give Peter tea biscuits. I wish Peter was here. He was the best dog I ever knew."

" We've got Black Douglas," Peter reminded him. " He's a happy sort of dog and very grateful for a walk.

Couldn't we take him up to the hillside where he can chase rabbits ? "

" All right, we'll do that after we've been to Bothwell's for the wireless things. Come along, young Peter. . . ."

Alison looked after the two boys pensively. " I s'pose," she said, " I'll have to go with Elsie and Quentin."

" What about coming with me ? " said her mother. " I'm going to tea at Hopewaterfoot, and I know Mrs. Strang wouldn't mind if I took you—in fact she invited you all. Amuse yourself for an hour, and then ask Ninny to put on your new coat and hat and I'll be ready for you."

Alison's round face immediately became wreathed in smiles. She dearly loved to accompany her mother on an expedition. Even Peter's scorn of the girl nature that enjoyed being dressed up and going out to drink tea and listen to grown-ups talk did not spoil it for her. So, to-day, she sat as good as gold with a picture-book until Ninny came to get her ready, and then she set forth in a brown velvet coat with a tippet trimmed with fur, and a hat to match, looking with her round placid face like a Victorian child. Indeed, when she walked into the Hopewaterfoot drawing-room, shyly holding her mother's hand, Mirren Strang greeted her with, " Our gracious Queen Victoria as a child," and swept a low curtsy, at which the abashed Alison flushed deeply, and seemed about to give way to tears, whereupon Mrs. Strang, remarking, " ' We,' said the Queen, ' are not amused ! ' " got out a little chintz-covered armchair which proved to be Alison's exact fit, and refrained from further pleasantries.

"Look at anything you like," she told the child. "Here's a scrapbook my grandmother made—that's her chair you're sitting on—and in that cabinet you'll find my great-grandmother's work-box and a whole set of dolls' clothes she made as a child. . . ."

There were so many amusing things to see that Alison protested when her mother said it was time to go.

"But you'll come again," said Mrs. Strang, "very soon, and I'll ask Fanny Home to come too." She turned to Jean. "Fanny's another small Victorian. How do you do it, you mothers? Is it the latest fashion or what?"

It made a very pleasant change, Jean and her secretary found, to have Mhor as a third at dinner. He ragged Miss Barton impudently, but she didn't seem to mind. He rattled off to Jean tales of escapades which made her remark dryly: "I don't think, Mhor, you can be quite the *badmash* you make out, or Eton would have dispensed with your presence long ere this."

Study Mhor frankly abhorred, but he admitted to reading a fair amount, anything from Thomas Browne to Edgar Wallace. Miss Barton took him to task for his idleness.

"What d'you propose to make of your life?" she asked sternly. "You seem to care for nothing but fiddling with wireless, playing games, and reading detective yarns. It's not good enough."

And Jean joined in with: "It's high time you woke

up, Mhor. Sixteen's a big age. You don't want to make Davy and Jock ashamed of you when you go to Oxford."

Mhor grinned disarmingly, and presently said :

" What d'you do here in the evenings ? Go to the Pictures ? "

" Certainly not," said Miss Barton primly. " We read history. If you would read aloud to-night, Lady Bidborough and I would both get on with our work."

" I'm afraid I couldn't go as far as *that*," Mhor said gently. " But I've a new Edgar Wallace. After so much history, wouldn't you be the better of a spot of crime ? "

Next morning they had another " spot of crime."

Breakfast was hardly over, indeed Mhor (who had decided that he would breakfast at The Rigs in order to get the benefit of Mrs. McCosh's cooking) was only just beginning, when the door-bell rang, and after a flurry of exclamations in the hall the two Miss Watsons appeared in the dining-room. They were not at all their usual neat selves, but were dressed in a medley of garments, and looked so odd and shaken that Jean cried, " Oh, *what* has happened ? "

" Balmoral's burgled," said Miss Teenie, and burst into tears.

" There, there ! " said Miss Watson, patting her sister's shoulder, while the rest of the company stared at the two little ladies.

" Come and sit down," Jean said, " and have some hot coffee."

" When did it happen ? " Mhor asked, full of pleased interest.

" Goodness knows," said Miss Watson. " *We* heard nothing. We were lying in our beds sleeping like logs while a burglar was creeping through the house."

Miss Teenie gave a smothered shriek at the thought, and Jean said, " But what a blessing you *didn't* wake. Think of the shock if you had ! "

" It would have cost us our lives," Miss Watson said firmly, " for I couldn't have helped screaming and he would have hit me with a jemmy."

" Or strangled you," said Mhor ; " that's quieter."

" Oh, mercy," moaned Miss Teenie.

Jean begged Mhor to be quiet, and asked if the burglar had taken much.

Miss Watson shook her head, drank some coffee, and said :

" We can't tell yet. The gramophone's away, and my mother's work-box, and all our rings, and Chrissie's wage that was lying on the dressing-table to remind me, and the money for the month's books . . . but I don't know what else. There's a pane cut in the scullery window to let him undo the snib. He'd tied Chrissie's door so that she wouldn't interrupt him, and he'd actually taken a meal—just fancy the cheek !—tongue and ham from the larder, and bread and butter and cider. And none of us heard so much as a sound." She looked rather bitterly at her sister as she added : " Teenie there always declares she suffers from insomnia, but whatever she has for ordinary she had a grand sleep last night ! "

"Well," said Miss Teenie, "if I slept last night I don't think I'll ever sleep again."

"I know," said Jean, "it's dreadful for you. But the man will be caught, and in time you'll forget it. Is your maid very upset?"

"Chrissie's wonderful," said Miss Watson. "The first we knew about it was hearing her shouting when she found her bedroom door fastened. We ran down in our bare feet, and she chased us back to bed, and got the fire on and brought up our breakfasts, and then telephoned for the police. She's got a head on her shoulders, has Chrissie. But what would tempt a burglar at Balmoral I *cannot* think."

"The treasures in the garret," said Mhor, digging into the honey jar: "the ostrich eggs and the Chinese scratchers. He was disturbed before he reached them, so he took the gramophone and retired."

"Havers," said Miss Teenie, visibly cheered at finding there was a comic side to this dreadful experience.

Miss Barton, coming in with some message for Lady Bidborough, had to hear all the details, then Mhor and Peter escorted the two little ladies back to their ravaged home.

"What an odd burglar," Miss Barton said, watching the procession go out of the gate. "What could he want with a gramophone!"

"What, indeed!" echoed Jean. "There's a Heath Robinson touch about the whole thing, but that doesn't make it any easier for these two poor little bodies."

CHAPTER XIX

" O, there be players that I have seen play . . . "

HAMLET.

AMONG other excitements Mhor came in for a meeting of Mrs. Duff-Whalley's Community Drama players.

Jean warned him about it at breakfast.

" Remember, Mhor," she said, " Mrs. Duff-Whalley takes this very seriously, and whatever you do you mustn't laugh yourself or make the rest of us laugh."

But Mhor's imagination boggled at the thought of Mrs. Duff-Whalley in conjunction with the Drama.

" But, Jean," he expostulated, " you don't mean that Mrs. D.-W. has started to produce plays and that you all sit round and do as she says ?   What does she know about it anyway ? "

" Not very much, I think, but it's Mr. Hamilton who's supposed to be producing the thing.   He's home from India, and has taken a sheep-farm, you know—Drykeld. A nice fellow he seems, and keen about acting."

" And who are the others ? " Mhor asked.

" Muriel Duff-Whalley, Barty, Rosalind Tweedie, and a boy called Malcolm Forbes—his people have bought Archfield."

" Oh !   Is Rosalind Tweedie as fat as ever ? "

" Rosalind's grown up very good looking.   You'll see

her to-night. I'm to be prompter, and I'm terrified in case I let them down. When people are nervous it's difficult for them to make out what's said, and I know I'll lose my head. However—what are you going to do this morning ? Barty has to go to Edinburgh. Wouldn't you like to go ? "

" It might be rather a scheme," said Mhor. " May Peter come too ? I could show him a lot of things."

Jean hesitated and then said : " Yes—but please be careful crossing streets. I'm terrified for the Princes Street crossings. Have you any shopping to do ? "

" Well, I've got most of my presents ; Peter and I had a busy day yesterday. Some of them aren't paid. I hope you don't mind, but our money went done and we told the shops to mark them."

" They said it was all right, Mummy," Peter broke in.

" Does that mean you've nothing for to-day ? " said Jean, reaching for her purse. " Now that's ample for you both. . . . See that Peter gets a good lunch—it's his dinner you know, so don't feed him up with rubbish. Go into the North British Hotel and have the *table d'hôte* lunch—that will be safest. Here's Miss Barton. Barty, you're to have company into Edinburgh. Could you lunch with the boys, or would you rather leave yourself free ? I know you've a lot to do."

" Yes," said Miss Barton, laying a businesslike leather bag on a chair, and looking over a list she held in her hand. " You want all these people called on person-ally, don't you ? and the parcels left. That'll take a bit of doing. I hope you boys don't want to hurry back ? "

They assured her earnestly that they had much business of their own to transact.

"Don't forget, Barty, that we've a rehearsal here to-night," Jean warned her. "Have you ever looked at the play?"

Miss Barton groaned. "I glanced at it last night: very poor stuff. . . . Is that everything, do you think? The morning's letters are on my desk: perhaps you may have time to look over them. And I put the sums of money you wanted into packets and laid them in the right-hand top drawer in case you want to take them round to-day. The keys are in the usual place."

"Thank you," said Jean. "I might go round this morning, only morning's not the best time to see people. They naturally object to visitors coming when they're doing grates. I'll do the letters now, and then see Mrs. Jowett, and do the rest of the visiting after lunch. . . . Run, Peter, and get your coat. And what about your nails? I thought they looked rather dingy yesterday. . . . Oh, yes, it matters, my son."

When the party had gone off in the car—Peter waving from one side, Mhor from the other—Jean played with Quentin and Alison until Elsie came to take them for their walk. Alison was getting used to Peter's desertion of her, and was philosophically turning to her small brother and sharing in his games.

Jean went to the kitchen to have her daily talk with Mrs. McCosh, always more of a pleasure than a duty.

"I'm glad," she said, sitting down in the low chair with the red cushion that stood in the window, " that

you're to have a quiet Christmas. These last months
have been a racket for you. . . . Are you sure you
wouldn't like a few days' holiday ? You know there's
nothing to prevent your getting away."

" Oh, I ken that, but I'd rather be here. I'm oot o'
acquaintance noo with the folk I kent in Glesgae.
Priorsford's home to me. . . . I thocht, if ye didna
mind, I'd ask the lasses at The Neuk to come here on
Christmas Day. Bein' English they pit great importance on Christmas, an' they're faur frae their ain folk
this year."

" But of course. I was just wondering what we
could do to make things a little festive for them. You'll
have turkey and plum-pudding, and all the things
here, and a good tea, and perhaps go to the Pictures
in the evening. And if it were a fair day Phipps could
take you for a drive in the afternoon. I know Mrs.
Elliot wants you all to go up to her party at Laverlaw
in New Year week. . . . I leave it to you, Mrs. McCosh,
to order everything that's needed, and I'll get the
crackers and sweets myself. What about asking Bella
Bathgate to join you ? "

Mrs. McCosh smoothed down her clean white apron
and shook her head doubtfully as she said :

" I'm no' sure. She's a queer body, Bella. Whiles
as pleasant as ye please and real entertainin', an' whiles
no'. She micht spoil the party. Phipps, bein' English,
is inclined to be jokesome, ye ken, an' likes a bawr with
The Neuk lasses, an' I'm feared Bella would pu' down
her lip at him . . ."

" She might, easily," Jean agreed. " Well, just as

you like. I depend on you to see that every one has as good a time as possible."

As Jean went on her way to The Neuk to look at her letters, she resolved to order a small Christmas Tree, which she and the children would spend the next day decorating for Mrs. McCosh's party. It would make the presents more inviting, and it would keep the children happily employed.

It was noon before she got up to The Knowe. Mrs. Jowett was, as usual, lying on the couch by the fire; but this morning the table by her side was heaped with books and cards and various articles, yards of ribbon, and little bunches of holly. After greeting her visitor she said: " I've been trying to wrap up a few parcels, but I'm not getting on very fast."

" Well, now," said Jean, " that's one thing I *can* do —make up tidy parcels. Let me begin right away. First I'll write down the names and addresses and what goes to each, and that'll keep me right. Perhaps you could write a word on the cards ? It would make them mean so much more. We'll get the parcels that have to go a distance away first : there's no hurry for the Priorsford ones. Who is this nice book for ? You're wise to choose books, they're so easy to tie up."

Mrs. Jowett gave a sigh of relief as she said: " Oh, dear, you don't know how glad I am to see a start made. Tim would have done it, but tying up parcels is not his forte, poor dear. He *will* argue. . . . And the maids are busy with their own work. They are very good, but I feel it is so dull for them to have me lying here day in and day out : no entertaining, no brightness. Every day I dread to hear that they're giving up in disgust."

" Oh, surely not," Jean cried, " they couldn't be such wretches. Never were servants treated with such consideration as yours, and that they would give up their places now because you are rather seedy would be unheard-of ingratitude. I think better of them than that. Don't worry, my dear, you set your mind on getting stronger. Once Christmas is over, spring is very near. Before we know where we are the snowdrops will be up, and that's the beginning of all delight." She worked busily and presently said : " There now, these are ready for the post. I'll come to-morrow morning and do the next batch. . . . Here is Mr. Jowett."

That gentleman clucked with impatience when he saw the pile of neat parcels.

" Perfect nonsense," he said. " I'm all against this present-giving. It's becoming a positive burden, and an unwarrantable tax. What's the use of loading things on people who don't need them ? We neither want to give nor receive, but we've got into a vicious circle and we can't stop. But if we all made a stand it could be brought to an end."

" It's good for trade," said Jean, and added rather feebly, " and it's only once a year."

" Now that's a silly argument," barked Mr. Jowett ; but Jean only laughed as she kissed Mrs. Jowett, and followed by her host, still declaiming, made for the door.

He walked with her to the gate, and as she left he said :

" I hate this Christmas fuss. It makes her feel her helplessness. Last year she was so happy with all her plans. . . . Forgive my rudeness about the parcels. It's not that I don't appreciate your kindness, but . . . Good-bye."

In the afternoon Jean and Alison chose a tree and laid in a store of decorations, and visited various old friends of Jean's down by the Water-side. It interested Alison to sit in a little kitchen with a bed in it, and play with a cat, while her mother listened to symptoms, and asked after young men and women she had known as children.

She would be told: " Ay, Agnes is in Canada. Daein' weel. Of course it's hard work wi' nae end t'it, but she likes it fine. Twae bairns—I've their likeness here." A framed post card was brought from the dresser. " Ay, they say the lassie's like me, but the laddie's like *his* folk. Na, there's no word o' them comin' hame ; they couldna leave the place even if they hed the siller saved. I'll never likely see ma lassie again. . . . Oh, I'm no' bad the noo, but I was rale hard-up for a while. An' hoo are ye yersel' ? I'll hae to tell Agnes ye were speirin' for her."

The party from Edinburgh arrived home in good time, after what appeared to have been a most successful day. Peter had seen, under Mhor's direction, so many *ferlies*, and heard so many strange tales, that his words tumbled over each other with eagerness as he tried to tell his mother all about it. As he went to bed they heard his tongue going to Ninny and Elsie.

After dinner Mhor helped Jean to arrange the seats

in the drawing-room while Betty Barton conned her part.

" D'you know it ? " Mhor asked.

" Not a word, I'm ashamed to say. I really forgot all about it—but I don't expect the others will be any further forward. It's utter rubbish any way. Listen to this . . ."

Mrs. Duff-Whalley and her daughter were the first to arrive, and the former enthroned herself in a high chair with arms, her feet on a hassock, and waited angrily for the late-comers.

Mr. Hamilton was only five minutes late. Rosalind Tweedie came rushing in, obviously inclined to giggle on the slightest provocation. Mr. Thornton apologized to Jean for being there at all, as he had no part and would be of no use. " The fact is," he confessed, " I just came for a pleasant evening."

" And very glad we are to see you," his hostess told him, " though as to a pleasant evening ! . . . Mhor, I don't think you know Mr. Thornton. . . . Where are the cigarettes ? . . . Mhor is renewing acquaintance with Priorsford after nearly ten years."

" Gervase," said Mrs. Duff-Whalley majestically, " you will know young Burton Bradbury at Eton ? His father is Sir Frank Burton Bradbury, and they have a most beautiful place in Cumberland. A show place. You remember, Muriel, the gardens, and the peach and pine houses ? " She turned to Rosalind Tweedie. " And the house is simply full of Old Masters."

" How nice," said Rosalind mechanically, then she added : " No, I don't think really it would be a bit

nice.   Old Masters are better in public galleries : you
can keep away from them there."

Mrs. Duff-Whalley proceeded as if she had not heard
this heresy.   " The tapestries in the hall were gorgeous
—I longed for time to study them, and the drawing-
rooms—there were actually *three large drawing-rooms*
—were full of treasures : cabinets of exquisite china,
jewelled boxes and——"

" Good place to burgle," said Mhor.   " Better than
Balmoral."

" Balmoral ? " said Rosalind.

" Absurd name," said Mrs. Duff-Whalley.   " He means
a small villa occupied by two maiden ladies known as
the Miss Watsons."

" D'you mean to say the Miss Watsons have been
burgled," said Mr. Thornton, looking much concerned.
" What a fright they must have got."

Miss Barton turned to him.   " Dreadful," she said
in her definite way.   " They won't be able to go upstairs for weeks without the thought of the man slinking
up.   It was a very cruel thing to happen."

Mrs. Duff-Whalley turned her gaze upon the girl.
" Who are you calling cruel, may I ask ?   Providence ? "

" I suppose so," said Miss Barton.

" Mr. Forbes is rather late," broke in Jean.   " He has
such a small part—don't you think we may as well
begin without him, Mr. Hamilton ? "

Mr. Hamilton and Muriel were seated together and
looked so contented that Jean felt herself a spoil-sport,
but somebody had to be sacrificed.

Mr. Hamilton consulted his watch.   " After nine," he

said. " We won't get much done if we don't start at once. May I arrange the scene, Lady Bidborough ? "

He pushed the furniture about, helped by the minister and Mhor, then gave the actors some instructions.

" A room in a home somewhere in Russia : a jail really—I wonder what local colour we could introduce . . . samovars—aren't they sort of tea urns ? Does anybody know anything about Russia ? "

He looked round but nobody made any response.

" Oh, well—fortunately the characters are English, except the Russian soldier, or jailer, or whatever he is. Forbes has to cope with that."

Rosalind giggled. " Haven't Russians blond beards ?" she said. " I've a notion I've heard that."

" The company discovered in room," Mr. Hamilton said. " Miss Duff-Whalley, will you come and sit here ? Miss Tweedie kneeling beside you. Miss Barton here. I've got a man to do the other part, but he can't come till after Christmas. *The Curtain goes up on a dimly lit room where the captives of the Soviet——*"

At that moment Malcolm Forbes came in :

" Terribly sorry," he said as he shook hands with his hostess. " I'm afraid I'm frightfully late, but the fact is we've been burgled." The boy gave an excited little laugh and they all stared at him. " I'm not ragging," he assured them. " It was done when we were at dinner to-night. A ladder from the green-house— or rather two ladders tied together and put up to my mother's window. As luck would have it, she was wearing nothing but her wedding ring, and everything else is gone."

" Everything ? " ejaculated Mrs. Duff-Whalley.

" Well, everything that wasn't in the bank. Her pearls and rings, and two brooches. All the things she valued most."

" My goodness me, we'll be the next," said Rosalind Tweedie, and laughed gleefully.

" It's no subject for laughter," said Mrs. Duff-Whalley severely, and turning to young Forbes, said : " What, may I ask, have you done about it ? "

" Done ? " said the boy. " We telephoned right away for the police, and they were up in a few minutes, but in the dark, with woods all round, what hope is there of finding anybody ! A description of the things stolen will be sent to all the pawnshops, but I don't expect the man—or men—will leave the district ; they're evidently doing a round."

" To-morrow morning," said Mrs. Duff-Whalley, " I'll get burglar-proof snibs on every window. Muriel, we must telephone the police-station to-night ; and if they've got special men put to watch and see that one walks round The Towers at intervals . . ."

The company looked at each other, and Mr. Thornton said :

" I can understand them burgling a place like Archfield, but why they meddled with the poor little Miss Watsons I can't think."

" Getting their hand in," said Mhor, that expert in crime. . . . " I'm afraid it's no good, Mrs. Duff-Whalley, getting new fastenings, a clever thief can always get in : cut out a pane and there he is."

" Instead of talking nonsense," said Mrs. Duff-

Whalley coldly, " you might ring up The Towers and tell them to send the car at once. I must be on the spot."

" Ring for coffee, Mhor," Jean said, " before you telephone. Oh, here it is. You will have a cup, won't you, Mrs. Duff-Whalley ? It's such a cold night. I'm quite sure there won't be any more attempts to-night. Those sandwiches are *pâté de fois gras* : I think the brown ones are fishy . . ." She took a bite of one. " Quite good they are. . . . Is every one being fed ? Mr. Forbes, you must make a meal, because I expect your dinner was spoiled."

The youth confessed that he was exceedingly hungry, and solidly sat and ate, to the delight of his hostess, who enjoyed few things more than feeding hungry boys.

When Mrs. Duff-Whalley left, dragging with her a reluctant daughter, the others gathered round the fire and speculated on this so sudden and unexplainable outburst of crime.

" For the moment it's wiped out Community Drama," Mr. Hamilton said. " I don't expect it's any use meeting again till the festivities are past."

" Meet here again in the second week in January," Jean suggested. " Has any one a calendar, till we find a date ? The 10th, does that suit ? The New Year will be quite warmed up by then. Mr. Hamilton, will you let the Duff-Whalleys know ? "

CHAPTER XX

"O winds, be calm, and earth, be mild,
 And let the heavens be sweet with light,
 Hush every stir and sound, a Child
 Comes to his Mother's arm to-night."

M. E. LOCHHEAD.

A LETTER written by Betty Barton from Laverlaw, on Christmas Eve, to her friend, Molly Secombe:

" . . . I am wondering how you and Susan are enjoying your Christmas abroad. It was a great scheme to take a cheap trip to the Riviera, and I'm hoping that you will find it worth all the trouble. I'm afraid you're right and I'm getting soft among the flesh-pots of Egypt, for I've seen the day when I'd never have hesitated about going with you, when I'd have enjoyed everything. Yes, even the crush and the crossing and the second-class carriages, but this year, somehow, the idea had no attraction for me. Partly, I suppose, because I'm in such completely different surroundings. You and Susan, the little flat, the gas stove, the scratch meals at home when funds were low, and the feasts in Soho when fortune smiled, seem almost too far away to be real. (That sounds vaguely rude, but you will understand!) I have settled down very comfortably into this corner of

Scotland, and the world may go round as it pleases for
me.

" That's like my egotistical way, isn't it ? (D'you
remember once saying, ' When I'm away from Betty
I like the thought of her, but I haven't been with her
five minutes before she says something that makes me
absolutely loathe her ' ?)   Anyway, there's nothing
selfish about you, my Molly, and I'm very grateful for
your letter, and the interest you take in your unworthy
friend. And a thousand thanks for the boudoir cap. It
is such a pretty one, and it was more than good of you
to take time to make it. I have it with me here, and
it matches beautifully with the rose-coloured dressing-
gown Lady Bidborough gave me, and the rose-
coloured slippers that I bought myself. I feel quite
fit, with my nice ' bath clothes,' to meet even the eye
of the most superior housemaid.

" You complain that my letters are only scraps and
that I tell you nothing about Scotland, the Land of
Romance. Well, I'll tell you what I'm doing now. I
am sitting in a turret-room in a Border Keep, one of the
castles on which they lit beacons to warn the countryside that the English were coming raiding over the
Border ! How's that for Romance ?

" The old ' Keep ' remains, but round it has been
built (it's taken several centuries to do it) an exceedingly comfortable country house, with central heating,
electric light, and abundance of bath-rooms. The place
is called ' Laverlaw,' and belongs to Lady Bidborough's
brother-in-law, Mr. Lewis Elliot, and we are here for
Christmas, the whole household of us.

" I explained to you—or did I not ?—that as a rule we live in the town of Priorsford, in the house in which Lady Bidborough and her brothers were brought up, a little old stone house looking to the hills, called ' The Rigs.' We have also a larger house just behind, where I work and sleep, and which acts as an overflow when the little house is overcrowded. There are three maids from Mintern Abbas, besides the nurses and the chauffeur, and at The Rigs there's a funny old housekeeper called Mrs. McCosh, so *utterly* Scotch that I can hardly make out a word she says.

" You must see Priorsford some day—when you get the little car and make a tour of Scotland : it is really beautiful : quite modern yet very reminiscent of far-away things. The very names of the streets, the East Gate, the North Gate, take one back to the time when men shut their gates against knaves and thieves. Walking along the streets, everywhere you get sudden glimpses of beauty. From the Post Office in the North Gate you look up to a green hill crowned by a white-turreted house like an old French Château, and standing on the wide bridge that spans the Tweed (dividing the town proper from what might be termed the suburbs), frowning down at you is Peel Tower, which was bombarded by Cromwell's soldiers, and once lodged Mary of Scots.

" Life at The Rigs is, of course, very different from life at Mintern Abbas. There, of necessity, there's a certain amount of pomp and circumstance : at The Rigs all is simplicity. At Mintern Abbas, though I'm supposed to take my meals with the family, I often

make excuses to have them in my own sitting-room.
There are so often guests, and anyway the meals take
too long and I prefer to be alone, but at The Rigs I
really am in the nicest sense of the phrase 'one of the
family.' We have the jolliest, cosiest times, and I'll be
honestly sorry when we have to leave Priorsford. And
I believe Lady Bidborough enjoys it too, although it's
very evident that half of her heart is on the other side
of the world. She loves being with her old friends—
she is still 'Miss Jean' to a lot of them, and goes in
and out among them as she did when she was poor and
of no consequence. There is something very steadfast
about her little ladyship. If ever I had to be dependent
on any one—which may God forbid—I'd choose to be
dependent on her. I can't say fairer than that, can I?

" It must be the spirit of Christmas that is making
me see things through rose-coloured spectacles to-
night, for I don't always view things so rosily. I don't
need to tell you that I have many moments of acute
impatience with life ! When one is poor and obscure
it is galling to live among people to whom money
simply doesn't matter, who are utterly secure in their
beautiful homes, born to high positions and accepting
it as their right. Mrs. Elliot's like that ; she always
makes me feel like being a Communist, but Lady
Bidborough, with all her possessions, remains 'poor
in spirit.' All she asks is that she may do good with
her money and not harm. She gets let down often
(when she *will not* take my advice !) but she never fal-
ters in her determination to *help*. She always says it
doesn't matter how often we fail if sometimes we

succeed. And sometimes we do score. We found one family lately, *pukka* gentlefolk, and I think we've made life a different thing for them. Most of the people I have to deal with are incapable, as well as lazy and greedy, and liars to boot, so you can imagine what it means to come on people who are absolutely above board. I'm supposed to do all the visiting and interviewing, but Lady Bidborough was so interested in what I told her of this family that she went with me one day to see them. Nobody knows better than you, Molly my friend, that I'm not lacking in a good conceit of myself, but I confess that that day I was completely out of it. I've a much better business head than my mistress—*she still counts on her fingers!* Do I hear you say, ' The darling ' ?—but I'm simply nowhere at all when it comes to making friends with people, when it comes to charming the hearts out of their breasts. Yes, that's what it amounts to! She walked into that shabby room, looking like a diffident schoolgirl, and laid some spring flowers on the lap of the woman she had come to see. Then she took a low chair beside her —Mrs. Gordon is an invalid, with a young son and daughter—and began to tell her what Quentin (the baby) had said that morning. From Quentin they passed to boys in general, and finally to Mrs. Gordon's own son, who is fighting his way through college. In a quarter of an hour she and Mrs. Gordon were fast friends. . . . It's a gift, I suppose, like being able to sing or act, that power of winning trust. I haven't got it. I'm too hard and polished—but you've *got* to be both if you've to make your own way in the world.

It's quite different if you're an heiress and the adored wife of a belted earl, or at least a belted baron. . . .

" You ask what the Priorsford people are like. Very like the people in any other country town I should think. They seem quite nice, all but one, a certain Mrs. Duff-Whalley, who keeps me rigidly in my proper place.

" Quite near us lives Miss Janet Hutton, the ideal spinster. When you meet her you feel, Here is what every unmarried woman would wish to be. There is nothing pathetic about her, no least appearance of having been cheated by life, rather she radiates a sort of serene contentment. I often slip in to see her of an afternoon, her house and herself are so beguiling, and she can tell one so much of the old life of Priorsford, tales of her grandmother's about the time when the French prisoners were in the town. She lent me the old lady's diary, which so fascinated me that I almost regretted I had not been born a Scot !

" Then we have a novelist in our midst—Mrs. Mirren Strang. Did you ever hear of her books ? I think *The Penny Whistle* is the best. She has a very pretty cottage in a big garden not far from Laverlaw. Her young husband was killed in the Boer War, and her only child—a boy of nineteen—in the Great War, so she's been hardly treated by fate. You see it in her sad, shrewd eyes, though she sounds quite gay. She is small and dark, with very nice hands and feet, and lovely teeth, but not pretty. She talks a lot, sometimes quite amusingly, and is cleverer than her books might lead you to believe.

"But I'm wandering away from this room, which I want to describe to you, knowing your interest in rooms.

"Picture to yourself an old house standing in a green glen through which runs a stream called the Laverlaw Water. There are lawns all round it, which run into the heather in the most enchanting way. The walled garden lies to the sun on the slope of the hillside, and, I am told, is a sight to see in its season, for Mrs. Elliot has 'a way' with flowers. She has also very definitely 'a way' with a house. It's so clever how she has preserved the feeling of age, or rather timelessness, and yet managed to introduce modern comfort. Each bit of furniture, each picture, each ornament is so well placed that turn where you will the eye is charmed.

"This room is panelled in oak—it was painted but Mrs. Elliot had it scraped—and has a thick blue velvet carpet from corner to corner, which makes it deliciously comfortable. Heavy curtains of dull gold and blue cover the three windows, and a Chinese rug like a square of sunshine lies before the bed. There's a bookcase filled with all the books one would like to read at bedtime, and a stand on the table holds some of the latest published. When the maid brought in my tea this morning—blue and gold china to match the room—I lay and watched the first streaks of light touch the Laverlaw Water. Where's your Riviera now?

"This is entirely a family party. Lady Bidborough and the children, with young Gervase Taunton and her two brothers. Gervase Taunton was brought up with the Jardines but is no kin to them. He is at Eton:

very good-looking ; a careless young pagan. Jock
Jardine is a *dear*. I couldn't exactly explain why, but
he is : everybody likes him. The elder brother,
David, I hadn't met before. I expect I was on holiday
when he came to Mintern Abbas. He isn't like the
other Jardines : much more of this world : slightly
inclined to be snobbish and very determined, one can
see, to make a success of life. There was something
faintly satirical in Mrs. Elliot's eyes as she listened
to him at dinner to-night. I'm sure his sister was
aware of it. She flushed, and one felt she'd shield him
if she could from criticism. Lady Bidborough stands
in rather an odd relation to those youths—not only
sister but parent. I understand that she was only
eighteen when she was left with three boys to bring
up !

" There was never a greater contrast between two
women than between these sisters-in-law, not only
in appearance but in character and temperament, but
they are devoted to each other. Mrs. Elliot is exceedingly nice to me, and couldn't be more thoughtful of
my comfort were I the most important in the land, but
with her it is simply beautiful manners, not interest
or human sympathy. At least that is what I feel, but
I may be wrong. Anyway, Mr. Lewis Elliot adores
his wife, and he is a darling—very bookish, very shy,
very kind.

" I've been helping Lady Bidborough to fill the
children's stockings, and I'm looking forward to to-
morrow with quite absurdly childish excitement.
Perhaps it's the thought of all the stockings hanging

8

up all over the world ! Christmas seems real this year.
Is it because I'm living in a real home ? I'm not sure
of anything to-night—not even of myself !

" Bless you, Molly,

" BARTY.

"You will be surprised to hear that this peaceful
neighbourhood is at present passing through an epi-
demic of burglaries. The question is, who will be next ! "

CHAPTER XXI

" . . . Sow in our souls, like living grass,
The laughter of all lowly things."

G. K. CHESTERTON.

CHRISTMAS Day had gone on its way, and the morning after saw the Laverlaw party gathered round the breakfast-table, none the worse, seemingly, for the yearly orgy.

Alison, seated by her Uncle Lewis, whom she dearly loved, was supping porridge as if for a wager. When she had finished she sighed and said :

" I had a nightmare last night. I thought there was a 'normous eider-down smothering me, and I pulled and pulled and couldn't get to the end of it, and I screamed, and when Ninny came I was at the foot of the bed, all twisted up in blankets."

" Undoubtedly a nightmare," Lewis said seriously.

" Two helps of pudding and a meringue ! " said Mhor, winking at Alison.

Lewis looked round the table in his short-sighted way. " What's happening to-day ? " he asked. " We thought of walking over Corhope, didn't we, Jock ? Have you any plans, Pamela ? "

" Nothing very particular, darling. Mirren Strang has bidden us all to a tea-party. I expect you men after your walk will find a hot bath and tea at the billiard-room fire more alluring, but the rest of us will go with pleasure. What d'you say, Alison ? "

" Yes, please, Aunt Pamela. Is Quentin invited ? "

" Indeed he is." Mrs. Elliot turned to her sister-in-law. " I gather that it's really a children's party. Kirsty Home is taking Fanny and Archibald, and Mrs. Brand at the Manse her small boy."

" That 'll be nice," said Jean, while Jock groaned dissent, and Mhor said in a high falsetto squeak : " How terrible ! "

" Oh, don't be so superior," Jean said. " It's not so very long since you were very grateful for an invitation to a party."

" Not me, Jean," Jock protested. " Be fair, woman. You know I had always to be dragged, and that wretched Davy wouldn't go at all."

David, who was peering into hot dishes, said :

" That's true, but now I think I'd rather like to go to a children's Christmas party, a sign of encroaching age, I suppose. . . . Will you take me, Pamela ? "

" Charmed," said Pamela. " I'm sure Mrs. Strang will give you a welcome. You know her, don't you ? "

Davy turned to his sister. " Do I, Jean ? I don't seem able to place Mrs. Strang."

" No," said Jean. " I don't think we ever saw her much ; she was mostly abroad when we were children, but I heard so much *about* her from Mrs. Hope and Miss Janet Hutton that I've always felt as if I knew her quite well."

David sat down at the table and unfolded his napkin, saying :

"She won't expect me to talk about her books, will she? I haven't read one."

"The loss is yours," said Jean. "But you needn't suppose that Mirren Strang is thirsting for compliments about her writing. I never saw any one with such a cavalier way of dealing with her admirers. You'll be wise not to pretend to a knowledge you don't possess, my lad. . . . Oh, the sun's coming out, and the wind's chasing the clouds away. You'll have a lovely day on Corhope."

Peter wanted to know if he might take the puppies for a walk, but his aunt told him they were too small. "But I'll tell you what, if Ninny agrees, we'll climb Netherlaw and give Black Douglas a glorious scamper. He's such a repaying dog to take out : every minute's a joy to him."

"He's a nice beast," said Mhor, who had been eating rapidly, taking no part in the conversation. "May I go, Pamela? Yes, I've had a huge breakfast. I want to see Veitch at the stables. Coming Peter?"

"Oh, don't drag Peter away ; he's not nearly finished."

"Yes, I am," said Peter, hastily gulping down his milk, for to him Mhor's slightest word was a command, and the two went off together.

"Business in Egypt," said Jock. "Peter's become a boy, Jean : in a night you might say. He was a baby going about with Ninny the last time I saw him and now he's rough and large."

"Oh, I know," said Jean, half-proud and half-regretful. "He'll be out shooting with you all directly. Biddy will find a great difference in them all. . . .

I'm glad Peter's had the sense to take his height from his father. I just hope Alison will."

Pamela watched her niece getting stolidly through her third piece and butter. "What's Alison going to wear at the party?" she asked.

"The same as I wore yesterday for Christmas," Alison said, in her uncompromising way; "it's my best."

Pamela smiled down the table to Betty Barton as she said, "I'm looking forward to my tea-party to-day as much as the children. I always enjoy going to Hopewaterfoot."

"It's very kind of Mrs. Strang to include me," said Betty.

"She specially mentioned you," Pamela assured her.

David broke in, "The point is, Miss Barton, have you read any of Mrs. Strang's books? It's a perilous thing to visit an author if you're ignorant of the very names of her books."

"But I'm not," said Betty. "I've read several. They're very nice: the sort of books you'd leave on the table if you expected the vicar to call."

"I see," said David, while Mrs. Elliot, regarding the girl, said:

"I expect you prefer stronger meat, Miss Barton: something to bite on. . . . When you're ready, Jean, I'd like to show you the print I told you about. It's in my room."

"I'll come now, and then I must write letters solidly till luncheon, the only hope is to begin at once before you forget who sent what. . . . Alison, Elsie's come for you."

The sisters-in-law had a talk in Pamela's sitting-room before beginning the day's work.

"How very pretty Miss Barton is," Pamela began. "I've never seen her before in the evening. She positively startled me last night. Of course it was partly the frock: lovely—but not very suitable, Jean."

"I don't see why not. Nothing could be simpler. As a matter of fact, I gave it to her: the stuff was so glorious; I saw Barty looking like a ballad in it."

Pamela lifted her eyebrows. After a pause she said:

"It's rather intriguing, the combination of glowing beauty and prim, cold manner. . . . Perhaps Miss Barton does it on purpose. . . . Don't you find men admire her?"

"Every one must admire Barty's looks," Jean said, watching Pamela rearrange her mantelshelf. "I haven't noticed particularly about men. She certainly never puts herself forward in any way. At Mintern Abbas she has a trick of disappearing when visitors arrive. She told me once that she much preferred her own room with its books and piano to sitting talking to people she didn't know anything about. One can quite understand that. In Priorsford her only opportunity for meeting men is the Community Drama Class! The Forbes boy is too shy, too troubled with his hands and feet to notice whether people are good-looking or not: Mr. Thornton's mind is too full of other things, I suppose; anyway he doesn't seem interested: and the only other man, Mr. Hamilton, belongs to Muriel Duff-Whalley."

Pamela turned quickly. "Seriously, Jean? And what does the Redoubtable One say to that?"

"She doesn't know. With such sharp eyes for most things it's amazing how she can miss what's happening near her. . . . I hope Muriel will have the courage to stand up to her mother, for this would be the making of her. I believe she would be absolutely happy and contented at Drykeld. But it's painfully obvious that Mrs. Duff-Whalley regards Mr. Hamilton as much beneath her level. Isn't it *ludicrous?* I wonder where she would find a more eligible son-in-law: a man who has seen the world and is settling down with a comfortable competence? It's this 'county' nonsense that gets between her and her judgment. As if 'the county' cared! What is 'the county' anyway? . . . Pam, I don't suppose you want to give a dinner-party and invite the Duff-Whalleys *and* Mr. Hamilton *and* the flower of the county so to speak?"

Pamela laughed and shifted a log on the fire. "I can't say I do," she said. "Why should I make things easy for Miss Duff-Whalley? In other words, what's Hecuba to me?"

"Nothing," said Jean meekly. "Only I thought, if you wanted to make good resolutions and begin the New Year well . . . But it doesn't matter."

Pamela looked at her small sister-in-law.

"Jean," she said, "there are moments when I'd like to shake you."

Mirren Strang may or may not have been a good

novelist, but she was a past mistress in the art of giving a party. Perhaps it was because she made preparations with such good-will, sparing no pains, inspiring others to work with something of her own enthusiasm. Some people make a party and no one would know it was a party until they reached the drawing-room and found it full of people. Mirren Strang's party began on the doorstep, where to the children's delight, the hanging lamp had become a presentment of the Man in the Moon. When the front door opened all was gaiety: a log fire burned in the black and white hall: the big blue jars on the oak chest were filled with what Alison called "magic lanterns," two handsome cats, Crian and Kitty by name, boasted scarlet bows.

The tea-table, glittering with icicles, might have come out of the Snow Queen's palace: snowballs lay at each plate: an enormous iced cake was guarded by scarlet-clad soldiers: the children ate and stared, stared and ate, bereft of speech.

The hostess in a bright red dress seemed everywhere at the same moment, but she got small assistance in her efforts from her companion, Rebecca Brand, who seemed to think she was only there to enjoy herself.

After tea they played such games as: *Oranges and Lemons*, *Have you any Bread and Wine?*, *Musical Chairs*, and in the midst of the laughter and noise Jean found herself beside Mrs. Home, with whom she had exchanged visits and found much in common.

"Isn't this fun?" she said. "I wish you'd bring Fanny down to play with Alison one day next week."

"Thank you. Fanny loves tea-parties, and there

aren't many about here; that's why it's so good of Mrs. Strang to trouble."

Jean looked at the absorbed face of her hostess as she helped Peter to explode a firework, described as a " parlour bomb," and laughed.

" I don't think she'd call it a trouble," she said. " At this moment Mirren's about Peter's age, and enjoying everything as much as he is. . . . It's such a pretty party."

Mrs. Home glanced at her companion with frank interest : " Aren't you loving being back in Priorsford ? "

Jean nodded. " Indeed I am. This winter among old friends is such a surprise, a sort of unexpected gift, an extra. I'm grateful for it, though, on the other hand, I'm missing a lot. I try not to think of that side of it. Count up one's gains, and let the losses go—that's the wise thing to do, isn't it ? "

" It's the way to be happy," Kirsty Home agreed. Presently she said, " Except Miss Hutton, who is a great friend, and Mrs. Duff-Whalley who calls at intervals, I don't know much about the Priorsford people. But I love shopping in Priorsford, the people in the shops are so particularly kind and obliging, and I long to be invited to tea-parties, they sound so deliciously Cranfordy as Miss Hutton tells of them. . . . But haven't you been thrilled by the burglaries ? They strike rather a discordant note in Priorsford ! "

" Our neighbours, the Miss Watsons, were the first victims," Jean told her. " An inexplicable thing, for it's the most modest of little villas, though it rejoices in the high-sounding name of Balmoral ! At the moment it has simply wrecked life for the poor little ladies. True, they have a dramatic story to tell, but to be themselves the heroines is almost too much for them."

" Have the police no clue ? " Mrs. Home asked.

" Evidently not. It looks as if the gang—if it is a gang—is still lurking in the neighbourhood. Rather a disturbing thought ! "

" Talking about the burglars, Lady Bidborough ? " Mr. Brand said, as he passed with his small son in his arms. " Let's hope they won't come up to Muirburn."

" If they come here," said Mirren Strang, her black eyes sparkling, " I'll just help them to look for what's worth taking. I certainly won't irritate them into hitting me with a jemmy."

" It's the long-continued unemployment," said Colonel Home. " There was bound to be an outbreak of lawlessness. But these men may be professionals from the city : they sound too clever for amateurs."

" But why come to this district ? " said Pamela.

" Because," said Mirren, " we're such a smug, comfortable-looking lot, we simply ask to be burgled. To be starving and see people rolling about in cars looking as if they fed sumptuously every day, it would be more than I could stand. I'd burgle like anything. But, anyway, I shouldn't be a bit surprised if we're all reduced to beggary quite shortly. You've only got to read the papers to see how things are going. Oh, I promise you we're going to see some queer things happen."

" Well," said Pamela, in injured tones, " you needn't

look so pleased about it. You'll go down with the rest of us."

" Ah, but my dear, some have to fall from a much greater height ! "

" Wretch ! " said Pamela. " I'm not a bit surprised that they stoned the gloomy prophets. . . . All the same, you've given us a lovely party, Mirren, and in spite of everything we love you."

And David, smiling at Betty Barton, said : " This is about the cheeriest Boxing Day I ever remember. It's generally such an anti-climax of a day."

CHAPTER XXII

" Who's there, besides foul weather ? "
                                    KING LEAR.

AT dinner that night the talk was all of evils to come.

" Lewis," Pamela appealed across the round candle-lit table to her husband—" Lewis, they're talking non-sense, aren't they ? You don't think it's possible that we'll all be beggared ? "

" Even so," mocked David, " did the fair ladies of France ask for reassurance when the black cloud of Revolution came rolling up ! "

Lewis smiled at his wife as he said : " I think I can promise you that there will never be a revolution. In this island, as some one has pointed out, we haven't got the sort of climate that produces revolutionaries, any more than it produces Cleopatras and Mussolinies ; but for anything else—it would be a rash man who would prophesy."

" But would it matter so terribly ? " Jean asked. " Of course it would be hateful to have to give up Mintern Abbas. I'd be terribly sorry for Biddy, but if they left us The Rigs. . . . I suppose they'd let us keep that ? "

Pamela shook her head. " You're too easily satisfied, Jean," she declared. " But of course nothing will really happen : it's only talk. The Conservatives will go back to power, and things 'll be straightened out ; trade will improve. . . ."

She paused and David finished for her. " The poor Indian 'll settle down and take an interest in agriculture : Russia 'll develop a conscience : employers and employed will come to an understanding—in other words, ' Jack shall have Jill, the man shall have his mare again, and all will be well ! ' Eh, Pamela ? "

Pamela helped herself to a savoury and said blandly : " Oh, I'm not going to worry. We've often been in tighter places—read your history—and we've always managed to wriggle out."

" I don't see," said Jean, " how any one can help worrying when there's such a weight of anxiety crushing the life out of so many people. Even a safe, sheltered little place like Priorsford's feeling it, and when one thinks of what some districts have been going through for years ! Take the miners. People say they're sick of the miners—but think how sick they must be of themselves ! Strike after strike, getting poorer and poorer, never any nearer a settlement. Working in danger for a miserable pay. And the miners are only one part. We hear such sad things, Barty and I, about people with little businesses, ruined through no fault of their own . . . but this isn't the moment to begin on that. Let's talk about something cheerful."

" Tell us about the party," said Jock. " Was it a good one, and did Davy shine ? "

Pamela laughed as she said : " Absurd creature you are, Jock. Yes, I think Davy did shine : he did conjuring tricks which were a great success. And Miss

Barton shone too, for she's so good at making games
go." She turned to her sister-in-law. " Don't you
think, Jean, that children like simple things best ?
They're simply puzzled by those ridiculous parties
when they're loaded with expensive toys."

" As if," said Jock," the little wretches hadn't nursery-
fuls at home."

" That's the silly part of it," said Jean. " Ninny
gets quite enraged when we're told it's to be a simple
party with games, and then finds an elaborate supper,
dancing, and all sorts of expensive presents."

" We once went to a party," said Jock : "—d'you
remember, Mhor ? Everybody was dancing in white
gloves, and after we'd stood about for a bit and got in
everybody's way, we withdrew to explore, and found
the best bathroom we'd ever struck, so we had a regatta
in the bath with brushes and loofahs and things. At
ten o'clock we dried ourselves and went downstairs and
had supper and went home after having spent a very
pleasant evening."

" All the same," said Pamela, " it was rather odd
behaviour for a guest ! . . . Oh, Lewis, Colonel Home
was there to-day and I'd quite a long talk with him.
Although he looks rather morose, I believe at heart he's
quite merry."

" And with reason," said Jean. " What a nice wife
he's got ! And I liked the look of Fanny and Archibald,
they might have walked out of the Fairchild Family.
. . . I hadn't met Mrs. Brand before, though I know
her husband."

" He's a good fellow, Brand," Lewis Elliot said, look-

ing up from the pear he was peeling : " We're very lucky
to have him, for he's not only a good preacher, but he's
interested in all sorts of out-of-the-way things. When I
was calling on him the other day he showed me a collection he has made of rare old books on witchcraft and
such subjects. One thing specially interested me, a
pamphlet on Mr. Robert Kirk, Minister of Balquhidder,
and afterwards of Aberfoyle, the author of *The Secret
Commonwealth of Elves, Fauns, and Fairies*, who departed
this life in 1692 to become, according to popular tradition, chaplain to the Fairy Queen."

Lewis calmly started again on his pear, while the
company stared at him.

" *Really*, Lewis ? " said Pamela, and Jock, grinning
approval, murmured :

" By Jove, that's the right sort of parson."

" Yes," Lewis went on, " and from the papers left by
Mr. Robert Kirk, her majesty the Fairy Queen was to
be congratulated on her good taste."

Betty Barton was apt as a rule to be rather silent
during meals, but now she was goaded into speech.
Turning, to her host she said: "You can't mean that
you actually think such a thing could *happen* ? To
begin with, there's no fairies."

" My dear Miss Barton," said Jock in mock horror,
" *think !* You'll be the death of Tinker Bell."

Betty looked round the table from one face to another,
as she said incredulously : " You mean to tell me you
think fairies exist ? "

Lewis Elliot smiled at the girl. " Be gentle with us,
Miss Barton," he begged. "If you had been brought

up in a green glen in the Borders, your daily bread tales of witchcraft, and ballads about wishing-wells and queens dressed in green riding on white palfreys, with silver bells jangling, you too would believe anything. . . . I admit it's rather an effort to conceive of a douce, middle-aged minister in the Fairy Queen's Court, but still——"

" You're laughing at me," said Betty.

Lewis protested, and Mrs. Elliot said to Betty: " You must see my husband's collection of the old tales of the countryside. You know, Miss Barton, this is a haunted sort of place. Merlin is said to be buried where Laverlaw Water joins Tweed. Thomas the Rhymer lived here, and quite near is what remains of the Black Wood, which had a very odd name in the countryside. It's easy to believe in nothing when you live in a modern London flat, but to sit of a night in that library and read these old books, and listen to the hooting of the owls and the noise of Laverlaw Water, full of cold reason as I am, I begin to wonder. . . ."

" And I," said Jean, " find it better to keep away altogether from these things. ' The conies are a feeble folk,' and I'm terribly easily scared."

David turned to his neighbour and said : " You really ought to see Merlin's grave, Miss Barton. Not that there's anything to see, but it's a grand walk to it over the hill. If to-morrow's fine we might try it. The next day I've got to be back in London, worse luck ! "

" Can't you stay longer, Davy ? " Pamela asked, as she rose from the table. " You're such a popular young man, so full of engagements, that we rarely see you."

"I only wish I could stay longer. It's been extra-
ordinarily jolly having Christmas here. I don't know
when I've enjoyed myself so much."

"That's good," said Pamela; "I was afraid you might
find it too quiet," and as she noticed the way David's
eyes followed Betty Barton out of the room, she thought
to herself that it perhaps was as well his visit was
not to be prolonged.

In the library they gathered round the fire and played
games with cards, but Jock cheated because, he said,
he was too sleepy to play fair, and Pamela, trying unsuccessfully to conceal a prolonged yawn, said she thought
tea-parties were almost too exciting for country dwellers.
"Hark to the wind!" said Mhor. "It fairly tears
through the glen. Nine o'clock! What about a little
news?" He turned on the wireless, and a bland voice
announced that a vigorous triangular depression in
Ireland was moving N.E. and would shortly cover the
whole of the British Isles.

"There's small comfort there," said Pamela. "But
isn't wireless real magic? I never get over the wonder
of it. To sit here in the stillness of the glen and by
turning a knob to be able to flood the room with music!
I'd rather read the news in the morning papers, I care
nothing about the weather report—it's bad enough to
have to bear it when it comes; it's only now and
again that there's anything on that interests me, but
I'd miss the wireless terribly, simply for the wonder
of it."

"I know," said Jean. "I always said I didn't want
one, but Mhor, assisted by Mr. Bothwell, has put one

up at The Rigs; already we absolutely lean on it, don't we, Barty?"

"Though I say it myself, it's a jolly good one," Mhor said modestly.

In a short time Pamela said, "What about one more round and then bed?" and there was no dissenting voice.

That night, as was her custom, Jean looked in at the children, lifting Peter, who was a restless sleeper, on to his pillow, tucking the sheet tidily round Alison, who had a habit of covering her face with it, and gazing at Quentin who, asleep, looked almost too good to be true. Then she went on to her own comfortable bedroom and slowly undressed.

The fire was so good she was tempted to sit by it for a while, dreaming, but presently she jumped up, and going to the window drew back the curtains. It was a wild night; she could hear the wind roaring round the house, but the other side was getting the force of it, so she pulled one window down from the top, pushed the other up from the foot, kicked off her slippers, threw her dressing-gown over a chair, and jumped into bed. She had *Penny Moneypenny* on the table beside her bed, and for half-an-hour she lived with Penny and Lorin, then she put out the light, turned on her right side and went to sleep.

The house was quiet now: only in the library, where Lewis Elliot sat among his old books, a light burned, but before midnight he too went up to bed, and all was dark.

Jean woke with that feeling of rising to the surface

that one sometimes has when wakened suddenly from sound sleep. Still dazed, she felt no surprise at finding one of the lights on, but a sound made her start up. A man was standing at the window, in his hand her pearl necklace, the case on the floor at his feet. Biddy's pearls! With a cry Jean sprang out of bed and made for the man, but in a second he was on the sill of the open window, and her hand smashed through one of the small square panes.

Then she found her voice. " Ninny! Jock! Lewis! " She cried for each in turn. It was only a minute but it seemed like a hour before Jock burst in with his head like a feather-besom, followed almost at once by Mhor and Lewis and David, then by Pamela and Ninny.

Jean stood in her night-gown holding on to the window-curtains repeating : " The burglars! " at intervals.

Pamela seized the dressing-gown that lay on a chair and wrapped her in it, and put slippers on her feet.

" My poor darling, did you see them ? Oh, your hand, it's bleeding. Run, Ninny, for hot water and dressings. . . ."

" I saw one," said Jean, " standing here by the window with Biddy's pearls in his hand. I tried to stop him, but he jumped out of the window."

Mhor, who was leaning out of the window, said : " The ladder's here sure enough. I'd better telephone for the police. They can't have got far."

He dashed away full of importance, while Lewis asked if the pearls were the only things taken.

Jean looked at the dressing-table. ". . . My rings

—all that I was wearing last night : my watch, a brooch. But nothing matters much except the pearls."

She sat down on the bed rather weakly, while Ninny proceeded to bandage the cut hand, and Miss Barton, who had slipped in, stood by to help.

" Do tell me what's happened," she said. " I heard a commotion and came."

Ninny, very fully clad in a tweed ulster, with a shawl wound round her head, said, " Commotion ! I should think so. I kent they'd come. I *kent* they'd try here. I said it this very nicht to Mrs. Plenderleith. ' Mark ma words ! ' I said, ' the rascals 'll try here.' Did they come in by the window ? " She gave a suppressed shriek. " Eh, mercy, mem, did ye *see* them ? "

" See them," said Jock, " she rushed at them."

Jean began to laugh. " Rushed," she said, " is too valiant a word. If I'd stopped to think I never would have done it, but I was out of bed before I realized what was happening."

" D'you think you could identify the man you saw ? " David asked her.

" Not I. I really didn't see his face at all, it was in the shadow, only his hand holding the pearls."

" Had he a mask, Jean ? " Mhor asked eagerly.

" I don't think so, but he vanished in a second. Indeed, I'd think it was a dream, if it weren't that the ladder's there and the pearls gone."

" You didn't see if he had a revolver ? " Mhor went on.

" Eh, I say ! " ejaculated Ninny. " Ye micht hae lost yer life, mem, and what wud his lordship say to me. Me bein' in charge like."

It wasn't long before they heard the sound of a car.

" The police ! " cried Mhor, who was having the night of his life, while Jock said, " They certainly haven't tarried by the way."

" If it's the polis," said Ninny, drawing her ulster closer round her, " I'm awa'," while Jock and Mhor decided to put on some garments to be ready to go out.

" Though," said Mhor, " I'm afraid there's nothing to be seen except the ladder and some broken ivy. But," he added, " I expect they'll find some finger-marks round the window."

" Very sleuth-like, isn't he ? " said David. " You're cold, Miss Barton. Do go back to bed. These fellows 'll have all sorts of questions to ask and notes to make. No, I'm sure you can't do anything. My sister must give all the information she can, and Mrs. Elliot will be with her. I'll take you along to your room. You're in the turret, aren't you ? "

When they reached it, David turned on all the lights, poked the remains of the fire into a blaze, threw on more logs, and turned to go.

" You aren't afraid, are you ? " he asked. " Jock's next door."

Betty shook her head. " Not in the least afraid, thank you, only horribly sorry for Lady Bidborough having such an experience. It was good of you to trouble. Good-night."

" Good-night," said David, and went out, carrying away with him the picture the girl made, standing in her bright wrap against the glowing curtain, her dark hair ruffled, her cheeks still flushed with sleep.

CHAPTER XXIII

"I have been so persecuted with visits . . ."
LETTERS OF DOROTHY OSBORNE.

AT Laverlaw next morning there was only one topic, and Jean was regarded by her family with admiring awe.

"Mummy's very brave," said Peter, proud of possessing such a parent. "She very nearly caught a burglar."

"I'd never have tried if I'd had time to think," his mother protested. But the fact remained that she had sprung after him, and in doing so had broken a pane and cut her hand.

"Didn't you hear him push up the window, Jean?" Mhor wanted to know.

"He didn't need to push up the window," said Jean. "I did it for him! I always like to sleep with a window up from the bottom. What I can't understand is, how I aimed so high as to get my hand through a pane!"

"What I want to know," said Jock, "is what Jean would have done with the man if she had caught him. I believe she would have let him away, as she used to let away the mice from the traps."

"Don't jeer at me, Jock," his sister warned him, "or I'll tell tales about you. D'you remember, Davy? . . . Oh, there's the telephone again!"

It had rung incessantly all morning with messages

from the police and inquiries from neighbours. They had all taken turns of saying : " No, *quite* a slight cut. *None* the worse, thank you. Yes, *wasn't* it plucky ? "

Jock, returning from this call, said, " Extraordinary unanimity in people's remarks ! That's the third that's said the same thing in the same sequence. Let's all go out. . . . This day's not going to last anyway. Look at the mist coming down over the hills : the snow 'll be on by lunch time. . . . Come on, Jean ; come for a walk with Peter and me, it'll do you good."

" Where are you going, Pam ? " Jean asked.

" I've a message in the village. The Rural are having their Christmas meeting to-day and I promised to send some cakes and things. You'd rather have a walk, I expect, as long as it's fine. David's taken Miss Barton to see Merlin's grave. . . . Alison, you'll come and help your aunt, won't you ? Lewis is going to stay in, in case anything happens."

" Aren't you coming with us, Mhor ? " Jock asked, as they stood at the front door.

" I'm going to have a burglar hunt in the wood. I believe they're bound to be there. A car 'd have been seen leaving, for the police have been watching all night. They couldn't have got away."

Peter was at once fired with a desire to help Mhor, but his mother shook her head. " No, Peter, I don't want you to. Come with us, Mhor. Leave the burglars to the police. I want the wind to blow away last night's nightmare. Come along, Mhor and Peter."

They came rather reluctantly, hanging behind, and as Jean mounted the hill with Jock, she said : " It's silly, but I can't bear to think of the boys spending their time prying about. . . . And I can't bear the thought of going back into that bedroom. I wasn't half sorry enough for poor Miss Teenie. . . . It won't be so bad when they're caught, but the thought of them lurking about to do more evil . . . perhaps quite near; perhaps, as Mhor says, still in the woods. . . ."

"Poor Jean! Of course you feel queer to-day: you're bound to. I think it's jolly plucky of you to be up and about. I'm sure heaps of people would have stayed in bed."

Jean shivered. "Oh, I don't feel as if I could ever go to bed again! I know I'll waken—if ever I fall asleep — screaming with fright. . . . Don't tell the others. I'll surely be able to pull myself together as the day goes on. This air's doing me good already."

"I tell you what," said Jock, "I'll stretch myself before your door to-night. And we'll fasten all the windows and draw the curtains and keep the lights burning. The first night 'll be the worst one; you'll soon get away from the nightmare."

"Oh, thank you, Jock. You always were my comfort."

"Nonsense. . . . By the way, Jean, doesn't it strike you that old David's rather enamoured of Miss Barton?"

"Oh, no, Jock. He's being very civil to her, trying to make her enjoy her visit, but——"

Jock turned and grinned at his sister. "You mean it's not likely he'd want to marry a girl with no money and all that sort of thing? I agree. But you never can tell—I wonder if Miss Barton would have him?"

"Most unlikely, I should think," Jean said with decision. "As a matter of fact, I don't believe domesticity appeals to her mind : she's rather keen on having a career. But indeed it's difficult knowing what Barty is feeling. She's rather proud of not allowing herself to feel anything ! She once told me it kept life from hurting one too much. Anyway, she's practically alone in the world and I feel responsible, and I'd hate if things were spoiled for her. . . . I never thought Davy impressionable."

"Oh, I don't know. I gather that he's rather a lion among ladies."

Jean laughed. "Well, you're not, Jock. D'you ever go to dances ? "

"Only when I can't help it. I went to Agnes Chatham's ball last week. Did I forget to tell you about that ? Oh, it was rather a festive gathering and I knew lots of the people, so it wasn't so bad. But I hate dancing—except with Agnes. She's got such a lot of amusing things to say, and it passes the time. . . . She asked a lot about you and the babes, and The Rigs, and she gave me a message for you—by Jove, it's a good thing I remembered it. Her people are going for a voyage to South Africa in January. Agnes says she's a bad sailor and she hates board-ship life, so she means to stay at home and visit, and she wants to know if she may stay with you a little in January. Will that be all right ? "

Jean looked uncertain as she said : " I'd love to have her, of course, but, Jock, please explain to her what sort of place The Rigs is, how *very* simply we live, and how very little goes on."

Jock nodded. " I'll do that. But she seems determined to sample life in Priorsford. She says she's sure it must be exactly like Cranford. You must have told her a lot about it, for she asked for Miss Teenie Watson and Mrs. Duff-Whalley in the most familiar way."

Jean took a flying leap over a burn that meandered down the hillside, and said : " Isn't she an absurd child ? She used to say, ' Tell me about Priorsford,' when she came over to spend the day with me, and play with the babes in the nursery. Being the youngest she was rather lonely. Before we left Mintern Abbas she said she would come to Priorsford. Does she really mean it ? "

" Indeed she does. She's determined on it. Will it bore you to have her ? "

" Of course not, but—well, think of Malchester and then The Rigs ! But I daresay the very difference will amuse her. I'll write to her at once. . . ."

It had only been the telephone in the morning, the afternoon brought callers, all clamorous to know every detail of the burglary.

Pamela sat in the drawing-room and wrestled with them, and later was joined by Lewis. Four different carfuls of anxious neighbours came, and, having heard all there was to hear, departed, but about four o'clock Mrs. Duff-Whalley and her daughter were announced, and it was obvious that theirs would be a long visit.

" Dear Mrs. Elliot," the elder lady said, clasping Pamela's hand very tightly, " I simply had to come whenever I heard of it. What an upset for you ! Out-

rageous ! What are the police for, I'd like to know, if
not to guard us from such attacks. And no word of a
capture as far as I can hear."

She sat down with an angry bounce in the chair
Lewis pulled forward for her, and said to him, " I'd have
thought you'd have been out searching. There's no
saying where the gang may try next."

" You think it's a gang ? " Lewis asked mildly.

" Undoubtedly. Desperate men, I should say, and
very expert."

" Well," Lewis said, " the ladders tied with rope
didn't seem very professional, and certainly they're
not ' cat ' burglars. I wonder where they'll try
to-night ? "

" Not The Towers, I hope," said Mrs. Duff-Whalley.
" We've snibbed all our windows since ever the scare
began. If we don't get fresh air neither do we get
burglars ! Is it true that it was Jean's room they entered
and that the man fired at her ? "

" The story is being added to," Pamela said. " When
my sister-in-law woke she found a light on, and saw a
man standing at the window with her pearls in his hand
and the case on the carpet. She sprang forward to
try and recover the pearls, but he got out of the window
and she stuck her hand through a pane of glass. Her
pearls are gone and one or two other things, but, fortunately, nearly everything she possesses was put in the
bank before my brother left."

" Where is Jean ? " Lewis asked.

" In the nursery with Ninny and the children,"
Pamela told him. " When she was out this morning

we moved all her belongings to a little room next to
the children, so she'll feel snugly surrounded to-night."

" I *heard*," said Mrs. Duff-Whalley, " that they had
also tried Drykeld—the farm-house, you know, where
that Mr. Hamilton lives."

" Hamilton," said Lewis Elliot. " That reminds me,
Pamela, that I lunched the other day at the Club with
a man who told me that a cousin of his had come to
settle in this countryside. Patrick Hamilton. He was
a planter in Behar, and has come home and bought
the sheep-farm of Drykeld. I promised to look him up,
for, oddly enough, his brother was with our lot in France.
He was killed on the Somme : a thoroughly good
fellow."

" Oh," said Mrs. Duff-Whalley, bouncing excitedly on
her chair, " then are Mr. Hamilton's people quite all
right ? "

" I should say very much all right," Lewis said.

" But how very nice for you, Lewis," his wife said,
" to have the brother of your friend settled here. You
must call on him at once and ask him over. Perhaps
he would dine some night next week. You must try
and fix it up. Jean knows Mr. Hamilton. Doesn't
he run your Community Drama stunt, Mrs. Duff-
Whalley ? "

" Mr. Hamilton," said that lady, with dignity, " is
producing for us. We quite like him, don't we, Muriel ?
And of course, having lived in India, and not being just
a common farmer makes a difference. One has to be so
careful in these days, has one not ? And in Priorsford
one false step is fatal. If we didn't select our friends

very carefully we'd find ourselves inundated with all
sorts of undesirables. We, of course," she added with
a little laugh. " associate almost entirely with the
county : the others are too hopelessly provincial."

" Oh, Mother," murmured Muriel helplessly, while
Pamela said :

" You must talk to my sister-in-law about Priorsford
people. She professes to find jewels of great price in
that little town."

" Oh, well, we all know what Jean is," Mrs. Duff-
Whalley replied in tones of kindly patronage, " almost
too willing to see the best in people ; but as women of
the world, Mrs. Elliot, you and I can see. . . . Oh,
here are the boys ! Gervase I've seen at The Rigs,
but it's years since I saw David and Jock. Dear me !
What wild boys you were ! I was terrified when you
came to the house ! "

Jock grinned, but David, who saw no point in being
civil to a woman whom he had always disliked, merely
looked coldly at her and turned to speak to Lewis.

Presently the gong sounded for tea and Jean and
Miss Barton came in, followed by Peter and Alison.

Pamela took Alison's hand, saying : " Tea's in the
Chinese room to-day by Alison's special request. Come
along, darling, and help me to pour out. Lewis, bring
Mrs. Duff-Whalley."

Jean, walking with Muriel, explained that the children
loved the Chinese room. " Largely because of the wall-
paper ! " she said ; " they study it for hours and make
up stories about it. Lewis had a forebear who had a lot
to do with China, and he brought back most of the trea-

sures. I hated the room as a child and thought it smelt of pigtails, indeed it was rather a grim chamber until my sister-in-law came here, saw the possibilities of it, and had everything carefully cleaned and done up, and now with the cabinets and lovely rugs, and the china arranged properly, it's quite a different place, and very charming, I think you will agree."

It was not a very comfortable tea-party, for there was only one topic on which Mrs. Duff-Whalley cared to converse—the burglars, and Pamela, aware of the dread in Jean's eyes, was determined to keep her off it.

Never had Pamela talked with more fluency, never had she appeared more interested in the concerns of her guest. She discussed with her at length the merits of wintering abroad, the difficulty of shutting up a house, and the question of board wages. The moment a pause occurred and Mrs. Duff-Whalley turned towards Jean, her ferret-like face sharp with desire to know every detail of what had happened, Pamela adroitly managed to draw the attention of the table to herself, or the children, or the dogs. At last Mrs. Duff-Whalley, baffled, rose to go. She shook hands with her hostess, then went with her quick purposeful walk across to Jean, who stood with Jock by the fire.

" I needn't tell you, Jean, how Muriel and I feel for you in this dreadful experience. I don't suppose you'll ever forget it. A burglar actually in your room! I think it would kill me. And this is such a lonely house. Does that water outside not give you nightmare? It would me, but of course I'm very sensitive. But don't *dwell* on the awful episode. Just put it out of your mind.

Did you actually *see* the man ? Could you identify him ?
Did he make any effort to attack you or——"

" Did you leave your coat in the hall ? " Pamela asked.
" Ring, please, Lewis, and see if the chauffeur's taken
the car round. . . . It was most kind of you to come,
Mrs. Duff-Whalley, you and your daughter. . . .
Good-bye——"

Mrs. Duff-Whalley settled herself in the corner of
her car with a very ill grace.

" I never will," she said, " be able to feel at home with
Mrs. Elliot. There's something about her. . . . But
it's a lovely house. That Chinese room was very *chic*,
and everything about the tea-table was just the last
word. And her dress. . . . D'you think that swathed
style would suit me, Muriel ? It seems the very latest."

Muriel looked doubtful. " Mrs. Elliot's so tall. . . .
What a good-looking lot they are—all except Jock.
What d'you think of David ? "

" Conceited puppy. Did you notice the way he
looked at that Miss Barton ? If Jean doesn't take care,
she'll lose a secretary and gain a sister-in-law ! "

" I wonder," said Muriel. " Of course Miss Barton is
very pretty, but I doubt if David's the sort of man
that would marry a penniless girl. . . . Jean looks
very shaken, poor dear. I'm glad she has so many
to comfort her. Mrs. Elliot evidently didn't want the
burglary discussed before her."

" Affectation ! " said Mrs. Duff-Whalley. " I've no
patience with that sort of thing. I got no details at
all, and there was so much I wanted to know. . . .
Well, it's not likely she'll go to bed to-night with her

window open! Those pearls of hers must have been worth a mint of money, but they were more concerned with Jean's nerves than the jewels. . . . By the way, they seem inclined to take up Mr. Hamilton. Did you hear Lewis Elliot say he'd known his brother in France? I was thinking we might ask him to dinner, Muriel, next Thursday with the Tweedies. That's to say if we're not burgled before that!"

CHAPTER XXIV

"O gentle lady, do not put me to't :
For I am nothing if not critical."
                                        OTHELLO.

On the morning of the last day of the year Mirren
Strang sat by her living-room fire, on her lap a pile
of papers, while her writing-pad and fountain-pen lay
on the rug beside her.

The door opened and the parlour-maid's gentle voice
was heard to say : "Could you see Mrs. Lewis Elliot
for a few minutes, madam ?"

Mrs. Strang wheeled round. "Why, of course. . . .
Come in, my dear. No. I'm delighted to see you.
I *welcome* interruptions. I'm only writing cheques.
I found I was in arrears with everything, and I hate
to leave things just anyhow when the Old Year goes
out. One ought to start the New Year with some
degree of tidiness. I remember how my grandmother
used to finish up any bit of knitting or needlework that
was lying about, and say, 'Finish the Old Year's
work. The New Year will have enough to do with
itself.'"

Pamela Elliot was regarding with interest a bundle of
newspaper cuttings that lay on her friend's lap. "Do
tell me," she said, "are these reviews, by any chance ?"

"Some of them," said Mirren. "American." She

took up one and read it. " . . . Look at this. A press-clipping firm sends it and says, does it not tempt me to join their Bureau and receive others like it. I don't know why they should think it so tempting : it seems to me decidedly nasty. The reviewer says my characters erect smoke-screens between themselves and life, and finishes with, ' A sweet book with which to read oneself to sleep.' Pamela, I've a good mind to write a *really bad book*."

Pamela chuckled.

" You think I couldn't ? I'm afraid you're right. I don't know enough bad things to write about. . . . No, I'm afraid I must go on enraging critics who like strong meat. Happily, very few of them even glance in my direction."

" If I wrote a book," said Pamela, " I'd care nothing what any critic said, I'd be so amazed at my own cleverness. I simply can't think how you do it."

" Neither can I," said Mirren. " Come and be comfortable. I'll put these things out of the way. There now ! . . . It looks a miserable sort of day outside."

" It is rather wretched. But you've a glorious fire. Where is Miss Brand ? "

" Gone to Priorsford in the car to do the week's marketing. The shops 'll be shut for two days over the New Year. Has your party departed ? "

" Yes, and I'm very flat. That's why I'm selfishly disturbing your morning's work. Generally it's something of a relief to see a house-party go, but a family party's different."

" Everybody wouldn't agree with you," said Mrs.

Strang. "To many people a family party means the last word in dullness: but I'm bound to say you managed to be very cheerful at Laverlaw—in spite of the burglars."

"Oh, have you heard?"

"Heard what?"

"They've got the burglar. The police telephoned yesterday morning, and he was brought out to Priorsford to be charged. Lewis saw him."

"Him? Was there only one?"

"Yes. It's rather anti-climax after our talk of gangs and London professionals and so forth! And the smallest little man! Lewis said he was handcuffed to a very large policeman, which made it more absurd. It seems he started life as a gardener, but began almost at once to burgle. He has burgled for twenty years, and spent a large proportion of his time in jail, but he takes great credit to himself that he has never carried a weapon!"

"But tell me, how was he found, and where?"

"In Edinburgh, in a pawnshop, trying to dispose of Jean's pearls. The girl in the shop was suspicious and asked him to call again when her father was in the shop, and when he went back the police were waiting for him. The pearls are intact, but he seems to have got rid of a lot of his loot. He'll probably tell where it is before his trial, to get a lighter sentence. It's rather pathetic, for he had got a job somewhere and had kept straight for quite a time, but the work he was at came to an end and he could get nothing else. He came to Priorsford, hoping to be taken on as a gardener, but there was nothing for him. He had been lying out for nights and was really starving—that's why he took the meal at Balmoral. Poor little soul!"

" And what does Jean say ? "

"Jean!" Pamela Elliot's smile was both amused and tender. "Jean is relieved that the man is caught and glad that her pearls are safe, but her heart is wrung for the wrongdoer. You'd think she and she alone was responsible for his downfall."

Mirren looked thoughtfully into the fire as she said :

" I suppose we're all responsible in a way. . . . I think I know what Jean feels. It was a thousand pities it happened to her. It would have done the Duff-Whalley good to be burglared, it would have done a host of others no harm, but Jean will take it hard."

" Oh ! hard ! " echoed Pamela. " She means to go and see his wife—probably a receiver or resetter or whatever it's called—to make sure that she and her children don't starve while the man's in jail. I pointed out to her that she is no more responsible than any of the other victims, but all she says is : ' I know it's foolish of me, but I can't feel like that,' and goes her own way. I sometimes lose all patience with her— then again I find myself taking her part when David, with his worldly wisdom, and his superior ' My dear Jean,' starts to argue with her. . . . Oh, well, that's the end of the Priorsford burglar, and now we start a New Year—a thing I simply hate to do."

" But why ? The years are very good to you surely. I know few people as happy as you and Lewis."

Pamela hastily touched wood as she said :

" Oh, I know, I know. It's just because I've got so

much that I'm afraid. We might lose our worldly possessions, and I shouldn't mind so very much : my prayer is, ' Leave me Lewis.' You see we missed so much of our time together : through misunderstanding we didn't meet for years : we were middle-aged when we married, and the years race past and we'll soon be old. If *only* it were possible to hold back the years and stop as we are ! ''

Pamela laughed at her own absurdity, and Mirren shook her head as she quoted :

> " Time, like an ever-rolling stream,
>   Bears all its sons away . . .''

" Be thankful, though, you feel like that, when others are so miserable that they seek for death as for hid treasure.''

" Not many of them," said Pamela. " I think most people enjoy life immensely—I mean, of course, ordinary, comfortable, healthy people—and grudge the years passing. And even with the quite poor, with whom it's always a struggle to make ends meet, just think how whole-heartedly they throw themselves into the pleasures of a public holiday, what a zest they have for living ! It's a good world for many, even now when trade is almost as bad as it can be, and there doesn't seem a single corner at peace. The only thing to do, it seems to me, is to try not to think of all the horrors that are going on, and if we throw our weight on the side of decency that's all that can be expected of us. So long as you help when you see help will be of use, it's foolish to make oneself miserable about the world at large—as Jean does.''

"Well, that's my way of thinking," said Mirren:
"it's also, I may add, most people's way! That's why
I have a secret admiration for Jean. There's only a few
of her sort, but they make a difference. . . . Pamela,
stay to luncheon. You'd be doing me a kindness."

"May I really? I was rather hoping you would ask
me, for Lewis is in Edinburgh for the day and I hate
to eat alone."

"Perhaps," said Mirren, "I should have warned you
before you accepted that you're likely to get a poor meal.
Rebecca Brand grows more morose with every day of
the dying year. She's been reading the newspapers—
things she never touched under happier circumstances
—and is much struck by the call of some of our members
of Parliament for national economy, consequently she
has been urging cook to send us up things like 'Shep-
herd's Pie'—almost meatless, and horrid concoctions
of baked beans: while eggs and butter and cream are
being cut down ruthlessly."

"Why do you stand it?" Pamela asked.

"I'm sure I don't know. Because I'm a fool, I
suppose. Fortunately it won't last long. Rebecca 'll
cheer up with the New Year and forget about economy,
and I daresay a fast's good for us after Christmas fare;
besides, cook may have rebelled to-day: let's hope so."

She picked up a book and held it out to her guest.

"Have you seen this? It's being much lauded.
I've only just begun it, and so far am not impressed;
but then I'm not much interested in the reactions of a
child of ten to a pig being killed."

"Oh, that sort of book!" said Pamela. "I'm afraid

I'd erect a smoke-screen, as your heroines are accused of doing by the reviewer. . . . Mrs. Duff-Whalley was rather delicious the other day about the Book Club. ' I joined it,' she said, in a sort of aggrieved way, ' because I haven't time to waste over rubbish, and I was told I could depend on having a selection of the best.' She gave a contemptuous snort. ' The last one they sent was about the lowest sort of people : people no nice person would care to read about : coarse : and the language . . .! I simply posted it back and said I wondered *at* them.' "

Mirren laughed as she said : " The Duff-Whalley always knows her own mind. By the way, are you going abroad this spring ? "

" I think not. Not with Biddy away. Though Jean doesn't really need us, we couldn't go away with easy minds. Besides, I'm enjoying winter at Laverlaw immensely, and it's pure bliss to Lewis. We were just wondering together last night why we ever go away in winter. Weather doesn't much matter to healthy people ; besides, so far, it's been an easy winter. I've seen such wonderful sunsets. . . ."

Mirren agreed. " My recollection of this winter is coming up the North Gate with the sun so full in my eyes that I couldn't recognize people—and that's no exaggeration. I had an argument with Rebecca about it only last night. She *threepit* with me that it had rained nearly every day since October. Such nonsense ! It may be true what she says, that she's never gone out without a mackintosh, but—oh, here she is—Hallo, Rebecca ! "

Rebecca came into the room clothed in a drab water-proof and in her hand a paper which she studied with a frown.

" I must say," she began, then stopped on perceiving a visitor.

" Good-morning, Mrs. Elliot. Mrs. Strang, did you want foolscap size or the other ? "

" The other," said Mirren.

" Well, I've got foolscap. And butter's up. I asked the girl in the shop what made it go up and down like that, but she said she didn't know. And Johnston had no decent pears or grapes—nothing but apples and bananas ; and only turnips and brussels-sprouts in the way of vegetables—not even a cauliflower. They were expecting everything in by the two train, but of course that was no good to me."

Mrs. Strang tried to soothe her worried companion.

" It doesn't matter, Rebecca ; we won't starve. Mrs. Elliot is staying to luncheon."

The news did nothing to raise Rebecca's spirits. " I wish I'd known," she said darkly : " it's not a visitor's lunch, but perhaps Mrs. Elliot won't——"

" Oh, I'm not what the seedsmen's catalogues call ' a gross feeder,' " that lady assured her. " Breakfast's my meal, and I can miss luncheon without noticing it if I see any prospect of a substantial tea."

" Same here," said Mirren. " . . . Do take off that coat, Rebecca : I can't bear to see you in it."

" Why, it's the most useful thing I've got. I simply live in it."

" That's what I object to."

" Besides," Rebecca continued, " what does it matter what one wears in this dreary weather ? "

" What one wears *always* matters to the people we meet, the people we live with, and most of all to ourselves."

Mirren stood on a hearth-rug and made her speech.

" A soiled dressing-gown and down-at-heel slippers must have a bad effect on one's moral nature. That drab mackintosh of yours colours your whole outlook on life. . . . When I find myself regarding life as a dismal dirty business, I go to my room and tidy my drawers, then I do my hair and my nails and put on fresh clothes, and come down feeling, no matter what the season or the weather, that the year's at the spring."

Pamela applauded, but Rebecca only sniffed.

" You can't," she said, " expect ordinary people to have the high falutin' ideas that writers have. I like to save my clothes until there's somebody to see them. Two women don't need to dress for each other."

She left the room pursued by groans.

CHAPTER XXV

" . . . the skirts of the departing year."

CHARLES LAMB.

JEAN could not help being slightly ashamed of her feeling of pleasure at being back at The Rigs. Pamela Elliot had been genuinely and understandingly kind, everything possible had been done to make the Laverlaw party a happy one, and if the advent of the burglar had poisoned all Jean's enjoyment, that was no one's fault.

" Although," Pamela had said to her sister-in-law in parting, " I must say I do think it is gross mismanagement on the part of a hostess to allow guests to be accosted by burglars ! . . . You're not going to let the thought of it worry you, Jean ? "

Jean had said many pretty things which came from her heart, and had driven away with Alison and Quentin —Peter was to follow later with Mhor and Jock— thinking how amazingly lucky she was in her " in-laws." She felt surprise that she was not more regretful about leaving Laverlaw, but on that dreary day The Rigs looked such a homely refuge, and Mrs McCosh, straight from cooking the lunch, standing on the door-step in her print dress and big white apron, looked as safe and steady as the Lea Pen.

" My," she said, " it's fine to get ye back," and Jean could have hugged her where she stood.

And when they trooped into the living-room, with its yellow walls holding sunshine on the greyest days, on the writing-table lay a pile of letters.

"These a' came this morning," Mrs. McCosh explained. "An' I *thocht* that was frae his lordship ; I pit it on the top."

But Jean had already sat down on the rug and was tearing open the envelope.

"There's a gey wheen parcels forbye what we sent up to Laverlaw," Mrs. McCosh went on.

"Oh, Mummy, let me open them," pleaded Alison. "Peter opened all the last."

Jean looked up for a second. "Ask Barty to help you, and don't mix things so that I shan't know who to thank for what," she said, and began again to devour her letter. Her way with a letter was to glance hurriedly through it to the end to make sure that all was well, then begin again at the beginning and go over it slowly, savouring every word.

Betty Barton and Alison unpacked the parcels in the dining-room, with Quentin and Ninny as an interested audience, and Jean was left in peace with the precious epistle from the other side of the world. She sighed in a satisfied way when at last she put it beside others in a drawer of the bureau. "To-morrow," she said to herself, "to-morrow I'll be able to say, ' next month Biddy comes home.' The end of February. We've got Christmas over, and he will see spring come at Mintern Abbas. Two more months. . . . If only every one keeps well . . ."

At lunch Alison remarked : "At Laverlaw it's lovely

and always like a party, but Mrs. McCosh's dinners are the best."

Jean felt it her duty to make some remark about comparisons being odious, then she smiled at Miss Barton and said : " Alison's like me, she prefers plain things, but few would agree with her. Mrs. McCosh is a good plain cook, but the Laverlaw cook is an artist."

Miss Barton laid down her spoon and said in her definite way : " Laverlaw is delightful ' for a stop,' as Mr. Salteena would say ; I confess I rather love luxury, I suppose because it's still new to me."

" Mr. Salteena," said Jean. " How much I adore that book. I never tire of it, and laugh as much every time I read it. No, Alison, you're not old enough. Some day I'll read it to you and Peter. . . . And, Alison, there's a letter from Daddy, and he says he may very possibly be home at the end of February or beginning of March. Isn't that great news ? "

" Oh, Mummy, may I tell Peter when he comes ? Quentin, d'you hear, Daddy's coming home and we'll all go back to Mintern Abbas."

Quentin regarded her solemnly over the glass of water he was drinking. Presently he said : " Quentin 'll stay with Mrs. McCosh."

Alison stared, horrified at her young brother, who was now busily engaged with a spoon in his right hand and a bit of bread in his left, shovelling minced meat and vegetables into his mouth, then turned to her mother crying : " He's not glad that Daddy's coming home."

" He'll be glad when he sees him," Jean assured her,

while Betty Barton said politely: "How is Lord Bidborough? Is he still in New Zealand?"

Jean nodded. "Having a very good time, I think. They've been staying with some friends of Major Talbot's and doing all sorts of interesting things. I'll read you some of the descriptions of places if it won't bore you. I think they ought to be in Australia now, and they hope to sail for home about the end of January or earlier. Tim seems marvellously well, and stronger than he's been for years. It *has* been worth while. And to think I was so unwilling to let Biddy go. No, not perhaps outwardly, but I know how unwilling I was in my heart. There seemed so many awful things that might happen. And even now—well, I'll never have a really peaceful moment till we are all together again at Mintern Abbas. But of course that's sheer silliness and mustn't be encouraged. If only I could cultivate a calm and tranquil state of mind."

Betty Barton helped herself to an oatcake, a ball of butter, a piece of cheese, remarking as she did so:

"Try reading Ecclesiastes: it's about the most satisfying book I know. I always go to it when I feel like despairing of life."

Jean could not but smile as she listened. Here was a girl, charming to look at, clever and capable, in the first pride of her youth, talking about despairing of life!

She looked at her secretary and said quite irrelevantly:

"Did you enjoy your Christmas, Barty?"

"Yes, thank you, very much." Miss Barton was again the perfect secretary. "Mrs. Elliot is such a delightful hostess she allows no one to feel out of it."

" And I'm sure she found you a great help, as well as a most appreciative guest. We're invited to dine at Laverlaw next Wednesday, to meet Mr. Hamilton. I rather think Mrs. Duff-Whalley and Muriel will be there too."

" Oh, that reminds me," said Betty, " there was a telephone message asking if Tuesday would suit for a rehearsal at The Towers. I said if they heard no word it would be all right."

" But I thought we arranged that the next rehearsal would be here," said Jean.

" Oh! Perhaps Mrs. Duff-Whalley feels she has more control over us at The Towers. What a nuisance that stupid play's going to be."

" I enjoy it," Jean confessed, " but, then, I've no responsibility. . . . Are you going out this afternoon, Barty? Too many arrears? I see. Well, it isn't very tempting, but I want to call on the Miss Watsons. I can sympathize with them now as I couldn't before. . . . It was so much worse for them. I could fly from the scene of my terror and come back to this kind, safe little house, but they've got to live in constant remembrance."

" They'll feel better now that the man's been got."

" I suppose so. Oh, Barty, have you got that address from the police? "

" I have," said Miss Barton. " It's an address somewhere in Leith. . . . I know, of course, that it's not my place to make any remark, but, honestly, I think it's most unwise to have anything to do with the woman. The man has often been in jail: she will have her own ways of managing, and, anyway, you are in no way responsible. However, if you feel you must do something, let me go and see the woman and find out what sort of creature she is. She may be worse than the man. It would be fatal to write; what's to hinder her telling you any old lie—half a dozen children and so forth."

"I daresay you're right," Jean agreed meekly. "You're full of common sense, Barty, but don't look with too jaundiced an eye on the poor soul. Oh, yes, I know I sluice pity about and am a nuisance to myself and my friends; I'm sorry, but there it is. . . ."

The Miss Watsons received their visitor with emotion.

"How little we thought," said Miss Teenie, "when you were so kind and sympathetic to us, that you were to have the same dreadful experience."

"The same!" said her sister. "Far worse. Lady Bidborough actually *clutched* the ruffian."

"No," said Jean, keeping very serious, "I didn't actually touch him; as a matter of fact, I aimed too high and put my hand through the window. I had gone to sleep with the window well up from the bottom —I doubt if I ever shall again!—or I might have been wakened by the noise of it going up and saved my treasures."

"And mebbe lost your life," said Miss Teenie. "It was all for the best."

"It's just a little disappointing," her sister said, "that it wasn't a gang, but only one man, and a wee one at that. I saw him, you know. Yes, I happened to be down in the town, shopping, and as I passed the

police-station a great big policeman came out handcuffed to a wee thin man. He was such a shilpit bit
creature that the handcuffs looked ridiculous. It
would have been liker the thing if the policeman had
led him along by an ear. You can imagine how I
stared. That was the villain that had come up our
stairs and walked about our rooms while we were
sleeping! I wonder what he's done with my mother's
work-box. The gramophone was found in the next-
door garden, of course, you know? . . . Lady Bidborough, I fair shuddered when I looked at him, for
it's always been a terror to me that I might get mixed
up with the demi-monde. You never know, and I
once read an awful book about a decent woman, just
like Teenie or me, who got mixed up quite innocently
in some plot, and found herself down among Chinamen
and trap-doors opening into the Thames. It made
your blood run cold, and though it all came right in
the end, I've never been able to think of that book.
D'you suppose it's true, Miss Jean, about those Chinamen and dope and gangsters and—and—— ? "

"The under-world?" Jean prompted, and Miss
Teenie broke in :

"Stop talking, Aggie, do. I want to hear all about
the Laverlaw burglary. We could imagine it all, for
we've been at Laverlaw twice : once about the Cripple
Children, once when our Sunday School had its summer
trip there. It's grand of course, but rather eerie-
looking. It just reminded me of the old ballad where
soldiers stood round the castle walls and a girl was
thrown out of a window on to the top of them—you

remember, Aggie, William Welsh used to sing it ?
. . . A fearsome place to have a burglar. You must
have been half out of your mind when you wakened
and saw him."

Jean laughed rather shakily and said : " As a matter
of fact, I made a great fuss, screaming at the top of my
voice. Happily the children never woke, so they got
no fright and thought it all rather good fun. I felt
I hadn't been nearly sorry enough for you."

" Oh, yes, you were," the ladies assured her, " and we
quite enjoyed our Christmas in spite of the fright. It
made every one extra kind, you know what I mean.
We were out to every meal."

" Every meal," echoed Miss Teenie. " Turkey three
times—that's unprecedented with us. And Mr. Elliot
sent us pheasants, and Mrs. Elliot sent us lovely fruit
as well as that bowl of hyacinths—aren't they sweet ?
—and she said we were to *keep the bowl*. I think
that was so thoughtful, for if you've got a bowl to return it's always on your mind. . . . Oh, are you going
already ? "

Jean explained that she wanted to see Miss Hutton
before the year was out, and in a whirl of words and
good wishes left Balmoral, and presently was being
admitted into her friend's parlour.

After greeting her Jean looked round the room she
loved. " How decorous you are, Miss Janet, with your
books piled so tidily, and everything in place. Not
quite so seasonable, though, as the Miss Watsons,
who have put all their cards on the mantelpiece, and
made all the pictures squint with poking holly behind

them. The presents are ranged on the window-seat, and they have so many bowls of bulbs that some have to stand on the floor. They are so happy about everybody's kindness that it has almost made up for their fright."

"And what about you yourself?" Miss Hutton asked. "I'm glad to hear the man's been got."

"Yes," said Jean: "a poor little half-starved creature. It seems so absurd all this fuss."

"But however small and starved he took the jewels, Jean."

"Oh, yes, and he'll pay for it by years in jail. It's quite right of course. . . . Miss Janet, don't you think I should go and see his wife? or at least do something about her?"

Janet Hutton let her knitting lie in her lap as she looked over her spectacles at her questioner.

"I don't see why not. But Miss Barton would be the one to go. She's more accustomed to dealing with people."

"You mean, not so easily taken in? I daresay you're right. And what sort of Christmas have you had?"

"A very pleasant one. I dined at Hopetoun, as I always do, and Mrs. Hope was in great form, and that made Augusta happy, and I don't know when I enjoyed an evening so much. I've been really quite gay, what with lunches and teas and people coming in with gifts and good wishes. . . . Now tell me about yours."

"It couldn't have been nicer. Pamela and Lewis were kindness itself, and Laverlaw is so lovely always, and the boys were there, all three . . . But do tell me, have you seen Mrs. Jowett ? How is she ? I got a poor account from the boys."

Miss Hutton's face was grave as she said : " Not very well, I'm afraid. I saw her for a few minutes on Christmas Eve, but she really wasn't able to speak to me. She ought to be in bed, but she drags herself down every day to that drawing-room couch simply to make things easier for ' Tim.' And she was going to try and sit at table and eat her Christmas dinner. It's martyrdom : but that poor husband of hers wilfully shuts his eyes."

Presently Jean got up to go in spite of her friend's protests.

" Jock and Mhor and Peter will all be back by this time, and I must get home, and oh, Miss Janet, Biddy expects to be back in the end of February ! Only two more months. He'll be sailing very soon. . . . I simply daren't let myself think about it : it seems too much of happiness. . . . Good-bye, dear Miss Janet. I'll wish you what I heard one man wish another in Priorsford—*The awfullest luck ever ye kent !* "

CHAPTER XXVI

" I have a journey, Sir, shortly to go,
    My master calls me. I must not say no."

KING LEAR.

JOCK spent New Year's Day at The Rigs and went back to London the next day. As Miss Barton was motoring into Edinburgh he decided to go with her and take the two-o'clock train. His sister suggested that the ten-o'clock train from Priorsford would be better, but he would have none of it.

He said, " I never want to be in London a minute before I can help it. With the two train I get back in time to go to bed. I wish I needn't go back at all. I've a good mind to settle down at The Rigs with Mrs. McCosh."

" And do nothing ? "

" I could work as well here as anywhere else—better in fact." He rumpled up his hair and said : " I'll never do any good in the office, Jean : the intricacies are beyond me, and if ever I did get any distance up and had to take control, I'd probably find myself in jail very shortly through sheer inability to understand the workings. . . . Mayn't I come to The Rigs, Jean ? "

Jean looked at her brother questioningly. Was he really in earnest ?

" Try it for another six months, Jock, dear. It would

be too feeble to throw it all up without giving it a proper trial. When Biddy comes home we'll talk it over ; he may have something to suggest. And of course you can have The Rigs any time, you know that. . . . Here comes Barty and the letters."

Jean immediately began to open envelopes, while Jock attended to Miss Barton's wants, and incidentally sought her advice about remaining on at the office.

" It's a good opening," Betty reminded him. " Just think how many there are who would be thankful for it."

" Oh, I know," Jock agreed. " There are dozens of men who were with me at Oxford, most of them better scholars, all of them quicker in the uptake, and they simply can't get a bally thing to do. And people rave about the youth of our country having lost the spirit of adventure, and asking why they don't all go to the Colonies and carve out careers for themselves. But these men have little or no capital, and the Colonies don't want them. And those who are lucky enough to have found jobs make so little as a rule that they literally can't afford to go out. One man told me that he couldn't go to dances because he couldn't afford the boiled shirts and the small expenses like tips and taxis. And the worst of it is they've no prospect of better things. Youth's having a pretty rotten time just now, as well as lots of others."

" Yes," Miss Barton agreed. " This generation had a pretty poor deal. You can't wonder that they're resentful."

Jean turned round with an envelope in her hand,

saying : " Here's one from Agnes, Jock. I wrote and told her we'd be glad to see her. . . ." She opened the letter—a long one—and glanced over the sheets. " The child says nothing—Oh, yes—she wants to come on the 9th. Will that be all right, Barty ? It's Lady Agnes Chatham. You know her parents have gone a trip to South Africa, and she's visiting about till they come back."

Betty Barton looked rather startled. " Lady Agnes coming here ! " she said.

" I know." Jean answered the tone rather than the words. " I'm afraid she may find it rather dull, but it's her own wish. She's always had a desire to see Priorsford, and has listened to so many stories about it from Jock and me that she knows most of the people by names, and asks familiarly for Bella Bathgate and Mrs. McCosh ! "

" Oh," said Jock, " you needn't worry about Agnes. She'll enjoy herself immensely. I wish I could be here and take her round and show her things."

" But can't you, Jock ? What about a week-end ? You could surely manage that ? "

" Ye—es, I might. How long is Agnes going to stay ? "

" As long as she likes," said Jean. " How pleased the children will be. Agnes was always the most welcome visitor to the nursery. . . . By the way, where are Peter and Alison ? "

" They swallowed their breakfasts and rushed off with Mhor," said Miss Barton.

" There must be mischief afoot," Jock said. " . . . What a day for a tramp ! Look at the white clouds

scudding. . . . I wish I were on the top of Cademuir
instead of on my way back to the prison-house. D'you
want to go now, Miss Barton? I'll rush round to The
Neuk and see if my things are all packed."

" There's no hurry," Miss Barton assured him. " If
we leave at two o'clock that'll be ample time. . . .
I'll rout out the children. I don't think they realize
you're going to-day."

" What'll you do till train-time," Jean asked.
" Barty's got to be back early or we wouldn't hurry you
away."

" Lots to do," Jock told her. " I want to go to the
Castle, for one thing : it's the sort of day Edinburgh
looks its most beautiful."

Miss Barton left the room, and the brother and sister
smiled at each other.

" Dear Jock," said Jean, " I wish you weren't going
away : it's always such a comfort to have you near.
It's been a nice Christmas, hasn't it ? "

" Couldn't have been better. Take care of yourself,
Jean, and don't worry about burglars or their depend-
ents. Learn to harden your heart, my dear : that's
the best advice I can give you."

" Thank you, darling, but I haven't noticed that your
own is adamant."

" Oh, bless you, I'm getting quite ruthless. Living
in London one gets taken in so often. . . . Well, I'll try
and come up for a week-end. I might get away on the
Friday night and that would give me Saturday and
Sunday."

" Yes," said Jean, " we'd send either to Galashiels

or Symington for you and you'd be here for breakfast.
We'd all love it, and Agnes would be pleased—you and
she have always been friends."

Jock agreed, adding, " We both hate the same things.
Well, I'd better be off."

When the car had departed for Edinburgh, Jean
hurried through her morning duties that she might
have time to see Mrs. Jowett before luncheon. Miss
Hutton's report had not been cheering, and Jean
wondered if the invalid would be able to see her at all,
but when she reached The Knowe the maid who admitted
her smiled a welcome, and said her mistress was " just
about it," and would she please come in.

The drawing-room was full of spring flowers and pale
January sunlight, but Jean's heart sank as she looked
at her friend. The week had made a difference : she
seemed to have receded a little further, her face was more
waxen, her lips a fainter pink.

She held out her hands to the visitor crying : " So
you're back, dear. We've missed you. . . . Oh, I'm
much stronger to-day and able to hear all your ad-
ventures. And you must look at all my pretty things
. . . presents, yes."

" You look like a crocus," said Jean ; " that mauve
with the pale yellow is lovely. . . . Do the crocuses
still come up round that beech tree on the lawn ? They
used to be so lovely, like a fairy ring."

" Oh, yes, more and more every year. Tim is so
proud of them. He had me photographed sitting among
them last spring ; he must show it you : it makes a
pretty picture."

" I must remember to ask," said Jean. " And here we are with a brand New Year, and the crocuses will be out again before we know ! "

" I liked Peter's present best of all," said Mrs. Jowett.

" Did you, I'm so glad. It was entirely his own idea. He said one day : ' I'll make a box for Mrs. Jowett,' and Mhor helped him a good deal. At present they are busy making a bank in the play-house at The Neuk. Mhor is so neat-handed, he's fitted up a wonderful counter. And you should see the cheque-books neatly printed by hand ! We've all been induced to contribute some capital to the Priorsford Bank, sums ranging from 2d. to 2s. 6d., but in spite of our fine cheque-books I doubt if we'll ever see our money again ! "

Mrs. Jowett laid her hand on Jean's as she said :

" I did so enjoy the boys' visit. Mhor is a great fellow, and absurdly good-looking for a boy. I remember those lovely curly lashes. Jock is just the same. I'm so glad I've seen him again. I used to wish I had a son like Jock. . . . I wish it more than ever now."

Jean put a cushion right, and tucked in the eiderdown where it had slipped and said : " I think I ought to go now. I'm making you talk, and that's so tiring."

" Oh, no, please stay and tell me what you did at Laverlaw. I won't talk ; I'll listen, and it gives me something to think about when I'm alone."

" Laverlaw was lovely," said Jean, " and Pamela did everything that was humanly possible to make things perfect for the children and for us all. Such a Christmas Tree ! Everything chosen with so much care and thought, not just ordered haphazard as so many presents are. And Mirren Strang had such a pretty party, and the burglar arrived! Altogether a most varied visit, and now that Christmas is over I feel as if I'd got over a big hurdle and can look forward to Biddy's home-coming. He *thinks* the end of February. Oh, dear Mrs. Jowett, *you* won't laugh at me. I can tell you how I'm longing for him. It seems like years since he went away. . . . They're all so kind, and they're always giving me advice, even my dear Jock, and of course I know it's for my good. 'Try and be this, Jean, or be that.' But Biddy doesn't want me changed, he likes me as I am."

Jean mopped her eyes and laughed at her own absurdity as she knelt beside the sick woman, who stroked the golden-brown head, as she said com-fortingly: "None of us want you changed, Jean, dear, but I expect your people don't like to think of you being taken in: there are so many cheating people in the world. . . ."

"Have you met many, Mrs. Jowett?"

"No, I haven't; I've been amazingly fortunate. I can't at the moment recall a single unpleasant person. Some, of course, one liked better than others. Mrs. Duff-Whalley used to make me feel rather jarred, she spoke one down so—but that's all over long ago, and she sent me a pot of calf's-foot jelly for Christmas, made by herself. That's one thing, Jean, about being ill, every one turns their best side to the invalid."

"They could hardly help it," said Jean, "when you are the invalid. But best or worst, it's high time I went ; I'm afraid I've overtired you sadly." She stood looking down at her friend, and Mrs. Jowett, smiling at her, said :

" Don't you know I want every minute I can get of my dear friends ? The time is short."

CHAPTER XXVII

" No epilogue, I pray you : for your play needs no epilogue."
                              A MIDSUMMER NIGHT'S DREAM.

THE New Year spurred Mrs. Duff-Whalley to furious
activity over the play they had entered for competition
in the coming Drama Festival.

" Simply nothing is being done," she told her daughter.
" Here is January, the thing takes place in February, and
not one of you is word perfect, let alone anything else.
Mr. Hamilton may call himself a producer, but so far
he's produced precious little. What's all this nonsense
of his about where people stand ? I'm sure he wasted
half an hour moving you all about because either you
were all in a line, or one obscured another. The great
thing, it seems to me, is that it should look natural,
like real life, and I'm sure in real life we must often be
standing all in a line, or obscuring each other. You'll
be like a lot of automatons before he's done with you."

" But after all," Muriel pointed out, " Mr. Hamilton's
the only one who knows anything at all about it,
except, perhaps, Miss Barton, and we must follow his
instructions. . . . I must say there's something very
silly about the way Rosalind Tweedie giggles, and that
young Forbes is quite inaudible, he somehow seems to
swallow his words. . . . Have you heard how many
teams are going in for the Festival ? "

Mrs. Duff-Whalley looked about for a letter, found it, and gave the desired information. " Seven. Three of them Rural Institutes."

" The Rurals are very good as a rule ; they're so keen. I shouldn't wonder if we were at the very foot."

" That's so like you, Muriel "—her mother's eyes were bright with anger—" always the inferiority complex. Like your father. That was his way. ' Oh, don't let's worry about bettering our position, let's be comfortable.' So feeble. Now, Muriel, when the players come here to-night try and get some spirit put into the thing. I want *you* to shine at the production. Don't let Miss Barton have it all her own way. Oh, I know she's very good-looking, and she gets very vivacious when she begins to act. It'll go down well with an audience, but I can't say I like it myself. Now you are quiet and distangy, but you would need to put more spirit into your part. . . . Isn't Mr. Hamilton bringing some one to play the young soldier ? It's an amazing thing that in a place like Priorsford so few men will come forward to act ! "

" Well, Mother, you ask so much."

" Merely, Muriel, that they should be of our class."

" Oh, class ! Very soon there 'll be no classes."

" And what a calamity that will be," said Mrs. Duff-Whalley solemnly, as she set off to see the cook. At the door she paused and asked : " Will one kind of sandwich be enough, along with egg and cress rolls ? "

Muriel considered, and said : " I should think so, but remember that acting's hungry work, and most of the players are young, so let there be masses of food."

She sat on in the dining-room after her mother left, sat on while the maid was removing the breakfast dishes. She was dreaming, in the way so often deplored by her mother, but it was noticeable that whereas her mouth had almost constantly had a downward turn, now it turned up as if a smile were not far away, and her eyes had a contented look, hitherto absent.

That evening Mrs. Duff-Whalley began as she meant to continue. As soon as the company had gathered she rapped on the table with a large tortoise-shell paper knife, and said in her best " committee " manner : " I would like to suggest that we keep our attention entirely fixed on what we are doing. We are just a little apt, are we not, to stray into conversation about trifles, gossip and so forth, which impedes the action of the play." She looked round and added kindly : " We can gossip over our coffee, can we not ? "

She sat down well pleased with her effort, and Mr. Hamilton, looking chastened, prepared to begin. He had brought with him a friend, one Nigel Montgomery, who lived ten miles or so down Tweed, to play a young English soldier, and he now told that youth to start with his lines.

" ' *Where can Brian be ?* ' " he read from his book. " ' *It is so long since they came for him I begin to fear some evil has befallen him.*' I say, isn't that rather wooden? I don't believe any English soldier 'd speak like that. Mayn't I change it ? I could say : ' *What's happened to that blighter Brian, he's been gone a long time.*' "

" All right," said Mr. Hamilton. " Now, Miss Tweedie."

The girl rushed at her first sentence, like a horse at a hurdle.

" ' I shudder to think what may have happened to him. It seemed to me that he had a premonition of doom.' "

The producer looked at her ruefully.

" Miss Tweedie," he said, " d'you really think those words would be spoken in quite such a jaunty tone ? Remember the position of these wretched people, caught trying to escape, in the hands of the Soviet, in hourly expectation of the worst happening. One of the company has been removed by a jailer, the others are waiting for his return, sick with anxiety. The play "—he avoided Mrs. Duff-Whalley's eyes—" is poorly written, but even through the stilted words surely you can feel the horror ? Say it brokenly—you know what I mean ? "

" I'm afraid I don't," said Rosalind, still radiantly cheerful. " D'you mean like this : ' I shudder to *think* —what—may have happened to him ? ' "

" No," said Mr. Hamilton, " not like that. Put some feeling into your voice."

" But who am I supposed to be speaking *to* ? " asked the girl. " Mr. Montgomery ? Or do I look round the circle so to speak ? "

" Look at no one," the producer told her. " You're speaking to yourself, as much as any one, so your tone should be low and intense. At present it's as high and clear as a schoolboy's."

" Oh, all right, I'll try again. ' I *shudder* to think ' . . . No, that's worse."

" Suppose," said Miss Barton, " suppose some one told you suddenly that your mother had been in a motor accident, what d'you think you'd say ? "

" I don't know, but I'd likely say, ' I hope to *goodness* she's not hurt.' But that's not the same, because, after all a mother's a mother, but as far as I can make out, this Brian's nothing to me. He belongs to Muriel, doesn't he ? You go on, Muriel. I'll practise at home."

" ' Something has happened,' " said Muriel, as Lady Elsie, in a curious falsetto voice, which, however, brought forth no adverse criticism from the producer. " ' He pretended that it was nothing, that they merely wanted some information they thought he had ; he was brave and gay, he jested as he went with the jailer, but we shall never see him again. Mother, oh Mother ! ' " She knelt at Betty Barton's knee, who regarded her stricken daughter coldly, merely remarking :

" ' *Hush, child. Remember who you are, and that England demands courage from her daughters. As a diplomat's wife, I have repeatedly been in danger but have never shown fear. We have great traditions, my child ; let us live up to them.*' "

Thus far she got, then stopped and addressed Patrick Hamilton :

" Couldn't we change if not the sentiment at least the language ? We'll never get that stilted stuff over."

Before the producer could reply Mrs. Duff-Whalley broke in with :

" What *can* you mean, Miss Barton ? *I* think the

10

language is beautiful, and most appropriate. Remember, please, you are acting a *countess*."

" Oh, I know," said Betty. " By the way, how did she happen to be there ? Rather tactless to imprison English people of rank. Altogether it's a very far-fetched story."

" Perhaps," said Nigel Montgomery, " it's really Communist propaganda. Some of the sentiments are so odd (not to speak of the English) that it might easily have been written by a Russian gentleman of Bolshevik leanings."

But Mrs. Duff-Whalley looked sternly at the young man as she said : " In view of what has happened, and alas ! is still happening in Russia, flippancy about that distressing country is most unseemly. I confess the latest of Russia's plans horrify me. Oh, by the way, Mr. Hamilton, I don't suppose I need ask your politics, for there is only one party a decent man can belong to in these days, and I want you to come to a meeting I am getting up. Our candidate and his wife are to be there, and several good speakers. Something must be done to protect our own country. Between Communist propaganda and the dole, one simply doesn't know what is going to happen. I keep protesting against these married girls furnishing their parlours off the dole, and all I get is abuse. I heard one say to another as I passed the other day : ' *There goes the old besom*,' but I don't care : I can't see my country go over the precipice without a word."

Mr. Hamilton assented, and after a pause said : " Perhaps we'd better get on with the play " ; and

Mrs. Duff - Whalley sat down in her chair rather flushed.

The rehearsal was got through at last. That it was a poor play there was no shadow of a doubt, but Patrick Hamilton managed to put some life into both it and his fellow actors. Muriel especially brightened amazingly when he was near.

They discussed the play along with the coffee and sandwiches.

" It's so odd," said Jean, " that with all the ingredients of tragedy, in the end it turns out to be comedy. Doesn't it almost sound as if the author had lost control and it had just happened so ? "

" I think," said Mrs. Duff-Whalley, " that it is a very nice piece, and will be a pleasant change both from these silly fantastic plays and the vulgar, would-be funny things that are so often produced. But of course," she eyed the performers sternly, " *everything* will depend on the acting. . . . When shall we meet again ? "

" We must rehearse twice a week," Patrick Hamilton put in.

" Won't you come to The Rigs ? " said Jean. " It's too bad to trouble Mrs. Duff-Whalley every time."

But Mrs. Duff-Whalley waved the suggestion away, saying :

" The Towers drawing-room is in every way more suitable, and as I started the project I must see it through. I never grudge trouble. Shall we make it Tuesday and Friday ? "

This was agreed, and Jean said to her hostess as they were leaving : " I'm to have a girl staying with me, a friend from home, may I bring her to a rehearsal? And perhaps you and Muriel will dine with us one evening? I want to give her a good time. Rosalind, Agnes Chatham's about your age, and you must help me to amuse her."

CHAPTER XXVIII

"... Had she been light like you,
Of such a merry, nimble, stirring spirit."
LOVE'S LABOUR'S LOST.

MRS. McCOSH was making the paste for an apple tart, when Bella Bathgate came into the kitchen with a shawl round her head.

"I just looked in for a minute," she explained, "to tell ye there's a missionary speaking at the Guild the night, and she'll be verra interestin', I've no doubt, so if ye can come I'll ca' in for ye."

Mrs. McCosh shook her head. "That's whit I canna dae, ma woman. We've a veesitor comin' the night—Lady Agnes Something-or-other, a Duke's daughter, nae less! Ay, ye may glower! We're risin' in the warld, it seems. We'll think naething o' Lords now that we've come to Dukes! ... Ay, she'll sleep here. Elsie's takin' Maister Peter an' Miss Alison to The Neuk—they're awfu' high about it!—an' the leddy 'll get the room that was auld Miss Alison Jardine's. It was a' done up when the electric light wis pit in, an' it's rale nice; the maids hev been gettin' it ready. Ma word! the fineness o' the sheets! An' pink and blue bath towels, and face towels like——" Failing to find a word she merely shook her head, adding, "Miss Jean aye likit things awfu' denty like even when they hed to be plain, but noo she can hae the best o' anything."

Miss Bathgate sniffed. " When I think," she said,
" of these noble women who give themselves to the
mission-field, and spend their life in the dust and heat
of the day, takin' no thought what they eat and drink,
never seein' a new fashion, and then look round an' see
the luxury and extravagance—well, it mak's a body
wonder ! "

" Oh ay," said Mrs. McCosh, regarding her tart with
her head on one side, " but ye can gang ower far wi'
that way o' thinkin'. If we a' made off for the mission-
field we'd be leaving work undone here : an' if a'body
wis content wi' a plate o' broth or porridge, a' the cook's
skill wud be lost. An' God wudna hae gi'en us the skill
if He hedna meant us to use it. It's the same wi' actin'
an' such like."

" Ay," said Bella, " I've heard that argument afore.
It's a gift, they say, and is meant to be used. It just
teaches them impidence, that's what I say ! I'm fair
sick o' thae Rurals wi' their plays an' their palavers.
There were nane o' thae things in ma young days.
We hed the kirk, and the prayer-meetin', and the
Y.W.C.A., an' the British Women—an' what mair
did we want ? . . . Oh ay, it's a braw tart, an' na doot
ye'll feed the Duke's daughter like a fightin' cock, but
there's mony a yin that hes nae food, an' for a' these
things ye'll be brought to judgment."

" Hoots. It's a' true whit ye say, Bella, but we
canna be thinkin' a' the time aboot ither folk. The
warld couldna gang on if we didna harden oor hearts.
Ye ken by yoursel'. When ye sit doon by your fireside
to enjoy your tea, are ye thinkin' a' the time aboot

the gangrels, wi' a' their wealth in a wee bundle, an'
nae comfort but a fire ahint a dyke, or a bed among
the straw in a barn? Not you! Nor me! I just
say, ' Puir sowls! ' an' pour masel' oot a second cup.
. . . I'll dae ma verra best for this Leddy Agnes, no'
because she's a Duke's daughter, but because she's
Miss Jean's guest. . . . She's only a young lassie,
I hear, so she'll like sweet things."

Miss Bathgate got up, wrapped the shawl carefully
round her head, and with the briefest of farewells,
departed.

" Puir Bella," said Mrs. McCosh tolerantly, " she's
a dacent cratur', but a wee thing narrow! "

Miss Barton and Peter went in the car to Symington
to meet the expected guest, and when they returned
with her the noise of their arrival disturbed the whole
neighbourhood. For Lady Agnes was accompanied
by two dogs, an Airedale and an Irish terrier, and when
they met the Black Douglas the impact was terrific.
The two strangers hurled themselves on Peter's treasure,
and in a second the three dogs were careering madly
round, inextricably mixed. They cleared a space for
themselves in the little hall and the household had,
perforce, to take the part of spectators. Fierce waxed
the fight, and might have ended disastrously, had not
Mrs. McCosh appeared with a pepper pot, and Phipps,
the chauffeur.

Lady Agnes threw her arms round her hostess,
crying, " Jean, I didn't dare tell you I was bringing
them, I hoped you'd forgive me when you saw the
darlings. I'd forgotten about Black Douglas. He'll

be none the worse, Peter. It was really only a friendly tussle : there's no malice about the dear things."

" They ran at Duggie," Peter reminded her, hugging that victim, who lay licking himself with a self-conscious air, "and it's Duggie's house : he was the one who should have done the attacking."

" Oh," said the new-comer, " I meant to be such a pleasant guest, and I've nearly wrecked your home at the very start ! Jean, darling, it was dreadful of me to bring them without leave. Mother would be furious if she knew—but they looked so pathetic and I wasn't sure if they'd be happy, for you've no notion how intelligent they are. . . . You don't really mind, do you, Jean ? They're called Ruth and Naomi."

Jean laughed. " I don't mind," she said, " so long as they don't kill Black Douglas. . . . Come now and see your room—Peter, it's high time you were in bed, Elsie's waiting for you. Ask her to tell Phipps to look after the dogs. Wouldn't you like to give him instructions yourself, Agnes ? "

Peace reigned again at The Rigs when dinner-time came. Betty Barton, wearing a new rose-red frock in honour of the guest, thought rather regretfully of the peaceful evenings with Lady Bidborough which she had so much enjoyed. She had met Lady Agnes often at Mintern Abbas, and had quite liked the handsome, rather untidy girl, but at The Rigs, where they were all in such close proximity, she felt that the new-comer would be almost as overwhelming as her high-spirited dogs.

But it was difficult not to warm to a girl who looked

at one so frankly, and said with such obvious sincerity :
"*What* a jolly red frock ! People with lovely dense
black hair should always wear just that shade of red,
except when they wear pure white or dead black."
She turned to her hostess. "Indeterminate things,
like you and me, Jean, can range up and down all the
shades. Isn't this fine ?" As she unfolded her napkin
she looked round the little dining-room. "Perhaps you
don't know, Miss Barton, but to-night one of my
favourite dreams has come true. Yes ! Since I was a
child—I'd be almost ten when Lady Bidborough came
to Mintern Abbas—I've loved to hear about Priorsford
and longed to see it. When Peter was a baby I used
to watch him being bathed, and listen to tales about
Mrs. McCosh and Bella Bathgate and the others. I can
hardly believe that I'm really here. It's such fun to
arrive in the dark, and see shapes of trees and hills and
know that Scotland's all around me."

Jean put down her soup spoon, and smiled across
at her secretary as she said : "I'm afraid Barty's
expecting you to be disappointed, Agnes. You may
find all my swans the plainest of geese. When one is
away it's so easy to idealize people and places. I've
got a bad trick of it. But you're an enjoying sort of
creature, and I think you'll be quite well amused. . . .
Tell me about the parents ? Are they having a good
trip ?"

Lady Agnes rattled on, for she had much to tell,
and there was no reading aloud that evening. As
they prepared to go to bed, she said, "Jean, do you
notice my Johnsonian English ? I've been practising

hard for weeks so as not to offend your ears and corrupt Priorsford with the latest slang! Say you're pleased, Jean."

" Absurd child ! " said Jean. " Your slang was always more funny than offensive, but it's kind of you to consider Priorsford."

" *And* Mrs. Elliot ! " said the girl. " Quite the most critical person I know. I always wish when I see her that I had better manners and a tidier head, and knew how to put on my clothes. Don't you find her very difficult to live up to, Jean ? "

" Go to bed," said Jean, " and think over that last remark. There's something about it not quite complimentary to your hostess. . . ."

Lady Agnes said at the end of her first day that it had been almost too full of thrills.

She was in to see Quentin on the way from her bath in the morning, and the house resounded with that young man's squeals and gurgles of delight. After breakfast, which was a hilarious meal, she convoyed Peter and Alison to school, and gave the three dogs, now happily friends and brothers, a run by Tweedside. Coming in, flushed and blown about by the north wind, she found Jean about to interview Mrs. McCosh, and accompanied her to the kitchen.

" Lady Agnes has heard a great deal about you," said Jean.

" Pleased to meet you," Mrs. McCosh responded in her hearty Glasgow way. " Those are nice dogs o' yours, if they wudna fecht."

" You were splendid with the pepper," Lady Agnes said, sitting down on the edge of the table and helping herself to a handful of raisins. " It was only the journey and finding themselves in strange quarters that made them wild. As a rule, they're as good as gold."

" Wee Douglas is no' a fechter, a canny beast if ever there wis yin. . . . What d'ye ca' yer dogs ? "

" Oh, Ruth and Naomi ; out of the Bible, you know."

" Mercy ! "

" Yes, it's not very appropriate, really, except that they're inseparable."

" I wudna like to cry to them, ' Ruth and Naomi.' It would sound kinda blasphemous-like, makin' free wi' the Bible."

" I think," said Jean, " we'll change their names for the time being to Rob and Wat. . . . That's all, I think, Mrs. McCosh. Now, Agnes, we'll proceed to Priorsford Highgate and do our marketing. Just wait till I get a coat and hat."

" Is it a fashionable promenade ? Must one be tidy ? I'm afraid I'm rather a mess. Ruth is so affectionate. Perhaps I'd better have a brush down. . . ."

The sun was shining as Jean and her companion walked across Tweed Bridge, and paused to look up at Peel Tower. The river was full with recent storms, and rushed wide and swift. Snow lay in patches on the hill-tops and at the back of dykes, but there seemed actually a hint of spring in the air, and the sunshine was heartening.

" It's lovely," said Agnes, " far lovelier than I'd pictured it. Whichever way you look—up to the castle

or down to the woods and meadows, it's perfect. . . .
Peter was trying to teach me some of the names of
the hills this morning. . . . But I didn't know you had
mills ! "

" How would we support our population ? Unfortunately we can't live by beauty alone—but the
mills aren't obtrusive, indeed I never notice them ;
but I suppose they must strike a new-comer. . . . This
is our principal street, the Highgate. It's a great
meeting-place of a morning, when Priorsford is doing
its shopping. D'you see that car over there at the
green-grocer's ? That's the chariot of Mrs. Duff-
Whalley."

" Oh," gasped Agnes. " Has she emerged ? Do let's
go and see."

Jean laughed. " We can't stand and stare. But
wait—I believe I've a list to leave—yes."

Although the Towers was only a short way from the
town and Mrs. Duff-Whalley liked to walk, she always
felt that it was more befitting to her dignity to roll down
in her luxurious car. She would not have missed her
morning shopping for a lot. She enjoyed shopping,
casting her eyes round in search of new things, and
quick to notice if anything but the best were offered
to her ; she enjoyed also giving advice to the shop-
keepers about how they should manage their business, but most of all she enjoyed meeting the other
shoppers.

When Jean and her guest entered the shop Mrs. Duff-
Whalley was laying down the law to Miss Hutton on
the subject of marmalade-making. The new season's

bitter oranges had just come in, and she had ordered a supply.

"The whole orange cut up," she was saying: " any other way is absurdly extravagant."

Miss Hutton's calm voice replied placidly: " I always keep to my mother's recipe, straining the juice and adding some peel cut into the thinnest snippets. Perhaps it's a little extravagant, but ours is a small household and we don't use so very much. I'm sure yours is a better way when quantity is a consideration."

Mrs. Duff-Whalley snorted. "Both quantity *and* quality, believe me. Oh—good-morning, Jean. We don't often see you in the Highgate."

"No," said Jean, " I took a holiday this morning to show my friend—Lady Agnes Chatham—Mrs. Duff-Whalley, Miss Hutton—who has come to pay us a visit, something of our town."

Lady Agnes shook hands, remarking, " I've been determined for years to see Priorsford."

"But why? " asked Mrs. Duff-Whalley suspiciously, as if scenting some sinister secret in this apparently innocent desire.

The tall girl looked down at her small questioner.

"Why? " she said. "Well, for one thing, it was Lady Bidborough's home, and I'd heard so much about it, and it sounded so much nicer than other places, and——"

"You'll be disappointed," said Mrs. Duff-Whalley firmly. "Bound to be. I don't say Priorsford isn't quite pretty, but views aren't everything, and it's very dull. If you don't just live for bridge there's nothing doing. The people are *not* hospitable, all very self-engrossed and lazy. You'd hardly believe the difficulty I have to make them stir themselves about *anything*."

As she declaimed Jean noticed that the other customers, as they chose vegetables and asked if the pears were soft, were listening intently, but that was nothing to Mrs. Duff-Whalley, who liked an audience.

" Yes," she went on, " I must work ; it's my nature, and I've more or less kept things going here for the last twenty years—with no thanks, I can assure you. However . . . I hope we'll see you at The Towers. You and Jean must dine with us. That will be pleasant. . . ."

When the order had been given and they were out on the street again, Agnes hugged Jean's arm and chuckled.

" What a *pet* ! Does she really play up all the time ? I'd have known her anywhere from your description. Nothing passes those darting eyes ! I can well imagine how she sat on you, poor Jean, when you were a little young thing—indeed she's mighty condescending still ! Jock hasn't forgiven her yet—*Oh*, isn't it lovely that Jock's coming for next week-end ! . . . I like your Miss Hutton. And where is Miss Smart's sweet-shop ? Oh, look, how lovely ! The hills shining through those funny little openings—what do you call them ? "

" *Pends*—that's the old Scots name for them. . . . Here is Miss Smart's."

The sweet-shop was already occupied by the Miss Watsons, who were resting on two chairs while their order for " pan-drops " was being made up.

The two ladies were all excitement on beholding

Jean and her friend, and made an effort, which Jean frustrated, to get off their chairs.

"We're so stiff," said Miss Teenie, "that it's quite an effort to come down to the town. My! I've seen the time when I was down two or three times a day!"

"We couldn't resist the fine morning," said her sister, "and we hadn't seen a soul for two days, and we felt we must have some news. We've just been asking Miss Smart if there's anything doing, but she says things are very quiet."

"Nothing very much happens in January," said Miss Smart, who looked with her smiling, rosy face the picture of contentment, "nothing but colds and influenza."

"Please don't discourage me," said Lady Agnes, "this is my first visit to Priorsford, and I don't see how it could be nicer than it is now."

Miss Teenie got carefully to her feet followed by her sister.

"I wish," said Jean, "I'd had the car to take you home."

"Not at all," said Miss Teenie, "it's better for us to use our legs. . . . We'd be awful proud if you'd bring your friend in to see us—that is, if you happen to have a free afternoon. Will she be here long?"

"Yes," said Agnes promptly, "a long time. There was no limit set to my visit, was there, Jean? You didn't say, 'Come from the 7th to the 14th,' or anything like that."

"So appreciative a guest deserves encouragement," said Jean. "We'd love to take tea with you one after-

noon, Miss Watson. . . ." She turned to Agnes.
" You've heard me speak of the parties the Miss
Watsons used to give for Jock and Mhor ? "

" Indeed I have," said the girl heartily, if rather
absently, for her eyes were roaming round the shop.
" . . . I never did see such a selection of boiled sweets
—they're my favourites ; and chocolates in such rich
abundance. And, oh, Jean, *Edinburgh Rock* ! One of
the happiest memories of my childhood ! May I get
some for the children ? And, please, I want to post
some to Jane's two : you can't get it in London."

" Well," said Jean, " I'll go on and you can follow.
You'll find your way back ? Luncheon at one. . . ."

The day closed with a dinner at Laverlaw, where
Lady Agnes met some young people, played games in
the billiard-room, and returned to The Rigs in such
overflowing spirits that Jean found some difficulty in
persuading her that it was long past bed-time in Priorsford.

CHAPTER XXIX

". . . Through long hours of labouring breath
You watched the world grow small and far,
And met the constant eyes of Death
And haply knew how kind they are."

J. B.

IT was a wet morning, not ordinarily wet, but an even downpour. Mrs. McCosh told the children that it was raining " auld wives an' strae brechums," and they stared uncomprehendingly.

Lady Bidborough sat in the living-room, correspondence spread out before her, and a distinctly worried look on her face. To begin with, she was sad at heart because her old friend Mrs. Jowett was drawing hourly nearer death. The only one who refused to see it was her poor husband. He blamed the weather.

" How can you expect any betterness in a Scots January ? I should have taken her away in October ; I wanted to, but Janetta herself objected to leaving home, and the doctors supported her. Said she'd be better at home. The fools ! They might have thought of the length of the winter in these parts. If poor Janetta would only rouse herself a little ; she's too apt to let go, and there's everything in having the will to recover. . . . However, the winter can't last for ever ; sometimes February is quite a decent month. She

305

seemed cheered to-day when I brought her in the first
snowdrops. If only we could get her out to lie in the
sunshine."

Jean, looking out at the downpour, thought how
miserably exasperated Mr. Jowett would be this morning. What a noise the children were making, playing
football in the little hall ! It was Friday, and Jock was
arriving next morning : also David. He had wired to
Jean, saying he could take a week-end off, and could she
put him up. Jean hardly knew what to think. She was
always glad to see David, but why was he coming just
now ? Was it Miss Barton ? And was he in earnest ?
Jean never pretended to understand the ways of the
youth of to-day. She knew herself to be old-fashioned,
and absurdly strict about things that other people took
lightly ; Davy had had the same upbringing, but it was
different with a man . . .

Deep in her own thoughts, Jean did not hear the door
open, and she started when a hand was laid on her
shoulder and a voice said, " Why, Jean girl, you do look
busy. What's worrying you ? "

" Oh, Pamela." There was relief in the tone. " I
am glad to see you. But what are you doing out so
early this bad day ? "

" Isn't it foul ? " Pamela drew off her gloves and
held her hands to the fire. " Lewis had to go to Edinburgh, so I motored down with him to the train. He
much prefers the train to a car always."

" Oh, then, you'll spend the day here—that's good."

" Alas, I can't. I've to get some things in Priorsford
and hurry back, for the Archfield people—at least Mrs.

Forbes and a friend—are lunching with me. Tell me, what's worrying you, Jean ? "

Jean flushed and said, " Nothing, Pamela : it's just silliness, really." She turned over some of the letters that were piled on the writing-table. " The appeals become more and more difficult to refuse—times, you see, are very bad—and what with everything . . . There's a wire from Davy asking if he may come down for the week-end. With Agnes here and Jock coming, I'm afraid it'll be rather a crush, and, anyway, why is he coming again so soon ? He always says it's so difficult to leave town."

" Yes, Jean, but Miss Barton's a very pretty girl. I'm afraid that's it. It was quite easy to see when you were all at Laverlaw that he was attracted by her, but I thought when he got back to London there would be no more of it. He's evidently more constant than I thought. What do you think about it ? "

" Does it matter what I think ? Davy must please himself. I suppose I ought to be glad if he is in earnest. . . . But isn't it rather impertinent of us to think that Miss Barton is ready to drop like ripe fruit ? I'm pretty certain it won't weigh with her, the fact that it's a comfortable down-setting. She's not that kind of girl. . . . I don't think you like Barty much, Pam, and I admit she has a manner that puts one off, but she's rather splendid in her way."

" Oh, I daresay. She struck me as being rather a difficult young woman. Probably that's what first attracted David—the difficulty, combined, of course, with her undeniable good looks. But, anyway, there it is. I tell you what, I'll wire to David to come to Laverlaw. You'd all come to dine on the Saturday night, and he could spend Sunday here. How's that ? "

Jean's face brightened. " Oh, Pamela, that's a good plan : it simplifies things a lot. We are all so much on the top of each other here, and the rain pouring. . . . Thank you, darling."

" I'm glad to be a little use. I'll go and wire now. . . . By the way, how is Mrs. Jowett ? "

Jean shook her head sadly. " Very far away. Yesterday she seemed hardly conscious."

" I'm sorry," said Pamela. " She was a most sweet, inoffensive woman, and her poor husband 'll be lost without her."

" Yes," said Jean. " It's odd, you'd think he was the most self-reliant of mortals, and that dear Mrs. Jowett only leant, but as a matter of fact it was he who did the leaning. He still tries to pretend to himself that the spring will put her right, but I think in his heart he knows that she will never see our spring. . . . Here's Agnes ! How are you going to get through this wet day, dear ? "

" Write letters," said Agnes. " I've neglected my parents shamefully since I came, there have been so many things to do. And I'm lunching with Rosalind Tweedie and going on to badminton."

Pamela smiled at the girl, remarking, " You're a nice guest, Agnes ! " She kissed her sister-in-law, picked up her gloves, and went off.

Agnes said : " What I like about Mrs. Elliot is, she doesn't waste words. Can't I help you, Jean. . . .

What a lot of letters, dull-looking things. Must you read them all ? "

" Barty generally goes through the letters and sifts out the possible cases, but as she's gone to Glasgow to-day I must tackle them myself."

" I suppose you can trust Miss Barton's judgment ? "

Jean nodded. " She's both kind and very just, and reads character in a way I never could."

" It's luck that you have her. By the way, what about your burglar's wife ? "

" My burglar's wife ? " Jean began to laugh. " Barty went to see her, for I couldn't rest, and found that far from wanting help because her husband was in jail, she was much relieved that he was again safe and in confinement ! She's a decent woman, with well-doing children, and says her husband simply can't keep straight. Barty thought she probably had an awful tongue, and certainly she seemed rather self-righteous, so the poor little man may be happier away from her, even though he is in jail. Anyway, he must be used to it by this time, and he can't mind it or he wouldn't go on burgling."

" That's true," said Agnes. " I expect he likes the excitement. But I mustn't keep you. . . . I'll be in to tea. Good-bye."

After luncheon Jean went up to The Knowe in the hope that she might see her friend, if only for a minute.

At the gate she met one of the nurses coming in from her daily walk.

In answer to Jean's inquiry she said, " Mrs. Jowett

is decidedly weaker, after a disturbed night. I don't
know if you would say she is suffering, but she is certainly uneasy. She slept for a little before lunch. The
doctor's coming back this afternoon. I'm going up to
bed now. I'll look in as I pass and see if you should go
in. . . . Oh, no, nothing would do her any harm now,
poor lady."

Presently the day nurse, a quiet gentle woman, came
out and told Jean that there was a distinct change for
the worse.

" She is wandering a good deal," she said, " though if
Mr. Jowett comes into the room she seems to know, and
pulls herself together. Yes, go in just for a minute or
two : she might know you."

It was a spacious, pleasant room, with a bright fire,
and nothing of the ugliness of illness apparent. Mrs.
Jowett was dying as she had lived, gently and decor-
ously. She lay on the wide bed—Mr. Jowett had a
passion against twin beds—so frail and small that her
body hardly showed under the cover : one hand was
under her cheek.

Jean stood looking down at her, her eyes hot with
unshed tears, then bent and kissed the hand that lay on
the coverlet.

The eyes opened, there was a puzzled look, and then
a smile. " You here, Jean ? I've been telling the
khansamah to get iced lemonade ready for Tim. He'll
be in quite soon now and he's so thirsty in the heat.
Quahai ! . . . These poor pansies, they'll never grow."
She looked out at the sullen grey skies and went on,
" The sun is so hot, so hot it parches everything."

Her eyes closed again, and after a minute Jean slipped out of the room. The nurse was moving about in the dressing-room, but she did not feel she could speak to her. Downstairs, she paused and knocked at the library door. There was no answer, and she was just going when she heard a slight sound in the drawing-room. The door was ajar and she looked in. It had the curiously bleak look which rooms so quickly get when the mistress is away or ill ; no flowers in the vases, the chairs set stiffly, the books unnaturally tidy.

On the couch before the empty grate, where his wife had lain all winter, Mr. Jowett was seated, staring before him. He seemed hardly to notice her presence. Presently she said : " I wish I could say or do something that would help."

" You can't," said Mr. Jowett, " there's nothing to say or do. Janetta is dying and life is finished for me. . . . You're a good child, Jean : you'd better go home."

So Jean went, walking blindly over the lawn that had been the pride of its owner's heart.

At the end of the drive she did not take the road home, but opened a gate and went down a path that led through the meadows to Hopetoun. She felt she simply could not go home yet to The Rigs, with all its exuberant young life. She wanted to be with people who had lived and suffered. Mrs. Hope and Augusta would understand.

The rain had stopped but the air was full of moisture, the clouds hung low, and from all around came the sound of running water, for every small stream was filled to overflowing with the weight of rain that had fallen. Hopetoun Woods were dank and dark: though it was only about three o'clock the daylight was going fast.

When she reached Hopetoun the servant who opened the door said Miss Hope was in, and she would see if Mrs. Hope was receiving callers, so Jean took off her wet mackintosh and tried to tidy her hair at a Queen Anne mirror in the hall. She was still rather woebegone when Augusta greeted her with : " Why, Jean, is anything wrong ? "

Whereupon Jean sat down in a chair and immediately began to cry.

" Come and see Mother," said Augusta, offering the greatest comfort she knew on earth. " Yes, she is really very well, and she was suggesting this very day that I might ring you up and ask if you could take tea with us. We've been missing you."

When Augusta opened the drawing-room Jean stopped on the threshold with a sigh of pleasure. Here was comfort ; in spite of the grey skies outside the room seemed full of sunshine, for everywhere were bright-coloured bowls filled with spring flowers, hyacinths, blue and pink and white ; daffodils, orange tulips, scillas with their heavenly blue. One or two shaded lights had been turned on that Mrs. Hope might read her *Times*, which she did with the aid of a magnifying glass, sitting very upright in her armchair with its curly legs. She was very glad to see her visitor, but exclaimed over the cold hands and her pinched appearance.

" A visitor is doubly welcome on a bad day, and you, my dear Jean, are something of a stranger."

" Not willingly," said Jean, " but I've a girl staying with me, Agnes Chatham, and we've had a good many engagements. I wonder if I might bring her to see you ? She's a nice girl, very young and joyful. I think you'd like her. It amuses her immensely to stay at The Rigs. They've a house about the size of Priorsford Hydropathic in the Cotswolds—her father's Duke of Malchester—and she loves the smallness of everything. She's never lived close to people before, and can't get used to the entertainment of seeing people live their lives in a row ! She reminds me rather of Pamela when she first came to Bella Bathgate's, only Agnes is more hilarious about it. She attends our Community Drama rehearsals, too, and gloats over our struggles. Mrs. Duff-Whalley is a never-ceasing source of delight to her—she's so elated over the fact that the Indomitable One can always be depended on to play up, as she puts it. . . . I expected a week would be about as much as she could stand, but she declares that nothing will induce her to go until she's turned out. . . . Jock is coming to see us for the week-end—he and Agnes were playmates as children—and Davy is to be at Laverlaw."

" Bring your friend to see me," said Mrs. Hope ; " any one who appreciates Priorsford—but, my dear, you look—have you been crying ? "

The question was too much for Jean, who laid her head on Mrs. Hope's lap, a place where she had often found comfort in childish griefs, while Augusta said :

" Jean has just come from seeing Mrs. Jowett, Mother. I'm afraid it's the end."

Mrs. Hope said nothing, only stroked the hand that clasped the arm of her chair, and presently Jean sat up, rather ashamed of her breakdown.

"Mrs. Jowett has been such a good friend to us always," she said, "and since I came back, and she's been ill, I've seen her constantly. . . . I think she must have known all the time that there was no hope, but she never hinted at it. No one knew if she suffered. Only once when I moved a cushion and said, ' That will ease you,' she said so sternly, ' I am never at ease.' She was a brave woman."

"A brave woman. Did she know you to-day ? "

"She smiled, and said ' Jean.' But she was far away. I think she thought herself back in India : she was giving orders to the *khansamah*, and said the sun was withering the pansies. . . . Poor, poor Mr. Jowett. She was the only one who admired him and had patience with him. I wonder if he'll be able to find comfort in committees. . . . Mrs. Jowett will be badly missed. People are only realizing now how much she did : she was so self-effacing. Life didn't amuse her, so she wasn't herself amusing, but she was good all through. And she never hurt any one with her tongue."

"Ah," said Mrs. Hope, whose tongue was still sharp after a ninety years' pilgrimage, "perhaps her husband would be less tiresome had her tongue been more of a weapon."

"Very likely," said Jean. "But, oh, isn't it sad that happy companionships have to be broken and homes made desolate ? I think of Mr. Jowett, with nobody of his own to be sorry for him or worry about him, going about always with the ache of loneliness, missing terribly his shelter—for that's what his wife has been to him. And that's only mild sadness. When one thinks of the tragedies that happen every day. . . . I'm sometimes terrified at the weight of pain there must be in the world."

" And yet," said Mrs. Hope, " life is worth it. I was re-reading Flecker's *Hassan* the other day. At the end the ghost of Pervaneh (you remember ? who died so terribly for love) is asked by the spirits of the unborn children, ' *What of life, sister ?* ' And she replies, ' *Life is sweet.*' . . . And after ninety years of it I say so too. My heart is full of thanksgiving for the good things I've enjoyed in the world, and also for the suffering that made living worth while. . . . But it's easy for me to speak, with the dust and heat of the day over, sitting here by the river waiting for the summons. You, dear Jean, are in the very midst of it, with great responsibilities and great anxieties ; sometimes I think you must almost feel like sinking, but keep a high heart, you're not alone ; thank God, you've got a husband who shares your burden."

" Yes," said Jean, " nothing is anything in comparison with Biddy."

" Not even the children, Jean ? " said Augusta.

" Oh, well, I can't separate Biddy and the children : we're all bound up in the bundle of life together." She turned to her old friend and said very earnestly : " You don't know what Biddy means to me. He's everything—and my best friend as well. And he's coming home! He's almost on the way now. If all goes well, he ought to be back in the very beginning of March."

The very thought of it made Jean's face lose its strained look and grow round and rosy. She smiled at Mrs. Hope and Augusta, and then with a glance at the clock on the mantel-shelf, sprang to her feet.

" You're not going, Jean? Surely when you are here you'll take tea with Augusta and me ? "

" No, thank you very much, but I must go back. Agnes has been out all day and is coming in for tea, and my secretary is in Glasgow for two days, and we've two stranger dogs (brought by Agnes) called Ruth and Naomi, and they complicate life greatly . . .! You've done me all the good in the world—the very sight of you and Miss Augusta and this room heartens one. Good-bye. Good-bye. And if I may bring Agnes . . ."

That night Mrs. Jowett crossed the River, and the waters were low for her.

CHAPTER XXX

"My father had a daughter loved a man . . ."
TWELFTH NIGHT.

THE week-end passed very pleasantly. The weather was good and Jock took Agnes for long walks : they all dined at Laverlaw on Saturday night, and David spent Sunday at The Rigs.

At breakfast on Sunday morning Jock asked if every one was supposed to go to church.

"Of course," said Jean.

"Oh, I'm not objecting," said Jock. "As a matter of fact, I rather like going to church. Is Thornton a good preacher ? "

Lady Agnes broke in with : "Yes, very good. I went with Jean to hear him last Sunday. It was the first time I'd ever been in a 'kirk.'"

"Poor heathen," said Jock, "I hope you valued the privilege."

"It's a nice restful service," said the girl. "I valued being allowed to sit down such a lot ! And I was interested in the sermon. Mr. Thornton preached as if he were trying to tell you something he'd found out for himself, not just slinging platitudes about."

"Mummy," said Peter, pausing in his pursuit of a bit of bacon that eluded his fork, "do ministers make up sermons out of their own heads ? "

" Well, they make them out of the Bible and . . ."

" Why don't they just tell a story ? " Peter wanted to know ; and added, " It would be easier."

His mother felt it her duty to improve the occasion.

" But that wouldn't be doing their job, Peter. They are there to preach the gospel of Jesus Christ."

" Oh," said Peter politely.

As they walked over the bridge Jean pointed out the Episcopal church to her guest, remarking that that was her spiritual home, but Agnes said that she preferred when in Rome to do as the Romans.

Jock enjoyed the service and joined lustily in the singing of the metrical Psalms he had learned in childhood—they were also familiar to Peter and Alison—but when the minister began his second Scripture reading, the thirteenth chapter of first Corinthians, Jock lifted his head like a dog on strange territory. Presently he turned to his sister and muttered, " What's he reading ? "

" A revised version ! Don't scowl so," Jean whispered back.

The sermon was short and excellent, Nicodemus coming by night, and very soon they were out again on Tweed Bridge.

" Wasn't it an interesting sermon ? " said Lady Agnes. " I'll remember Nicodemus now. I always confused him with the man up the tree."

Jock smiled pityingly at her. " My poor child, that's not the way to discuss a sermon ; the proper thing is to get down to the fundamentals. . . . Jean, will you please tell me what the minister was reading ? That chapter of all chapters, almost the loveliest in literature. '*Charity vaunteth not itself*'—What did he read— '*Love does not put on airs*,' or words to that effect!"

"Jock," said his sister, "you're just like Bella Bathgate, who says she doesn't like 'new toots on auld horns.'"

"It will always spoil it for me," Jock grumbled. "'*Charity vaunteth not itself*.'"

"Are you *allowed* to change the Bible?" Peter asked.

"It should be made a capital offence," said angry Jock.

"But, Mr. Jardine," said Betty Barton in her cool tones, "you must remember that you are in a small minority. People don't want Elizabethan English, the bulk of them don't, it merely puzzles them, they've no time for it; the simplified version means much more to them. Quite lately some one was talking to me about this version, and instanced that very chapter in Corinthians as being so beautiful."

Agnes laughed at the helpless expression on Jock's face, while Jean said: "Never mind, Jock, I'm with you. We are the old die-hards, demanding that the things we love should be let alone. . . . But, Jock, the fact that Mr. Thornton chose to read that version to-day proves to me that it must be of value. We must talk to him about it, you and I."

"And now," said Agnes, "let's walk up the Drove Road and take the dogs. It isn't nearly luncheon-time."

"Come on then, Sprats," cried Jock to the children; "let slip the hounds!"

"Perhaps I'd better go in," said Jean. "Davy may come early, and I've got some letters to write. . . . . Are you going to The Neuk, Barty? We'll see you later. Luncheon is one-thirty to-day."

David was in high spirits through the meal, and Jean wondered if they had merely imagined that he was specially interested in Betty Barton. Certainly he listened with deference to what she said, and addressed most of his conversation to her, but that, Jean thought, might be simply a tribute to her mind.

Betty did not look in the least conscious when she greeted him, and agreed with the greatest calm when he suggested that they should climb Cademuir in the afternoon.

Jean excused herself on the grounds of a Sunday lesson with the children, and the two girls went off alone with the two young men.

After dinner David and Jock motored into Edinburgh for the London train.

It was oddly quiet that evening after all the talk and bustle of the day. Betty Barton went off early, and when the other two were left alone, Agnes coaxed Jean into telling her all about Lord Bidborough's coming to Priorsford.

"And did you fall in love with each other just at once, Jean?" she asked. "On that very first night when he walked in and found this room all untidy because Jock and Mhor had been having a play? Oh! how I wish I'd been here!"

Jean laughed and went back to her book, while the girl sat on the rug and looked thoughtfully into the fire.

Presently Jean looked up and said : " Are they worth a penny, Agnes ? "

" I'm only thinking," Agnes said simply, " what a darling Jock is." She added, " And so terribly young. Wasn't he funny about the chapter this morning ? An angry little boy who hates changes. . . . Although I'm three years younger, I'm really heaps older." She sighed. " Jock doesn't think about anything that matters. Let him watch the ways of birds—that's a topic that excites him—or anything to do with Nature stuff. . . . *Beetles*."

" Parasites on shrimps ! " said Jean. " I found him poring over an article on that soul-stirring topic."

Agnes laughed somewhat ruefully.

" Will these things always come first with him, d'you think ? "

" I hope not, darling," Jean said, and bent and kissed the ruffled head beside her knee.

CHAPTER XXXI

"One man in his time plays many parts . . ."

AS YOU LIKE IT.

AFTER a week of nightly rehearsals, and much writing and wiring about clothes for the Soviet soldier, the "Tweeddale Players" held their dress-rehearsal in the Town Hall of Priorsford.

Mrs. Duff-Whalley had refused utterly to have the team called the "Priorsford Players." "Absurd!" she said, "as if it were a mere town affair. Why, it's almost *entirely* County, and the village Institute can't object. They're welcome to take any name that pleases them. How many are competing? Seven, didn't we hear? I wonder what they're all doing?"

"It was in the local paper on Saturday," said Mr. Hamilton. "Sounds quite an interesting selection, and there is an original attempt by a village team in Roxburgh, 'The Wayside Players.'"

"Absurd!" said Mrs. Duff-Whalley. "What sort of a play could a village playwright produce! . . . I really can't agree with you about the ladies' dresses, Mr. Hamilton. They were people of consequence and would naturally be well dressed."

Patrick Hamilton looked stubborn. "They would, no doubt, to start with, but you must remember that they had been flying for their lives when caught, and

when we first see them they'd been a week in jail,
with no opportunity of changing, or even washing——"

" Oh, disgusting ! D'you mean you're going to make
them look *dirty* ? How could you expect an audience
to have any sympathy with a dishevelled, unwashed-
looking heroine ? Art's all very well, but you can carry
it too far, and realism too. . . . I saw a film the other
day where a Russian Princess, escaping with nothing
but a handbag, appeared in a series of wonderful garments. That, of course, was absurd, but I must insist
on my daughter wearing a becoming dress and having
her hair waved as usual. I couldn't permit anything
else. Miss Tweedie and Miss Barton must do what they
think best."

Mr. Hamilton attempted no further protest. Mrs.
Duff-Whalley had chosen a play—a bad one ; if she
liked to ruin any little chance it had, then she must do
it. She seemed to see no absurdity in a perfectly tidy,
well-dressed young female with her hair waved to a
nicety, crouching in a Bolshevik prison.

It so happened that the Community Drama Festival
fell that year to be held in Priorsford. It also fell to
Patrick Hamilton to make arrangements for the different
companies, to fit the performances into afternoon and
evening, and as, given a choice, each company would
have preferred to play in the evening, a ballot was re-
sorted to.

The " Tweeddale Players " had seemed fairly sure of
themselves in The Towers drawing-room. They had
learned how and when to put certain expressions into
their faces and tones in their voices. Miss Barton, as

Lady Elsie Davenant's mother, managed to make a feeble part quite amusing, Muriel was sweet and pensive as the heroine, Nigel Montgomery was good, Patrick Hamilton was all that a gallant lover should be, but Rosalind Tweedie and Malcolm Forbes were still very uncertain in their actions, and shaky in their words, with a tendency to turn their backs to the audience.

" Well," Rosalind complained, " how can I remember where the audience is when I can't *see* it. I'll be all right in the hall."

" I hope so," said Mr. Hamilton sceptically, and as it turned out he had reason for his doubt. When Rosalind found herself on the stage, so dazzling were the footlights, so strange her surroundings, that everything went from her and she could only gape. Young Forbes was worse, for, deprived of the familiar articles of furniture that had guided his uncertain movements, he was lost. When he made his first entrance he had to appear to push open the door roughly (but really with great caution) and rudely summon one of the wretched captives to the Tribunal. He got on the stage and stood utterly at a loss for a second, then muttering some words to no one in particular, instead of pushing Nigel Montgomery rudely to the door he made for it himself, gave it a violent push outward, instead of inwards, wrenching the frail thing from its hinges. That finished him for the evening.

" Never mind," said the producer, " you won't make the same mistakes to-morrow. . . . Perhaps you don't realize it, but we're jolly lucky to have a chance to rehearse on the stage we act on. . . . Forbes, you'll be careful, won't you, about your entrances and exits ? These doors are *cutcha* affairs, not nail-studded oak ! "

" Oh, I know, I'm sorry," said the boy. " Somehow I couldn't get my bearings at all. Everything seemed to be turned round about."

" Yes," said Rosalind, supporting him, " I had got to think of the audience as in the fireplace."

" I'm sure you were told often enough to play to the big end window," said Patrick Hamilton patiently.

" Perhaps, but I always *felt* it to be in the fireplace. I was bad enough to-night, but to-morrow, when there really is an audience, I'll be stricken entirely dumb."

" I hope not. Lady Agnes, how did it sound from the back ? "

" I heard you quite well, and Miss Barton, and Mr. Montgomery. Miss Duff-Whalley was apt to let her voice go down a little at the end of a sentence. . . . I didn't hear much of what Rosalind said, for her back was to the audience. . . . And, oh, when Miss Duff-Whalley says, ' What lights are these ? ' no lights appeared for almost half a minute after she said it. You'll have to watch that they're in time. What are you using for them ? "

Nigel Montgomery showed her. " It's not satis-factory," he said. " It's either over too soon, or not on in time."

" Then," suggested Rosalind, " let Muriel say instead of ' What lights are these ? ' ' Where *are* these lights ? ' Wouldn't that do ? "

" No, it wouldn't," said Mr. Hamilton shortly. " We'll try it once again : it only takes half an hour."

Mrs. Duff-Whalley looked at her watch. " Nine-thirty," she said. " Can you wait, Rosalind ? "

" Oh, that reminds me," said the girl. " I've forgotten to telephone for a car from Veitch's to take me home. My mother, you see, is one of those people who would serve strangers hand and foot, warm and feed and comfort them, while her nearest and dearest go barefoot. Our car's away with six members of the Rural Institute to some beano in Langhope, and I'm cast upon a cold world."

Mrs. Duff-Whalley frowned disapprovingly at the girl, and advised her not to be disrespectful. " Your dear mother," she said, " is a pattern to every one ; so public spirited."

" And we had dinner at half-past six," Rosalind went on, " and I'm so hungry. I'll have to go home and gnaw a crust, for cook is off to the Rural orgy."

" Poor ill-used creature," said Jean, " come home with us. Mrs. McCosh has promised us morning baps with fried bacon inside. Agnes 'll tell you how good they are : and we'll drive you home afterwards. That is, if you're sure your mother won't be anxious."

" My mother won't be home. I'm afraid I'm being a frightful lot of bother, but it's too tempting to refuse. Thank you very much, Lady Bidborough."

They ran through the play again, and this time it went fairly smooth.

" To-morrow at seven prompt," Patrick Hamilton warned them. " We're first on the evening list, the performance starts at seven-thirty, and you've all to be made up before that."

" I'm glad we're first," said Jean.   " We'll be able to listen to the others in comfort."

" What about the afternoon performance ? " Muriel asked ;   " are we supposed to go to that ? "

" It would be nice of you to go," Mr. Hamilton said. " I'm afraid there won't be many there."

" *Of course* we must go," said Jean, " it would be too disheartening for the teams to have to play to a scattered few."

" I shall certainly go," said Mrs. Duff-Whalley, " not from sentimental reasons but because of my interest in Community Drama.   I shall take notes."

Unfortunately the next day was February at its worst.   Snow had fallen most of the night and was rapidly turning to slush, while a bitter East wind tore at miserable wayfarers.

" It doesn't matter," Lady Agnes said cheerfully, as she supped porridge and cream, " we've no way to go."

" *We* haven't," said Jean, " but think of the others down Tweed.   The one you like the sound of, ' The Wayside Players,' have to come in a charabanc about forty miles.   I wonder how they arrange about food ? "

" Their expenses are paid," said Betty Barton, " and they can get a meal at any of the shops."

" Then they're not to be pitied," said Agnes, " for I never tasted better bakemeats than you have in Priorsford.   Rosalind Tweedie took me in and gave me coffee at a place, Miss Somebody's, and I made a positive beast of myself.   Don't worry, Jean, the snow's disappearing, and they'll only have to contend with mud. . . . Aren't you terribly excited, Miss Barton ?   You're far and away the best, of course ; and Mr. Hamilton does his best to make the thing sound possible, but oh! Mr. Forbes as a Russian ! Such a gentle Bolshie. Let me make you up, Miss Barton. I'm doing Rosalind Tweedie. I'm really quite an artist at it, aren't I, Jean ? "

" Thank you," said Miss Barton. " I'll be glad if you will. I'm not much good at it."

They all went to the afternoon performance, Peter and Alison, Ninny and two of the maids, not to speak of Pamela and Lewis Elliot, who had been lunching at The Rigs.

Patrick Hamilton had seen to it that the performers had as good a chance as possible ; the hall was properly darkened, and the stage was as perfect as he could make it.

Three pieces were given, all very commendable, carefully studied and produced, but all lacking the something that would have made them live. Two were unfortunately chosen, the third was good of its kind, but that kind was not high.

They all went home to tea discussing the plays and the actors.

" I only hope," said Jean, " that they're all getting a decent meal."

" Well," said Agnes, " whoever starves it won't be ' The Wayside Players.' When I was in Mitchell's to-day there was such a nice woman in a sealskin coat ordering tea to be ready at five o'clock for that company. Fish she ordered, also sandwiches and cakes. ' A really good tea,' she kept saying, and Mrs. Mitchell assured her she would see that they got that. I expect the Sealskin

Lady is the fairy godmother of the team. So, you see, they'll be in fine trim for their evening performance."

" I was hearing about that team," Jean said. " It's a lady who trains them, a Miss Adie. They choose their play in the spring, and work at it all year. They've very little time, for they're all busy, the women in their houses and the men in the fields, but they're as keen as can be. I'm looking forward to their evening play."

The hall was packed that night when the curtain went up on the palpitating players in *Noblesse Oblige*.

Patrick Hamilton could only hope that a few of the precepts he had tried to instil into them at rehearsals would remain, when all else was from them drifting. Sheer fright put the necessary intensity into Rosalind's voice when she wondered what had become of Brian. Malcolm Forbes growled through a flaxen beard, and was as gingerly with the door as if it had been a high explosive. Muriel, the heroine, quavered out, " What lights are these," but alas ! no lights appeared ; instead sounds were heards of strong men struggling for a word.

They got through somehow, and the curtain fell to the accompaniment of polite applause.

Mrs. Duff-Whalley had engaged a row of front seats, and the players put on wraps and prepared to enjoy the rest of the evening.

The next play was a pretty thing of Cranfordish flavour, with crinolines, and poke-bonnets and curtsys.

(" Rather feeble," was Mrs. Duff-Whalley's comment in her note-book.)

Then came a more ambitious attempt, which, how-

ever, was so involved that the audience was left in a
maze as to what was supposed to have happened.

Lady Agnes whispered in Jean's ear : "Ours is best
so far."

Then the curtain rose on the last piece : *Departure,*
by "The Wayside Players."

The scene was a cottage kitchen : the old wag-at-the-
wa', the china dogs, with painted gilt chains, on the
mantelpiece, the dresser with its brightly coloured bowls,
were all there. In the midst of her possessions a woman
sat, shapeless and stiff and old, but in her eyes the wist-
ful look of a child inquiring why. Various characters
came in and out, and it became evident that the woman,
ill and alone and helpless, was to be taken that day to
some sort of Home. The kindly neighbours, the brisk
efficient nurse, having said their say, went out, and the
woman was left alone with a young girl who had been
doing the work of the cottage and who understood something of the utter desolation this departure meant. The
two talked together, the old woman gazing at her loved
possessions, telling herself the history of each, and linger-
ing on the blue jug that her man Jimmie had bought in
Kelso when they were first married.

"Rax it doon for me, Jeanie," she said, "I'd like to
feel it in ma hands again," and when she got it she
crooned over it while the young girl stood and watched
her pitifully.

Then the girl's mother came bustling in and exclaimed
when she saw the blue jug, "Ye'll break it, Mistress
Weir, an' it's a braw jug. See, I'll put it back on the
shelf." She snatched the jug from the trembling hands

and—in a second it lay smashed on the floor. With a cry the old woman rose to her feet, and then sank down in her chair with a sigh, and was still. When the nurse bustled in to say that the car was at the door she found that the feeble heart had failed, and that the old woman would trouble no one any more.

It was a simple little play, most movingly acted, and Jean's eyes were wet as she turned to Agnes, saying, with a sigh of relief, " Anyway, she hadn't to go ! "

" That wins," said the girl : " at least it deserves to. . . . Here comes the Adjudicator ! My heart's absolutely *pounding*."

The Adjudicator was very tall and quite young. After a few little pleasantries he got down to the business of the evening. He was not unkind, and no more sarcastic than he had a right to be. He told the " Tweeddale Players " what they already knew, that theirs was a poor play, without form and void, but he commended the acting, particularly that of Miss Barton and Mr. Hamilton.

The winner was *Departure*, and no one cheered more heartily than the defeated Priorsford team at the decision.

Only Mrs. Duff-Whalley reared an insulted head.

" Scandalous ! " she said. " It's quite obvious that that young man knows nothing of his job. To put that *common* little piece first. Any one could see that *Noblesse Oblige* was in a different class from the others. They moved and spoke like gentlefolk : surely that should count. Of course the old woman was very natural, and I've no doubt it was all very like the thing, but I've no use for kitchen drama."

" Oh, I wouldn't say that," Lady Tweedie demurred. " It was very touching. I know exactly what the poor dear felt about ' the bonnie blue jug.' It was a great tribute to the acting that we were so vastly relieved when she died comfortably and quietly in her own kitchen before the nurse returned for her. . . . *Noblesse Oblige* was very good, I thought. Miss Barton did *very* well, and Muriel looked sweet. . . . *Poor* Malcolm Forbes ! "

Afterwards in the dressing-room, when every one was packing up different " properties," Jean got an opportunity to congratulate Miss Adie, the originator of " The Wayside Players."

" Yes, I am glad," she said. " My players are such *triers*. They work all day at their jobs, and come full of zest to practices at night. Some of them cycle miles in the dark. Come and meet Mrs. Wilson who played the old woman : she's our postmistress ! "

Jean was amazed to find herself confronting a tall, good-looking woman about five-and-thirty.

" But how did you do it ? " she gasped. " You looked at least seventy. How did you get that heavy, immovable look that an old sick woman so often has ? It was a splendid piece of acting."

Mrs. Wilson shook her head. " Na," she said, " I didna do well. I was feared. Miss Adie aye tell't me to take two long gentle breaths at the end. I de'ed ower loud."

CHAPTER XXXII

"In the great hand of God I stand."
MACBETH.

Two days after the Community Drama performance, Peter came in to breakfast looking rather pale and heavy-eyed. His mother watched him anxiously but said nothing, not even when he pushed away his scrambled eggs, a favourite dish.

"Saucy!" said Alison. "Ninny says if we don't make clean plates now, when so many people haven't enough food, we'll come to want."

"Don't be a prig, Alison," her mother advised her: "eat your own breakfast. I expect Peter has got a little cold. Elsie will take you to school to-day, and Peter'll stay warm by the fire."

"We'll do a Crossword Puzzle, Peter," Lady Agnes said. "That'll be better than lessons."

Ninny reported that Peter had complained of earache. "But," she said, "he's a queer laddie, he'll no tell if onything ails him. No' like Alison, who squeals afore she's hurt."

"If we keep him warm in the house," said Jean, "I expect he'll soon be all right. Have you taken his temperature?"

But as the day wore on it was obvious that the child was suffering, and when Dr. Dalgleish came, and Jean rather apologetically said that she was uneasy, he assured her that she had done right to send for him. He said very little, however, except that he would be back in the morning.

Peter was put in his mother's room, and all night he tossed and moaned and was so distressed that when day broke they telephoned for the doctor. He came at once, and after he had examined the boy, said the word they'd dreaded—mastoid.

"I'll arrange to have him taken into Edinburgh at once."

Jean, outwardly calm, asked if there was any reason why the operation could not be performed at home.

The doctor pointed out that in a Nursing Home they had everything at hand, that it was infinitely more convenient, and so on.

"Still," Jean persisted, "it *could* be done here, couldn't it? This house will be kept utterly quiet. If you telephoned now for nurses they'd prepare everything."

"Yes," said Dr. Dalgleish reluctantly. "Of course it *could* be done, though I'd advise you to go to Edinburgh myself."

"Oh, I know, probably you're right, but Peter has never been among strangers, he's really very shy, and I can't bear to send him away. . . . Of course, if you tell me that he'd have a better chance in a Nursing Home——"

"I don't say that," the doctor grumbled, "but it will mean an enormous amount of trouble for you and surgeons coming out specially."

" I'll be glad of the trouble, and this is a time when expense doesn't matter. If the surgeon will consent to it."

" Then," said the doctor, " I'll telephone from here. Irvine's the man I want, and I know two special nurses. If they're free——"

" Oh, Dr. Dalgleish," said Jean, " I'm so thankful for you. You saw us through all our childish ailments."

In a very short time all arrangements were made, and a room was being got ready for the operation.

" If only Biddy were here," Lady Agnes lamented, but Jean said : " I think I'm almost glad he isn't here. . . . How lightly I used to talk about this one and that one having an operation. I didn't know that it meant—this."

In the kitchen Bella Bathgate shook her head. " No' mony recover," she said. " Poor Mistress Reid lost her wee Annie. Ay, ay, hoo quick trouble comes."

" But it passes as quick, Bella," said cheerful Mrs. McCosh. " Bairns are like bells in a dub, soon down and soon up. We'll hae Maister Peter runnin' aboot again ere it's long. If we just hed this day over. I fair hate operations ; unnatural things. . . . They'll be here at two o'clock. God help poor wee Miss Jean. . . . I'm gaun to turn oot a' ma presses, just to keep ma hands busy."

" Ye'd be better on yer knees," said Bella.

" I'll be prayin' in ma he'rt." Mrs. McCosh gave a short laugh. " I doot I'm like Mistress MacGlashan. When she heard that there was a specialist comin' in to see her Willie, she stertit whitewashin' the kitchen !

I thocht at the time she was daft, but noo I can understand. . . . I wish I could think o' something to fill
Miss Jean's hands. . . . Hoo lang will it tak' ? "

Bella shook her head.

Jean sat in the living-room with Pamela and Lewis
Elliot. They seemed to have been sitting there for an
age, and Lewis, that naturally silent man, had spoken
almost without intermission. Jean smiled and responded, apparently quite composed ; only, when a
silence fell, and footsteps were heard coming downstairs
did she go deathly pale and clutch Pamela's hands for
support. . . . It was over, and, so far, the surgeon was
satisfied. He was a young man with a lean face and
steady eyes, and Jean had trusted him from the moment
she had seen him. Now she was loth to let him go. He
had to go, he told her, but he would be out again in the
evening.

" Dr. Dalgleish will be with you, and if I should be
wanted he'll let me know at once. And the nurses
know their job thoroughly. Try not to worry, Lady
Bidborough. Good-bye. . . ."

When he left the room Pamela took Jean in her arms,
crying : " Thank God, darling, that it's over ! And if
all goes well he will soon be out of danger. . . . We'll
take Agnes back with us. You won't want her with
nurses in the house. I expect she'll want to go on to
her next visit now that this has happened. . . . Cheer
up, darling ! Peter won't be a scrap the worse ; stronger
than ever probably. And we shan't need to say a word
about it to Biddy. When does he sail ? "

" I've been expecting a cable saying he'd sailed," said Jean. " He hoped to leave this week."

But when the Elliots, with Lady Agnes, got back to Laverlaw that evening they found a cablegram from Major Talbot saying that there had been a motor smash, and that Lord Bidborough was lying unconscious with a fractured skull.

" We can't tell Jean," said Pamela. " It isn't as if she could go to him or do anything for him—Oh, *Lewis*."

" I doubt if we can keep it from her," Lewis said ; " it's her right to know. . . . We'll see what the morning brings."

The next day was one that all her life Jean was to look back on with horror.

When the surgeon came out he was not satisfied. Peter's temperature was rising, it looked as if there might be a fresh mischief. With a sick heart Jean realized that they might have to operate again. " I *can't* bear it," she said, staring at the anxious faces round her without seeing them. " If Biddy were here —Pamela, would it be cruel to cable to him ? He can't have left Australia or I'd have heard."

Pamela, quite unnerved, began to cry.

" Oh, Jean," she sobbed, " my poor darling. We've had a cable from Tim. They've had a motor smash and Biddy's knocked out for the moment with concussion. . . ."

" You mean he's unconscious ? "

" Well, yes, but——"

" Just how bad is it ? Tell me, please."

"His skull is fractured," said Lewis, "but that often doesn't mean much. I expect he'll be all right in a day or two."

"But," Jean said, "Tim wouldn't have cabled if the doctors had thought that."

No one spoke, and Jean's mouth folded firmly. "Well!" she said, "there's nothing to do but wait. We can't help Biddy, we can't help Peter. . . . Have you cabled to Tim?"

"I'm just going to now," Lewis told her. "There may be another cable from him, but not likely, concussion takes time, and . . ." He looked miserably at his wife as if begging her to try and think of some comfort.

"What time is it?" Jean asked. "Ten o'clock! The day's only just begun."

The hours dragged leaden-footed. What a changed little house. Last week full of happy laughter and children's voices and the noise of busy feet running all about ; now silence and hushed tones.

How grief shuts one away from the world, thought Jean. It wasn't that the people outside were callous and unfeeling, simply that there was no point of contact with them. Jean felt as if glass enclosed her. Meals came, almost apologizing it seemed for their presence, and Jean attempted to eat and make conversation with the nurse not on duty. She spoke of everything but illness : she could not risk hearing of cases.

As luck would have it spring paid a fleeting visit to the world that day. When Jean went round to The Neuk after lunch, the sun was quite hot on the lawn, where Quentin tumbled with Black Douglas and the Inseparables.

Alison ran to her mother crying, " Is Peter better, Mummy ? When 'll I see him ? I went with Barty and bought him a present. It's a minnow to fish with : he always wanted one, but they cost a lot."

Jean regarded the fearsome object and assured Alison that she would take it as soon as Peter was able to look at it.

" But he has to be kept very quiet, darling. Peter's very ill."

" It's all right though, Mummy, I'm saying him in my prayers."

" And Daddy ? " said Jean, " you're ' saying ' him too, I hope ? "

She turned to watch Quentin racing round the lawn with the dogs. His laughter was as gay as the sunshine. No, she wouldn't let herself think of Peter at that age, paddling about the wide lawns at Mintern Abbas, playing ball, getting a ride on his father's horse, sitting at the steering-wheel pretending to drive the car. . . . Peter and his father had been inseparable. Were they to go together ?

At last it was evening. Mr. Irvine came out, but said little. The reply to Lewis's cable was " no change."

Everything was prepared for the night. Mrs. McCosh was putting sandwiches and cake beside the tea-things in the room next Jean's for the night nurse's refreshment.

" Ay," she told Jean, " she likes rich cake. I askit her what she fancied, thinkin' to masel', sponge cake, or mebbe gingerbread, but she said plum cake. . . . I've pit chicken sandwiches and tomato. . . . She's a rale nice body, the night nurse. So is the ither yin."

" Here's Ninny," said Jean.

" I'm no' gaun oot o' this hoose the nicht," said Ninny defiantly. " Elsie's wi' the bairns and Miss Barton, an' I'm gaun to bide wi' ma wee laddie. I'll no' mak' a soond, I've on felt slippers, but I'll sit by his bedroom door. Dinna say a word, please, Mem, for I canna help it. . . . Eh, an' isn't this an awfu' calamity aboot his lordship ! I kent what wud happen. When folk gang awa' in ships across the sea they tak' their life in their hands. . . . But never you heed, Mem, we'll be gettin' better news gin morning. . . . Ye're worn oot. Get to yer bed, Mem, an' lay yer heid on the pillow, an' mebbe sleep will come. We're in God's hands."

Jean nodded. " If anything would make me sleep it would be the thought that you're watching, Ninny. Promise you'll come for me if Nurse says there's any change ? "

" Oh, I'll come." There was something reassuring in the very tones of Ninny's Tweedside voice, and Jean, vaguely comforted, went to her room.

She ached with weariness, but misery made her restless, and she pulled up her blind and leant out of the window. The Kips stood up sharp in the moonlit world : how safe they looked and enduring. They had seen generation after generation live and love, suffer and depart, and seemed to say that nothing really mattered. And Jean, looking out at the peace, tried to make herself believe it. It was comparatively easy to agree that her own suffering did not matter, but it was a different thing when it came to being philosophic about her husband and son. . . . Suddenly it was too much for her. " Biddy, Biddy," she cried, throwing herself on her knees by the bed, and breaking into bitter weeping which she tried to stifle in the bed-clothes.

Exhausted at last and almost sick with fatigue, she tried to say her prayers.

" God," she began, and got no further.

God. With the saying of the name it came to her that this great trouble which had overtaken her had come from God the Father. She had been given so much, a brimming cup of happiness ; the hand that gave had surely also the right to take away. "*Shall I receive good at the hand of the Lord and shall I not receive evil ?* "

Jean shut her eyes and clasped her hands. " O God," she prayed, " Thou knowest what is best for them. If it seems the worst to me, help me to say Amen."

After that she slept.

CHAPTER XXXIII

" Still nursing the unconquerable hope . . ."
MATTHEW ARNOLD.

JEAN needed all her courage, for next day Peter still lay perilously near the edge. No word was said, but Jean read in the silence of the surgeon, in the pitying eyes of Pamela and Lewis, in the nurses' carefully reassuring tones that the danger was great.

A cable came early from Australia, but merely said, " No change."

So another strange day began at The Rigs.

" It's queer," Jean said to her sister-in-law, " but already this seems to have gone on so long that I can hardly remember anything else." She gave a dreary little laugh and turned to her secretary :

" Barty, I thought I had such sympathy with sufferers. It was sheer impertinence. I hadn't a notion what suffering meant. When people were in torture I said, ' Poor dears,' and sent them flowers and peaches."

Betty Barton, perfectly neat and tidy, but weary-eyed, said : " Don't blame yourself, Lady Bidborough. Even when one is in torture little things help. . . . Have you looked at your letters ? There is one from——"

But Jean had turned quickly to the pile of letters that

lay on the writing-table and seized the one that lay on
the top. She held it jealously against her, almost as if
she feared her companions might want to snatch it from
her.

" I shall read it—later," she said. " Is there anything very pressing this morning, Barty ? "

" Nothing much. I thought I'd take the children out
now and let Elsie help here. Ninny should lie down,
she was up all night. Of course it was quite unnecessary,
with two nurses, but the poor soul's miserable if she's
out of earshot."

" She brought him up," said Jean, " it's her right to
be with him. . . . Thank you, Barty, it's good of you to
take the children. They're all right, are they ? "

" Oh, very much all right. As you know, Quentin
only cares for food, and though Alison has sad moments,
she's helped by feeling important. . . . I'll take them
by the back way up the hill and will avoid being be-
sieged by inquirers. The telephone never stops at The
Neuk, nor the door bell. What a blessing you're away
from them at The Rigs. Even Mrs. Duff-Whalley would
hardly venture to come here."

" I should think not," said Pamela, but Jean, holding
her letter, said, " They mean to be kind : don't be too
brief with them, Barty. . . . I'd better see Mrs. McCosh
before I go upstairs—Pamela, dear, go back to Laverlaw
with Lewis ; it's miserable for you hanging about here,
and it isn't as if you could do anything. We'll ring you
up at lunch-time, and perhaps you'd both come down in
the evening for a little ? "

Pamela nodded. " Agnes wondered if she could come

down this afternoon to say good-bye? She travels south to-night."

"Oh! D'you know, Pamela, I'd almost forgotten about Agnes. Of course she must come. I'm so sorry her time has been spoiled."

"For that matter," said Pamela, "she was due at her aunt's about ten days ago, and simply stayed on here because she liked it. I'll bring her about three. The child was very forlorn at the thought of not seeing you to say good-bye. Bless you, darling. Good-morning, Miss Barton."

At last Jean could lock herself into her room with her letter. Generally she was in such a hurry to get at the contents that she tore open the envelope, but now she slit it with a knife, and carefully studied every letter of the address.

The letter was a long one, and full of details of what they were doing, especially of a visit to friends of friends, who had a wonderful farm.

"It's a glorious free life," he wrote, "though I could never of choice live in a country where in a drought they have to let the animals die: it must be ghastly."

He wrote of coming home. "No home-sick school-boy ever ticked off the days more eagerly than I do. The odd thing is, much as I'm enjoying seeing this wonderful country, I'm in a fever to be gone. Sometimes it seems as if the days will never pass. I'm obsessed with the most childish fear that something will prevent us from starting. I watch Tim—now a picture of rude health and exasperatingly contented with his present position—like a cat and a mouse, and I'll be

a thankful man when we find ourselves safely bestowed
in our cabins on the *Orotava*, and our faces turned
towards home. After that I'll be more content, and
even if Tim insists on dawdling a bit by the way, I'll
be home in time to see the spring. . . ."

Jean let the letter slip from her hand as she thought
of the vision the words conjured up. England in April !
Mintern Abbas in springtime ! Cowslips in the meadows,
the Crow-Wood carpeted with primroses and anemones :
the birds' sweet clamour : daffodils blowing in the west
wind. . . . Would Biddy ever see it again ?

Locking away the letter, she smoothed her hair and
presently went cautiously to the door of the sick-room.
There was a screen just behind the door, and she could
see without being seen. The bandaged head on the
pillow was still for the moment. Peter was asleep.
His mother tried to count the hurried breaths as his
chest rose and fell. The nurse, with a duster in her
hand, was going round the room, tidying here and
there : the window was wide open, and cheerful morning sounds came in. Jean turned away and went downstairs.

The day passed somehow. Agnes came and wept,
collected Ruth and Naomi, and departed. A wire
came from David saying he would arrive the next morning, and would like the car to meet him at Symington.

" It's kind of him," said Jean, " but it's a pity he
should trouble."

" Well," said Pamela, " I expect he feels that it's his
place to be here just now. Don't give it a thought :
he'll come to Laverlaw."

"Tell Phipps to go to Symington. He does nothing but take the nurses for drives, he'd be glad of a job. Pamela"—Jean looked full at her sister-in-law—"Pamela, did Mr. Irvine say anything to you about Peter?"

Pamela's face grew a shade paler as she replied:

"Only what we know, that he is very anxious. If the temperature doesn't go down . . . Oh, my dear, don't look like that. Children can fight through *anything*. I knew a child, Kitty Tressider's girl, who had double pneumonia and then mastoids, and got perfectly all right. It's quite a common thing. There's no need to despair. It's not like you, Jean, to look at the dark side, but it's the double anxiety, you poor child. . . . I was speaking to Mr. Irvine about Biddy, and he said, what, of course, we all know, that he may lie unconscious for days. Indeed, it's as well with a fracture, for he'll be utterly inactive. I can remember the business I had to keep his head on the pillow once when he had a spill hunting and a slight fracture. Oh, Biddy's come through a lot."

The surgeon came out again after dinner and went straight up to the sick-room, while Jean, sitting with Pamela and Betty Barton, worked stolidly at a chair seat she was embroidering. On her lap was a book, and Pamela looked at it.

"*Scott's Journal*," she said; "I might have known. In every crisis of life Jean flies to that book; and indeed there are few more comforting."

"It has helped me often," said Jean. "It's so full of courage that it makes one ashamed."

About ten o'clock that same night Mrs. McCosh went round to Bella Bathgate's back door and entered without knocking.

Bella was sipping a glass of hot water before retiring to rest, and had wound round herself a large grey shawl, for the night was chilly. She stood upright when she saw her visitor and sadly shook her head, asking in sepulchral tones, "*Has he passed away ?*"

It was not often that Mrs. McCosh lost her temper, but at that moment she surprised her friend.

"Ye're a great gomeril, Bella Bathgate," she said bitterly. "Who's speakin' aboot passin' away ? The laddie's better, I tell ye. The temperature's gone doon a wee bit an' the surgeon's pleased wi' him. . . . Oh me ! I've been seeck a' day wi' the fear that they'd need to operate again, an' I couldna gang to ma bed this nicht wi'oot tellin' somebody the guid news ! An' mair than that, there's a cable come and it says his lordship is conscious. . . . Passed away ! No' verra likely ! "

CHAPTER XXXIV

" Say that you love me not, but say not so
In bitterness."

AS YOU LIKE IT.

THOUGH perhaps Mrs. McCosh's jubilation was a little premature,—a fluctuating temperature gave them many anxious hours at The Rigs—yet Jean rose up the next morning with a heart that was light in comparison with what it had been, and was able to greet David, when he appeared, with a smile.

And David was very anxious to be kind and helpful to his sister in her anxiety. He was rather a self-centred young man, spoiled a little by having things made too easy for him, with a high respect for his own abilities, and no doubt at all about his power to accomplish whatever he set out to do, but to Jean he was still the Davy she had played with and petted and admonished, and she merely smiled at his conceit.

" It was good of you to come, Davy," she said, and David, honestly shocked and saddened by the ravages anxiety had wrought on his sister's face, said, "Oh, Jean, you've been having a perfectly rotten time. I thought you'd be glad of some one of your own beside you. . . . I didn't know what I was going to hear this morning, but it was all right when I saw Phipps's face : it wore a grin ! Poor old Peter ! I bought him an air-gun.

. . . And Bidborough too! But now he's conscious
he'll be all right. You're looking pretty pulled down
yourself, Jean. It's the worst kind of luck having him
so far away. Tim was an ass to cable : you need never
have known till he was better."

" I expect," said Jean, " they sent the first cable by
way of breaking it."

" Oh, well, perhaps. Things probably looked worse
than they really were, and then, of course, there's the
great difficulty of keeping things out of the papers.
Here is Miss Barton."

The secretary came in carrying a bundle of papers,
and David leapt up to greet her eagerly.

" You've all been having an anxious time," he said.
" I thought I'd come up and see for myself how things
were."

" Yes," Betty said gravely. " . . . I'm sorry to
interrupt you, Lady Bidborough, but d'you think you
could look over these some time before the post goes ? "

" Of course," said Jean. " Don't let me neglect
things, Barty. I'm really glad to get a job, something
that must be done. Is everything right this morning ? "

" Oh, yes. We've been down in Priorsford paying the
books, Quentin and I, and doing the day's marketing.
We had Black Douglas with us."

" He'll be lonely," said Jean, " without Ruth and
Naomi."

" *Who ?* " David asked.

" Didn't you see them when you were here last ?
Agnes Chatham came accompanied by two dogs,
whom she had christened, very absurdly, Ruth and

Naomi. . . . Oh, Barty, doesn't it seem an age since
the night she arrived. The dogs fought and there was
such a clamour."

" Yes. . . . I'm so thankful to hear from Nurse that
the news is good. Has Mr. Irvine been out yet ? "

" No," said Jean. " Not yet. That in itself is a good
sign. Dr. Dalgleish was here by eight o'clock, and was
very cheerful. The very sight of his weather-beaten
face does me good : he has a lifetime of experience
behind him."

" What kind of night had you ? " Miss Barton asked.

" Oh, all right. I was too thankful to sleep."

" Well, do lie down all this afternoon, won't you ?
. . . Forgive me butting in like this. I'm going to
take Quentin up the hill as long as the sun shines."

As the door closed behind her secretary Jean said :
" Barty has been a tower of strength. She doesn't
say much, but without any fuss she goes quietly about
keeping things straight, and is always there when she's
needed."

" That's good," said David. " Well—I think I'll go
for a short walk. It's a pity to waste such a jolly morning. Won't you come, Jean ? "

" Not now, I think, thank you. I'd like to get these
letters done at once. But you'll come here to luncheon.
I must see *something* of you ! "

David's walk led him past The Neuk, and he quickly
forgathered with Miss Barton and Quentin, and made
himself useful by riding his small nephew on his shoulder,
and controlling the wild spirits of the Black Douglas.

" I like to see him tearing about," said Miss Barton,

when they reached the freedom of the hill-side. "It must be wonderful to feel as free as that; for I don't suppose that he remembers for an instant that he's really cabined and confined. We poor humans never lose sight of that."

"Oh, I don't know," David demurred. "We can all do what we like in reason."

"Yes, I daresay, but the trouble is that some of us want more than is reasonable."

David turned and looked at his companion. "But you, surely, are an eminently reasonable person."

"Not always, I'm afraid. Sometimes I'm terribly dissatisfied, without reason."

"Oh, well," said David, "it's a mean soul that's satisfied. We must all struggle towards something."

"And find when we reach it that it's not the thing we wanted," said Betty.

"But isn't that all to the good?" David asked, quoting:

> " ' Never the thing attained,
>   Is the thing we struggled towards . . .' "

"I'm glad you're so pleased with life," said Betty.

"Which means, that you think I'm very well pleased with myself?"

Betty laughed but did not deny it.

She looked so pretty sitting there on the heather, with her brown coat and skirt and bright red jumper and cap, that David did what was most unusual with him: he acted on impulse. He had been strongly attracted to Betty during the Christmas holidays, and the thought of her had been constantly in his mind since then. She was not the sort of girl he had meant to marry. He told himself that he had meant to marry a girl whose connections would have been a help to him, a girl not only well-featured but well-dowered, but, hang it all, a man must, up to a point, follow the dictates of his heart. She was lovely, this Betty. He liked her reserve, her cool manner. She was clever, too, and would help, not hinder, him in his career. . . . But of course he had intended to think things over very carefully before he threw the glove.

He was betrayed by the beauty of the early spring morning, by the mocking smile of the girl at his side, by the youth in his blood, and to his own great surprise he found himself, with his heart beating wildly, tumbling out some sort of incoherent proposal.

It was received very coldly.

Betty, with an eye on Quentin and the dog, said :

" Are you by any chance asking me to marry you ? "

" That," said David, " was rather my idea. Betty, you do care for me a little, don't you ? "

Betty gazed at him critically but kindly, as she said :

" My dear sir, I like you immensely, to walk with and talk with, to dance with and play with, but as a husband—no."

Her tone was quite calm and very final, and David grew a little pale. It was rather unbelievable, for when he had rehearsed the scene to himself it had always finished with a ready, grateful acceptance. But he put a good face on it and managed a smile—withal a somewhat wry one.

" I'm sorry I troubled you," he said. ". . . Shall we go farther up the hill, or do you want to sit here ? "

" We'll soon have to be strolling luncheon-wards," said Betty. " Don't let us keep you : you want a walk."

But David was not going to be dismissed.

" I'm very content here, thank you," he said, and began to talk about the trouble that had come so suddenly on his sister. No one would have believed to hear him that a minute or two before he had been ardently offering marriage to the red-capped maiden at his side, and was, truth to say, not only a hurt, but a most astonished young man.

" Pamela Elliot says the surgeon has good hopes now of Peter's complete recovery. . . . I got an awful scare about the poor little chap. I only hope the illness won't leave any bad effects. He won't be deaf or anything, will he ? "

" They hope not," said Betty ; " they think not. Mr. Irvine is wonderful. So sure. The very sight of him put comfort into us through those terrible days, and Dr. Dalgleish was a rock to lean on. . . . I simply don't know how Lady Bidborough kept going. The agony of seeing the child suffer, the dread of a further operation, and behind that the thought of her husband lying unconscious. If ever a woman was on the rack . . . And there was nothing that any of us could do to give her ease. She was so quiet ; it made me afraid."

David had been picking bits of withered heather and scattering them about ; now he said : " Why should calamity be full of words ? Jean is a little sentimentalist, with tears to shed for every ill-used child and animal and poor mortal buffeted by fate, but she won't cry for herself. *Little* Jean."

Had Jean heard her brother's words and tone she would have been both touched and pleased, but they roused Betty Barton to fury.

Many things went to contribute to her outburst: the strain of the preceding days, an ever-increasing loyalty to and affection for her employer, and, perhaps, certain misgivings about her hasty refusal of the young man at her side.

" Little ! " she said. " It's always ' *little* Jean,' ' dear *little* Jean '—I'm sick of it. Can't you see that she's the biggest thing among you ? I've been with her now for more than a year, lived with her, seen her daily life, seen her kow-towed to and flattered, seen her tired and disappointed though never disheartened, but through everything she's the same, gentle and kind, quite seeing how comic life is, yet not making a mock of it ; never bitter, always pitiful. . . . And what would you and the others have been without her ? I don't mean the money and position—that was merely luck ; but she brought you up, didn't she ?— a child herself and made a home for you—Miss Hutton has told me. I'm glad, anyway, her husband has the sense to appreciate her . . . Now we'd better go home."

It was rather an anti-climax for Betty to be politely helped to her feet by the object of her tirade, who, indeed, still looked somewhat dazed.

As they went slowly home he said : " I'm sorry you should have thought I needed such an admonition.

Though we may seem rather dense, we are not unaware
of my sister's 'bigness' or ungrateful for what she has
been—and is—to us all. Believe me, Jean needs no
defender from her own people."

Betty flushed and bit her lip. "All right," she said,
"I asked for it. It was the most rank impertinence.
I apologize."

"Please don't," said Davy coldly.

Something of the old peace came back to The Rigs
that night, and dinner was quite a cheerful meal.
Peter's temperature was keeping down, and his mother
had been allowed to sit with him for an hour. Another
cable had come to say that Lord Bidborough was now
going on well.

"It will be at least three weeks before he can be
moved," Jean said, as she and Miss Barton sat sewing
together after the nurse had left the room. "What
a blessing he'll have the long voyage to restore him!
And Tim's a capital nurse. It's rather funny that the
situation should have been reversed on the way back!
. . . Ninny's going to get her innings at last, Barty:
Nurse Livingstone's been recalled; Dr. Dalgleish says
that Ninny may help with the day nursing. I know
we're not out of the wood yet—I'm not going to begin
to hallo!—but Mr. Irvine was very satisfied to-night.
He chaffed Peter, and Peter grinned at him under his
bandages. How small his face has grown in these few
days. Think, it's not nearly a week, Barty. But every
day has seemed endless."

Miss Barton agreed. "One couldn't work," she said.

" I found myself writing nonsense : and putting wrong dates. I simply had to stop it and take Quentin out ; that seemed my only usefulness."

" You were splendid, Barty. I was telling Davy this morning how good you had been. Don't you think it was nice of Davy to come up ? He said he felt responsible, with Biddy away." Jean held her work out and looked at it critically as she said : " You know, Barty, when boys grow up one is apt to lose hold of them, they seem so far away, full of interests you know nothing of, intimate with people who are strangers to one. . . . Davy was such a dear schoolboy, and when he went to Oxford he used to save his spare shillings —and they were very few—to buy us all presents. . . . I've often wondered if Peter Reid's money was a bad thing for him. Perhaps it made things too easy ; boys are all the better of having to struggle. . . . To me he'll always be the beloved little brother who depended on me, but I know Pamela sometimes thinks him rather conceited : too sure of himself, thinking he has only to ask to get."

" Well," thought Betty to herself, " he won't feel so sure of that to-night," and was surprised to find that the thought brought her no comfort. Hers seemed a singularly barren triumph.

CHAPTER XXXV

" I'll be as patient as a gentle stream,
   And make a pastime of each weary step
   Till the last step has brought me to my love . . ."
                    TWO GENTLEMEN OF VERONA.

THREE weeks later, though still bandaged about the
head and rather weak about the legs, Peter was up and
about, able once more to enjoy a game with Black
Douglas.

Mrs. McCosh, watching him from the kitchen window,
turned with a sigh of thankfulness to Bella Bathgate,
who had run in on some small errand, and said : " It's
me that's the thankfu' woman ! I hardly dared hope
I'd see the laddie oot again. . . . An' his lordship's
sailin' for hame this verra day ! "

" We get more than we deserve," Bella said piously,
but without conviction. She was suffering from neu-
ralgia, all her spring-cleaning was before her, she was
going back now to prepare for the sweep, and there
seemed at the moment very little to be really thankful
for.

" Oh, I wudna say that," Mrs. McCosh objected.
" Maist o' us are real deservin' ; we dae oor bits o'
jobs as weel as we can, an' when ye think o't we dinna
dae muckle ill."

Bella looked bitterly at her friend's placid face.

" I wonder to hear ye," she said. " If you'd been at the League o' Nations meetin' last night (an' there was nothing to hinder ye), ye would hev felt fair affronted at the peace and comfort we enjoy. Are the Russians no' as deservin' as us ? An' yet they can only get one meal a day, an' whiles no' that, an' as like as not are shot afore they get it. If I hed been born a Russian . . ." She finished with a shudder.

" Uch, Bella, I wudna' think o' onything sae awfu'. For one thing, ye could niver hev learnt the language. . . . An' I wudna tak' on aboot it if I wis you. I used to read in ma school books aboot Russians :

' Only a soldier sire, they said,
    Only a soldier dead . . .'

They were aye bein' persecuted : they'll hae gotten used to it by this time."

But her friend's cosy philosophy made Bella shudder the more. " Ye ken nothing aboot it : yer thochts never get ayont Priorsford."

" Weel," said Mrs. McCosh, " if ye can dae naething to help, whit's the good o' thinkin' ? An' ye ken fine that if ye stertit bringin' Russians ower here it wud be an awfu' turn-up. *D'ye mind the Belgiums?* An' if ye want to vex yersel', ye needna gang farther than oor ain Britain. I fair hate to read the papers noo : if it's no' one thing it's another : I'm grieved to the he'rt aboot ma country.'

" Ay," said Bella, with something of gloomy satisfaction in her voice, " it's just slidin' to destruction."

" I dinna believe it. There's ower mony righteous

men in't. If God saved Sodom for ten, surely He'll save Britain that hes thousands—I ken a wheen masel'."

" In Priorsford I could verra near count them on ma fingers," said Bella.

" Awa' wi' ye," laughed Mrs. McCosh. " Ye'll mebbe get a surprise some day, Bella, ma woman, when ye find wha's sittin' quite comfortable in the Golden City ! No' the folk *you* expect. Weel, I suppose we'll soon be back to the auld quait ways, an' ma he'rt's like lead to think o't. The weans will be an awfu' miss, an' me and her leddyship hes sic fine cracks ! . . . I wis lettin' masel' get into auld ways afore they came, thinkin' I wisna able for this an' that, but I see noo I'm as able as iver I wis, an' I want Miss Jean to gi'e me some work to dae. She says she'll send me folk that need rest and up-making, mebbe a lassie no' fit for work after an operation, or some wife worked to death. I'd enjoy fine cookin' for them and lookin' after them for twa or three weeks."

Miss Bathgate sniffed. " When does the family leave ? " she asked.

" Oh, no' yet awhile—mebbe a fortnicht or three weeks. They want to be a' settled doon afore hes lordship arrives. . . . There's Phipps wi' the car. Miss Jean's gaun oot to her tea. She's lookin' mair like hersel', an' that's a new hat she's got on. It's a wonderfu' support to a woman a new hat."

" No' to me," said Bella, rising. " I'm thankfu' I can do wi'oot such support. Good-bye to ye, Mistress McCosh."

" Only three more weeks in Priorsford," said Jean,

and even as she said it, it seemed to come the last day.

The last week was spent paying calls.

" They're not duty calls," Jean told Miss Hutton, " they're calls of gratitude. All of them, the Tweedies, and the Olivers, and that nice Mrs. Forbes at Archfield, the Homes, and even Mrs. Duff-Whalley have been kindness itself to me at this time. I'm only beginning now to realize it."

On the last afternoon she went to Hopetoun. She had been dreading parting from her oldest friend, but Mrs. Hope made it a cheerful, happy visit. As she was leaving, Augusta said: " Dear Jean, your visits have been a great delight. Having you and the children near has shortened the winter for us. And now, I hope, you are going home to be very happy."

" I hope so," said Jean soberly. " But I'll not take happiness so much as a matter of course now. I think I'll walk softly all my days."

Mrs. Hope smiled at the girl she loved so well. " Good-bye, my Jean, I wish you everything that's good."

" And I wish you——" Jean began.

" What is there left to wish me ? " asked Mrs. Hope.

" There's still the best," said Jean. " I wish you—*safe lodging, holy rest, and peace at the last.* . . ."

When Jean reached home she met Mirren Strang at the gate of The Rigs.

" What luck ! You were coming to see me, weren't you ? "

" I was, but if you've been out all the afternoon you won't want visitors."

" I want *you*. . . . I've been to Hopetoun to say good-bye, and it was borne in on me, as Great-Aunt Alison used to say, that it would be the last time."

Mirren was silent for a minute, then she said : " She's had a wonderful old age, but I'm sure she'd be glad to finish now. She once told me that as her memory dimmed to ordinary things, everything connected with her young husband and her boys stood out more clearly than ever. Haven't you sometimes noticed her look out to the lawn with a smile, as if she saw young lost forms play there ? . . . Augusta has no life apart from her mother : a pale shadow, she will fade after her. Hallo, young sir," to Peter, who ran out to meet them, " you take a very odd way of amusing yourself ! Feeling all right now ? That's good."

" Thank you," said Peter, " for the puzzles you sent me. I did them all. . . . Come on, Duggie, and help me to pack. . . . I don't believe Duggie wants to leave Priorsford."

" Do you want to leave Priorsford, Peter ? "

" Ye—es," said Peter, rather shamefacedly. " You see, we've a lot of things to go back to. . . . And Daddy's coming home : he *belongs* to Mintern Abbas."

" I see," said Mirren, " you think he couldn't be fitted in at The Rigs ? But there's something very gloom-making about seeing you all prepare cheerfully to depart, like swallows at ' the hint o' hairst.' "

" But you're going off too, aren't you ? " said Jean.

Mirren nodded. " I always go at this time, to let myself see an English spring. As you know, spring comes but slowly up this way, it's a lovely but reluctant thing : it's June before the hawthorn is out, and the bloom golden, and the rhododendrons in full glory. So I go off in my little car every April to Warwickshire—I have friends there who make me welcome—and unless the weather is very spiteful, I can feast my eyes on orchards all pink and white with blossom (or flourish, as I prefer to call it) and hear the larks sing in a blue sky, and listen to Shakespeare's words in his own town."

" Why," said Jean, " you will almost be passing our very door. Children, d'you hear ? Mrs. Strang will be our first visitor when we go home. Yes, but you must. . . . What is it, Alison ? Miss Hutton at the gate. Run then, and bring her in."

" I've had tea," Miss Hutton announced. " I thought this might be a time when you had a few minutes to spare, but I know you must be very busy."

" Not a bit busy," Jean told her, " and delighted to see you. We've just been hearing that Mirren is to be in Warwickshire in April, and we're trying to persuade her to come to Mintern Abbas. Miss Janet, is there any chance of your being in the south soon ? It takes away the pang of parting when one can look forward to another meeting."

" Janet," said Mirren, " every year I try to persuade you to come with me and every year you say ' No.' Say ' Yes ' for a change. The little car is really very comfortable : we'd take it by easy stages : a night perhaps in Kendal, and another in Shrewsbury. I don't believe you know anything about the beauties of England—you've spent far too much time abroad—

and I know you'd enjoy every mile of the road. You're steeped in history. Just think of the castles we'd visit, the cathedrals we'd worship in—and then at the end Jean in her own home."

"Oh, I admit it's very tempting," said Miss Hutton. "Give me time to think it over and——"

"No," said Mirren, "that's fatal. Always decide on the spur of the moment."

"Then it's ' Yes,' " cried Miss Janet recklessly.

"Hurrah," said Mirren. "Oh, here come the Miss Watsons."

The little ladies came in very apologetic, both talking at once.

"I'm afraid this is an intrusion on your last evening —you've got visitors, please forgive us—but we were out when you called, and we couldn't bear not to say good-bye. . . . So good of you to write to us in your anxiety."

Jean led them to comfortable chairs and assured them that they were welcome. "I meant," she said, "to look in in the morning. I couldn't have left without thanking you personally for your great kindness. Those daily parcels you sent to Peter were the greatest help : he looked forward to opening them all day. How did you manage always to find something fresh ? "

"Oh, nothing," said Miss Teenie, waving away the subject, "nothing at all "; while her sister said, "We were glad to do *anything*. How is Lord Bid-borough ? "

"By this time," said Jean, "I hope he's almost quite well. They got away all right, and the voyage will be splendid for him. We expect him home about the middle of April."

" My, but you'll be thankful," said Miss Watson. " Teenie and I were fair miserable when the news was so bad. We couldn't settle to anything, could we, Teenie ?"

" Indeed we couldn't. You'll not forget your winter in Priorsford, Lady Bidborough. It would have been awful if—— But we won't think about that now. We're rejoicing with you, Aggie and I, though we can't bear to see you go. . . ." Miss Teenie poked a parcel tied with pale blue ribbon into Jean's lap, remarking, " It's a bag. We made it for you : perhaps it could hang on the bell in your own room ? "

Jean's pleasure was obvious : she called on every one to admire her present, and Miss Teenie, much gratified, said :

" Well, I'm sure, it's a small return for all you've done for us." She turned to Miss Hutton and said confidentially : " You know, at the beginning of winter we were just feeling that we were done—our legs and our sight—and as we were less useful, people weren't bothering with us. I don't blame them. Then Lady Bidborough came to The Rigs and everything seemed different. She gave us a new interest in life and we forgot our age—we're not so very old either, when you come to think of it ! Between Lady Bidborough and the burglar scare (which shook us up, though it nearly killed us), we feel quite young again and brisk. Indeed, we're going to do a very daring thing—*We're going to London !* "

" Oh, Teenie," said her sister faintly.

" Yes. You see we'll not get any younger, and we'll likely get a lot poorer, with so many things ceasing to pay, so if we don't go now we never will. And it's sort of paltry never to have seen London, so we're going to stay for a week in the Regent Hotel. Our rooms are booked. I'm told it's noisy but very bright, and there's hot and cold water in every room. It'll be amusement enough for us to watch the people. No, we've no friends there, but we'll look at the shops."

" And go to the play ? " Mirren suggested.

" Well, we might go to a morning performance, but we'd never think of going out at night. We might never find our way back."

" I wonder," said Jean, and hesitated. Her eyes met Mirren's eyes, which were bright with malicious amusement.

" I wonder," she went on, " if you'd care to come and spend a day with us at Mintern Abbas ? We'd send a car for you and take you back—if you don't mind rather a long run."

Miss Teenie gave a sort of gasp and then said, " I can ride all day in a motor, it's not often I get the chance," while her sister murmured, " *Far* too kind . . . wouldn't think of troubling you . . . perfect nonsense. . . . Teenie, we couldn't think of accepting. . . ."

" When do you go ? " Jean asked. " The 5th ? Then you're too early for my husband. But the children and I'll do our best to entertain you, and I *would* like you to see our home."

A Saturday was fixed, the 8th of April, a day that ever afterwards shone like a star in the Watsons' firmament, a day that was talked about and discussed so long as the little ladies had breath and memory; and Jean was just remarking, "Now I call that great luck," when a voice said, "May I come in?" and Pamela Elliot appeared at the door.

"Oh, my dear, come in," cried Jean. "Have you had tea? Sure? I hoped you'd come."

"I'd have been earlier, but one thing after another happened to keep me. . . . Oh, don't let me drive you away, Miss Watson. How are you? Quite recovered from the fright of the burglar?"

"Oh, yes, thanks, though I can't help feeling thankful that the light nights are coming. We still feel queer going upstairs to bed, but Teenie says the shock shook us up, and perhaps it did."

Mrs. Elliot laughed and said, "That's a nice way to take a trial."

"We're going to London," said Miss Teenie, too full of the great event to keep it to herself. "For a week. To the Regent Hotel." She let that sink in and added, "And Lady Bidborough says that she will send a car to London for us so that we can spend a day at Mintern Abbas. I can hardly believe it. Aggie and I have wondered and wondered what it could be like, but never in our wildest dreams did we ever think we'd see it."

Pamela looked at her sister-in-law with rather a cryptic expression, but it was a very kind look that she turned on the Miss Watsons as she said; "I hope you'll have a splendid time. London is at its very best in April, the shops are so gay and everything is fresh. And I'm so glad you are going to pay my old home a

visit. Will you come and see me when you come back,
and tell me all about it?"

A little dazed, the Miss Watsons murmured something,
and almost immediately departed. Ninny came and
fetched away Peter, who was still regarded as something of an invalid; Alison went with him, and the
four women left in the room drew into the west window
to watch the marshalling of the pomp of sunsetting.

It had been a noisy March day, but the wind had
dropped, and a shining peace lay over the little town.
Sounds came up to them as they stood by the open
window, the voices of children at their spring games:
far off some one was playing the pipes.

Pamela linked her arm in Jean's, saying, "Sorry to
go, darling?"

"Take her away," said Mirren Strang, "before she
invites the whole of Priorsford to visit her at Mintern
Abbas."

"Nothing would give me greater pleasure," said Jean,
"than to see all my Priorsford friends there. Just
think how good they've been to me."

"Oh, I agree," said Pamela. "I'll never again talk
of the 'Priorsford rabble.' And if it gives them the
slightest pleasure to come to Laverlaw they're welcome.
Even Mrs. Duff-Whalley herself!"

"And you can't say fairer than that," mocked Jean.
"You sent the Miss Watsons away very happy anyway."

There was silence for a little while, then, "What an
evening," sighed Mirren. ". . . Jean, you're looking
at Priorsford as if you'd like to put your arms round it.
I admit at the moment it looks an abode of peace, but

we all know it has its gossips and back-biters, the people are both good and bad as poor humans are everywhere ; in fact, it's just a very *ordinary* town."

" Not to me," said Jean firmly, " never ordinary to me. Of course there's a lot of gossip. Wherever you get women whose minds are unemployed though their hands are busy, there's bound to be gossip. They don't believe it themselves, but it livens up things for them to tell each other the most unlikely stories. And of course the people aren't perfect, but as Mrs. McCosh says, *Faigs, they're no' bad.*' At the moment I can't think of a single person who is downright nasty. And how could Priorsford be ' ordinary ' with the situation it has, with Tweed running through it, with Peel watching over it, with the hills encircling it ! I shall miss the hills——"

" Oh, and the burns, Jean, the burns," cried Mirren. " Think of Laverlaw Water, and the Manor, and Hope-carton——"

" There are streams of water in the south," Pamela reminded them. " What of the Evenlode ? The Dawn ? The Windrush ? Are these not lovely names ? "

" But," Mirren objected, " these are only sluggish English streams with mud for a bottom instead of silver sand and shining agates. . . . Oh, but I must tear myself away and go home and work. I've a book to finish before I leave home."

" D'you mean to say," said Jean, " that you're going to sit down and *make* yourself write ? I thought authors had to wait for inspiration."

" I'd wait a while," said Mirren grimly. " No, the

only way I know is just to peg at it. . . . I had two writers staying with me for the week-end, the kind that need inspiration."

" Oh, yes," said Janet Hutton ; " how did you get on with them ? "

" Well—the girl had plucked eyebrows, and her mouth looked as if she had been drinking some one's blood ; her nails, too, were disgusting, but when you got over those drawbacks she wasn't at all bad—you should have seen Rebecca Brand's face as she took in all the details ! The husband is a clever fellow : he looks like Beverley Nichols and writes rather like Charlotte Yonge."

" But how did you even manage to meet such people ? " Pamela asked.

" Well," said Mirren, collecting her gloves and bag, " I was asked to a writers' dinner in London, and I met the Orwells and heard they had to come to Edinburgh to do something, and asked them to Hopewaterfoot, and . . . Oh, my goodness, here's Mrs. Duff-Whalley. Let me go ! "

There was a general exodus, and presently Jean found herself alone with the new-comer.

" I've hardly time to sit down," she said, " for we're dining out to-night, but having missed you when you called—we were down Tweed lunching with Lady Scott—I simply had to rush in and say good-bye. And how is Peter ? . . . I'm thankful to hear it. Of course I don't think he'll ever be quite strong again, poor little fellow ; that operation nearly always leaves *something*, but I'm sure after this you will be very careful of him, and he may grow out of it. . . . And Lord Bidborough has sailed! Well, there, you've a lot to be thankful for, Jean. I just hope it will be a lesson to your husband not to go flying off across the world with sick friends and leave his wife and children! But husbands are so restless nowadays, any excuse and off they go. I'm afraid this unhappy episode will quite spoil the thought of your time at Priorsford. It has *aged* you, Jean."

Jean laughed, and Mrs. Duff-Whalley continued: "I really came in to tell you a little secret. You have always been so interested in dear Muriel. She is engaged to Patrick Hamilton. Yes, I am very pleased, for though my girl might have done better in a *worldly* sense, it is much more important that she should obey the dictates of her heart."

" Oh, surely," Jean agreed, rather in a maze.

" And Patrick is really a delightful fellow. Such a good old Edinburgh family: W.S.'s in the time of Sir Walter Scott, and personal friends, I believe. And his uncle, his mother's brother, is Sir Duncan Macpherson, Governor of some part of India. And of course, what weighed with dear Muriel was that at Drykeld she wouldn't be far from The Towers and her mother."

" Oh," cried Jean, in all sincerity, " I think it's perfectly ideal. Everybody likes Mr. Hamilton, and Muriel will be so happy at Drykeld. When is the wedding to be ? "

" That hasn't been spoken of yet : they only got engaged last night. They've gone to Edinburgh to-day to choose the ring. I offered them the Rolls, but they're

away as happy as birds in Patrick's dilapidated Austin !
Ah, Jean ! these young things. You and I can sympathize with them."

Jean, a little startled at finding herself promoted to
being a contemporary of Mrs. Duff-Whalley, murmured
vaguely, and presently the visitor rose to go.

"I'll write to you," she promised, "and give you all
the details about the wedding. Dear me ! I'll be
busier than ever now, with another household to super-
vise, but it's the breath of life to me to have my hands
full," and with a peck at Jean's face Mrs. Duff-Whalley
bustled out of the room.

Five minutes later, while Jean was still sitting thinking happily of what she had heard, steps came flying up
the flagged path, and presently Muriel herself ran into
the room.

"I've only a minute," she said, "but I couldn't bear
to pass. Patrick wanted to come too, but I sent him
away. I had to have you to myself. Jean, we're
engaged. Look ! " She held out her left hand. "I
didn't want him to spend too much on it, and it's just
what I like best. . . . I'm so *happy*. It seems far too
good to be true : I keep thinking I'll waken."

Jean hugged the excited girl. "It's perfect," she
said. "I couldn't imagine anything nicer than your
Patrick. And what fun to be a farmer's wife ! "

Muriel gave a blissful sigh. "*How* I'm looking forward to it ! It's the sort of thing I've always wanted.
But please don't mention ' farmer's wife ' to Mother ! "

"Your mother has just been here to say good-bye,
and told me about it. She seems very pleased."

" Well—reconciled. She was furious at first, poor dear, and said I was tearing down the house that she had erected—meaning our social position ; but Pat talked her over. . . . And very soon she'd made herself believe that it was her idea from the first, and that she managed to bring it to pass. Poor Mother."

" And all the preparations for the wedding will be such a joy to her," Jean said ; " I can just imagine how she'll throw herself into them. She's a wonderful woman, your mother."

" Oh, wonderful," said Muriel. " . . . Jean, Pat says he fell in love with me the very first time we met."

" I'm not surprised."

" Jean, don't laugh and don't tell any one, but I'm so *grateful*."

Betty Barton came into dinner looking rather tired after a day of finishing up things.

Jean told her the news, which she received without surprise, merely asking how Mrs. Duff-Whalley was taking it.

" It seems she was angry at first, but she spoke to me as if she were very pleased."

" Well, she certainly brought it about," said Betty. " It was the Community Drama rehearsals that gave them the chance to meet."

" So it was," said Jean. " Well, Muriel is the happiest thing you ever saw. It's a delight to see her. And what a good wife she'll make. . . . I only hope Mrs. Duff-Whalley won't try to impose her will on the household and make mischief."

"She won't be allowed to," said Betty. "I think Patrick Hamilton can be trusted to see to that."

"I daresay you're right. I don't know when I was so pleased about anything. Isn't it a very pleasant happening just as we leave?"

"Oh, very," said Betty listlessly.

Jean looked across at her secretary and said:

"When we get back to Mintern Abbas you're going away for a month's holiday. You've earned it, and you need it. What about a cruise somewhere? If you're a good sailor that might be quite interesting, and you'll be the better of meeting a crowd of people, all different, after having been cooped up with us for a year. But you must take a friend with you; half the fun is having some one to talk things over with."

But Miss Barton shook her head as she said:

"It's very good of you, Lady Bidborough, but I don't feel in need of a holiday."

"Well," said Jean, "I'm not going to tell you (as Mrs. Duff-Whalley told me this evening) that you are *aged*, but you certainly look as if you'd be the better of a change. I don't feel it's fair to Priorsford that we should go away all looking, more or less, wrecks! . . . The first thing I must do is to see about new clothes—lots of them; and then I'll be ready to greet the spring—and Biddy!"

CHAPTER XXXVI

"Now is the winter of our discontent
Made glorious summer . . ."

RICHARD III.

APRIL had come to the Cotswolds, not in uncertain glory, but casting favours as royally as June.

Mintern Abbas never looked more beautiful than in April, and as Jean stood by the open window of the dining-room, and listened to the rooks among the swaying elms, and saw the wide lawns, freshly mown, stretch to the full bright river, she wondered if any one in the whole wide world that "sunshine morning" were happier than she.

Biddy had come back the night before, seemingly not a penny the worse of his accident, and now they were all together, and at home.

She turned as the door opened and her husband came in. He had been out for an early morning ride, and, though thin, he looked brown and well.

"Well, darling, I've had a glorious gallop. It's good to be on Alan Breck again. . . . He lifted the covers of the dishes on the side-table. "Aha! sausages. If there was one thing I longed for all the time I was away, it was Mrs. Watt's sausages."

"This is bitter hearing," said Jean, glancing over her letters. Then, "How d'you think Peter looks?" she asked.

374

" Much better than I expected. Pulled down a bit, of course, but as merry as a grig. And hasn't Quentin come on! He's a great fellow. And my little square Alison. . . . What are you having, darling ? "

" Oh—anything."

" Is that the way you've behaved at meals in my absence ? No wonder you're thin."

" Mrs. Duff-Whalley said I'd aged."

Lord Bidborough looked at his wife, standing in her green frock, with the spring sun finding out the golden lights in her curls and in her eyes, and smiled.

" Almost as ' aged ' as a wild rose in June," he said. " How is Mrs. Duff-Whalley ? "

" Oh ! most exciting news. Muriel—— What is it, Simson ? "

Simson coughed apologetically, then said : " Mrs. Turner on the telephone, m'lady : could your ladyship see her for a few minutes at ten o'clock. And a message from Malchester : Lady Agnes Chatham will come to luncheon if it is convenient."

Jean hesitated. " Say to Mrs. Turner, yes, certainly. I'll give you a message later for Malchester," and as the door closed behind the butler she turned to her husband and cried, " Oh, I *did* want this day free. Agnes must come another time."

" She certainly must. Look here, at eleven by the clock I'm going to pack you and the children into the old Humber and we'll go off for the day, somewhere, anywhere, it doesn't matter so long as we're together, and away from people. Now don't tell me that you've half a dozen engagements, for I don't care. When I lay in that Nursing Home in the blazing heat, I kept myself alive by thinking of you and the children, meadows full of buttercups, running water, beech woods. To-day I've promised myself that I'll have them all. So off we go—d'you realize, woman, that I've been in a parched land and I'm *thirsty*."

Jean laughed. " You silly old Biddy, it's such fun to have you home. . . . Last night I could think of nothing but the great serious things like life and death. I had no words : I could only hold you to make sure you were really there, that you had come back to me. . . . And now, this morning, the old dear life's begun again as if there had been no parting. Yes, let's all go off in the old car and find beech woods and buttercups, and we'll take our lunch and tea with us, and make a fire and be ' gangrel bodies ' for a day and forget that we've any responsibilities . . . Oh, remind me before we go to send a wire to Davy with the name of Barty's hotel. She's in London for a couple of days before embarking with her friend on the cruise that is to be her holiday, and Davy writes this morning for her address. I expect he wants to take her to a play."

" I'm glad Miss Barton's to have a good holiday. She was rather a prop, wasn't she, at Priorsford ? "

" Indeed she was. I got to know her, and the more I know of her the better I like her. D'you know, Biddy, those months of separation taught me a lot."

" What they taught me," said Biddy, helping himself to cold ham, " was that I couldn't live away from Jean, my wife."

" Well, of course," said Jean, " I've always known

I couldn't live away from you, so I didn't need to learn that, but I learned many home truths about myself, how I aggravated people and so on——"

" Who had the impertinence to——"

" It was only too true, I'm afraid ; but the chief thing I learned was that you and I are in danger of settling down too soon. Yes. I heard some one use the expression ' gone cosy,' and I thought it rather described us."

" Upon my word, Jean . . ."

" Oh, I'm the one to blame. I know that I love the fireside feeling too much, the safe feeling, which will be all right when we've earned it. . . . The children will soon be grown up and out in the world, and I want them to be adventurers in the best sense of the word, not just always playing for safety. . . . Biddy, *you* know what I mean, though I express myself badly : you were no pedestrian till you met me."

" And d'you think you've condemned me to the dust of the common highway ? Why, my dear, you've always seemed to me like an Alpine meadow."

Jean gave a contented sigh as she said : " Oh, thank you, Biddy, for that kind word. You don't know how grateful I am for it. I've had nothing but advice how to make myself different since ever you went away. And I didn't like it. You've spoilt me, Biddy. But I'm really going to try to make myself strong and very courageous, so that if Peter comes to me and says he wants to go out and fight giants, I'll be able to say, ' Go, my son.' "

Biddy nodded as he took some marmalade, and Jean

went on : " I've been thinking, and it seems to me that the only thing we can do to help our country is to bring up our children as well as we can. I mean to try to give them a sense of duty and a firm hold on the eternal decencies, and then they will, perhaps, carry the light on. . . . Don't you agree ? "

" Oh, yes, I agree."

" Then why are you smiling like that ? "

" Was I smiling ? I was thinking of Great-Aunt Alison. Forgive me, darling, I don't mean to be flippant. You're perfectly right, of course, and it's our job to do our best for the children. I think myself they've quite a chance of growing up fairly decent, but—— Hallo ! . . ."

He rose and went to the window, followed by Jean.

An angry scrimmage was taking place on the lawn. Quentin had managed to seize Black Douglas by the ears, and refused to let go though Peter beat him lustily on the back and Alison slapped his fat legs. The dog squealed, Peter shouted, Quentin roared, and Alison wailed, so the noise was prodigious.

" You'd better separate the future light-bearers," said Jean.

And on her face was an impish, schoolboyish grin which her husband found irresistible.

Lord Bidborough kissed his wife.

PRINTED IN GREAT BRITAIN AT
THE PRESS OF THE PUBLISHERS

NELSON'S NOVELS

Select List of some of the most famous modern novels. These volumes contain as much reading matter as the full-sized novel now issued at 7s. 6d. net. Set in clear type, and strongly bound.

At 1s. 6d. net

BELL, J. J.	Wee Macgreegor
BENNETT, ARNOLD	Helen with the High Hand
BENTLEY, E. C.	Trent's Last Case
BOWEN, MARJORIE	A Knight of Spain
BUCHAN, JOHN	John Macnab
BUCHAN, JOHN	Huntingtower
BUCHAN, JOHN	The Path of the King
BUCHAN, JOHN	Midwinter
BUCHAN, JOHN	Prester John
BUCHAN, JOHN	The Three Hostages
BUCHAN, JOHN	The Gap in the Curtain
BUCHAN, JOHN	The Blanket of the Dark
BUCHAN, JOHN	Salute to Adventurers
BUCHAN, JOHN	Greenmantle
BUCHAN, JOHN	Mr. Standfast
BUCHAN, JOHN	Witch Wood
BUCHAN, JOHN	The Dancing Floor
BUCHAN, JOHN	The Runagates Club

[Continued

NELSON'S NOVELS AT 1s. 6d. net

(*Continued*)

BUCHAN, JOHN	The Courts of the Morning
BUCHAN, JOHN	Castle Gay
BUCHAN, JOHN	A Prince of the Captivity
CONRAD, JOSEPH	Romance
CULLUM, RIDGWELL	The Saint of the Speedway
CULLUM, RIDGWELL	The Man in the Twilight
CULLUM, RIDGWELL	The Luck of the Kid
CULLUM, RIDGWELL	The Riddle of Three-Way Creek
DOUGLAS, O.	Penny Plain
DOUGLAS, O.	The Setons
DOUGLAS, O.	Pink Sugar
DOUGLAS, O.	Ann and Her Mother
DOUGLAS, O.	Olivia
DOUGLAS, O.	Eliza for Common
DOUGLAS, O.	The Proper Place
DOUGLAS, O.	The Day of Small Things
DOYLE, A. CONAN	The Refugees
HEWLETT, MAURICE	The Queen's Quair
JACOBS, W. W.	Ship's Company
JACOBS, W. W.	The Lady of the Barge
JACOBS, W. W.	Many Cargoes
JACOBS, W. W.	Sailors' Knots
JACOBS, W. W.	Deep Waters
JACOBS, W. W.	A Master of Craft

[*Continued*

NELSON'S NOVELS AT 1s. 6d. net

JACOBS, W. W.	At Sunwich Port
JACOBS, W. W.	Night Watches
JACOBS, W. W.	Sea Urchins
LENNOX, GILBERT	" X 14 "
LESLIE, NORMAN	Winged Victory
LYNDON, BARRY	Speed Fever
MASEFIELD, J.	Lost Endeavour
NORRIS, FRANK	The Octopus
NORRIS, FRANK	The Pit
PARKER, SIR GILBERT	The Battle of the Strong
PARKER, SIR GILBERT	The Seats of the Mighty
PHILLIPS, H. LAWRENCE	The House of Secrets
PHILLIPS, H. LAWRENCE	The Tangle
PHILLIPS, H. LAWRENCE	The Park Mystery
" Q "	The Ship of Stars
" Q "	The Splendid Spur
SABATINI, RAFAEL	The Sea Hawk
SILBERRAD, UNA L.	The Good Comrade
SOMERVILLE AND ROSS	
	Some Experiences of an Irish R.M.
SOMERVILLE AND ROSS	
	Further Experiences of an Irish R.M.
SOMERVILLE AND ROSS	Some Irish Yesterdays

[*Continued*

NELSON'S NOVELS AT 1s. 6d. net

THYNNE, MOLLY	The Murder on the " Enriqueta "
THYNNE, MOLLY	The Case of Sir Adam Braid
THYNNE, MOLLY	The Crime at the " Noah's Ark "
TWAIN, MARK	Huckleberry Finn
TWAIN, MARK	Tom Sawyer
VACHELL, H. A.	The Other Side
WALPOLE, HUGH	The Duchess of Wrexe
WEYMAN, STANLEY J.	Count Hannibal
WEYMAN, STANLEY J.	A Gentleman of France
WEYMAN, STANLEY J.	The House of the Wolf
WEYMAN, STANLEY J.	The Red Cockade
WEYMAN, STANLEY J.	The Wild Geese
WILLIAMSON, C. N. and A. M.	The Lightning Conductor
WILLIAMSON, C. N. and A. M.	The Princess Passes

THOMAS NELSON AND SONS, Ltd.

London, Edinburgh, New York, Toronto, and Paris